Darren Coleman
author of the Smash Hit 'Before I Let Go'
Presents:

Lost &

Turned

Out

D0110851

a novel

by Zach Tate

®

An Nvision book *in conjunction with* **Power Play Media**
Published by Nvision Publishing
A division of **Nvision incorporated**
P. O. box 274, Lanham Severn Road, Lanham, MD 20703

Nvision Publishing and the above portrayal of a boy looking to the moon and the stars are trademarks of **Nvision Incorporated.**

Cover design by Darren Coleman.
Cover Art by Anthony Carr
Graphic photography by Curtis Kitrell
Cover layout and graphic design by Les Green

Library of Congress Cataloging-in-Publication Data;

Tate, Zach
   Lost and Turned Out: a novel/ by Zach Tate
   For complete Library of Congress Copyright info visit;
   www.nvisionpublishing.com

ISBN 0-9724003-4-6
Copyright © 2005

Lost & Turned Out

a novel

by Zach Tate

introducing

Power Play
Media

in conjunction with

Nvision Publishing

Acknowledgements

To the world of the lost and turned out, love sometimes comes in ways you'll least expect. Hold on, it will come to you too.

To the high, exalted Queen, Dimples, my Jubbie. You have endured what others cannot. You gave me strength when I was weak and kept me focused when I was losing my mind. One day baby, all this writing will prove its' worth. Even then, I will still kneel before you. My world is yours Mami, NEVER FORGET THAT.

To the Prince and Princess; this is all for you! Big Sis in Florida; we doing it again. You are the wind beneath my wings... I have nothing if I ain't got you. Bre-Bre & Joe Joe, I make it so you can take it. Ma, your boy's out there acting like a fool again. Be proud. I love you. Uncle David, the Don, simply, Florida's finest. Thank you for everything. Aunt Marie; I promise they won't have to call the cops this time. I never forget that you love me. Kareem Unique ... still your daddy, boy! My agents and inspiration, Renee B. from Accord. Chloe Vanderbilt, thank you for believing in me and being the ONLY one who listened when I needed that ear. This is only the beginning. Wait until we get to Hollywood.

To Darren Coleman; for remembering the lost! Stay up playa. Check it, "You have a collect call from 'The Truth', PRESS 3! You just don't know how much that means. Let me do my thing and take this book thing over.

George F. 3810, you spoke when I was deaf. I can hear you now.

To the staff at Nvision Publishing. Lisa Richardson & Angela Oates. Anthony Carr, you are magic on that canvas. Les Green, thanks for all the tactical, graphical. Leslie German, Tressa Smallwood, Enid Pinner & Yolanda Johnson. To the newcomers, Danette Majette and Eyone Williams, represent.

Thanks to Natti and Afrikan World Books. To Karen at A&B, you are a gem. D loves you. Thanks to Eric and Gayle. Shout out to Massamba on Jamaica Ave. Ryss... Sistas Uptown, James at Dynasty Books, rep me. Tru Books in New England. Special thanks to Karibu Books and the staff. You all set the standard for black booksellers, period.

Shout out to Vickie Stringer, K'wan, and Tyrone Wallace. Rockelle at Harper, thanks for the look. In for a penny, in for a pound, I'll see ya'll in a bit. To Crystal Winslow and Nancey Flowers. One.

To Queen Alicia & Baby Born the consultants; Hairs to You! Cecile Anthony, my executive assistant, thank you from the bottom of my heart, the check is in the mail. Zioness Dawn, my media and executive Jah-guide! Johnny O, the realist. Keep throwing them jabs and see what I do! Mr. Jade, You the Biggest Homey from the B.K., the biggest, Duke, the biggest! The Ambassador of Queensbridge, Fall Guy, the God Supreme, a.k.a. Derick. You was famous, I made you infamous. Love you Gee. Butter, I told you. Mr. Mance; what they gone do when Big Heavy from St. Nick comes for you? You know I really love you.

P.R.-Addict, what more can I say? Little Lord, guess who? Respect goes a long way, thank you. Peggy Ann, from the 6th floor, still love you. Jason, blue eyes don't look well, under a ski mask. Johnny Hustle, yeah, somebody might as well write a book about your life, who better than me? Love you, bro. Sharieff Clayton, I don't want a girl with a bone in her nose, I like them M6's and Mauri Gators too much. Powerful, this ain't a memoir, so just stop it. Mikey Cheese … you rat bastard. Gee Man, the past is in the past. Peace. Vera, the clothing line is simply smashing. Diane, "Dem can't bloodclot judge me. Tell dem fe goway. Jill, thanks for the permission. To the rest of the crew, we went from *No Way Out* to being *Lost & Turned Out*, can you believe what's next still causes unreasonable doubt.

J-Rock (A. Davis), the writer who taught me how to write, you just don't know what you did when you was rude. Thank you over and over again. Don Corleone-Fort Greene's fiercest. Kill them with your mind. It's much more rewarding. The infamous Minister of Information… shhhhh. Big Daddy the Chef, thanks for the ink. Kirky, you know I appreciate everything. G.O. Solo-won-Konobi, S. dot Weston III, watch what happens when they see us at the U.S. Open, "Somebody, call the cops." It's a bird, it's a plane, it's West-Man! Hi, Marge, B.O, Biggie Smalls (R.I.P), Tank, N.A., Rock, up in this motha. Una, they don't know the 1-7-Ohhhh like we know! Intelligent Allah. Boo Bear, this is a beautiful thing! My boy, Black. Good morning, Z-A-R. Bumpy. EL. Regulator, you got my mind hurting. Mr. Jackson, you touched me, thank you. Brook, I love your support. The K. Azim-Zima, Shiesty Ave. Dre, the poet who comes from the place where 'Little kids play freeze tag with bullets'. Martha Stewart, sorry, baby, but I got your back. I told you it would be over before you knew it. Little Kim, Me, Hustle Hard, and Cinobe... got your back. Casino Mike, man, just listen, damn. Rel, you are so real. Maino, we go you.

The old College Crew – 166. Y'all just don't know how bad ya'll messed up. Dirty Poe and Oyster, you the only ones that kept it real.

To all the Yard Massive; Big Up and X amount of titanium respect fe de love!!! You nuh have fe like de sex part, but dem real. Nuh get red eye pon me! Gwan go chat me now. Tony Turner, Cousin Boots. Bya, Charlie. "See Boops de."

To the HATERS, you make me so damn great. Keep up the good work. Flamingo, rest in peace. I'm still crying to this day. I love you, baby.

"Don't look back and don't cry."

- El Hajj Malik El- Shabazz (Malcom X)

Lost & Turned Out

a novel

by **Zachary Tate**

One

Summer of 1991

"Yo, you ready to do this?" Webb asked as he pushed shells down into the clip of his Para Tac-four. His eyes focused on the pistol with the type of adoration a man usually reserved for a woman. Webb prided himself on having the best pistols on the market.

Trying to calm Webb down, Jason replied, "Webb man, relax. I got this. Stop buggin'."

Webb glanced around, checked his watch to signal that he wanted his partner to speed up.

"Alright homey, run this thing down to me," Jason spat.

Webb could smell the grime escaping the loud garbage trucks that cleaned the city streets in the morning. He rubbed his sweaty palms together while he removed the black leather gloves from under his bulletproof vest. While he slipped them on, he watched as Avenue D came alive with pigeons flying overhead in the already baking sky. He pushed Jason's back to the wall next to him, and stared at the bodega.

Webb said, "Homey, our man is an Italian cat. The connect says he'll be on foot, dressed in a suit carrying a brief case."

Webb looked at his watch and said, "Should be any minute now. So take your position, bang him out, and do your thang, my nigga. I'ma hold you down and do my thing if them fuckas come out of the bodega. I'll see you in the Bridge when we done. If not, you know what to do."

Webb looked around the corner and down 8th Street. In between the assorted working class folk who were commuting on foot to their jobs and the dope fiends who were ready to cop their morning's fix, he saw a young Italian man fitting the description his connect had given him.

He slid around the corner onto Avenue D and said, "Here he comes. The rest is up to you."

Jason slid his mask around and braced himself against the wall. He peeped around the corner and saw a man that resembled a movie star. Oddly, a part of him felt sorry for the man, because he was sure that his face would not hold up when he put his Golden Gloves skills to work. Then just as quickly his mind drifted back to the dough he needed.

In that instant he turned to Webb. They tapped their gloved fists together and Jason from behind his mask chanted, "You in the game, then the hustle stay the same…" as he took off to meet the Italian.

"If you ain't a full-time crook, you square up and turn lame," Webb finished their chant and pulled his bandana up and over his nose. He patted his small blowout Afro down and removed one of the pistols from his waist while looking out for the police.

The people on Webb's side of the street saw the masked man approaching and did an about face. The traffic in the street continued to move.

The Italian man looked up at the red canopy and the flashing lights to make sure he had the right place. When he put one foot up in an effort to step into the bodega, his peripheral vision caught a figure dressed in black. Instinctively, he reached to his waist to draw for his own weapon. Jason had startled him and the fear caused him to stumble as he tried to back away. In a fraction of a second, Jason pounced on the man and attacked like a lion leaping from the bush.

The first punch to the temple dazed the mark. Each subsequent punch served only to completely disable him. Jason wasn't cruel, but often got carried away once he slipped into work mode. Jason always treated victims as if they were opponents in the ring and rained blows on them as if he were trailing in the twelfth round of a championship bout needing a knockout to win. His fists were flying and connecting and the blows began ripping the man's flesh from his face like a meat cutter on a side of beef, even though the man was trying to cover up. When he collapsed under the pressure of the barrage of punches Jason lifted the man to his feet and snatched his .38 from his waist. Barely able to hold himself upright, the victim dropped the case.

Jason smiled and threw one last punch into the man's rib cage and watched him fall to the ground dizzy from the beating. Jason reached for the silver case and ran swiftly. Out of the corner of his eye, he watched, surprised as the man climbed to his feet and stumbled into the bodega. As Jason drifted away from the scene, he placed the pistol into his pocket, slid the briefcase into his messenger bag, and tightened his straps for his long ride. He imagined that by now the victim would be calling the men in the back of the store for help.

Jason's eyes scanned across 8th Street looking for Webb, in an effort to let him know that he was expecting company. No announcement was needed. Webb stood in the middle of the street to cover Jason.

Just when Jason cranked the gears to his mountain bike, Webb took aim and waited for the men to come running out of the bodega. The first two ran out, pistols in the air, looking in every direction except in front of them. Webb laughed at their lack of finesse. He made the first two men pay as bullets from his silenced pistols ripped through the side of the first man's head and ricocheted, hitting the second man's ear, taking it completely off.

Webb laughed louder as the men's screams echoed up the block. The next men who appeared in the door were obviously unarmed. As soon as they heard the window crash out of the bodega they ran for cover.

Jason was gone without a trace. All reasons for Webb to stick around were gone. Webb turned his attention back to the bodega where the one-eared gunmen tried to escape back inside to safety. Webb caught him in the back twice and ended him. Without hesitation, he emptied his clip into the bodega simply for good measure. He then turned around, and headed for the six-story abandoned tenement.

Two at a time he took the stairs that led to the roof, avoided the rats, and reloaded his tool. The red, steel, roof door was open like he'd left it the night before. Webb looked over the ledge and saw that the traffic below was at a halt. The flashing police cars were pulling up one after another. Bystanders and witnesses alike pointed to the building Webb had escaped into.

The police took too long to respond just like always. Webb hopped three roofs and jumped down two stories onto the roof of the buildings that faced Avenue C. By the time he was done playing leapfrog with the buildings and scaling a fire escape, there wasn't a squad car in sight. In no time at all, he was crossing 7th Street on Avenue C. When he passed the red brick building under construction on the corner he felt a sense of relief. He popped the lock to his ride, jumped in and sped off.

Six hours after the robbery, Jason and Webb exited their apartments on 12th Street to meet and celebrate their success.

"Yo, homey, did you see that cat going for his heater? He almost caught me slipping," Jason told Webb while inhaling on a blunt.

"That's 'cause your ass *was* slipping. You was getting sloppy wit yours, Duke," Webb said.

While they both laughed, Webb played with his Rottweiler, Butch. Webb was about to get into another sermon when they both saw a brand new white, 92' 300E Mercedes Benz turn the corner at Baby Park onto 12th. When Jason saw the car, he pressed his leg against the building, looked to the sky, and began to shake his head.

"Aww shit, Duke, now here come your broad and her scandalous crew. I bet she keeps that ass motivated when it comes to getting this paper," said Webb.

Before the words were out of Webb's mouth, Jason saw Tasha get out of the back seat of the Benz, with both hands filled with shopping bags. Her two girlfriends sat in the car.

"Baaaby," Tasha yelled in her strong Cali accent from across the street. Webb despised Tasha. For one, it was clear she was a gold digger. And two, she had his man Jason open from the start. The only reason Jason hadn't gone totally insane and married her was because of Webb's constant warnings. Time and time again Webb had told him that becoming too emotionally involved could prove disastrous in the game they played.

To avoid having Tasha come too close to Webb, Jason walked over to her, peeping her attire. Her sun-kissed skin was baked bronze from the summer heat. Her straight nose supported the designer frames that covered her doe-shaped eyes. Her thin lips gleamed with gloss, as she smacked on Double-Mint gum.

Jason saw where his money was going. Tasha wore a pair of tan, skin-tight jeans made out of Gucci material, a white T-shirt that was tied to the side revealing her belly button, and her hair was braided in extensions that showed off her new gold and diamond earrings.

He loved to see his woman look the way she did, but he hated the fact that the cost was always at his expense. He shuffled over to her and was met with disapproving eyes. Tasha's girlfriends sat in the front seat of the Benz and looked at Jason like he was begging for food. Ignoring her two girlfriends, he walked up to his girl, zoned in on her shades and said, "How you?"

"Don't be handling me like I'm one of your friends," Tasha yelled out making a scene as usual. She pointed her chin in Webb's direction, "Especially that buster over there," she grunted.

"So what up?" Jason asked filled with impatience.

She smiled, "Guess where I'm coming from?"

"Out spending my dough like always," he replied.

"Stop silly. You always playing when I want to holla at you about serious biz."

"A'ight, a'ight, make it quick. I got Webb waiting."

"Don't be rushing me for your hoodlum friends," Tasha said turning her nose up. "But nah, Boo, on the real we was up at Paramus Mall over in Jersey. After we left, we stopped off at the Acura dealer on route 17. Shauni's man gave her nine gees to put down on a new green Legend coupe and since Darlene got the Benz, you know I'm gone need a ride, so what up, Boo?"

As she spoke, he wondered to himself why he even dealt with a girl like the one he had. She kept her hand out, but he couldn't imagine finding a woman with better sex. Instead of pissing her off and saying 'no' right then and there he answered with, "Tasha, slow down, we live in the projects, let's get a crib first, and then move on to the vehicles."

Her head began its wag back and forth in trademark black woman fashion while her fingers snapped. "Listen, Jason Faust, I told you from jump, I was a high maintenance bitch. In the last five years, we went from my mom's house to an apartment in the hood. Did I deny *you,* when you ain't want to put up with your drunk ass moms upstairs?"

She went on, "Hell no, I didn't. I asked my mom if you could chill at our house until you came up. Now we got our own spot. Our apartment is phat and fo' real, I like the hood. So if you can't handle your business, I'll find another man to get me my Benz." Tasha had raised her voice and her friends were all ears.

From the expression on Jason's face Tasha sensed that she might have gone too far. Switching her tone up, she said in a cuddly little girl voice, "Nigga, you know I only messed with you when you was broke 'cause a dem blue eyes." As if she hadn't just finished attacking his manhood, she went on in a whole different direction. "I know our baby is gonna be all that whenever you handle your biz in that department." Then it was back to business, "Baby, so am I gonna get my whip or not?"

Jason's hand was balled into a fist. He was watching across the street as Webb laughed and nodded his head at Tasha while pointing his .45 at Tasha's head behind her back. All Jason had to do was nod at Webb and she would have been history. "Go upstairs, we'll talk about this later," he said.

"By the way, I'm going out tonight, can I hold the car?" she asked referring to Jason's Nissan 300ZX with the chrome Hammer rims.

Instead of flat out denying his girl, he tried to bargain with her. "Tasha, why you need the car if Darlene is driving hers?"

With her eyes glued to his and through clenched teeth she said, "I'm not trying to even let you embarrass me out here with your silly ass questions." She pushed her designer frames in position and said, "Now, I'm going to take a shower. You can come if you want to, or maybe Webb will volunteer to suck your ding-a-ling instead?"

Her proposal made him nervous, so he hurriedly looked over at Webb. He knew if Webb would have heard what she said, her brains would have been on the sidewalk.

Jason's eyes zoomed in on Tasha's ass as she walked off. Then he turned in Webb's direction. "Yo Webb, I'll be back in an hour," he said as he ran to catch Tasha. He recognized from Tasha's being so loose with her mouth that nothing could have been more important at that moment than showing his girl how he could indeed handle his biz.

TWO

Tasha had called him out and Jason responded by trying to blow her back out. "Oh yeah, yeah, yeah, right there. Boo, don't stop, don't stop."

Tasha was bent over grabbing her ankles in the shower while drops of steaming hot water hit her back. Guy's, *Let's Chill* was blasting in the background. Jason was purposely choking her with the heavy eighteen-karat gold link chain. Mixed into his grip along with the chain he had a handful of her braids and was yanking them with all his strength while pounding his manhood deep into his woman.

Jason got rougher with her, causing the top of her head to bang up against the wall several times. He purposely ignored the cries of pain that were mixed in with the ones from pleasure. It only turned her on more to be dogged out by him. "Oh shit, baby …Oh…Oh…I'm about to, I'm gonna cum…I'm cum…I'm cummminnng." In hurried breaths she screamed, "push it harder, Boo… I'm … almost there. Jay…talk that shit to me… I like… talk that shit."

While Jason contemplated saying something to her romantic she grew impatient.

"Talk… that… shit… to… me…now… Boo," Tasha yelled.

"Oü pa en yen, Mwen swété outé on bagay," Jason spoke in the Patwa dialect that he'd learned as a child. It turned Tasha on to hear it.

"Yes, yes, motherfucker…cum for me Boo, cum for me," she panted out.

Reaching his climax, Jason pulled his manhood out of Tasha while letting her out of his chokehold. He hopped out of the tub in a frenzied state, spun her head around, and ejaculated on her lips and face. When his toes uncurled and his breathing was at a normal pace, he snatched her by the hair again.

To Tasha's surprise, he then cocked his arm back and pimp slapped her with all the power his one hundred and sixty five-pound frame could muster. "You got a slick mouth. Don't ever talk that shit about replacing me," he reprimanded her. She said nothing and the blank expression on her face gave no clues of what she felt.

He grabbed a washcloth to wipe the excess sperm from his dick. When he looked into the shower, Tasha was smiling at him as she licked the sticky liquid off the side of her face.

After he exited the bathroom he walked into the spare bedroom where all of his belongings were and he opened the closet. Although they slept together, Jason kept a separate bedroom. He called it his office.

As he was choosing his attire for the evening, the chill of the night air was slipping through his window and reminded him that he needed a jacket, so he grabbed the jacket to his Air Jordan sweat suit, and a pair of Gap jeans. He then grabbed his bulletproof vest, a pair of socks and as usual, a fresh pair of dark blue nylon knee-high woman's stockings.

After laying out his outfit, he reached in the closet to remove the lose floorboard. He reached in and grabbed a thousand dollars in cash, his jewelry, and a snubbed nosed .357 with two speed loaders. He was set for the night.

Jason dressed and when he looked out of his window, he could see the florescent green glow of the car-phone in Webb's tinted out 300ZX. He headed out to meet him. They'd decided to buy the same car but the difference between the two was that Webb's was black with all black rims. Webb had added stash compartments to his for his guns, and a high-powered quad exhaust with a computer chipped fuel injection. On a bad day, he could get up to 140mph in less than seven seconds.

Jason and Webb were going up to Bay Plaza in the Bronx to see the new Terminator 2 movie, and then to The Rink over in Teaneck, New Jersey to watch the ladies roller skate.

"Where you going, Boo?" Tasha asked while she was naked, fixing her hair.

"Why, Tasha? You making sure I don't bump into you tonight?"

"Well *I know* you won't, but I'm just checking on my man, that's all."

As he walked out towards the front door, he avoided stepping on the pile of bags she had on the living room floor. When he looked down, he saw bags that were marked with Gucci, Chanel, Polo and Fendi. He turned to her and said, "How much of this stuff is for me?"

"Um…I planned to get you something from Tommy Hilfager but it slipped my mind," She said with embarrassment on her face. "You know I was out with the girls, Jay, and you know how it gets when we're spending money."

He thought about the three grand she had just spent and how she hadn't pulled one caper to get a dime of it. Then he thought of her two girlfriends and figured they would all probably be out later trying to catch some new rich fish so they could have new cars by the fall.

Tasha was persistent, "So can I hold the car tonight?"

As he walked out of the front door he said, "No, and be home by two."

Her face turned sour. "No? What you mean *no*?" she began to protest. "If your broke ass would buy me my own ride, I wouldn't have to ask you for yours," she stomped towards him.

"Alright then, I'll just find me a big Willie that'll make sure I ain't got nothing to complain about." Instead of blowing his mood and taking the time to give her a beat down, the door slammed in her face.

As he strolled down the stairs with his gun in hand, he thought of how easy it would be for Tasha to find another man to buy her what she wanted. He headed back for the door.

As he opened the door, he reached for his key ring and threw them in her direction. She looked down and picked it up. Jason walked out, slamming the door once again behind him. She ran behind him in the dark rank hallway wearing a sheer nightgown. Tasha smiled as she gripped the back of his head, shoving her tongue so far down his throat, he almost choked. Seconds later, she squatted down sliding her hands into his pants. Unable to control his passion, Jason drooled like a junkyard dog. She pulled his out his jimmy and began to give him a blow job right in the hallway.

When he stiffened to his maximum length, she stopped sucking on him and said, "Don't forget what you got at home waiting for you tonight." She stepped back into the apartment laughing.

Jason fixed his pants and headed down the stairs with thoughts of his twisted mate.

"Yo, yo Duke, how you gonna have me waiting all night?"

"Tasha be tripping, Webb."

"How many times I got to tell you bout that girl, man? That bitch is the devil in disguise…"

"Alright, alright," Jason cut him off. If he let Webb get started, he would have to hear it all night. Webb was the one who convinced him not to marry her when he was ready to the first time. He felt Jason was too young to settle down, amongst the other thirty reasons why. First and foremost was that Tasha just wouldn't make a good wife.

They pulled off in Webb's car headed for the multiplex. Jason removed two fatly rolled Phillie's Blunts from his pocket and slipped in a new DJ Kid-Capri mix tape. It was the best sess Queens had to offer. They bobbed their heads to the sounds of Naughty by Nature's hit song, *O.P.P,* as they lit and puffed.

Tasha's words were ringing in Jason's head about her wanting a new car and what she was willing to do to get it. Jason turned down the sound system. "Yo, I got to get some real house paper, homey."

"Chill, homey. What, you dreaming again?"

"Yeah, man, my dream is a ticket out of here. I'm stressing over this paper, 'cause right now mines ain't long enough."

"I know you got at least thirty gee's left over from the last heist, plus the eighty we split today."

Jason was calculating that he really had forty-two thousand dollars from the last robbery he and Webb pulled off. In that heist there were a couple of Albanian casualties, but the take had equaled sixty grand apiece. He said, "Yeah, but I'm tired of living in the hood, it's time to get house, money."

"Yo, just relax. I got something lined up. Just enjoy the night and I'll break it all down to you later," Webb reassured.

By the time they reached Bay Plaza in the Bronx, they were feeling mellow and ready for some Arnold and some Terminator 2 special effects. When Webb stepped out of the car, Jason laughed at how much they were alike. Webb adjusted the two Glock 17's behind his back. He was also dressed in dark clothing with his bullet-proof vest underneath.

The movie was all that they expected to see. A few women admirably peeped at Webb and Jason. They both sported Presidential Rolex's, and Jason's diamond pendent was definitely an eye catcher.

Some local thugs looked their way and Webb's smirk indicated that he was ready for the thugs to make a move. Jason, on the other hand, was hoping that if any of them did make a move, that they came his way first. He was sure that not too many people in that theater had the boxing skills he had, not even Webb. The difference between the two was that Jason would send you to the hospital, and Webb preferred to send you to your grave.

With '*It never rains in Southern California'* playing in the car, Webb went over the Tri-Borough bridge and onto the Brooklyn-Queens Expressway. When they made the left at Flatbush Junction and parked in front of the world famous Junior's, Jason knew that Webb was going to buy his favorite black and white cheesecake. He decided to order a strawberry one since the weed he smoked made him feel he could eat every dessert in the window. As they headed out the door they saw Q-Tip from the new rap group, A Tribe Called Quest, walking into the restaurant with a dime piece on his arm.

They nodded at one another. Webb commented, "Yo Duke, remember when you could tell rappers because of all the gold them niggas wore? I wish I would catch one of them studio gangsters rocking some of that shit again. Remember that night we caught what's-his-face leaving the club?"

Jason laughed out, "Yeah."

"I took that nigga's shit right in front of his bodyguards." Webb chuckled like a demon. They climbed into the car and pulled off.

Jason knew it was too late to head to Jersey. Webb must have come to the same conclusion. He kept driving straight until he reached the heart of Bed-Stuy. The car stopped on the familiar corner of Nostrand and Gates Avenues.

Webb was originally from Brooklyn. His mom died when he was twelve and his father was doing forty in Sing-Sing for a variety of crimes. He was forced to leave Brooklyn when the welfare system tried to send him to live with a foster care family at twelve. Instead of being away from his eight siblings on the system's terms, he wandered over to Queens. He fended for himself while living in a back room of a married couple's apartment. They were hard-core addicts and allowed Webb to stay there as long as he came up with rent. Webb got himself a knife until he could afford a gun and started his career as a stick-up artist.

The neighborhood rumor had it that when he was fifteen the junkies he lived with tried to molest him and sell him off to an old white fag who was into young black boys. A week later the husband was found dead in the East River. It was also rumored that the body of the woman was buried in the floor of the apartment that he still occupied. No one actually believed that, but at the same time Webb could be counted on to do almost anything to anyone who got him wrong. Whenever Webb felt like getting away, Bed-Stuy was where he could be found.

Webb got out of the car, and Jason followed. The regular gang of hustlers were out there playing Celo for small bankrolls. B.O, Dog, Tank, and Biggie played for a hundred dollars a roll. For the rest of the night they hung out drinking bottles of Möet and smoking plenty of weed, blunt after blunt. At four a.m. Jason was ready to go.

On the ride back Webb was playing the Kid Capri tape in an effort to stay awake. When 'My Mind is Playing Tricks on Me' by The Geto Boys came on, he made an effort to wake Jason up. He blasted his sounds and put his three amps to work. Jason awoke and hurried to cut the sounds off.

"Homey…yo Jay, I'm glad I got your attention."

"What up man?" said Jason as he cut the music down.

"Listen, listen." Webb had a bad habit of saying most things twice. "Duke…Duke, that caper we was building on earlier. It's on for Monday morning. You gonna need to meet me with two gees in your pocket. We got a lot of work to do on Monday Duke, so get some rest tomorrow, and don't tell that scandalous ass chick about our plans either. You hear me, homey?"

"I heard, now shut up so I can get some sleep." Jason rolled over to face the window.

"No time for sleep, no time for sleep, we here already, and you walking with me from the garage."

When they rolled into the garage on Queens Plaza, Jason's parking space was empty. It was close to 6 a.m., so he figured that Tasha parked in the projects. As he and Webb were walking into the projects, he thought he saw a man in what looked like his car zoom past behind him. It looked just like his car, but he wasn't certain. He didn't mention anything to Webb. He knew Webb would have a fit and wind up screaming a bunch of I-told-you-so's. So he shook it off, thinking that he was paranoid from the weed. He reasoned that Tasha was probably at home waiting for him to return.

Webb went into building 4107, and Jason into building 4112. It was early in the morning, but he pulled out his .357 anyway. He refused to be caught slipping. There had been too many homicides done where the killers were waiting for the victim to come home tipsy only to get caught off guard.

When Jason opened the door to his apartment, he could feel someone's presence. He cocked the hammer back to the revolver, and inched his way towards the back where the three bedrooms were located. When he reached his bedroom, he saw Tasha in bed sound asleep. He immediately tried to figure out where his car was, but before he had a chance to wake her, Tasha jumped up.

"What time is it?" she asked with a sound of alarm in her voice.

In a whisper he asked, "What the hell is your problem? And where's my car?"

She had a surprised look on her face as if she was caught with her hand in the cookie jar. Hurriedly, she changed her expression. "Oh…um…don't even start tripping, your car is safe. I just parked it on the other side because I wanted to go grocery shopping early so I could get back in time to make you breakfast in bed."

He felt like she was lying, but he wasn't in the mood for arguing and was too tired from the weed to walk outside and investigate. Ever since Webb disturbed his sleep in the car earlier, he had been dying to get into his king-sized bed. He didn't want any drama early in the morning. Then Tasha's pager went off by the bed.

"Who the hell is beeping you at 6:15 a.m. in the morning?" Jason asked.

As she rushed out of bed she said, "Stop tripping, that's Darlene beeping me so I can get up early and catch Pathmark before the Sunday crowd gets in there."

"Whatever," Jason said as his head hit the pillow. Seconds later, he heard Tasha leave the apartment.

It was one o'clock when Jason finally awoke. He heard someone coming through his front door, so he jumped up with the revolver that he kept under his pillow. When he saw Tasha, he put the gun away. His intuition told him that she had been up to something, because she carried a small bag. Still fighting to get some rest, he decided to lie down for another hour instead of starting an argument. He never put in work of any kind on Sundays. He always tried to do something to ease his mind from his dangerous life, and not even Tasha could interfere with that.

At a quarter til' two, he was startled to consciousness by a warm feeling on his manhood. Tasha dripped warmed caramel on his dick and balls as she sucked up and down like she was bobbing for apples. Jason loved her sexual appetite, but he was starving as he came to consciousness. "Yo, baby, ummm, damn. Let me eat first," he yelled, almost knocking the food off the bed.

Tasha pinned his chest with her hand and put him flat on his back without coming up for air. She stopped for a moment. "Talk that shit to me Boo," she moaned and commenced to sucking. She loved making niggas scream her name like a bitch.

"Ou sé on pil kaka...Ou sé on pil kaka," Jason watched his foreign words drive her crazy.

She pushed her Ralph Lauren panties to the side. Her fingers strummed her vagina like a pro. In and out her fingers moved, until she reached her climax. She gulped his cum as he reached his peek right behind her. He watched as his girl took it all in her mouth, spit it out into his belly button, and then suck it all back up in what seemed like one simple move.

"Ti bou zin ou sé on pil kaka," he said, as she prepared for a second orgasm. What she failed to realize was that she was being insulted. Those Creole words meant that she was a good for nothing slut. Jason felt no remorse. He meant every word.

As he ate he wondered to himself why he kept her around. The only answer he could come up with was, besides the fact that she was fine as hell, her sex was off the hook. As far as he was concerned, Tasha was too ghetto and manipulating to be treated like a real queen. She was like a bad apple; shiny on the outside, but rotten to the core.

By the time Jason was done eating, Tasha had rolled him a blunt. He smoked it until it disappeared. "Change the sheets," he commanded Tasha. Jason hopped like a little boy towards the bathroom. He ran his water, dropping in a few bath crystals. He burned the scented candles that lined the edge of the tub, and slid into the soothing water, one foot at a time. He closed his eyes thinking about his and Webb's next scheme. As his body adjusted to the temperature he began to relax trying to think of only good thoughts. A day would come when he'd be out of the hood with enough money to never come back. He'd have a real woman by his side. One he could love *and* respect.

Just then he heard Tasha's laughter outside of the bathroom as she cackled to one of her friends on the phone. Just like that his daydream had come to an abrupt end.

Three

Jason expected Webb to be outside by the time he got there, but he was nowhere in sight. The projects were still quiet except for the junkies and the earliest risers headed off to work. Hating to be kept waiting, he began to walk across the street. He stopped suddenly when he saw Webb striding towards him. He carried a carton of Tropicana orange juice and the *New York Law Journal* in the same hand, while eating a banana. Suited down, Webb looked more like a lawyer than a criminal. Jason was impressed.

The two men treaded toward the Queens Plaza garage. Webb insisted that they take Jason's car so he could read his newspaper. Jason agreed, opened his car door, and noticed a Newport cigarette on his floorboard. His seat had been pushed back. Jason looked at Webb without giving away his thoughts. Neither he nor Tasha smoked cigarettes. Something was up, and he planned to get to the bottom of it when he got home.

They hit the 59th Street Queens-Borough Bridge and headed for midtown Manhattan. Jason's mind raced with thoughts of what Tasha was doing behind his back. He knew that he pleased her in every way possible, so she had no reason to cheat on him. Getting her a new car was the reason why he was so anxious to pull the move today. Knowing that if he didn't have his mind on what he was doing, things could go wrong, he immediately shifted his thoughts to the robbery Webb had planned. He hoped that his take would be large enough for him to purchase a home and buy Tasha a new car.

Webb directed Jason to 9th Street at Sixth Avenue. He told Jason to park in front of Barney's clothing store. "We need to cop a couple of suits, no fly shit either. We gotta look like businessmen," Webb said.

After Jason got out of the car he was filled with anxiety. He knew that two thousand dollars was not going far in Barney's. He also knew that whatever Webb had planned must have been a legitimate establishment since they needed suits.

Upon entry into the store, the security guards looked them over once and then looked away. A salesman helped Jason choose a few pieces, until Webb drifted over toward them, put his arm around his shoulder and said, "Homey, summer material, single-breasted suit. Dark colors. Either blue, dark gray or brown. No pinstripes or distinctive marks. No pretty shirts or loud ties. We got to be invisible in midtown, invisible in midtown, homey."

Jason connected the dots immediately. They would hit a firm in the financial district. In his best uppity impression, he mimicked in a British accent, "Excuse me chap, can you tell me the most popular color for this season?"

They made two more stops. One, for non-prescription eyeglasses and then a second for ankle high dress shoes. They chose Bruno Magli lace-ups because of the rubber soles. In case they had to do some serious running, they would need the grip and the comfort.

Jason parked in the basement of the World Trade Center and they took a walk to 40 Wall Street. When they reached the building, they walked a complete circle around its perimeter and then to Pine Street.

"All right, homey. We gonna hit the twenty-ninth floor, got it? The twenty-ninth floor. Manufacturers Hanover Trust. Eight minutes, eight minutes, baby boy, and we out. Caps on when we come through the door. No heat flashing unless we have to. Room in the back is mine. Cash drops on the wake-up. You got the floor, watches and necklaces only. No eye in the sky and security is nada. Silent alarms fo' sure. Eight minutes, baby boy. We roll at nine forty-five. In and out. I go left, you go right, back door to Pine, car service on the low. White car. I come straight out the front. Down on the Path train to Jersey, drive back to the QB and see you at my crib. You get bagged, send Tasha over like the last time. You don't see me at the crib, check the second precinct, and make that lawyer chick, what's her name?"

"Yancey, Troy Yancey," Jason replied.

"Yeah, make sure she bring me something to eat and a fresh pair of clothes."

As they headed back home, Jason was thinking about Tasha and what he was going to do to get the truth out of her. He didn't like putting his hands on women because he thought of his abusive mother. But Tasha had told him flat out once that she would not respect him if he didn't. As always, Jason gave her whatever she wanted.

As he wrestled with sadistic thoughts, Webb broke him out of his daydream when he said, "Duke, you gonna crash at my crib tonight. I don't want that scandalous chick fucking wit' your head when we got to go to work tomorrow. I'll give you one of my heaters to carry or you can use the burner you have on you. But you staying with me until that car comes to get us at seven thirty. Don't forget, you got to drive me to Jersey City and back by four in the morning."

Jason knew Webb was right. Tasha didn't know how lucky she was, so he put his plans to deal with her off until tomorrow night. He did realize that his whole life could change in just one day, and it was always possible that he would never get the chance.

Four

Webb and Jason sat up 'til midnight going over the plans for the next day. Neither of them used drugs the night before a big caper. In order to get to sleep faster, they worked out. Webb's routine was too much for Jason to handle, and by the time Jason reached a hundred push-ups, he was ready to pass out. Webb saw that and began to do push-ups even faster chanting, "I'm a soldier, I'm a soldier. The more you sweat in peace is the less you bleed in war." Jason wasn't interested in what he was saying, because his head was in the toilet as he vomited from over exertion.

By 3:00 a.m., Webb was up and Butch was licking Jason's face. They dressed and headed for the door. They strolled towards the parking garage where they picked up their cars. Webb led Jason over the Queensborough Bridge, down the F.D.R. Expressway across 42nd Street, and into the Lincoln Tunnel. They exited the downtown Jersey City ramp.

Webb parked his car right outside of Penn Station, and jumped into Jason's. Jason fought to stay awake, but managed to reach Queens Plaza in less than a half-hour.

Back at Webb's apartment, Jason briefly considered stopping home and checking on Tasha, but he changed his mind. He knew how important business was and he didn't want to hear Webb's mouth. When Webb went to walk Butch, Jason called her, but to his surprise, no answer. He then paged her because he remembered that she'd kept her pager by the bed. He didn't get an answer, and figured she was probably hanging out earlier and was at home sleeping hard.

In their suit pockets, they each had the stocking caps they made to cover their faces. In other pockets, they had their gloves and in their boots, they had stashed razor blades in case they ended up jail on Rikers Island. If that happened, things on the Island would be a lot easier for them if they split someone's face wide open as soon as they walked through the door.

Before leaving the apartment they synchronized their TAG Heuer watches. The last thing they did was stand in front of each other to inspect each other to make sure nothing about the other blatantly stood out.

The white car showed up on time. They slowly walked down the project steps geared up. Webb had two Glocks, and Jason, a fifty-caliber Desert Eagle. When they reached the desolate street, there was a Lincoln Town Car parked out front. Webb turned to Jason, "Homey, this is Roger," he said. "Roger this is Jay. Yo Jay, Roger's gonna wait on Pine Street for you."

"Roger, we gonna need to keep you on call until noon at least. When we go to take care of our business meeting, if Jay don't come out by 10:30 a.m., you can leave Duke," Webb said while putting a small roll of bills into the driver's hand. "Here's an advance payment."

In anticipation of what they were about to do, they went through their rituals while Roger quizzically looked back and forth at the two men through the mirror. The car entered Manhattan and they eventually stopped at a diner on Chambers Street, across from City Hall, so they could eat breakfast.

Webb was in a zone. Tapping on the table, he laughed and hummed to himself. Jason was praying that he wouldn't have to kill anyone and asking God to forgive him for the crime that he was about to commit. When his prayers were over, he sat at the restaurant booth and thought of every way the robbery could go bad. At 9:15 a.m, the men left the restaurant and headed to take care of their business.

Instead of pulling up in front of the intended Wall Street building, Jason exited the car on one corner, as Webb got out on the corner two blocks down. As Jason closed the car door and adjusted his briefcase, he caught the eye of a striking Latina. Although she wore a pair of dark, Armani shades, Jason could tell she was staring into his eyes. He always got that response out of women. The glance caused the gorgeous woman to bump into a passerby and she dropped her briefcase losing all of its contents.

He was breaking a major robbery rule deterring from his course, but he bent down to help the woman.

"Shit...thank you," she said as she squatted to retrieve her belongings. "Do you see what you made me do?" The lady looked up at Jason.

He wanted to walk away and take care of his business. Despite it being the precise time he had to meet Webb at the elevator, he reached down to help. "My fault, huh, well I guess I owe you one?" he said flirting.

With a voice laced with natural sensuality she said, "Sure it's your fault. Being so handsome and striking, what's a girl to do? Since you helped me, I guess I owe you one too, huh?" Handing her a folder, his hand touched hers and he noticed that her skin was like silk.

He looked down at his watch and began to rush off. "No sweat," he said. He tried to focus on what he had to do, but her sensual voice, soft touch, and scent had thrown him off. It was 9:35 and he was late. He moved faster to reach the escalators of the building.

The huge glass mirrored doors of 40 Wall Street were open when Jason stepped through. Webb moved in right next to him. They rode as any two strangers that shared an escalator would. When they reached the top landing, they both walked in opposite directions to reach parallel elevator banks. Now back on time, Webb and Jason both pressed the twenty-ninth floor in their separate elevators. As the doors opened and closed on what seemed like every floor, both men kept their heads pointed towards the floor. They counted the time down on their watches, knowing that the other was doing the same exact thing.

The elevator rang at the twenty-ninth floor. The alarms to their watches rang. It was 9:42. Jason and Webb met up at the entrance to a long hall that lead to the double oak doors bearing the logo of Manufacturers Hanover Trust. As they walked down the empty hall, they looked at their exit path, then at the service elevator, set their digital stopwatches and the countdown began. Their pace quickened and they slid on their gloves, and stocking caps. Gently they opened the thick brown oak doors.

Jason entered first and saw an empty reception desk. Past that was a room filled with workers at their cubicles.

Webb slid a black lounge chair in front of the door and made a beeline for the back room with his guns drawn. As he walked, a few of the shocked employees looked at him without giving any verbal response. Jason stood at the door, opened his briefcase onto the floor. An executive walked from his office with a mug of coffee in his hand. He didn't see Jason until it was too late. He was greeted with an uppercut and a left hook and fell backwards into the wall. He snatched the portly man by the tie and stood him against the wall. He then pulled out his cannon and announced, "May I have your attention please. I need everyone down on the floor and all of your cash, watches, necklaces, and diamond earrings in this briefcase in less than two minutes. I will randomly check your pockets and desk. Anyone holding back will be shot."

He turned to the man that he hit and said, "You. Collect the items. And if you move too slowly I will put a hole in you."

While Jason was working, Webb moved right on schedule. The first room was empty and there wasn't a safe to be found. The second room Webb entered had two large stacks of cash and a money counter on a table. A black woman who resembled Dionne Warwick was signing papers for the armored express drivers, who had their backs to the door. As soon as the woman saw Webb she screamed, "Oh my God."

The two security officers were stunned. When they turned around, they found themselves looking down the barrels of Webb's pistols. "If you move carefully and quickly you will all make it home to your families. If any of you wants to be a hero, I *will* kill you all, understand?"

They all nodded. One of the drivers said, "Listen, just stay calm. We aren't going to do anything to stop you."

"Yo, shut the fuck up and put the money in the case before I blast you." The man quickly closed his mouth. The safe was open already and Webb ordered their assistance. There was too much to fit into his briefcase so he ordered them to pack only the hundreds. "Throw the stacks with the twenties and fifties over here to me." Webb was going to stuff as much as he could into his waist and suit pockets.

As soon as they finished, the guards cuffed themselves to the table at Webb's orders and surrendered their keys. Webb took their pistols, packing them into his waist further humiliating them.

He walked into the main office, and Jason had everyone silent on the floor. The lounge chair that was blocking the office door was moved, and together they walked out of the office without saying a word to each other. The whole robbery took seven minutes.

When they returned to the long hallway, Webb made a right and raced down the exit steps. Jason made a left and tried to take the service elevator, but it was locked. It was supposed to be his getaway and open at all times, but instead of panicking, he went to the other set of stairs. When he heard the faint sound of footsteps running up towards him, he knew security had to be on the elevator and coming up the other stairwell Webb went down. Jason was trapped.

He was too professional to panic, and didn't worry about Webb. He knew there would be no surrendering or retreating for Webb. Once again, Jason had to violate one of his robbery rules. He and Webb never used the same route to escape. If the police caught up with them, it made little sense for both of them to get captured, so they always went separate ways.

As Jason opened the door to the exit, he heard security coming up the steps. Immediately he went down the opposite stairwell that Webb used. He put his stocking cap and gloves in his briefcase, put the gun in his waist, and then opened the entrance door one flight under. When he hurriedly stepped out of the door he felt a bump, heard a thump, and a woman yell, "Christ Jesus. Not again."

Jason looked down to see the gorgeous Latin woman in a pink suit with her coffee spilled all over her skirt. Her head was down as she was making sure her papers didn't get wet. Since all eyes looked his way, he scratched his ear, held on tightly to his briefcase, and bent down to help the woman up.

In a low tone filled with anger she asked, "Is this your idea of a joke or something?"

With nothing else to do, but think fast, he pulled the lady closer to him. "I guess this is destiny's harsh way of saying we had to meet each other. I don't want to see what happens if I choose to ignore next time. Hi, my name is Jay."

They squatted to pick the papers up from the floor. It was déjà vu.

Her attitude disappeared. "Oh, so you think you can get off that light with your fast talking, huh, Jay?" She extended her limp soft hand as she examined her skirt. "My name is Zeida. Zeida Carro, and we definitely know now who owes who, big time. Look at what you did to my skirt, you," she smirked. Jason helped her up and watched as security entered from every angle on the same floor.

Security studied everyone suspiciously. Jason knew that the victims could tell by his voice that he was black, so security had to be looking for two black men with suits on. That description fit too many people on Wall Street. Jason looked at his watch and saw that it was ten o'clock. He still had some time to spare.

Zeida stopped talking while watching security run about causing panic. She then looked into Jason's eyes, squinted with hers, and then looked him up and down. He watched her eyes, and with her chin, she pointed to his briefcase. One of his gloves was sticking halfway out of the case and security was heading his way. When Zeida saw the security guard approaching, she put her leg closer to Jason's crotch and covered the sight of the glove with her body.

A young man with a blue uniform, silver badge, and baseball cap said, "Excuse me sir, madam, we're looking for two black males who..."

Jason slipped his hand closer to his waist when security approached. Zeida saw him reach for his waist, so she turned to the security guard, and in a loud voice she looked him straight in the eyes and said, "Are you questioning us because we are the only two minorities standing here?" She looked down at her watch. "This gentleman and I have been standing here for the last twenty minutes. And it's obvious that you don't know who I am? I am the chief financial officer for Douglas A. Warner III, need I say more?" She pulled out her pen, and held the coffee stained paper and finished with, "By the way, give me your name."

The security guard, thinking salary over supercop, smiled at the two. "Ma'am, I apologize. There's no need to be upset. You two have a nice day."

Zeida and Jason watched as he gathered the rest of security and left the floor. She then turned to Jason with a witty grin. "So by the way mister, time is ticking, and I know you're in the middle of something."

Jason knew he was busted. With a sly grin on his face, he said, "I don't know what you're talking about, but yes, I do need to bounce."

Zeida leaned on her heel as she held onto the bottom button of his shirt. "Is that so?" she said. Well, let me escort you down the elevator. You can give me your information so that I can send my shopping bill to you. This skirt is ruined and it's gonna take two suits to replace it. I have a twelve-hour day ahead and just enough time to catch Nordstrom's.

Jason was not about to argue with the gorgeous woman. On the way out of the building she kept commenting about his eyes. She told him that a man with eyes like his couldn't be trusted, but that didn't stop her from giving him her info. He slid her card in his pocket and Zeida stood mesmerized. She watched as he left 40 Wall Street and made the first left at the corner.

He checked his watch and saw, Roger, the driver of the getaway, looking around for him. Looking back over his shoulder Jason saw that the NYPD was all over the building and scurrying about the perimeter. He stopped at the tattered newsstand on the corner, bought a Wall Street Journal, and tucked it under his arm so that he looked the part. While rushing to get to the parked car on Pine Street, he saw an officer catch his eye. Jason hoped he wouldn't call him, but he heard someone say, "Hey guy...hey."

He didn't turn around. All he had was a few more steps until he reached the car, but then he heard his alarm go off and saw Roger put the car into drive. With the police officer calling behind him, Roger must have heard the cop, because he looked right at Jason's face, and Jason winked at him. Jason reached for the car door and placed the briefcase on the floor. Seconds later the police officer caught up to him and grabbed him by the elbow.

He had one foot in the car, turned around, and in a voice imitating a British aristocrat, he asked, "My gosh sir, what seems to be the problem?"

Shocked by either the blue eyes or the British accent, the officer breathing heavily, stopped as his backup circled the area. The officer said, "Oh...um...I was going to inform you that there was a robbery in the building you just came out of and I wanted to ask you if you saw anything."

While the officer kept looking at Jason's eyes and shaking his head in disbelief, Jason said, "Heavens to Betsy, was anyone harmed?

I'm Prime Minister Mark Anduzé. I was just visiting my dear friend, Douglas Warner III in that very same building. I have an important meeting at City Hall with Mayor Dinkins, but I'm sure he'll understand if I'm late." Jason smiled then looked at the officer and asked, "What is your name? Oh, I see by your tag, officer O'Ryan is it?"

The officer began to turn red in embarrassment. He looked at Jason and then at the rest of the officers and said, "Forget it. You can go on your way, sir. I just wanted to inform you and make sure that you weren't victimized, that's all. Sorry for the interruption."

"Well you gentlemen have a merry day. I hope you catch the crooks. I'll be sure to mention you men to the mayor," Jason said as he sat in the car and slammed the door. He opened his paper as the driver sped off. Immediately after Roger made the first right heading towards the West Side Highway, Jason said, "Yo homey, get me the hell up out of here."

Five

Jason pulled into Queensbridge at eleven thirty. When he reached Webb's place, he could hear Butch on the other side of the door waiting to eat an intruder. To be on the safe side, he put his hand to the bottom of the door so Butch could smell his scent. He then put his spare key in the lock and stepped into the apartment. Butch happily greeted Jason at the door.

Jason laid the briefcase on the table and began to transfer the contents onto a strip of black velvet cloth. Butch jumped on the table with his two paws and nose in the case. Jason didn't dare push the massive dog away. Webb had a special language that only he and his dog knew. Webb had trained Butch that a command from anyone other than him meant to attack.

After he hid the empty briefcase, he went to the radio and cut on 10.10 WINS AM, the all news station, to hear if the robbery was mentioned, or if the authorities had apprehended Webb. He removed his clothes, threw them in a garbage bag, and sat the bag in the corner. Jason put on the clothes from the day before, and sat on the couch to listen to the news. As he lounged back, thinking about how much money they made, his mind switched gears and thoughts of Zeida slid into his mind.

Just as he was beginning to see her face and recounting the curves that he could remember, Butch came over and began to sniff between his legs. He looked down at the dog, and the moment he was attempting to push his head away, Butch looked at him and growled. Butch was too close to his prized possession. He sat still with some measure of fear as the dog continuously sniffed and licked in between his legs. Jason was looking up at the ceiling and prayed for Webb to walk through the door.

For close to five minutes Butch continued to sniff him and there wasn't anything he could do about it. Finally, Butch jumped up on Webb's couch with him. He sat his head on Jason's lap and went to sleep. Jason had to use the bathroom at the time, and considered trying to push the dog's head off of his lap. But as long as the beast was sleep he figured he was safe.

Patiently he sat on the couch listening to the news. He perked up when he saw the flash that MHT was robbed. When reports of the amount that thieves had gotten away with were mentioned, Jason figured that the company had probably tripled the amount that was stolen in order to bilk their insurance policy. When he heard the newscaster say that the police had no one in custody and no suspects at the present, he knew it was just a little longer before Webb walked through the door.

As he sat waiting, Butch's ears suddenly pricked up. He ran to the door, took a sniff, and then ran back into a corner and played like he was sleeping. That's when Jason heard Webb's key in the door. He couldn't believe that the dog was outsmarting Webb.

"Where the hell you been, Bro? I just heard about it on the news." Jason said.

With a look of exhaustion, Webb said, "Duke…Duke, you had the easy part, Duke. What the hell took you so long to come out of the building, Duke?"

"*Easy part*? Man you ain't never gonna believe this." Jason said.

Web unbuttoned his shirt, "Parlay, parlay. Let me switch up first."

Jason watched as Webb dumped the contents of his briefcase onto the table. He wiped both of the brief cases down, and threw them, along with his clothes into a garbage bag. Jason waited as Webb jumped in and out of the shower in ten minutes and came back to the living room. Webb said, "Spill it homey."

"Yo, check it. When we broke, I went to the service elly and the joint was dead. I was about to be locked down up in that piece so I got on some ol' McGiver shit, right? I went down the other steps, but I heard the Poe-poe running up. I figured then that they was on the elly too. I just knew I was surrounded homey."

"Yo…Yo Duke, get to the end of it," Webb was losing his patience.

"Yo, chill," said Jason. "I decided to jet down the steps one floor, while security was coming up the same stairwell. As soon as I came through the door on the stairs, I bumped into this fine honey." Jason described Zeida's body with his hands, "She was like bang-bang-bang. Definitely a fifty-cent piece. No sooner than I got down there, security was everywhere. I was about to bust some caps, but I just grabbed honey and pulled her to me on some real playa-type moves. And when one of the rent-a-cops was ready to question me, she stood up for a brother." Jason did the *Whop* dance and said, "She chose a playa like me on the spot. Know what I'm saying? So I told her to walk me downstairs and I might give her my number, and like a trooper, she walked a playa out like I was her pimp and she was my...."

"Duke, Duke, Duke you getting carried away. What was the chick's name?"

"I got her card right here," he said while reaching into his pockets. "It says Zeida Carro, CFO to Douglas A. Warner III of JP Morgan and Chase and Co. She even gave me her home address."

Webb held up his cannon. "So now we got to go push her wig back so she won't identify you?"

Jason's jaw dropped in shock. "Damn Webb, why you always want to kill some some shit?"

"Alright, another chick got you open already? Or do you want to turn her out and find out where her boss keeps his paper?"

Jason looked to the ground with his hand to his chin and said, "Aye Yo, I didn't think of that... what the hell am I saying? I'm trying to make this chick my piece. Just forget about her Webb. She's baby mama material."

"Oh yeah, then I want to meet her, I want to meet her, fo' sho'. Any chick that'll make you think about dropping that scandalous ho, Tasha, I'm cool with already, Duke."

After Jason was done exaggerating his version of the events, Webb explained that the robbery was for three hundred thousand, but they only had thirty thousand in cash that wasn't ruined, from loaded dye packs. He then explained to Jason that they had to take the jewelry to their connection, and split the cash.

Jason was completely disappointed to hear about the money being ruined. He needed a big pay off to get the house he wanted. He also wanted to give Tasha the car she had been bugging him for. Now that he would only be receiving fifteen thousand dollars, problems from his woman were going to multiply. He shrugged his shoulders and figured that fifteen thousand was pretty good for a day's work and no one got killed.

"Duke, meet me here at seven-thirty after rush hour, so we can go downtown and meet the connect."

With Tasha on his mind, Jason gathered his things, put the stacks of cash in his waist, and headed out the door.

Tasha was on the phone when he entered the bedroom. She looked up at Jason and into the phone she said, "Scratch that, my man just walked in the door and ain't been home for two days so I'm gonna be in for the night. But I'm gonna definitely let you hold that when I see you."

Tasha hung up the phone with a smile on her face. She wore a multi colored two-piece Victoria's Secret negligee. Her talons were airbrushed to match her toenails, and her body was well-oiled. Through the side of her panties, he could see that her pubic hairs were groomed. She tied her extension braids into a ponytail head, and Jason was aroused immediately.

"Who was that on the phone?" he asked.

"Damn Boo, I been here worried sick, thinking you was locked up or something, and that's all you can stress me about. I stood by the phone all last night waiting for you to call. I even went to your mother's thinking that you called her or something, but she was too drunk and started cursing me out, calling me all types of bitches and stuff. She needs to stop drinking."

"And you need to stop lying," he said as he threw the stacks of money on the bed. He was taking his clothes off when he said, "Put that in my stash, set my bath, and make me something to eat."

He left his clothes on the floor, thinking about his anger for Tasha the day before, but the way Tasha was dressed and her lace thong reminded him of why he was hooked on her.

When his bath was ready, he pulled his Walter PPK machinegun from under his mattress and sat it on the side of the tub. He lit half of the blunt he had on his windowsill and carried the LeVert *Rope a dope Style* CD into the bathroom.

For most of the album he sat in the hot water and thought of Zeida. She was the complete opposite of Tasha. She was the type of woman that deserved a home and a good man to take care of her. Sitting in the water, he imagined what it would be like to marry a classy woman like Zeida.

He was lost in the thought until Tasha interrupted to announce that his food was ready. Tasha stopped at the door, and sucked on her bottom lip while she looked at her man's nakedness. She cut the bathroom lights off and sat on the side of the tub while she lit a small red candle. While Gerald LeVert was crooning away, she slid into the tub without removing her negligee, and straddled Jason. She passionately kissed all over him, saying in a whisper, "Why was you out all night, baby? You know I need you to be next to me, I'm yours for life. She pulled the top of her negligee down and said, "Here," as she put her long brown nipple into his mouth.

While he licked her breast she kissed the top of his head and massaged his manhood. When he began to devour her, she moved her panties to the side, slid on top of him, and very slowly she bounced while her two hands firmly held the back of his head. The warm soapy water splashed and gave more lubrication. She rode him steadily for five minutes all the while making splashing sounds as her ass hit the water. Tasha bit her lip, controlled the pace of her movements and whispered, "Nice and slow, Boo, nice and slow. Let me work this Boo, let me work this."

Jason couldn't hold back any longer. She felt that he was about to burst, so she sat up, squeezed his tip, and then mounted him again. Slowly she leaned back without breaking her motion. When both of her feet were on top of his shoulders, while he was in the sitting position, she leaned her head back. With her extended hands and feet, she pushed the wall and the surface of the tub so Jason's shaft could move in and out of her. He wondered where she learned all the freaky things she did to him, and her moans caused him to explode. Once he released his pent up stress, Tasha washed in between her legs, got out of the tub and left to prepare to serve him his feast.

Rice and her attempt at baked chicken, waited for him. He hardly ever let Tasha cook him anything besides breakfast. Her cooking was horrible in comparison to his.

He had learned how to cook from his sister Daisy when he was younger. Daisy was more like his mother when they were growing up. When she became a born-again Christian and Jason decided to run the streets, or as she'd said, "Serve the devil," she stopped communicating with him altogether. On special occasions Jason visited his mother, hoping he could catch his sister there. But his mother was always too drunk for him to figure out if Daisy had come through or not.

By seven o'clock, Jason was dressed in slacks, a Coogi summer sweater and his Polo boots. He had all of his accessories with him and a snubbed-nosed .38 in an ankle holster.

"Where you *think* you going, Boo?" Tasha asked, sounding like an interrogator. She stood in front of him clad only in a black lace bra and panties. Tired of having to seduce Jason just to keep him in the house, she asked, "I know you aren't leaving again?"

"Tasha, what did I tell you about questioning me?"

She charged towards the room shouting, "To hell with you Jay. You were gone all night. If you got another bitch, then say so. Don't have me sitting at home waiting on your ass all day like I don't got other places to go."

He tried hard to stay calm and promised himself that he wasn't going to let her get him upset.

With a hand on her hip she yelled, "You fuckin' New York buster, do you hear me? I don't even know why I put up with your ass. I need to go back to Cali and find me a real nigga. You think..."

His hand slapped her across her mouth with a loud crack before she had a chance to finish her statement. Normally she would have burst into tears and tried to lock him out of the room, but this time Tasha reacted to the sting of the blow and punched Jason with all of her might and then spat a bloody glob of saliva in his face. With that, he lost control. He'd sworn that he would never make a habit of punching Tasha or any woman because he knew his hands were weapons. But Tasha was showing that she had the need and desire to be physically abused. Even seeing his anger didn't stop her. "Jay, you ain't shit. You don't got enough paper to put your hands on me. I'm a queen and you ain't shit. It's plenty of motherfuckers that would pay top dollar for this pussy and I need to start ..." She spat out before he retaliated.

In that instant, he grabbed her by her hair with one hand and with the other he began to pimp slap her over and over. She screamed loudly when she realized that she had gone too far. Her high yellow skin was the color of beets when the flurry stopped.

In a rapid blur, he dragged her by her hair into his private bedroom. He pushed her to the floor and opened the trunk he kept in the closet. Over her protest, he pushed her face down into the floor, and pulled out a rope. He grabbed a pair of handcuffs from out of the trunk, and cuffed her behind her back. He then picked her up, stuck a sock in her mouth, and duct taped her mouth shut. The thought of putting her out of her misery was a brief consideration, but he quickly gained control. He held her leg and dragged her to the third empty bedroom. Her body drooped to the floor. Like he did in countless robberies, he duct taped her legs, and cuffed her to the cold gray radiator. Rapidly, he closed all the windows in the small muggy room. Jason then unplugged all the phones, took the battery out of Tasha's beeper then turned the heat up. Tasha was in shock when the door slammed shut.

It took Jason minutes to gain his composure. He exited his building to meet Webb, and was greeted by the masses of blunt smokers and forty-ounce beer drinkers. Hip-hop serenaded the projects from the car stereos as little boys tried their best to play basketball in the dark. In an attempt to hide his emotions, Jason bit down hard on his lip and headed toward his partner. Webb stood on the corner of 12th Street waiting, with a large garbage bag.

Without a word, Webb handed Jason the velvet bag of jewels. Side by side, they walked the tree-lined street. They crossed the busy intersection of 21st Street, and stopped in front of a warehouse at a large green dumpster. Webb deposited the garbage bag into the dumpster, to dispose of the evidence.

"Click," the two men heard the sound behind them and both recognized the sound.

They both spun. Webb's hand automatically fell on the small weapon hidden in his jock strap. Jason, stunned, froze like a statue. A tall dirty-looking black man in a faded Grambling University T-shirt pointed the .44 Magnum right at their faces. The man had popped up out of what seemed like thin air. They both prided themselves for always being on point, but he had gained the advantage over them with the element of surprise.

"You, give me the watch. You, the bag and the chain," the drug hungry man said. Familiar with how the game is played, they knew who was in control.

The robber wanted Webb's expensive Hublot watch, and Jason's diamond encrusted chain and pendant. The thief's jittering hand was a serious threat.

Jason thought for a minute about Tasha. She would die of heat exhaustion if he didn't make it back home. Webb, on the other hand, was confident he was about to take the crack-head out of his misery forever.

"I ain't gone tell y'all again, run the jewels," the addict scowled.

Jason said, "Yo, we gonna let you walk away alive if you put that gun away and break out. I know you want to get high, but you picked the wrong ones."

Sweat dripped from the face of the walking corpse and the would-be stick-up man shouted, "Shut the hell up and run the jewels," he shouted as his shaky hands shook nervously.

"You always talking, Duke. You always talking. Why you ain't just twist his cabbage?" Webb yelled at Jason. By the look on his face, Jason knew he had to move fast. Webb was about to kill.

Jason pulled the long chain off his neck and held it out to the man. The zombie reached for the chain but Jason's quick hands caught his wrist and yanked with the strength of a gator snapping down on its prey. The force of Jason's pull nearly gave the man whiplash and while trying to take aim the man dropped his gun, but held his hand as if he still had it in his possession. Webb jumped on the man. First a knee to the mid-section dropping him to the ground and then a stomp from his Air-Force 1's to the side of the man's head. Jason swung a kick to the junkies mid-section and heard the man heave. Then he grabbed the gun and began to walk away.

This wasn't nearly enough for Webb who by this time had removed a small medical scalpel from the strap on his sneakers and with all the care a Chinaman gave a fish at the Warf, he put the small shiny blade to the man's throat and slammed the blade in and out five times.

"Noooo," Jason shouted, just loud enough to create an echo throughout the dilapidated buildings.

Webb stood up and began to stomp the man's head. After roughly ten kicks, Jason felt sympathy for his attacker. He lightly pounded Webb's shoulder, letting him know that was enough; it was time for them to break out.

Jason looked up and down the street, and then pushed the man to the curb. He put his chain back around his neck and walked away like nothing ever happened.

When they arrived at the garage, Jason watched as Webb pulled the entire back of his car seat open to reveal a secret compartment. Webb took the gun from Jason and slid the .44 into the space and snapped it shut. With one foot out of the car, he started the engine and pushed in Ralph Tresvant's cassette. Jason zoned out, not hearing a sound going on around him. He turned to Webb. "We just going to see the connect and we out right?"

"Yeah, why? What up?"

"Nah, I got to clear my head, so I'm a drive my car and I'll follow you. Where we going anyway?" Jason questioned.

Webb slammed his door. "Just follow me homey, if your put-put can keep up?" he kidded.

"Let's do it," Jason said.

Webb cut through Times Square, and Jason wondered where he was going. But when he pulled up to the Marriott Marquis, his question was answered.

Inside of the Marriott were the best businessmen and hustlers, sleeping high above the street dealers, some of whom held the same desires and used very similar business practices.

Jay and Webb took the hotel elevator up to the Presidential Suite. They walked through the regal doors, and there was the man himself, Johnny Hustle, waiting for them. Wearing a black silk bathrobe, with his hands extended, he spoke, face frowned, "Y'all brothers have come at a bad time, my ladies were about to give me my bath, so let's make this quick."

They felt like they were standing in Hugh Heffener's mansion. Webb and Jason stared at the three naked women beside him. The naked white female was built like a swimsuit model. The woman to her left, was mulatto with red hair and a body like a fitness trainer. And the third was an older sistah, who to Jason, seemed a little plain in comparison to the other two.

Johnny conducted business like it was nothing to have three naked women in the room in front of strangers. Webb explained to him what happened with the cash and the dye packs but Johnny already knew. Jason looked at the women in awe and wondered how a man was able to get all three women to live in harmony. He had a lot to learn.

The stolen jewels glistened when Johnny peaked into the bag. His face grimaced in disbelief. "Nephew, this don't look like it's even thirty grand. My partner down in Atlantic City... I ain't even gonna waste his time with this." He shrugged his shoulders and handed the bag to the mulatto. "Oh well, I might as well give this to my wives and keep the watches for myself. You win some and you lose some. "I owe y'all one," he said.

Jason knew they really owed Webb's uncle, for coming up short. Everyone was supposed to come off with much more. He was disappointed in himself, because no matter what, his uncle always looked out for them. Jason also admired Johnny's ability to remain humble, considering his rags to riches story. Johnny went from sticky fingers to stacking cash. The 'Big Willie' lifestyle had not gone to his head.

Johnny asked them if they wanted to stay. He offered to call some of his women up to entertain them. "Naw Unc, we're cool," Webb replied.

Webb pulled Jason to the side as they entered the parking garage. "Yo, in a minute, I'm gone do some business in the Cayman Islands. You hear, the Cayman Islands, Duke. Let me know if you in or not. Seven Mile Beach homey, gonna leave the hood for a while, you game?"

Jason couldn't think straight. He felt discouraged. He needed to do another major robbery in order to reach his goals. Putting one foot in his car he said, "I don't know. I'll let you know soon."

Webb nodded, jumped in his car, and sped out of the parking space. Jason hit Broadway, and headed up Eighth Avenue.

Six

The Harlem streets were bustling with those who lived for the nightlife. During the summer nights, Uptown always brought out a parade of women who put on a fashion show of sorts along with hustlers draped in jewelry and exotic cars. The overpriced chrome wheels were mandatory. Jason's 300 ZX fit right in.

White buckets lined the small block. The soapy water cooled the sticky pavement. A group of addicts owned the establishment, and the lined cars were advertisement for the dealers meeting place.

Jason recognized the old man. "Hey, Pops, do your thing." He handed the man his keys, "I'll be right back."

Like a locomotive, he darted towards the hair salon. Because his hair was semi-straight, he wondered if a woman would be able to give him a better cut than a male barber would. When he walked into 'Hair's to You', he saw a group of women gossiping about Harlem hustlers and what concert they were going to later. All talking ceased when Jason stepped in. He was striking and they salivated over him like he was prime rib.

"Blow whoa! Me never inna me life see a black mahn wit blue eye yet. And how you hair look like it wan turn red?" a Haitian women said, nodding at Jason. "Who you come fe see?"

Jason recognized the Haitian accent immediately. He had fond memories of kickin' it with Haitians in his old school, Jamaica High.

"I need to know if any of y'all can cut my hair. I want a fade on the sides, and the top to be smoothed out."

"I'm Diane," the Haitian said as she wiped her chair, spinning it towards Jason. "Well, you come to de right place. If it can grow, me can cut it. Me nuh like mahn, but damn you face pretty, so come sit inna me seat before somebody come."

She gave him a wash and rinse. While his hair was still wet she put it between her fingers and cut until it was evened out. She then blow dried the sides and put the clippers to it. She gave him a triple layer fade. When she was done, she lined him up and applied a gel to his hair that made it both wavy and curly. The whole shop stared in amazement of the transformation. Knowing that the others wouldn't hesitate, they each jumped to be first to give Jason their number.

Jason was impressed. He turned to Diane, peeled off a hundred-dollar bill and said, "My name is Jason, I'll be back in a couple of days. You did a good-ass job."

Diane extended the bill towards the light to check its authenticity. "Yes, Mr. Ja-son. Me like how you spend. You come back and ask fe Diane. One love, me deer child."

The old man removed Turtle wax off his rims as his helper put the finishing touches on the inside when Jason approached. Jason smiled, as the old-head applied Armor-All to his Yokohama tires. Calm, cool and collected, he eased in his car, and pulled out Zeida's number in hopes that she would answer.

After the fifth ring, the answering machine picked up. He felt warm all over when he heard her message, *You've missed me, but you still got my voice. Leave a message after the tone. Thank you.* When it was time to leave his message, he became nervous. "This is Jason, the guy you met earlier, I just..."

"Hey handsome, still spilling coffee on strangers?" Zeida picked up laughing.

"Nah, love," he couldn't stop smiling through the phone, "So what you doing?"

"Thinking about you," she said seductively. "When am I going to see you again?"

When he heard her response, he said to himself, *You see, you see, that's what I'm talking about? Why can't Tasha be like this*?

"And don't forget that we have a date to go shopping to replace my suit?" she added.

"Fo' sure, fo' sure," he said smiling while he leaned back in his car seat. "When you ready, I'm ready."

"Well, I'm sure you're not ready for what I'm ready for, but whenever I see you again we can talk about that."

"What's wrong with right now," he asked hoping she would say *nothing*.

"Oh, touché. Nothing is wrong with right now if you can get to my house before I go to sleep."

"Well, I have the address, but don't know where it is. You were in a rush and I can't read everything you wrote, so tell me and I'll see how far away I am."

He figured that she lived somewhere in Manhattan. He wanted to surprise her with how fast he got there, until she said, "Oh, I live in the village of Scarsdale."

"Scarsdale?" Jason asked in shock. "Where the hell is that?"

"Well to get to my side, it's best if you take the Major Deegan to Central Park Avenue. It's past Yonkers Expressway. Get on Central Avenue, then 54 Crane Road. Ask for Ms. Carro and I'll buzz you in if you get here on time. See you later, love."

"Hold up…" was all Jason was able to get out before he heard the click. He called the old man over, handed him a fifty-dollar bill and told him to finish immediately. In less than a minute the old man told him the last tires were done. Jason revved the engine and sped off leaving black parallel streaks in his wake. He made an illegal left turn on 125th, and then made another left on First Avenue. He drove over the Willis Avenue Bridge to the Bronx, until he hit the Major Deegan Expressway.

He sped through the city like a raging lunatic. The Z flew through the Bronx and cut off to Central Avenue when Jason reached Westchester. From there he pulled over at the gas station, got directions to Crane road, and pulled up to an exclusive condominium complex.

One look at the fancy, brown, eight-story building and Jason was reminded that he was far away from home. The parked cars he passed made the lot look like an imported car dealership. From Alfa Romeos to Bentley's, his Z fit right in. He was greeted at the lobby, by an elderly bellman. "Hi. You're Jason, right?"

He figured that Zeida must've called down in advance. Even though Jason's skin was light, he figured by the look of the place that young black men were not regulars in the neighborhood. With the same phony British accent that he used with the police officer in the robbery, he said, "Yes, that would be me."

"Okay sir, apartment 317. The elevator attendant will take you there."

The elevator doors were open, and a short black man was waiting for him to step in. The man had the shiniest head he had ever seen, and his droopy eyes revealed years of pain or experience.

When Jason stepped in, the man looked at Jason from head to toe, and in a raspy voice said, "Hey, brother." Jason grinned and nodded. The old man went on, "We don't get too many of us up in here."

The door opened on the third floor and Jason peeped that the narrow hallways were lined with red carpet. Gold and cream paisley paper adorned the walls.

Door 317, vibrated from the music playing inside. He rang the doorbell and Zeida appeared. She wore painted-on Guess jean shorts with the top button undone, and a violet tank. Her long hair rested softly on her cleavage. Jason scoped her body becoming instantly aroused. Dazed from her appearance, he stood stiff in the doorway. "Come on in. Mi casa es su casa," she said, breaking his spell.

He couldn't move. He thought earlier that maybe Zeida had more white in her than anything else. But now the Barry White playing along with her ample curves were a dead give-a-way and revealed an ethic background.

Zeida turned to place the glasses she held on a small table behind the door. Jason got a good look at her ass and went wild inside. Taken by his behavior, Zeida grabbed him by his shirt laughing. "What, no comprende? Come in out of the hall."

Her apartment was top flight. When he stepped into the marble foyer he could see a small kitchen to his left. Its rich design revealed wealth. "Little lady, you live like a queen," he managed to say.

"Oh, you like? Well let me give you a tour of the house before I scare you off," she giggled. "If things go well maybe you'll be spending plenty of time here."

He was thrown slightly by her aggressiveness. He knew for sure that she could have any man she wanted and he was flattered that she seemed to be feeling him.

"You look nice with that fresh cut, and I must say that suit you wore earlier was the very essence of a stylish man. I hope to see more like it. My man must always leave a lasting impression.

"Follow me," she said. "This is my kitchen, where I make dreams come true."

Zeida's kitchen had an urban attitude. The enclosed, mahogany cabinets were dressed with glass-panels and solid doors. The high ceilings opened it up, making it feel spacious. Jason was impressed.

She waltzed him to her living room. It was filled with a black leather couch, and a leather love seat, leopard-skin rugs, a gas fireplace, and a sliding glass door that led to a terrace that allowed in the muggy August air.

"Follow me."

Jason trailed her down a beautiful beige wallpapered hall. Monet paintings decorated the walls. To her right, she opened a door and Jason saw a king sized bed.

"In here is where some more dreams can come true *if* you're serious about what you need in your life," she winked.

On the fast track, she possessively held on to his hand. "Behind us is another bedroom. I will make this my child's bedroom, when I find the right man. Right now I use it to store all my shoes and clothes. Now let me take you to the bathroom."

The bathroom revealed a marble counter top with his and her sinks. In between the sinks stood a pillar shaped fish tank filled with various tropical fish. It complimented the pink and black bathroom. Her Jacuzzi was large enough to fit three people. The standing shower was perfect for a strip show. The glass door exposed two gold showerheads and enough space to accommodate a wild sexual escapade.

He promised himself that when he bought his house that it would look just as good as Zeida's place. He entertained the thought of having her decorate the place, but then Tasha would probably commit a homicide if she found out, so he scratched the thought.

When they stepped back into the living room and sat on the couch, Jason could hear now hear Latin music playing. Even though he didn't understand all the words the woman was saying, he liked the way she sang. "Who is that? What is she saying?"

"Oh, that's Anna Gabriel. It's *Balaba*, she's singing about a lover she lost and how she won't be the same until he comes back. I hope I never have to sing that song."

"Yo that's nice. I like her voice." He looked in her brown eyes and said, "Listen, what's up you? I hear you dropping mad hints my way and I *know* you got a man, so what's the deal?"

Zeida blew a hair from in front of her face and sighed when she said, "I was hoping you would be mature about it, but I hear where you're coming from, so here's *the deal* as you say." She looked Jason directly in his eyes and with a voice of conviction she said, "I get what I want because I work hard and bend what rules I have to. Just like you, I think destiny bought us together, and either it's gonna be for a reason, a season, a lifetime, or at the very least hopefully for some good sex?" Then she laughed. "Seriously though, Jason, I won't front. When I saw you, I liked what I saw and I want to get to know you. I'm not worried if you have a girl, because I'm a woman. And you're smart enough to know what's best for you..." She moved in for the kill and laced her tone with seduction and said, "All I ask is that you just be straight up and not play games with me. I'm usually the one turning people down. And no, I don't have a man, so hopefully you can be that special someone. Anything else?"

Jason was stuck for words. He didn't know how he always attracted aggressive women, but he knew a good thing when he heard it. "Listen, I was hoping you would take a quick ride with me. I need to clear my head. I feel like having a little company," he said avoiding her request.

Zeida was silent. She moved slowly but cut her music off and grabbed a tape. She marched through her living room, closed her terrace door, threw on a pair of sandals, and brought the glass of Lancers white wine she was drinking.

Happy as a gay bird, the elevator man interrupted. "Hey, honey bun. I brought this fine young man up to your floor earlier. I had no idea he was coming to see you. I'm glad though, because I can tell he's a fine young gentleman."

As Zeida kissed the man on his shiny head, he gave Jason a wink. They reached the parking area, and she walked right up to his car with confidence.

"How'd you know this was mine?" he asked.

She impatiently held the passenger door. "I know all the cars in this lot." She pointed, "That white car over there is mine. You should have bought the twin-turbo, you would have gotten more for your money. If you ever have any problem with this one, don't take it to the Nissan dealer, they'll only gyp you. Bring it to me and *I'll* fix it for you."

He looked over and saw an all white Alfa Romero Spider with a quad exhaust and low profile racing rims. By the looks of the car, and the way she talked, Jason suspected that her car could give his a run for its money.

"Oh, I see you changed the exhaust too? Good move," she said after he cranked the engine. He put the car in drive. "Um, and you dropped the suspension and added the cams? I see you did a little homework," she said.

He laughed to himself. *Damn, I'm getting a two-for-one,* he thought. Zeida felt like a homeboy and looked like a gorgeous runway model. As they turned on to Central Park Avenue, Zeida slipped in a little blues. "Who's that?" Jason asked.

"It's Etta James singing the blues." She put her finger to his lips. "Shhhish, listen to the words, baby, and clear your head," she said.

He didn't know who Etta James was so he just focused and did what he suggested. She pushed her seat back, slid her feet from her sandals and placed them on the dashboard. He pushed his five-speed transmission to the limit.

After speeding through the Bronx, and into Queens, he jumped onto the Long Island Expressway. When Jason reached the town of Elmont, he drove through the quiet streets, listening to the love ballads of the woman named Etta sing a song called *At Last*.

Jason pulled over and asked Zeida to stay in the car. He ran up to a white colonial home. The house appeared dead until a lamp came on behind the large wood door. An older man with a salt and pepper afro emerged from behind the door. Jason shook the man's hand, handed a stack of bills to him, and bid him farewell. He paused before entering the car. Jason stared at the for sale sign on the lawn as he moved back toward the car. He shook his head, and jumped back in the car.

He had another stop to make. Jason parked the car on 21st street and asked Zeida to wait there.

As soon as he entered his building, he pulled out his gun and ran up the stairs. When he entered the apartment he could feel the heat coming from out of the room where he left Tasha. He opened the door and heat came rushing out the door like a tidal wave. Tasha was leaning against the wall nearest the radiator with sweat dripping from her body. Her extensions were frizzled at the roots. Her body showed signs of heat exhaustion.

Jason was relieved that she was still alive. He turned the heat off, cracked the window an inch, and removed the gag from her mouth.

Tears in her eyes, she cried. "Boo. I'm sorry Boo. Damn, I thought you left me for dead." She inhaled the fresh air from the window, and with raised cuffs, whined, "I won't ever disrespect you again baby, please untie me, I got to use the bathroom."

Jason leaned close to her ear, and in an evil whisper replied, "You see, bitch, since you like coming slick out your mouth it was time I showed you how things can be. I tolerate your shit cause I want to, not because I got to. Now think about that the next time you start spitting that bullshit. I'm a leave your ass cuffed right her a little while longer because you still need some time to think."

He peeled another small piece of duct tape off the roll and put it over her mouth. He could hear her muffled screams, but he closed the door and raced back to the car. Zeida looked like she was glad to see him. Instead of questioning him about his whereabouts, she said, "You all right?" he nodded lying through his teeth.

On the drive back to Zeida's, the interrogations began. "Cut the music off," she said. "I want to talk with you."

She began to ask questions about who he really was and instead of lying, or avoiding the questions, he told her everything she asked. He didn't like to be questioned, but he was intrigued because no other woman had ever wanted to know who he really was.

He told her his real name, how he grew up with an abusive mother, how his eyes were blue from his red-haired grandmother in Haiti marrying a blue-eyed white man who went there to rebuild the country after a revolt. The man was an engineer for a company called Tate Industries, and she told him that she was familiar with the company. Twins ran in his family and his mother had a twin brother that died when they were children. The emptiness stayed with her forever and it became another of her psychological issues that caused her to abuse alcohol. His father had abandoned his mother and him at birth, and now Webb and his sister Daisy were the only family he had been able to count on and now he and Daisy were estranged. Jason did the unthinkable and even told Zeida about Tasha and the constant drama she brought on him. Last, he told her that they drove through Elmont because he wanted to buy a home there and couldn't wait to leave the ghetto.

Zeida was stunned and excited because they seemed to have so much in common. They were both born in April, two days apart, and her parents were of varied ethnicity as well, coming from Brazil and Puerto Rico. She explained how she grew up on Hughes Avenue in the Bronx, where her mother still lived and refused to move after her father died from sclerosis of the liver.

Her brother was part of a motorcycle gang called the Ching-a-lings. She explained that she used to run with the gang and help them launder money that they stole from armored cars, and the fact that she had lived a life of crime in her past was why she helped Jason get away rather than turn him in. Unlike most people who turned their lives around Zeida hadn't forgotten where she'd come from. Then as they continued on the ride, she reluctantly told Jason about her ex-boyfriend Rico, who was obsessed with her.

Rico was still a member of the gang which ran the neighborhood she lived in. Hearing rumors that he had a hit out on her kept her from ever going to see her mother. She had offered to move her mother from the hood many times. 'Everyone I know is here, Zeida,' was always her mother's response.

Ending with talk of her schooling at NYU she explained how education had been her ticket to leave the ghetto. Though she had turned her life around, gotten her MBA and landed a great job with Douglass Warner, she wanted one day to design her own clothing line, hopefully with a daughter by her side.

They talked in her parking lot 'til four in the morning. "So are you still interested in me or what?" Zeida asked after sharing details of her life story.

"I should be the one asking those questions, so what up?" Jason asked.

"Listen, I give my all when I love, and I love hard so if we decide to do this I hope you can handle it. I'm going out on a limb, but I can handle it. All I ask is that you give up the life of crime and pursue your dreams."

Jason reminded her of Tasha. "You know my situation."

"You ain't no fool, Jason. That I know. That said, you'll take care of that in due time I'm sure."

"What makes you so sure?" Jason stared into her eyes and then leaned towards her.

"Don't be shy. Come a little closer," Zeida said with a seductive smile. "I'll show you."

Jason's lips met hers and they slowly melted into one another's. Zeida caught his bottom lip with hers and then she parted his lips with her tongue. This excited Jason and he reached for her neck but she pushed his hand away. She was in control for now. She instead held his face and he could smell her perfume. As they kissed he began to feel lightheaded. It was the first time a kiss had ever felt so satisfying for either of them. They continued to kiss passionately for five soul-stirring minutes. When they broke away Jason was hard and Zeida was wet.

When Jason walked her to the door, he felt like he wanted to stay and never go back to the projects. Instead of goodbye, they parted with the promise to hook up again.

Seven

Zeida's kiss was still fresh on Jason's lips when he pulled into Queensbridge. After leaving Scarsdale, he paid particular attention to the filthy conditions that surrounded him. He couldn't help but compare its shortcomings to the neighborhood he'd just left.

Jason crept into his house with his gun in hand. Furniture was turned over, and things were not the way he left them. Slowly and quietly he crept in the kitchen. He eased over to the cabinet under the sink, and removed the hollow bottom under the cleaning fluids. His hand reached in and pulled out a Mac-11 sub-machine gun with a silencer. He stayed low as he left the kitchen prepared for action.

The silence was unsettling. He was certain that someone had broken in, seen Tasha tied up, and found his cash. He aimed the red beam from the laser as he inched towards the room. The closet door was open and the inside of his trunk was in plain view. He eased closer to see if his cash was history. He knelt down on the side of the trunk, and in that split second he heard the cock of a pistol. He knew he was in grave danger. He spun around aiming his beam at the figure in the door.

"Hey, Boo?" Tasha said, holding his Glock in her hands.

She stood in a do or die pose. Her smile was crazed looking. Half of her hair was out, her immaculate nails were broken, and dark marks circled her eyes.

"Tasha, be easy or I'ma put you down," yelled Jason.

"Put me down like a dog, Boo? You had me clawing as scratching up in this motherfucker," she hissed with the thick Cali accent. "I know I'm a bitch at times but you ain't have to treat me like a dog," she said with a suddenly suspicious calmness.

Tasha was one sudden move away from becoming a memory.

"I'm gonna tell you one time. Put the burner down, and I promise to I won't hurt cha'," yelled Jason.

As a tear rolled down her cheek, she put the gun on the windowsill. "Now what?" she said with her hands spread wide.

49

With the red dot still glued to her forehead Jason spat, "On the real, you're wasted. You can pack your things and find shelter elsewhere. Go on and get one of them big willies you always talking about or take dat ass and go live it up with Darlene and Shane," he suggested. "Do your thang, boo. I'm through."

Her eyes were locked on him and the truth was revealed. The tears began to fall when she said, "I'm sorry, Boo. I learned my lesson, I know I be going too far, but you always get me like that. I don't want to leave, I want to make up and make love to you til' we stink." She sniffled twice and licked her lips.

Jason put the gun down and the idea of banging her out ran through his mind. "Mmmph," he huffed. "Your ass is trippin'."

Tasha moved toward him and said, "Jay, on the real, all that rough shit you did, it kinda got me going."

Tasha just confirmed why he had to work his way out of his relationship. Jason debated whether it was he or Tasha that was mentally ill. She eased closer to him and then she dropped to her knees. She tugged at his clothes after she unfastened his belt. She opened wide and the foreplay began.

That night they made love aggressively, until early morning. Jason banged her hard as she begged him to. The only time he slowed down to anywhere near a caring pace was when he imagined that she was Zeida.

The next time he opened his eyes, Tasha had been watching him sleep with his Glock in her hand. She wasn't aiming the weapon at him, but he knew that he was outsmarted again.

"What up?" he asked in a raspy voice.

"We need to talk," she said with a sinister grin. "You was too busy digging my back out for us to finish our little discussion."

"What up?" he asked again impatiently.

"I know I been acting up, but I'm a bitch and that's what I been doing from day one. I see you getting tired of it so you wilded out on me. That's cool, but I want you to know that I love you and ain't no other out there for me. I *need* you, Boo. You the only one that can keep me in check. I'm just letting you know I'ma be good. I just ask that you do one thing for me."

"What up?" Jason asked, hoping she would get to the point.

Tasha sighed and said, "I'm just asking that you cop me a whip so I can represent you in dem streets. It hurts me to be riding in somebody else's car. So *please* think about it?" she begged.

She handed Jason the gun, pointing the tip to her head. Her tongue worked from his chest to his stomach. When she found what she was looking for, her lips starvingly caressed his manhood. He immediately told himself that he'd better hurry up and get some cash, so he could fulfil both of their wishes.

With the gun still to her head, Jason scolded, "You want your car? Then *know* this, I'm gonna be out for days."

"While I'm out, I want you in this house by sundown. You say any slick stuff out of your mouth, and you gone."

"I'm not putting my hands on you no more, Tasha. Now have my clothes ready by the time I get out of the shower."

In the shower, he actually prayed for a changed life. As he replayed the event from the night before he thought to himself, *A chick like Tasha meant serious problems.*

Twisted as it was, he felt good inside thinking about the punishment that she craved from him. Then he wondered if it was really love that they shared for one another or if it was merely some sick obsession.

Jason's beeper went off. It was Webb. He reached Webb's house dressed in an Armani suit, no tie and a pair of Gucci shoes. Two Gucci bags sat at the door when he entered.

"Where you going, homeboy?" Jason playfully asked.

"Duke…Duke, what's wrong with you, Duke? I told you I needed you to take me to the airport, Duke."

"Yeah, but I didn't know you meant today?"

"If you knew, then anybody else could know, and you know I don't get down like that. You know I don't get down like that," Webb bragged and laughed.

Jason knew that he was right. He always moved in silence and kept everyone around him in limbo.

"Yo, what's in the Cayman Islands anyway?"

Webb sighed. "Since you gotta know, I met this chick from down there and she work at one of them banks you can hide paper at. She says its nothing for some of them white collar crooks to bring suitcases of cash down there. All I need is a connect at the hotels they check into and I definitely *think* we can get some paper from down there, Duke. They can give it up easy or hard. You know how we do."

Jason shook his head as he thought about Webb and him out of the country tying niggas up like the shit was free. He knew then that Webb was crazier than he thought. "What time your plane leave?" he asked.

"We need to break out in about twenty minutes, so lets go," said Webb. "Make sure you feed Butch. I told him that it was okay," Webb said and threw a playful jab to Jason's midsection. "So, you know where his food is, and don't let nothing happen to my dog, homey, or I'll have to body you. I'll be back in three. Don't let nothing happen to my dog."

Jason dropped Webb of at Kennedy Airport. "Be safe, homey," he told him as he pulled off. Webb followed up with a head nod. It wasn't odd for Webb to go on trips, but for some reason, this time Jason felt something terrible was going to happen. He didn't like the fact that he wouldn't be there to keep Webb out of trouble.

On his way back, Jason got stuck in rush-hour traffic. He sat so long, he caught himself dosing off a couple times listening to Miki Howard. As he approached the projects, he saw Crackhead Mike. His big head, dirty tight clothes and dark shades, made Jason sick to his stomach.

Mike met Jason as he got out of the car. "Whoa, back up," Jason said reaching for his gun. He took two steps back and smiled with two front missing teeth.

"Hey, Champ. You know I'm your man. Oooo wheee, you got a mean ride, so why don't you let me wash it, wax it, or watch it for you all night? Just twenty dollars and Mike's your man." Mike stood a few spaces away. The fiend smelled like shit. Jason could taste the foul odor that reeked from Mike's mouth.

The episode happening was yet another reason why Jason wanted to escape the ghetto. He couldn't wait for the day when he could enjoy the safety of his possessions in the same way he'd seen residents in Elmont.

In the meantime, it wouldn't hurt to have someone watch his car, so he pulled out a fifty-dollar bill, ripped it and gave half to Mike. "See you in the morning. Don't try to wash it with that dirty ass bucket of water you got. I'm taking it in the morning. Something happens to my car and that's your ass."

Mike danced to his mythical music. "Oh, no...no...no, Champ. Mike's your man with the master plan, put cash in my hand, and I'm your man, yes I am, yes I am," he sang.

Jason walked into the building amazed at how Mike was going to get high off of credit. He knew he wouldn't move from in front of his car. When he reached his door, he could hear Tasha on the other side talking on the phone. Instead of walking right in, he put his ear to the door and he thought he heard her say, "Oh yeah? They don't call you Powerful for nothing? Yeah, we might see. What? Oh, Powerful, you crazy."

He slung the door open and looked her directly into her eyes, but she didn't show any signs of being busted. She continued her conversation. "My husband just walked through the door, hold on." She then turned her eyes back to Jason. "I got your favorite shrimp Parmesan with garlic bread delivered. It's in the microwave, and I sent Darlene for some of that Chocolate Tai-stick from Branson's. It's on top of the T.V."

She continued yapping on the phone. He took notice of how clean the place was. Tasha had it spotless from front to back, just the way he liked it.

Tasha called to Jason pulling the phone away. "Boo, if you in for the night, try and take a nap cause I'ma want to keep you up for a few hours later. I love you, baby."

Each word she spoke raised his suspicion. Any other woman would have had him in jail for tying her up, but Tasha was showing him more love than she had in a long time. He couldn't understand it, and really didn't want to.

As she promised, that night was another of rough and rugged nasty sex. Tasha woke Jason in the middle of the night sucking every inch of his body.

The next morning, Jason's pager went off at 8:00 a.m. He looked at the readout and didn't recognize the number, but replied immediately. To his surprise, he heard Zeida's sexy voice.

"Good morning, handsome," she said in her seductive voice.

Jason looked at Tasha sleeping in his arms and said "Yo man what's up? You up mad early. Where you at?"

"Yo, *man?*" Zeida asked. "Oh, I take it that your little girlfriend is right next to you where *I* belong, huh?"

"Ah huh," he mumbled

"Oh well. I'm at the gym and I have the day off. They're redecorating my office. I was hoping that after I drench this sweaty body in some water, you can come dry me off. Then…let me see, lotion me down, and then…you ready for this?" she said.

His erection awoke from her sultry voice. "Yeah, then what?" he said.

"Then, take me shopping," she laughed hysterically.

Tasha woke up, stretched and came down on his penis. Her head bobbed in slow motion.

"On the real Jason, I feel naughty and I want to see you today," Zeida said on the other end.

A threesome, he thought, *what a great way to start a morning.*

He focused on everything he could to have an orgasm and get it over with. When he did, she did what she loved to do, and claimed it helped her nails and hair to grow after swallowing. When she was done with her breakfast she rolled over and went back to sleep.

Jason rushed out of the bed and took a quick shower. Before his body was dry he put on a pair of Ralph Lauren slacks, and a Hugo Boss shirt. Strapped with his piece and three grand, he grabbed his sports bag, filled with a change of clothes. He liked keeping a change in the car at all times. Being prepared was a must.

Crack-head Mike stood in the same spot doing the same dance that he'd been in twelve hours before. Jason pulled out the other half of the fifty dollar bill. Mike snatched it and said, "Okay Champ, car's safe, did my job, gotta go, gotta go, gotta go," and he took off running up the block like Carl Lewis, all the while looking around as if he owed someone he didn't want to pay.

By 9:30 a.m., Jason was on 127th Street getting his car a quick wash. He walked over to 'Hair's to You', and when he reached the door he heard, Diane calling his name. "Jay-son, ho you come back so soon, mahn? Boy you hair grow too fast," Diane said as she dusted off her chair.

"Yes, come now, me know how unnu big money mahn stay, so mek me fix you up early inna de marning."

"Just the mustache and any strands sticking up. I want to look perfect."

Diane moved her professional hands with speed, and by 10:05 he was easing his way down 125th Street so that he could make it to Scarsdale. Zeida's world was like a dream come true, and he thought that he could escape the rest of the world through her. During the drive he wondered how her sex would be in comparison to Tasha's.

Zeida's door was open when Jason arrived, and the smell of vinegar and olive oil was fresh in the air. She gently kissed his lips wiping her lipstick from his mouth. Her smile showed how happy she was to see him. Her body spoke the language Jason knew all to well. Zeida was flawless. Her supple breasts were like juicy pears. Jason was speechless.

"Ai Papi, you have to eat before we go." She led him into the kitchen.

The table was set with fried eggs, plantains, home fries, mango juice, and slices of grapefruit and kiwi. The food was still hot and he loved that. He dined with fine China. When he was done eating, Zeida handed him a brand new toothbrush and told him to leave it on what was now *his* side of the bathroom when he was done. "Hurry up Papi, we have to go."

Five minutes later Jason was all brushed and ready. Zeida grabbed her Moschino purse and shades, and they headed out the door. She asked for the keys. "I'm doing the driving," she said. He looked at her like she had two heads. She threw him her set of car keys and said, "I crash your car and you keep mine, deal?" she asked.

He looked over at the new Alfo Romero Spider and moved over to the passenger seat. She adjusted the seat to her comfort, slipped on her driving gloves and prepared for take-off.

Zeida pushed his Z better than any man he knew. As she drove with the confidence of a getaway driver, Jason was awestruck. He wished at that moment that Tasha wasn't in his life. No woman had ever seemed so sexy, confident and intelligent to him before. He had to ask himself if he was falling in love because he'd never before experienced what he was feeling for Zeida and he hadn't even made love to her.

Soon they were in the city looking for a garage. They parked the car and walked up the sidewalk. Jason noticed the stares as men were taken by her beautiful face and body. A woman handing out coupons for one store stopped them to ask if they were models. "You two look like a match made in heaven," she said.

They stepped onto Fifth Avenue headed for Lord & Taylor's. Zeida picked up three business suits by Calvin Klein, Carolina Herrera, and Bill Blass. The saleswoman directed the total to Jason. "That will be twelve hundred and sixty two dollars."

Zeida left him at the counter to pay the bill while she was off to the side looking at shoes. Jason thought how Tasha could spend the same amount of money, but on hoochie project wear. Zeida took the bags and kissed him on the lips. "Thanks, baby," she said as she wrapped her arms around his waist.

In high spirits, she hailed a yellow cab. Jason couldn't figure out why they needed one, until he heard her tell the cabby, "To Macy's, please."

They walked into the 34th Street entrance of the store. Her head scanned from side to side until she stopped at a tall black man, who was the head of security. When she stood in front of him he didn't look down at her, he looked directly at Jason instead.

"Carlton, what is happening, mahn?" Zeida said in a horrible accent. The man hugged Zeida while looking in his face. Jason was surprised, but he was even more surprised when he heard Zeida say "I need an assistant and I'm pressed for time, so can you call Marilyn down for me." She handed him her bags and said, "And here, hold these bags for me, darling."

Zeida waited while the security guard was on the phone talking to the woman she asked for. In less than five minutes a short white woman appeared and Zeida said, "I'm headed all over this place, and I'd like to pay for everything at once, so I need your assistance."

The lady was smiling and telling her that she'd be delighted. Zeida put her hand in Jason's and walked off to the Versace Versus section where she picked up a couple of shirts. When her selections were made, she walked over to the Ralph Lauren's men section and started looking at suits until she found the perfect ones. A section away in the Izod Lacoste store and Zeida selected slacks and a few polo shirts. When she was done in the shoe department selecting multiple pairs of shoes for her and what Jason assumed was for him, she handed the items to the woman and told her they were done.

The assistant escorted them to an elevator that went to the basement. The hidden lounge area had a cash register and security posted, and when all the clothes reached a grand total, Jason's eyes popped when he saw the $3,300 bill. He was about to tell Zeida that she was spending too much of his money, until she walked over and handed Marilyn her American Express card.

While the clothes were being bagged, Zeida removed one of the Hermes ties, put it around his neck and tied it while she was laughing and putting her tongue into his mouth. Jason was impressed with the woman that was kissing him, and for the first time in his life, he was on the receiving end. Someone took the time out for once to consider *his* needs.

They stepped out of Macy's with the bags. Zeida stopped another yellow cab and told the driver to take them to the Four Seasons restaurant. On the way there, Jason said, "I didn't even know you could get an assistant in Macy's."

"Usually only celebrities can," Zeida admitted. "With the right image and a little finesse, the bustling city can be in the palm of your hands. For instance, that guy Carlton and I first met ten years ago when he caught me shoplifting in Macy's. He was new on the job and gave me this long speech about changing my life around. On that day, I told him that one day I would come in there and spend a lot of money on my clothes and he wouldn't be able to touch me. I kept my promise a hundred times and he always reminds me of how proud he is of me."

Jason was blown away by her story. Though she kept telling him that she'd come from humble beginnings, he found it hard to relate the past she spoke of to the woman before him now.

After a first class meal with Zeida, Jason was too stuffed for dessert. He silently vowed to never eat food at a regular restaurant again. Like most cats from the projects, even having money hadn't given him class. A meal prepared by a gourmet chef was a new experience for him; one that he wanted more of.

On the drive back to Zeida's house, Jason blurted out, "You know, I like the way you live life."

"Well, why don't you be a part of it?" To his surprise, she added, "I enjoy being with you, and even though you have some obvious thuggish ways."

They entered Zeida's house and she led him with all the bags he carried to her spare bedroom. Both closet doors were open and all her clothes were transferred from one closet to the other. She began to unpack his clothes into the closet before she touched her own.

"Zeida, you sure we're not moving too fast for this?"

She took a deep breath, and exhaled, "Listen Jason, do you want to appreciate a good woman and allow her to take care of you or what?"

"Yeah, as a matter of fact, hell yeah," he answered without much thought.

"Alright then as long as we keep it real, because I'm not about games. If you don't like the way things are going then you put it on the table. We straight, Papi?"

Her ability to go from intellectual sophisticated woman, to the girl from the hood was a major turn on for him. He smiled instead of answering the question.

Zeida returned the smile. "I take that as a yes, so come here."

She walked over to him and gave him a passionate kiss that made him feel like she was taking his breath away. When she slid her tongue down the side of his neck he was feeling dizzy. He tried to touch her and be aggressive the way he was with Tasha, but Zeida whispered and moved his hands to his sides, asking him not to move.

Jason's tie came off. She unbuttoned his shirt, and then licked and nibbled on his chest. When his upper body was fully naked, she seductively sucked on his hairy belly button. He couldn't resist his desire to touch her, so she pulled his hands behind and tied them with the tie. Slowly she led him into the bathroom. Jason watched as she cut on the water to her tub, dropped the bubble bath solution in, and then led him to the shower where they made love for the first time.

Later that night, Zeida's forty-inch television awoke Jason. He looked up and saw her ass in front of the screen. She slipped a video into the VCR above the set. She glimpsed over her shoulder and saw him staring. She blew him a kiss and walked out of the room. Moments later, *Good Fellas* was on screen. He propped himself up with her thick white down pillows.

Zeida reappeared with a silver food tray. "Watch the movie," she said as she fed him escabeche fish and rice.

By nightfall they were wrapped in each other's arms taking in the sounds of the *Quiet Storm*. The long search had finally come to end. They each found what they were looking for. Zeida found balance and Jason it seemed, a way out.

Jason was awakened by a crazy dream at 5:00 a.m. Butch, Webb's dog, threatened to eat him whenever he came to feed him. He jumped out of the bed, tripped over his feet and fell into the door. He scrambled in the dark for his clothes startling Zeida.

"What's wrong? Why the rush?" she asked.

"I got to feed and walk the dog." Jason replied while stumbling to get dressed.

"What dog?" Zeida asked while yawning.

"Webb's dog, he's gonna kill me."

"Whose gonna kill you baby?" she asked, ready to come to his aid.

"The dog."

"The dog?"

"The dog." He shook his head. "You wouldn't understand even if I explained it.

He fixed his gun in his pocket and kissed Zeida goodbye. "I'll call you later."

"Okay," she said. "Oh, one more thing. Saturday night there's a ball at Carnegie Hall. The Deltas are having a function, and I would like for you to come. It starts at six, and you need to wear a tux.

He had Butch on his mind and didn't have the slightest idea what a Delta was. "If I can make it, I'll wear my tux," he said knowing he didn't have one.

Eight

Jason sat idle in traffic for twenty minutes. Pedestrians walked their dogs and ran their morning errands. A green Chevy station wagon was doubled parked on the busy street blocking his path through. Jason was tempted to beep his horn before noticing two men, stroll by. The first one carried a black duffel bag on his back. Jason took a closer look and several items wrapped in silver duct tape were sticking out of the bag.

"Oh shit," he said to himself as his mind began to race. Jason glanced in his rear view mirror.

He watched the second of the men climb the stairs to a private house across from the car. Jason had a hunch. In his line of business, a hunch was the difference between being broke and getting rich.

Fumbling to get his sneakers off, he removed the stockings he wore and held them in his hands. He put his sneakers back on and grabbed an oily towel he had behind his seat.

One by one he slid the stockings over his face. He reached into his glove compartment and slid on a pair of black golfing gloves. He checked all around to see if there was anyone who would witness the work he was about to put in. Not person in sight so he did a U-turn in the middle of the street and pulled his car over. Next he pulled out his gun and crept across the street like a thief in the night. They were in the doorway of the house preparing to secure the premises while he snuck up on them like a leopard on a gazelle.

When he reached the backs of the two men, he pushed them through the first door, closed it behind him, and wrapped the oily towel around the front of his Beretta. The door slammed, and one of the men spun around in shock, forcing Jason to flinch. Jason aimed low and hit the man in his hip. The silenced bullet broke his hip and the man dropped to the floor with a thud.

Jason didn't know if there were more people in the house, but from what he could see, the house was empty. For his own protection, he hit the other man in his right temple with the butt of his gun, bringing him down next to his partner. Jason did a search and found matching Sig. Sauer handguns between the two of them. He put the two guns into the pockets of his fatigues. In an effort to silence the man that was shot and still yelling, he stood over the man and applied a knockout punch. Jason opened the duffel bag and almost fainted from surprise.

Twenty packages of what looked like cocaine filled the bottom of the bag. Instantly, he grabbed the bag and put it on his back, arms through the straps like a backpack.

When he took a closer look at his surroundings, he noticed that all of the windows were covered with black garbage bags. It wasn't his first time robbing a stash house in Jackson Heights, Queens, so he knew what to expect.

Door by door, and room by room, Jason searched only to find two bedrooms with mattresses and televisions on the floor. He figured that the rest was empty, until he kicked open the last door in the back of the house. His heart pounded when the pile in front of him revealed itself. Stacks of cash were on a table, and below the table were piles of empty boxes. Jason was robbing a big time operation. He did a quick calculation by sight but had no idea how much dough was right there. His new house was clear in his mind.

Hearing one of the men stirring he dashed back to them and placed the pistol to the back of the man's earlobe. He flinched as he popped the man. But with the amount he was stealing, he could hear Webb's voice telling him, "Duke, Duke, you know you can't leave either man alive." He extended his arm to the other man and executed him just as quickly though with some remorse, then he dragged both bodies into the basement.

In the basement, he saw a card table with a triple-beam measuring scales, a roll of heavy-duty garbage bags, and a few chairs down in the cold, damp, crevice of the house. The smell of burnt oil and gasoline permeated the room.

His heart pounding, Jason raced to the basement, grabbed the garbage bags, and then raced up to the room filled with money.

When he reached the room, he slid the bag off his back, he pulled out the two guns he had in his pockets and laid them on the table. He made sure they were full of bullets. At any minute, someone could walk through the front door.

He doubled the four garbage bags, and threw in the loads of cash. Avoiding his sweat from dripping on the floor, he opened the window. He wished Webb were there.

One by one he dropped the garbage bags out of the window. Hurriedly, he closed the window, put the duffel bag on his back, and was heading down the steps. He reached the landing and had a flash for precaution. Instead of walking directly out the front door, and possibly into the arms of drug traffickers or the law, Jason walked into the living room. Carefully he parted the only curtains in the house and looked out of the living room window. The coast was clear and his double-parked car was unharmed.

With no time to waste, he put the two weapons in the front of his pants, took the stockings off of his face, and slipped them in his pockets. Like any native from the neighborhood, he walked to his car like he lived there his whole life. He dropped the stolen duffel bag into his trunk, sat in his car, and drove off with half of his job done.

Jason thought he should have waited until later that night to do what he plotted in his mind, but it was either all or nothing. He made the first right at the light and then made another right on the next corner. Casually he pulled up into the alleyway of the house, backed his car down the driveway and popped his trunk. He was expecting the owner of the home to come out, but figured he'd deal with that when the time came.

With his fortune in his sight, he jumped over two short fences and made two trips before he had the garbage bags in his trunk. As he was closing the trunk to his car, he heard the sliding of a window rising above him. "Ey whaddaya doing?" the Italian voice asked.

In a fake Italian accent, Jason avoided eye contact and said, "Joey sent me over to pick up the leaves, it's nott'en, fogettabout it."

The man in the window heard Jason's response, shrugged his shoulders, and said, "Tell Joey that Mikey Cheese sends his regards, okay?"

Jason said, "Will do. Take it easy," and headed on the road to the life of the rich and famous.

He drove away as fast as he could without breaking the law. He drove extra careful through the streets of Queens and took the newly cleared highway until he reached Queens Plaza. He parked the car, ran into the QP's flea market, and bought a shopping cart and giant sized laundry bags. He raced back to the car and drove directly to the projects. When he cut the corner of Baby Park in Queensbridge, he saw Crackhead Mike and beeped his horn. Mike saw the yellow car and followed along dancing until Jason parked in front of Webb's building.

Jason lined the laundry cart with the laundry bag and dropped the garbage bags in. He said, "Mike, I got a hundred dollars for you. Come here."

Mike's eyes almost launched from their sockets. "What? Champ don't get me killed, but for a C-note, I'm your man and will slap Tyson if you tell me to."

"Just help me up the stairs with the cart, and then come down and watch the car."

When the cart was full, he put the duffel bag of cocaine on top. Mike looked down at the bags in the trunk and said, "Damn Champ, I would of did your laundry for you, you can trust Mike, Mike's your man, yes I am," he said looking down at the cart.

Together they carried the cart to the floor beneath where Webb lived. Jason sent Mike down to the car. He managed to carry the cart on his own to the next floor. Butch was at the door, and Jason sensed that the dog had an attitude with him from the menacing stare he received from the animal as he made his way through the apartment. Jason hid the cart, locked the door, and knew the cash was safe because *no one* from the projects wanted to face Webb's repercussions if they violated his space. Jason took Butch for a walk up the block. The entire time his heart and mind was racing with excitement. He couldn't wait to tell Webb and at the same time he felt leery about the robbery. What if one of the Italians had gotten his tag number?

When Butch was done taking care of his business Jason headed back upstairs, he locked the door, and carried all the bags into the bedroom Webb used as a gym. He stacked all the money from the heist on the weight bench, preparing to put it in the money counter.

Each stack rolled, counting the different denominations. Jason discovered that he owned $875,000 in cash, as he wrote the amount down on a sheet of paper. With no emotion, he calmly went into the bathroom to wash the sweat from his face. He dropped to his knees and thanked God for getting him out of the ghetto.

In the room, he opened one of the drug bags, poured the powder into aluminum foil, and saw that it was cocaine. When he put the drugs and money together he calculated that he had ten kilos worth of drugs and another half a million dollars in cash, if he put the drugs on the street and sold it retail.

Jason counted out a hundred and seventy five thousand dollars. He walked over to Webb's bedroom where he had a steel gate installed in his closet. Jason was the only person who knew where the key was, so he opened the locks to the closet door, and the gate. Once the gate was open, he put the cash and the drugs on top of Webb's safe.

After cleaning up, he took the rest of the cash into the living room. He went to the kitchen and emptied a two-day supply of dog food on the floor and left Butch a pail of water to wash down his meal. The dog gave him a puzzled look.

Jason grabbed a kitchen knife, and finely cut one of Webb's leather couch pillows. He put five hundred thousand dollars in the neatly squared tear. He re-placed the pillow in a way that would not leave a trace. "Come here boy," he whistled to Butch as he patted his thigh. He positioned the dog on top of the money, where it would be safest.

With the minor part out of the way, he went into Webb's hall closet and pulled out a black MCM bag. Trying to fight his anticipation, he stuffed two hundred thousand in the bag. After rechecking that all was well, he put his gun in his hand, left the house.

Around noon, Jason busted into his house and slammed the door, behind him. Tasha stood in the bedroom doorway with his machine gun ready to bust a cap. She immediately noticed the sweat running from his temple. Paranoid, she asked, "Who you kill? What happened?"

He walked up to her, pulled her close to him, and put his mouth to her ear. "Listen real carefully," he said calmly. "Get all the money out of the stash. Put on some classy looking shit, like you got a job."

When she hesitated he continued, "and for the first time in your life just do exactly what I tell you. I want you to go to the House of Grossman on 34th Street in the city. I want you to take the money from the stash and I want you to put a down payment on furniture for four bedrooms, a dining room, a kitchen, a living room, and lounge furniture for a basement. When they ask for an address, tell them you'll call back with it."

Tasha interrupted his speech. "But we don't have a basement, and there ain't nothing wrong with…"

"Shut up," he demanded, squeezing her hand.

"I want you to go to ABC carpet and put a down payment on carpet for all those rooms and two flights of steps. Then I want you to go to Macys and pick out all the appliances a house needs, and get two of those big screen TV's. Bag these clothes up, and get all the guns around the house and put them in one of my Gucci bags. Do not tell dem scandalous friends of yours about none of this. Just go by yourself, and come straight back here."

Tasha never saw her man that serious before so she did as she was told and he jumped into the shower. Jason got dressed quickly. For the first time in a very long time, he didn't wear stockings, or carry a gun. He knew he was carrying a lot of cash, and he wasn't about to loose his fortune by getting caught by the police with a gun on his possession. His first task was to get rid of the car, because the Italian man in the window could surely identify it.

He walked out of the building and handed Mike two hundred dollars. While Mike was dancing in the street with the hundred dollar bills in his hand, Jason was turning the corner in his car. He headed for Queens Boulevard.

Paradise Auto's was filled with a rainbow of foreign cars. Jason parked his car next to all the other cars on the lot.

"Which one now?" the dealer asked, appearing from the trailer.

Jason searched the dealership and found a car he figured would be good for Tasha. "Oscar, the new white 325," he said.

The man nodded and then went back into the trailer to handle his paperwork. "How much?" Jason asked.

The man said, in a deep Israeli accent. "You got the system, you got the rims, you got the high-performance, I'm gonna need $32,000 for it."

"I'll give you twenty seven-five."

"Jason," he said stretching his name. "You're killing me."

"Twenty eight, that's it or I have to keep shopping."

"Okay, my man. Deal."

Jason wasn't thinking of himself or Webb as he peeled off the stacks of money until there was twenty eight grand on the desk. That was until Oscar asked him if he would need an identical one for his partner. He put his face to the glass of the trailer and looked out on the lot to see what he would like to buy for himself. He looked all around until his eyes spotted a red Porsche 911 Carrera.

He told Oscar, "Give me that one, and How soon can you have another one for Webb?"

"I actually have a black one on Northern Boulevard so I can have it here by tomorrow morning. That one goes for fifty grand to someone I don't know, forty-five for family. For you, just give me $40,000 for that and I give you both for say… $70,000. I'll fix the paperwork how you like, you give me the name." He knew Oscar attained his cars through illegitimate means, but the paper work always cleared and Oscar would save him from the IRS or any other law enforcement official that came snooping around.

Jason handed Oscar another forty thousand dollars. He figured that Webb could afford his own car, and when he picked him up from the airport in the morning, he could make the decision.

"Listen, Oscar, I need to leave the Z on your lot until later tonight." Jason had already coordinated with Roger, the getaway driver from the Hanover Trust job, to meet him later. Roger would follow him as he drove the car out into Jersey over to Brick City where he would have the car set on cinderblocks and torched beyond recognition.

"No problem."

He picked up the car keys, grabbed his bag of cash, and then looked at Oscar and said, "I'll see you in the morning."

Security notified Johnny Hustle that Jason was on his way up without his nephew.

"Youngblood, where's my nephew?"

"He's out of town, but I need you to call your people and do some washing before the banks close."

Johnny looked at his watch. "You want me to do a miracle in an hour? How much we talking?"

Jason dropped a hundred and fifty thousand dollars in cash on the dining table. "I need a new social security number." He grabbed the cash from the bag, held it up to show him his payment. I need a driver's license and a place of employment so when the realtor calls she can verify it all through the bank and the job."

Johnny looked at the money. "Man, I thought you had some real paper, have a seat. You want somebody to keep you company while you're waiting?"

Jason was always offered one of Johnny's women. The women loved Jason's eyes and did whatever Johnny ordered. But he turned down his offer, just wanting to get his business handled. He watched as Johnny made a phone call and explained to the person on the line the information he needed taken care of.

After waiting forty-five minutes, one of Johnny's women walked into the suite and handed him an envelope that had the Chemical Bank letter head on it. Johnny slid Jason the envelope and said, "That's a hundred and ten in there. Your bank code is there, and the account the transaction came from is there. You did some consulting work for this hotel and when they ask, you're the head of overseas marketing for the Marquis. Give them this number here on the top of the letter as the contact. At the end of the year you have to file taxes on that as Jason Baptiste, your new social and license will be here within another hour." Johnny snapped his finger at one of the women, and then said to Jason, "Go take a picture against that wall."

One of Johnny's wives opened up a black suitcase and set up like a professional. She took his photo with the same background they used at the Department of Motor Vehicles. He watched as the lady took the camera and headed out the door.

He picked up the remote to change the channel to *The Box.* He bobbed his head to the beats of Ice Cube. Another one of Johnny's wives walked into the hotel suite wearing a business suit, with a briefcase in her hand. She walked over to Johnny and gave him a passionate kiss, and did the same to the mulatto woman that stood next to him. When she opened the briefcase, Johnny congratulated her and said, "Hey son, come over here and see if you want to pick out something for your lady."

Jason looked in the briefcase and saw that the case was filled with Laurence Graff diamond jewelry. A diamond necklace caught his eye. He looked up at Johnny. "What you want for this one?" he asked.

"From a Jewish businessman that will be here at six, I'd want fifteen large, knowing he's gonna make another ten on it. But for you? I'll take five and a favor."

"What's the favor?" Jason asked.

Johnny started laughing with his wives in unison. "Well how am I supposed to know? Whenever I need one, I'll find you, and you do what you can do."

Jason reached into his bag, which was now almost empty, and pulled out five thousand dollars. The woman that brought the jewelry in handed him a velvet necklace box. As soon as he was done with the transaction, the woman he was waiting for walked through the door. She was the gorgeous white woman whose hair was cut short. She handed Jason a brand new driver's license and social security card. He thanked Johnny and then left in a hurry.

While driving on the highway he headed straight for Elmont, Long Island. He called the number from the business card that was tucked away in his wallet for over a year.

"Mrs. Clarke, this is Mr. Baptiste, you know the face, but not the name."

"The black guy with the blue eyes?" she asked.

When he heard the recognition in her voice, he gleefully said, "Yes, I see the property still hasn't been sold? I'm ready to purchase it, cash."

"Yes, I know the banks are closed, but do you think you can meet me at the house within an hour? Yes, I know you're working until seven. Yes, I'll be right there."

Jason sat in awe of the multicolored brick house that he believed was built just for him. He did everything he could behind the scenes to make sure the house wasn't sold.

When he reached the Long Island street, he pulled the BMW up to the driveway and then walked to the house across the street. Inside of the house lived the black retired police officer that he'd been paying to keep other buyers away. When the man answered the door, they laughed and joked as Jason gave him what he hoped would be the last payment of a thousand dollars.

While Jason stood out front taking in the view of his new neighborhood, Mrs. Clarke pulled up in her old burgundy Dodge Caravan.

"Is the property available for viewing," Jason politely asked. "And can I get the keys by tomorrow."

"What you're asking, sir, is impossible," she said.

Jason sweet-talked her as he explained that he was ready to move in the next day. "What would it take for me to keep the keys," he said, licking his lips. Jason was not taking 'no' for an answer. "I guarantee that I have the money and thinking of the last of the money he had in his car he said, "I even have some little green thank you notes right now that will be on top of your commission."

The black woman blushed as he spoke, staring into his eyes. "Okay, I'll make an exception this time. But please understand that this is not common practice."

Jason smiled and ran back to the car to grab it.

They stepped across the door, and he handed her twenty-five hundred dollars as a token of his appreciation. He softly held on to her hands the whole time, and asked her would she like to join him for dinner.

Impressed by the bribe she said, "I can get the bank to verify a check on a Saturday, but I can't do any transactions." She smiled as she leaned on her heels. "But, I'm gonna go against policy and give you the keys. I can probably have you go to settlement by the middle of next week. Until then if anyone stops by, just say that you are doing work on the house."

When he heard the news he hugged her and kissed her on the cheek. The lady kissed him back and thanked Jason for the tip. They flirted with each other a little more while he filled out all of the paperwork. He then led her out of *his* house with his hand rested on her behind all the way to her car. When she pulled off, Jason knew he had just closed the deal of his lifetime.

Nine

Jason stood over her body shaking her, "Tasha wake up, Tasha wake dat ass up."

She awoke with saliva on the side of her face and an old silk scarf wrapped around her head. "Damn, Boo, it's mad early in the morning." she said as wiped the cold out of her eyes.

"Yeah, put on a sweat suit and some sneakers, you got to drop me off."

"Come back to bed, Boo," Tasha said as she tapped the bed. "And then we can do whatever you want after. You know I like it in the morning."

"Do you want your car or not?" Jason asked.

When Tasha heard the word 'car' she jumped out of bed like a 'Price Is Right' contestant. "We going to get my car?" she screamed. "Boo, I'll be ready in two and two."

"Nah," Jason shook the car keys in front of her. "Your car is already picked out and paid for. Meet me in front of the building in five minutes, I got to go to the plaza to get it."

As Jason stepped across the street, he looked around the projects and it seemed different. Maybe because he knew his time there had finally come to an end.

He walked up to Webb's apartment, hurried to feed Butch, and then he snatched the money out of the couch. An old black and white MCM bag held his future safe and secure. The diamond necklace he bought from Johnny was slid into his side pocket. After going into the kitchen and stuffing his pants pockets with new Zip-lock bags, he was out the door.

When he pulled up to the building, Tasha looked disheveled, dressed in pink sweats and a jean jacket and her braids were stuffed underneath a Liz Claiborne baseball cap. She saw the car, and her hands reached for the sky in victory. She started to do the *Running Man* on the sidewalk.

"Damn Boo," she yelled when she saw the white convertible, attracting attention.

She ran into Jason's arms. "I love you, I love you, I love you. You the man Boo."

"Oh wait till you come home *tonight.* I'm a put it on you. Ooooou Wee," she whispered, tugging at his crotch.

Jason patted her on her ass, and in his business as usual tone said, "Come and drop me off, then you can do what you want to do. I need you to take care of some business Monday, so don't you be hanging out like you done lost your mind ."

She jumped in the car and looked all around inside. She adjusted her seat, the radio, and with a new level of confidence, she drove the BMW with authority. During the entire ride she reminded Jason how they met, and how much she loved him from the start, and that no matter what, that he could count on her to be there for him forever."

He expected her to talk that way and considered it the truth. Whenever times were hard for him, she always found some way of providing what he needed emotionally.

"Drop me off on Queens Blvd," He commanded.

For the first time, Tasha asked no questions. "Okay, Boo, whatever you want," she said.

When they reached their destination, Tasha slammed on the accelerator and bolted off before Jason could get out of the car. Jason knew she was excited to go show off her car. Jason walked onto the lot and Oscar greeted him, "Good morning, my man." Oscar had all the paperwork ready for both vehicles with his old address in the projects. He planned to keep the apartment in the projects. He wasn't going to let anyone know where he lived except Tasha.

With his new plates on the car, and everything in order, Jason was ready to see if his money was well spent. The Porsche was all Jason expected it to be. He sped on the L.I.E headed for Elmont with a half of million dollars on him. He had a lot to do in the next couple of days, and the first thing was picking up Webb, who'd beeped him and let him know his flight number and time of arrival. Webb had called him just as he and Roger pulled out of Jersey. Jason had felt a little remorseful about torching his car, he could have painted it but he knew that after a million plus job and a description from Mikey Cheese, whomever he'd stolen from would be searching every paint shop and dealer in the five boroughs and Jersey. He couldn't chance it.

He pulled up to the quiet Long Island street and people were out mowing their lawns and working on their houses. Before the week was out he would be one of those homeowners, Jason thought. Instead of parking the car in the driveway, he drove into the garage.

He first checked the plumbing work he had done the day before. He'd had a fake sewage system installed in the house. The large cast-iron pipe that hung from the ceiling went into the ground blended in with the old plumbing system. Water would never see those pipes. They were for one purpose only. Jason knelt to unscrew the cap that was at the end of the pipe. He pulled the large Zip-lock bags out of his pants pocket, and dumped all of the cash from the MCM bag onto the floor.

Stack by stack, he put in forty-nine bags, totaling ten thousand in each Zip-lock bag, and stuffed pushed them into the pipe. He screwed the large three-inch brass cap back on and left the basement with ten thousand dollars in his pocket. He felt secure with his new hiding place.

Jason hit the highway and headed for the airport. He pulled into the TWA terminal at Kennedy Airport, and saw Webb, standing by the Redcaps. He glided the Porsche right past Webb, but Webb didn't notice him. He knew Webb was looking for a yellow Z, so he beeped the horn, and rolled down the window. "What, you gonna sit out there until I get a ticket?"

Webb's gold teeth glistened from the morning sun. By the look on his face, Webb approved of the car.

"Yo, yo, homey, what you done did?" Webb said as he jumped in the car. "Did you empty your whole stash to pay for this?" He looked at him in disappointment. He reached into his suit pocket and pulled out seven, ten thousand-dollar stacks of cash, and handed Jason two stacks.

"I blew up the spot down in the Cayman's," he laughed. "Can't go down there no more, but there you go homey, get back on your feet."

Jason looked at the cash and thought of his friend's undying loyalty. "Nah, Bro. You keep that." He handed the money back. "I got a major surprise for you too." Jason drove Webb straight to the car dealer. Webb asked twenty questions about how Jason bought the car. Jason never responded. "Just chill fly guy," was all he said.

They pulled up to Paradise Auto and Jason got out of the car, pointed to the red Porsche, and said, "That's yours if you wanna trade your Z and ten G's for it. You can give Oscar the paper for it now, or you can use the paper I got at your crib for you." Webb looked at Jason in confusion. Jason was about to burst when he said, "I caught the mega-lick and got one-seventy in the crib waiting for you."

Webb took a minute to register what his partner told him. "Nah, homey, nah," he said waiting for Jason to admit he was joking. When Jason kept a straight face he hugged Jason like a little boy on Christmas morning. Webb gave Oscar the ten and the keys to his Z. Oscar had two of his mechanics follow them out to the projects to retrieve Webb's car. Oscar didn't need to see it. He knew what kind of shape Webb kept his vehicles in. Fifteen minutes later, they were both cruising off the parking lot in their new rides.

As they sat in the house, Webb counted all the money while Jason told him how the heist went down. Since he did it on his own, Webb didn't question or want to know what he made for himself. Whatever consequences came from the robbery, Jason may have to handle it on his own. Webb was grateful that his partner thought of him the same way he thought of his partner.

After the drugs were tallied up, Jason said, "Yo man, I'm out. I want to knock this off quick cause I don't want my hands in this."

Webb looked at Jason twisted. "Duke, Duke, you in this Duke. Ain't no choice, homey, we gonna ride this together. I just don't know what to do with it? What we gonna do with it?"

"Damn, I wish Fall Guy or Butter was here instead of doing all that time. They could move it fast." They were speaking of two Queensbridge legends, that they looked up to, who got fifteen to life for selling crack. "Yeah, homey, I know fo' sho that Fall Guy could make it happen, but I'ma check P.R. or Little Lord. They can probably move it in the hood by the card tables on the forty-first side."

Webb scratched his chin and said, "Yeah, that's what I'ma do Duke, give them an offer they can't refuse. Give them an offer they can't refuse, all we want is the paper homey."

He drove to 38th Street on 10th Avenue to Ultrasmith audio center. The familiar face of the owner and his two Alaskan Husky dogs reminded Jason that no instructions were needed. He dropped five thousand on the owner's desk, and he told Jason that he would see him in eighty minutes.

Jason hailed a yellow cab on 11th Avenue. He received a warm welcome when he entered Brooks Brothers. He remembered he needed a tux for Zeida's affair. He chose a Walker Wear tux, and a pair of patent leather lace up Bruno Magli shoes to match.

"Oh, I see you have exquisite taste," the salesperson said underestimating Jason's fashion sense.

Jason's response was wrapped up in his smile.

Jason returned to Ultrasmith only to find his car sparkling like new money. With a new system, and a new phone, he cruised to meet his favorite girl. Since he met Zeida, he'd been exposed to new things, music, food and events. She was definitely refreshing. Seeing her was on his mind so much that he almost forgot to call her to let her know he was on his way.

"Howdy do Ja-son? You look damn good inna you suit." Diane's big smile greeted him. She had a pink substance on her hands while she tended to the hair of a high yellow woman that couldn't keep her eyes off of Jason.

Jason nodded to the owner Alicia, then rubbed his head and said, "Hey Diane, I need you to tighten me up before I go on this date."

"Yes mahn, five minute more and me soon come."

After he browsed through the latest Essence magazine, Diane was ready for him.

As Jason was seated and draped with a red smock, Diane began her show. "Me see you want to be me best customer, eh? What a way you take care of yourself? Me know fe sure no woman a let you go Jason. You a go look so good when me done, you might mek me want you fe me mahn."

Everyone laughed at Diane's joke as he explained to her that he wanted the top of his hair to grow out so she could let it get curly on top to give him a more, mature look.

"So you have an older gal, eh? Boy, you bossy, nuh?" Diane said, as she began to cut.

"Nah, I'm cool," he said laughing.

When she was done, she shaped his bushy eyebrows, something he'd never had done before. His new grooming gave more depth to his face, and more intensity to his eyes.

He handed Diane a hundred-dollar bill. "Thank you, keep the change."

As Jason turned, Diane grabbed his wrist and said, "Your cut is twenty dollars. You a give me a eighty dolla tip? You do de same ting last time?"

Jason smirked. "No sweat. Things are good right now. One day I might need you to look out for me, right? Plus, nobody ever cut my hair like you," he said.

Diane's eyes welled up. She kissed him on the cheek and said, "Thank you, you nuh know what dis mean."

He shrugged his shoulders, heading out the door to Scarsdale.

Zeida answered the door wearing a black silk panty and bra set. She had a black sequin Azzedine Alaïa gown laying on the back of the couch, and a pair of Chanel black ankle-strap pumps nearby on the floor. She kissed him, and handed him a set of keys. "Your lunch is on the terrace."

He looked at the keys in his hands. "What are these to?" he asked. Looking over to the terrace, he caught a glimpse at a huge bowl. Before she could answer, he said, "And what's this in the bowl?"

Zeida held two sets of earrings in her hands, trying to decide which ones to wear. She glanced over her left shoulder. "Those are the keys to the house. Don't call before you come anymore, that way I don't have to stop whatever it is that I might be doing to answer the door. Security already knows that you have the run of the place. The food in the bowl is crab and corn chowder with turkey bacon and Chanterelle mushrooms. I made soup' cause we have to eat at the ball and I didn't want to stuff you."

While eating, Zeida walked over and took his blazer off. When she draped the jacket over the top of the chair she felt something heavy in his jacket. She patted the pockets and asked, "What's this, blue eyes? You carry your gun everywhere?"

"As a matter of fact, that's for you."

She reached into the jacket, saw the black velvet case, and then opened the box. Her eyelids stretched to the fullest. Zeida was stunned. She took a seat next to him, and in a voice filled with liberating emotions said, "I knew from the moment I looked into your eyes that you were the one for me. Don't ask me to explain it, but my soul told me what my heart didn't know, and now I don't ever want you to go. Jason, the things you do to show me you care are why I have no problem being vulnerable to you. I know that it's soon but I swear I love you."

His spoon scraped the bottom of the bowl when she reached into his zipper and began to massage his manhood. After rubbing his tip in the palm of her hands, she put her head in between his legs and gave him oral pleasure as he stiffened in her mouth.

"Go get a condom," Jason said, his eyes spinning in the back of his head.

She came up for air. "No, Papi. I want all of you this time."

Jason interrupted Zeida and pushed the table back. He lifted her out of the seat, moved her to the cold steel rail of the terrace, and pulled her panties down. She leaned over the terrace, and he entered her nice and slow.

In erotic ecstasy, they panted and moaned as the afternoon sun baked their naked skin. Sexin' on the open terrace free for the world to see. They were hungry for each other and after stroking her for a while he pulled out, and dropped slowly to his knees. He gently kissed her ass, headed for downtown. She dripped with anticipation.

Zeida caressed her breast as he took her vagina by storm with his kisses. "Aye, Papi, use me," she screeched.

He sucked on her until he could stand it no more. Zeida turned around and faced him. Her back was up against the rail and Jason quickly moved into her. Their eyes were locked on one another as he moved his muscular body in and out of her. Zeida's face frowned up, not in displeasure, but because an orgasm was approaching her and she was losing control. Jason was approaching his peak as well and began to pound harder into her. Her eyes watered from the sensations that he was giving her as well as from the beating that he was giving her body. She felt like she was being ravaged and worshipped at the same time.

One magical stroke and the tingling started in the back of her thighs. She began to hump him fiercely and call out his name. "Ohhhhh, Jaaaaasssssonnnnn. I love it, I love it, yessssss, pleassssse don't... don't stop. Iyyyyeeeee," she screamed out. "I'mmmm cummming all over your .... All ... over ... your ... dick."

With that, Jason exploded inside of her and banged her until every drop had shot inside of her. Panting he tried to tell her that she was incredible.

"Shhhhh," she said. "Just don't move for a minute." They stood still on the terrace in the heat until their hearts stopped pounding.

Zeida reapplied her makeup and fixed her ruined hair after she showered. She had to rush in order to get herself together. Originally, she wore her hair long and flowing back, but the sweat she worked up forced her to pin it up.

When she was done turning into a Latin queen, he slipped the Laurence Graff twenty-carat necklace onto her neck. To match his gift, she slipped on a pair of pear shaped studs in her ears and a diamond Rolex.

When they walked out of her building she asked, "Jason, where's your car? Don't tell me you took a cab," Zeida said.

He laughed at her and pulled out the car alarm. He pressed one button and the doors unlocked. When she realized it was the Porsche, she pranced over to the driver's side on her heels with her hands extended for the keys. Jason shook his head "no" as he moved her out around the car. There was no way he was going to let her drive his car when he hadn't had a chance to push it to its limits yet.

"So what did you have to do to afford this?" she asked on the highway.

"All I can say is that I'm out the game. I'm done. I have everything I need right here with me, and you don't have to worry. My days will be spent pleasing you, and you're gonna figure out how to make me triple my earnings since you want me off the streets, right?"

She laughed and said, "The work ain't hard, baby boy."

Ten

As they stepped onto the huge ballroom floor, Zeida held Jason's arm tightly. He did the whole senator Anduzé voice and strutted like an aristocrat. He entertained the women all night. Zeida's sorority sisters fell head over heels in love with him.

"I sell estates to the extremely wealthy," he told one of the not-so-attractive sorors, who hung onto his every word. Of course he lied about his career. Jason didn't know how Zeida would take him toying with her ultra bourgeoisie sisters but surprisingly she laughed it off, enjoying his acting performance.

Dinner was served and they ate pan grilled New York strip steaks with green olive tapenade and creamy potato gratin, served with a bottle of 1987 Chateau Latour elegant Bordeaux. Jason was confused about what silverware to use, so he carefully watched Zeida use a silent code with her hands for him to follow her lead.

On the way home, it was clear Zeida was drunk. She was saying full sentences in Spanish before she realized that Jason didn't know a word she was saying. She did it more than once, and every time she did it, they would burst out in laughter. Zeida played with Jason while he drove, and in the middle of their conversation she stopped. She turned the music down, and looked him straight in the eye. "Will you marry me?"

Jason laughed. He thought she couldn't possibly be serious, until her silence showed otherwise. He didn't want to hurt her feelings, so he said, "This is all moving kind of fast. Why don't you just give me some time to think about it?"

Zeida didn't show her surprise, she used what she had to get what she wanted, and pulled out his penis and said, "Let me give you something to help you think."

They reached the parking lot and had sex on the hood of the car. They kissed all the way up to her place in the elevator. Zeida was loving him like a woman possessed. She was determined to use whip appeal to capture his heart and make his heart weak for her. She had no idea that Tasha had that tactic mastered already and owned pieces of Jason that she would never willingly surrender.

When the sun began to creep through the window signaling the dawn of a new day, they both pulled the covers over their head knowing that they hadn't enough energy left between the two of them to close the blinds.

Jason was up early Monday morning arranging his afternoon appointment with Mrs. Clark. She'd been able to move his settlement up to the afternoon. A cash deal was rare and she didn't want to blow it once she'd verified his funds. Jason had even paid up the property taxes for the next several years. All was set. With the new news, he called Samson movers for a truck and a small van to pick up the furniture from House of Grossman.

Tasha had been on the go since Jason had copped her the Beemer. It took everything Jason had just to get her out of bed.

"Tasha," he yelled as he shook her. "Get up. We got a lotta shit to do today." It was this lazy mentality that made Jason consider leaving his ghetto queen right there in the hood. Zeida could definitely be the wife he needed to go with the new house.

"Come on baby, I'm tired," she moaned.

"Bring ya' ass home sometime and maybe you'll be able to get your lazy ass up."

"Damn, Boo, okay, I'm up, shit."

"Get all my guns and the cash, put on a suit and meet me downstairs."

What should have taken Tasha thirty minutes tops, turned into an hour. Jason was pissed and on the way to Grossman's Jason said not one word to Tasha.

"That will be thirty thousand dollars," the salesman said. Jason nodded and Tasha handed the money to Mike.

"The chair, ottoman and dinette chairs are on back order," said the assistant manager. "There is a four to six week wait."

Jason's persistence to have the furniture rush ordered did not move Mike. So he put the negotiations in Tasha's hands.

Once Tasha unleashed the dragon from within, they were ready to do anything to get the unruly black couple out of their establishment. When they discovered that five thousand dollars of the money he gave them was in singles, they didn't count it. They were too busy trying to get him out of the store.

When he gave the movers the address in Long Island, Tasha was furious. She thought Jason was buying everything for someone else. It took him awhile to calm her down without revealing his plans.

At ABC carpet, Jason offered two thousand dollars to four Latino men to lay his carpet the same day. They agreed.

With the smaller moving van, Jason went to pick up all of his electrical appliances. That cost him another ten thousand dollars. After he bought curtains, chandeliers, and new locks to be installed, he'd blown through all of the money he had on him.

He raced to his new house in an effort to get there before the moving trucks. During the drive there, Tasha was arguing and trying to figure out whose house he was spending all his money on. Since Jason wouldn't tell her, she thought it was for his mother.

The BMW pulled up to the quiet street of the Elmont community, and when they reached a front house with a big front and back yard, Tasha was filled with wonder when she asked, "Damn, Boo, whose crib is this?"

Jason smiled, opened the car door and said, "Mine."

Her eyes popped open in shock and then she dashed from the car breaking her gold fingernail, and hopped around in the suburban street shouting, "I can't believe it" as she kissed and hugged Jason.

Eleven

Two months to the day after he moved into his house, Webb told Jason that Crackhead Mike had told him that he thought he'd seen some cat name Powerful going in and out of his old apartment. If that was the case then, Tasha had violated to the utmost and Webb told Jason that he was going to kill her and the dude on sight. Distraught but wanting to find out for sure, he told Webb to chill and let him handle it.

"What? Chill? I ain't feelin' dat. Duke, you slippin'. Duke, you definitely slippin'," had been Webb's response.

On top of her disrespect, Jason found birth control pills hidden under the sink. Over the years, she led him to believe that he was sterile, since she had never gotten pregnant. When he confronted her about the pills she fed him a bunch of lies. "Boo, I just started taking them to ease my cramps."

Jason left the house and was headed to the projects to do a stake out when Zeida paged him. He dialed her back.

The phone rang once and Zeida yelled into the phone "We're pregnant," while Jason's whole life flashed through his mind.

He was stunned and whimpered out, "Are you sure?"

"Oh yeah, I'm very sure. I waited when I didn't get my period, and now this month I missed it again, so I went to see the doctor." Zeida started singing, "Papi, you're about to be a daddy. I wish you would hurry up and marry me and stop playing games."

Jason thought about her words while his heart was banging through his chest and said, "I'll be right over." He hung up the phone, turned the car around and headed back into the house.

"Back so soon?" Tasha asked like a smartass.

He ignored her and went into his room to change clothes.

Since he was going to see Zeida he needed to change his clothes. She always preferred to see him in suits or slacks at the least and he had gotten used to the idea of always looking fresh. Zeida had changed him for the better at least as far as his look. "Baby, if you're going to have business about yourself then you need to look the part," she'd say. Long gone were the days where he wore stockings and a gun on his hip as if he had a license. Jason naively believed that he was done with the life of crime.

Before he left, he followed his intuition and went to the basement to get a hundred thousand dollars. He knew with the news he just received that everything had to change. He was going to give Zeida the money to invest at her job, in a business of her own, or for her clothing line. Jason wanted the best for his soon-to-be child.

He had learned in a short while that having the house was overrated and a large liability. On the way to Zeida's house he thought that he should move Tasha back into the projects that she loved so much, and sell the house so he could live with Zeida.

Money in hand Jason rushed to the soon-to-be-mother of his child. When he walked into the bedroom she was holding her stomach and puffing her cheeks out, trying to figure out what she would look like in just a few months. He put his arms around her waist then moved them to her stomach.

"So we gonna do this, huh?"

"Are you happy?"

"I couldn't be happier," Jason thought as his mind was filled with a thousand and one thoughts. He was going to have to let Tasha go. He had a winner in Zeida and now she was about to give him a family. Then he went on, "I'm happy about the baby, but I'm happier about you."

Zeida began to cry tears of joy. She told him that she didn't want to be stressed out during the pregnancy, so she asked for him to be at home with her more often. She also told him that she wanted her baby to have *their* name, so consider her marriage proposal or just say no.

"Yes, baby." Jason announced with a smile on his face.

"Yes, you'll consider it right?" Zeida asked.

The smile left his face when he said, "No...I mean yes, I'll marry you before the baby comes. Just let me get rid of the drama in my life so we can be alright." He dropped the money on the bed and said, "That's a hundred thousand right there. Put it up, invest it, or start your business cause we're gonna need money real soon."

Zeida wrapped her arms around his neck and kissed him. While their lips met over and over she said, "I have money Papi, but if you want me to start my own business, let's wait until after the baby is born."

They kissed some more until they removed all their clothes and they made love until they were fast asleep.

At midnight, the phone rang. When Jason awoke he could tell something was wrong. Zeida was talking a mile a minute in Spanish. When he looked over to ask her what was wrong, she palmed the receiver and said, "I have to go to the Bronx. My mother's really sick and she won't go to the hospital."

Jason sat up and said, "I'll get dressed."

"No," she said with urgency in her voice, holding up a finger for Jason to wait while she ended her call.

When Zeida cut off the phone, Jason demanded, "I'm coming with you. You can't go down there by yourself."

Zeida was silent as she held her hands as if she was praying and said, "Okay." Before Jason could move to get dressed she blurted out "But there's something I have to tell you if you really want to go." She folded her naked arms and looked at the white carpet when she said, "After I tell you, if you don't want to stay, then I will understand."

"What is it?" Jason asked with paranoia running through his veins.

Zeida exhaled. "It's my ex-boyfriend, Rico. The reason he has a hit out on me is because I had an abortion without telling him. I was starting school and a new life. I had a lot of pressure, and I wasn't ready to be a mother to a child whose father was the leader of a gang. I wanted out, and that baby would have kept me lost in that hood and hooked to that man. Anyway, my brother told him what I did because he's more loyal to the gang than he is to his own blood, and if we go over there it could trouble." She pulled the covers off of her body. "So now, you may think differently of me, but I have to go."

Jason waved her off relieved that she didn't give him some horrendous news about her past. Compared with the drama Tasha gave, what Zeida told him was nothing, so he thought. He went into the closet to put on a pair of jeans, shoes, and a sweatshirt. When he came out, he saw her in sneakers and a baseball cap for the first time.

He wished he had a gun on him, and he knew there wasn't time for him to go to Long Island and come back, so he had no choice but to go as is.

Jason's Porsche stuck out on the street. The desolate block was flanked with tenements and private houses. The neighborhood told a story in a language that Jason understood well. It was a tale of poverty that most would call hell. When he and Zeida pulled into Hughes Avenue in the Bronx, they saw a row of twenty motorcycles lining the street. As the Porsche crept its way through the darkness, Jason could hear whistles from one street corner down to the next. He knew the whistles were a code that announced a stranger was in the mist. He exited his car and a welcoming committee was there to greet him. Zeida fled. She put her head down and rushed into her mother's building, hoping that no one would recognize her. Jason took his time to survey the block, wishing he wasn't driving his Porsche for once.

Apartment 5F was crowded. As they entered the cramped space, Zeida's brother rushed past them. He wore a Ching-a-ling biker's jacket. Three more beer-carrying bikers appeared seconds later, leaving in a rush. Since nothing jumped off right on the spot, he foolishly figured that Zeida exaggerated about her ex-boyfriend wanting to kill her.

He and Zeida walked into a cluttered bedroom that had enough statues of Saints to fill the Vatican church. Ms. Carro was stretched out in her bed and Zeida tried to convince her to go to the hospital. Half of the people in the small room told her she should go, and the other half told her not to go. When the cursing started, Jason eased his way into the kitchen. A toothless man smiled, handed him a bottle, and plopped down in the chair. Jason eased in the adjacent chair, sharing space with cockroaches.

After listening to ten minutes of screaming and yelling, from the other room, Zeida appeared in the kitchen begging for a hug. She snatched his cold beer, and took it to the head.

"You alright?" he asked concerned.

"Si, Papi, they just have their old fashioned ways and I'm ready to go. My work is done here," she said exhausted.

The distant voice of familiarity echoed Zeida's name. "That sounds like my old home girl, Dotti, from back in the days," Zeida said smiling as she opened the window.

Jason studied Zeida as she pranced to the kitchen window. The moment she reached it, her facial expression went from that of a happy child to the fear of an abused woman.

His heart pounding, Jason instantly shut his eyes. He had what seemed like an out of body experience. In a split second, a loud boom shattered the window. He felt the vibration of the thump near his feet.

"What the..." the toothless man cried. He took off running to the bedroom.

As Jason slowly opened one eye at a time, his worst nightmare had come true. There, the mother of his unborn child lay clutching her shoulder. Zeida was stretched out on the floor covered in blood.

He should have, but for some reason Jason didn't panic. Instead, he stepped over her body and went to the window. Roughly twelve bikers lined the street. Their hands were extended. He was outnumbered. In an instant, a volley of shots rang out like flying cannons.

Jason cut out the lights, hit the floor, put his mouth next to Zeida's ear and asked, "Where are you hit?"

She was losing consciousness as she struggled to speak. "I don't know...but...my shoulder is hurting. Papi, I'm dying, call the ambulance. "

Jason knew what to expect. He had been on the wrong side of a gun twice before. He pulled her shirt down, and saw a gaping whole where the bullet made contact. Hurriedly, he grabbed a dishtowel and placed it on the wound. "Press as hard as you can," he said. As the last word left his lips, all of Zeida's family members appeared frantic. They yelled for someone to call the police. "Baby, are there any other phones besides the one in the kitchen?"

"No, that's the only one," she whispered.

Jason snatched the phone from a young attractive girl. "Look, everyone calm down. I'll handle this. Hold on baby," he said. "What's the number here," Jason asked Zeida. She whispered out the number.

"Why the hell are you dialing all those numbers. Call 911. Call 911," her uncle shouted.

"I'm gonna get her to the hospital chief, but right now I'm calling the answer to our problem."

Jason paged Webb with the 5-4-5-5 code, each numeral spelled out the letters in the word *kill*. Without delay, Webb called back. Jason gave a detailed account of the events as well as the location.

"Hey, Duke, get an ambulance for your girl, and let me handle the rest. Yo, stay posted while the building still stands."

Jason dialed 911 and said, "My mother is having a heart attack, come quick." Jason hoped that by telling that lie, the police would come quickly.

Ten minutes passed before Jason heard the sound of the ambulance. As he crept to the shattered window, his Porsche was being stripped right in front of his eyes. The knock at the door broke his rage.

"EMS," they shouted through the door.

Jason opened the door. "Over here, sir," he said guiding the chubby man to the kitchen.

"Someone reported a heart attack not a gunshot wound."

"Sorry," Jason spat. They went to work and Jason was so frantic standing over her that he had forgotten that he was in the middle of more than one battle. "Will she be alright," Jason asked.

"Back up, please. We won't know until we get her to the hospital and run some tests," the female paramedic responded. "She's lost a lot of blood Jim, hand me the towel," she added, turning towards her partner.

Jason removed all of his cash from his pockets and placed it into on of the overworked ambulance driver's hands, and convinced him to wrap a sheet over her body as if she were dead. Once he explained it was for the safety of the EMS workers as well, they complied. A sheet hid the oxygen mask that covered Zeida's face.

His scheme worked. The onlookers assumed she was dead. People stood around shouting, "Who is that?" After he explained to her family what was going on the chaos in the house subsided.

"You need to leave. We don't want any trouble," the uncle said.

"No chance of that yet," Jason replied. Jason barricaded the door to the small apartment, and ushered Zeida's family into her sick mother's room. He waited in the dark for his savior to arrive. After an hour's wait, Jason recognized the special knock at the door. Webb entered wearing an all-black preacher's attire. He laughed uncontrollably as he put down the large Bible in his hands. No one understood Webb's laugh but him. In his laugh, Jason found comfort.

In Webb's other hand rested a large black duffel bag that he dropped on the floor. Jason immediately removed the items inside. One after the other, Jason pulled out two seventeen shot Glocks, a snub nosed 357, a Mac-11 submachine gun, and one of Webb's Tanto blades.

He slid two Glocks, one on each hip. Web was already wearing a bulletproof vest. He motioned for Jason to put one on. Jason strapped the snub nose with the bulldog handle onto his ankle. Webb then removed an Army-issued grenade from the bag. Jason was shocked. "Never bother a man's money, car or woman," Webb laughed out.

They looked out of the window and the Ching-a-lings were still hanging out front as if they dared the police or anyone to come for them. Periodically they yelled up boasts about what they'd done to the Porsche. When Webb and Jason were dressed, Webb laughed, and Jason prayed. He didn't think that too many people would come out alive once his friend was done. This was one time he didn't care.

Webb said, "Okay, Homey, it's time to pop off. We got to make it to the parking garage on Tremont Avenue. The keys are in the car in case I don't make it. Now, you know I only know how to get down one way, so here's my plan. Here's my plan homey. When we walk outside, we don't run Duke, we don't surrender, and we don't retreat, Duke. We don't leave until everything is murdered, or when we run out of bullets, so lets make it happen."

Fear gripped Jason, but he had no time for that. He ignored the sweat that danced so freely down his back. "I just got one thing to say. Try not to hit any bystanders."

"Anyone standing out there when I hit the ground is as good as dead, Duke. They good as dead."

"Thanks for coming for me, man," Jason said in a sincere tone.

"You da only family I got, Duke. You go, I go."

They slapped hands and walked out of the fifth floor apartment. As they were walking down the steps, they could see from the windows in the tenement hallway that the crowd outside was multiplying. They knew the police stayed away from gang territory unless one of there own was involved, and Jason was counting on that.

Side by side they walked in a straight path out of the building. They spotted Zeida's brother. He stood with a confused look.

"You in the game, then money stay the same..." Webb stated while clasping the grip and removing the pin from the grenade.

By the time Zeida's brother realized the two men were armed, it was lights out. Jason fired in his direction and filled his head with three groupies from his Mac-11. A brother that would allow his sister to be shot got what he deserved. Jason's only regret was that his death had come too quickly. As Jason moved toward his body to confirm his kill Webb threw the grenade at the row of motorcycles, and watched in amazement as if what happened had not been his intention. One of the bikers, who was overweight, had been unable to get off of his bike and when the grenade went off his bike exploded into flames with him on it. His flaming corpse was sent hurling backwards toward a tenement.

By this time, Jason was aiming at the men as they tried to scatter. Anyone baring any symbol of Ching-A-Ling was served. Webb enjoyed hitting the moving targets in the back. Some of them attempted to return fire but it was obvious that they'd never been attacked so ruthlessly. One by one Webb put holes in them. He did so without fear and paused only to throw a cocktail into Jason's Porsche. It erupted in flames and with it any link to them burned.

One of the bikers peeped out from an alley. He thought that Webb hadn't seen him so he took off running trying to reach the alley on the other side of the street. It proved to be a fatal error. Webb easily hit the man in the side of his head. The man's body went limp as he slid do the ground missing half of his skull. Webb was a ghetto marksman if ever there was one. More than having the guns though, Webb had wet dreams about using them. He spent weekends in the woods near Albany learning how to fire the guns with a group of Arabs who claimed to be terrorists. He'd met them through one of his weapons suppliers. They got a kick out of the crazy, gold tooth-wearing, black man. "You should fight with us and bring this country down. America has no love for black man," they would say.

Webb had even thought about it until they told him that no money was involved. It was all for Allah, they'd told him and lost him right there.

"Ya'll wanna fuck with Rico. You wanna bang weeth the Ching-a-lings?" The leader of the Ching-a-lings had spoken in the voice of a deranged lunatic and revealed himself. Rico stood on the hood of a Caprice like he was holding court. Jason was filled with anxiety as his chance to end it all was in front of him. He jumped from behind an ice cream truck and took aim at Rico. Jason got two shots off but the Mac jammed and fear washed over him. Rico laughed. He hadn't flinched when Jason fired. It was apparent to Jason that he was high on something. Jason threw the Mac to the ground and tried to grab the two Glocks from his hips but he wouldn't have time.

Rico aimed his Desert Eagle at Jason and gritted his teeth as he prepared to end his life. Fired with bad intentions, the shots erupted in six loud bangs. All six shots hit Rico in the back and as he fell forward off of the car. "Gotcha," Webb yelled out. "Gotcha ass," Webb ran around the car and looked down at Rico and put his foot on his back. Two more shots blew bone threw his neck where his Adam's apple had been.

Jason ducked and spun when bullets flew from a window behind him. They looked over and saw a woman yelling out the window. *Hell,* he thought *that's a broad.*

It seemed like the whole neighborhood was shooting at them. A bang came from another direction and Webb fell. Jason ran to him. "You alright?"

His eyes opened wide, he glared at Jason in embarrassment. "Duke, Duke, get off me Duke. I'm a soldier, I'm a soldier."

Webb was hit in his vest and was too deep in a zone to be stopped or feel the pain. He stood up, stumbled, and then chased four of the armed men into a building with his bullets. "Come on, we gots to get out of here," Jason feared that they had underestimated the gang's depth. "We can come back and smoke them another day."

As Webb climbed to his feet, a child about twelve years old shot at him, so he aimed for his legs and put the kid down as he yelled out, "You Fucker."

Jason and Webb fled like Batman and Robin. To avoid being shot, they ran in zig-zag patterns on opposite sides up the street.

Back at Webb's they sat in front of the television as Webb iced his chest down. The news reporter announced that six men were dead, two more were on life support and one was in critical condition. In the press conference, the chief of police, Roberto Maglioco, informed the reporter that it was possible that the gunmen were military trained, and that the violence could have possibly been retaliation for the molestation of a white girl in a bar by the gang a few days before.

Twelve

Jason broke night with thoughts of Zeida and the massacre from the night before weighing heavy on his mind. Jason left Webb's house early in the morning. As he left Webb's building, Tasha was pulling off with someone in the passenger seat of her car. She had tinted all of her windows, so he couldn't be sure. In a wasted effort, he called out to her, but she was turning the corner and he was too tired to give chase.

Jason walked down to the Laundromat at the center of the projects and called her car phone. When he didn't get an answer, he paged her and put his emergency code in. After ten minutes of waiting, she called him back. Instead of arguing and complaining, he explained to her that he didn't have his car and he needed hers. Jason was fed up. He'd made up his mind. He was taking her car from her and moving her back into the projects.

After waiting for an hour, Tasha drove past him, headed in the direction of their apartment. Jason walked up the street with fire in his eyes. When they met up, she was dressed in her lime green sweat suit. He walked over to the driver's seat. "Get out," he said nothing more.

Tasha began her usual protest when she said, "Wait Boo, I'll take you where you wanna go, I just got to take care of something, so you can't have the car yet."

Jason didn't say a word. He hauled off and punched her in the mouth. "Bitch, I saw you earlier with a nigga in this car. My fucking car."

"No, you didn't," she was scooting away from him. He stepped toward her. "I ought to let Webb come out here and do what he's been dying to do for the longest and blast your fucking ass right here in the street."

"Boo, how can you say that to me?"

Jason lunged at her and was about to beat her down like he was Iceberg Slim but when she screamed, "Noooo," at the top of her lungs, he said to hell with it. He had to get to Zeida so Jason moved her out the way, jumped into the car and left her on the sidewalk. He adjusted the seat, fixed the radio, and headed to find out what hospital Zeida was in.

Jason was still furious. It was over. As soon as he found Zeida he was going to change the locks and Tasha was history. He turned the radio on and a tape was in the deck. A mix tape featuring Pete Rock and CL Smooth came blasting through the speakers as he hung the corner of 21st Street in an effort to get on the bridge. Jason switched lanes suddenly and his path was cut off. "What, the..." he yelled.

Unmarked cars pulled out of thin air and surrounded him. Jason reached for his pockets and remembered that he didn't have his gun. Fears of catching six bodies for the shooting in the Bronx quickly crossed his mind.

About ten officers had guns in his face. "What's this about?" Jason asked.

"Shut the fuck up." They pulled him out of the car and told him to get face down on the ground.

He was clean so he cooperated waiting to hear if they were about to question him about the shootings. He wondered if they were arresting Webb at the same time. While on the ground he watched a muscular black police officer pop the trunk to the BMW and yell, "Bingo."

Jason was confused and his nerves became rattled with each moment. He looked up wondering what they were talking about, until the bulky steroid freak picked him up. They walked him over to the trunk and showed him four Zip-locked packages in one of his Gucci bags. He looked at the officer and in foolish innocence he said, "So what? It's a bag?"

The officer stuck his knife in one of the packages, pulled out a brown powder, tasted and then spat on the floor before he said, "Yep, it's heroin."

"Heroin?" Jason asked in disbelief. "I know you didn't just plant that on me?"

"Look, buddy. We got you now. You might as well make it easy on yourself." a white officer with liver spots on his face said, "We been trailing this vehicle since you left here this morning, and came back from Far Rockaway. Unless you want to confess.... anything else you have to say, make a statement or tell it to the judge."

Jason's mind began to spin. He became nauseous. He felt sick as he took the ride to the Queens Tactical Narcotics Team's headquarters. He wondered why Tasha had drugs in the car. He knew the Gucci bag was his and remembered the day he and Webb went to the outlet to buy the complete set. So he wondered how the drugs got in there. He bought her everything she wanted, so he was sure she wasn't transporting for money. So why were the drugs in the car?" he asked himself. He hoped she would have a good explanation whenever he talked to her.

Two hours after Jason was busted, Webb was on his way to check on the progress of his new drug business with Little Lord and P.R.

TNT officers had him pinned in handcuffs. P.R.'s short body was off to the side in the lobby. He tried to signal Webb to reverse his steps, but one of the officers recognized him from a description his snitch gave him.

"Hey, Webb. Hey, Webb, come here, homey," the pink faced officer called.

Webb walked at a brisk pace trying to get to his apartment. When the officer ran up on him, Webb smoothly reached into his waist, removed two .50 Desert Eagles, and aimed one hand above the vest, and the other below. The triggers were released.

The other officers heard the shots. Their bodies dropped to the dirty cold pavement into the same position they put so many people in before. When they looked up, their worst fears came to life as their fellow officer lay dead with wounds to the head and thigh. Webb had downed an officer and was headed their way. Webb reloaded and took cover behind a tree.

In a fit of panic, one of the officers put Lord on his face and sat on his back so he wouldn't escape. One of the other officers grabbed his radio but was too afraid to speak. Webb blasted like a mad marine in combat. In an act that no one in the projects had ever seen before, the police retreated into a piss-infested building for cover. They weren't prepared to be attacked.

Webb took off and headed for his apartment. He had planned ahead in case a situation like the one he was in ever occurred. When he reached the apartment, he ran into his room and emptied his safe. He grabbed two bags, and with his bulletproof vest in hand, he snatched Butch and headed to the door. Before he left the house he opened the hall closet, sparked two wires on a car battery that was on the floor, and the whole house began to smolder. He was in and out of his house in less than two and a half minutes.

When he reached outside, the streets were empty but approaching sirens were blaring. He looked across the street to the forty-first side where he laid the officer down. There were two female officers pointing his way. He kissed Butch on his head and then sent the dog to his death sentence, but he was sure his companion was taking someone with him. A helicopter was above him, and the police had all exits from the projects closed off. Webb took his time to walk in the only direction he could. He eased through the fence of Baby Park, and with the helicopter above he jogged on the R&R train tracks. East River and Manhattan were in his vision. He had temporary cover when he reached an overpass. The helicopter swirled around and tried to regain a visual but couldn't. Six cars arrived and they saw no trace of Webb. One wondered if he'd jumped into the water to commit suicide.

"It was as if he disappeared into thin air," said one cop.

Little Lord was brought into the same precinct as Jason, but they were kept in separate holding tanks. From the vents in the cell, Jason could hear an informant telling the police that Webb and Jason were partners, and that Lord sold coke and not heroine. The voice sounded like Crack-head Mike. He also told the police that Jason was a thief and not a drug dealer. Once the police received that information, they were more concerned with finding Webb. Right in front of Jason's cell the police discussed how to use him to get his partner. They mentioned that they were letting Little Lord go for lack of evidence.

Two hours later, Jason was interrogated. They tried to get him to rat on Webb about the drugs. The thought didn't even enter his mind to cooperate with the police. He knew he would have a hard time living in prison, but he decided that he would stay strong and suffer whatever consequences. Once they gave him a bail, he would be home, he unwisely thought. He tried to reach Tasha, but he didn't get an answer. He then called his lawyer, Troy Yancey.

Over the phone, his lawyer explained that she was going to get his case heard in front of a judge that day and speed him through the system the way all high profile cases were done. She didn't ask for a retainer or discuss any money issues. All she wanted was for her client to be released. Jason knew from the sound of her voice, that he and Webb had picked the right attorney.

Jason's case was heard and he was given a bail for $100,000. Everyone in the courtroom wondered why he smiled, but he knew something they didn't. He planned on being in the company of his girl Zeida before the night was out. He just had to do the impossible task of finding Tasha first.

Thirteen

Powerful's idea of being lenient was saying, "Yo, suck my dick while I think this shit over." He was in a bad mood and the blow job hadn't done much to change it.

Once she'd finished he grabbed her by her hair and yelled, "Bitch you better have my money."

With tears in her eyes, she pleaded, "Powerful, how you gonna have me driving around with drugs all this time without telling me? I love you Boo, how could you do this to me?" she asked right after swallowing his cum.

The big muscled man sat on the bed that Jason and Tasha had shared with the lower half of his body exposed. He smirked with death eyes and showed his diamond and gold grill. In a Southern accent mixed with a Brooklyn roughness he said, "Forget all that. I need my money. That's close to a half of million worth of stuff your man got popped with cause of your dumb ass. I told you to drive straight to Jamaica. Why you come here in the projects?" He looked around the once immaculate room. "Just find your man's stash and pay me my money, and me and you is cool." With a player's flattery he said, "You know I love you, Boo, but you gonna get me killed if I don't have that paper."

Tasha didn't realize she'd been used as a mule by Powerful from day one. Every time she drove into Edgemere Projects in Far Rockaway, she was working without knowing it. Since he needed a way to transport the drugs from Rocaway to Jamaica, he used Tasha every chance he got. He told her that she was transporting money for him, nothing that would get her into trouble.

In an effort to impress Powerful, she let him drive whatever cars she drove. At first it was the 300ZX, and then it was the BMW. With his slick fast country talking style, she quickly became his sex slave from day one. He had the rough edge she wanted. Tasha wanted money, and Powerful wanted a woman that was familiar with the Jamaica area to take drugs back and forth for him. He would ask to borrow her car, drive it around the corner where his workers would fill it with drugs, and then drive back around and tell her to meet him in Jamaica with his money. When they reached Jamaica in separate cars, he would tell her that he wanted to drive around to make the drop to his stash, and do the same thing to get rid of the drugs. Since he was the biggest dealer in Far Rocaway, he promised her big money and a *real* future. Tasha easily became Powerful's toy.

The first day in jail passed and turned into night. Jason was sent to the Queens House of Detention for men and was placed under Central Monitored Case-Maximum Security status. When he reached the sixth floor, he was well respected. The inmates had heard about he and Webb's acts on the street. This afforded him special privileges, like extended phone calls.

All night he called and couldn't get Tasha. He called his old phone number and someone hung up the phone when they heard his voice. Jason's mind was playing tricks on him, and he was sure he dialed the wrong number. He called his house in Long Island, but again, she wasn't at home. Without his pocket computer or phone book his was lost. He wished that he remembered phone numbers well, and he only had Zeida's beeper number, but it was impossible to page someone from jail. He was losing his mind. He needed a change of clothes, and he needed some basic necessities.

The next morning he called, he reached Tasha at home. She went hysterical and denied ever having the drugs in the car. He told her to come and visit him immediately giving her instructions on what to bring.

Within the hour, he was being called for a visit, and he knew Tasha was the one that would always be there when he was down. During the visit, he told her where to go in the basement to get the money for his bail. He then told her how to get in contact with his lawyer, and that he would be home that day if she hurried. Like a partner for life, she told him how much she loved him, and that she left him an abundance of things that he needed. She promised that no matter where they sent him, if he had to do time, that she would be right there for him till the end. His hopes were high, and he knew he would be home soon.

A week passed and Jason still waited for Tasha to post bail. He had no way of contacting Zeida, and everyone in the jailhouse was tired of him getting on the phone trying numbers he never got through to. He ended up breaking one guy's jaw. His mood was growing darker by the minute. The guys he was in with liked jail, but he was only concerned about going home. Two days later, he was transferred to Rikers Island.

Rikers Island, the biggest jail in the world, sits out in a body of water like Alcatraz, and the grime stained building resembles a tortured city of suffering. Some of the guards, Jason thought, must have been recruited from hell.

As soon as he got there Jason was sent to the dungeon. He reached the cellblock knowing the men down there were the condemned who were never going home. Only the ruthless were sent down there. He was confident that he would survive on a physical basis, and with the cash and clothes Tasha left, he was comfortable. He was still trying to reach her, but he didn't get an answer. Jason didn't realize at that point that she left him so many things to survive in jail, because she had no intentions of ever getting him out.

The following morning as he tried to reach Tasha and his lawyer, he saw a ghost coming through the steel bloodstained door of 1B. Jason was sure now that he was losing his mind. The muscular body and ferocious swagger were a little unfamiliar. The man he'd known was never this large. He didn't turn away and when he recognized the bowlegged bop of the man, he knew a new savior had arrived.

"Jason?" His eyes scanned Jason's structure from head to toe before he yelled out, "Damn you put on some weight young'n."

Jason was filled with joy. "Yo, Fall Guy, what up? You don't know how glad I am to see you."

The man observed his surrounding with suspicion when his soft spoken voice said, "Young'n, you have to call me the God Supreme now."

"Oh yeah, I heard about that. No doubt, no doubt. You with the Nation of Gods and Earths now…what you doing down here?" Jason asked.

"These devils had to reverse the case of the God. I'm starting from scratch all over again. We going back to trial, but what you doing here? I heard you and my man Webb was doing y'all thing out in the world?"

Jason told Supreme the whole story of what was going on. Jason was sensing that he'd been foolish to tell Tasha about his money. When he was done talking, Supreme said, "I got to get on the phone. Lets track your girl down and get you up out of here, so you can return the favor."

A path was cleared for Supreme to get on the phone. He called up a couple his contacts in Queensbridge to put an APB out on Tasha. People still feared him, so the search was definitely on. His connect dropped some news on him.

He walked Jason into the day room recreation area, and sat him down on the cold steel gray picnic bench and put his hand on his shoulder. "Young'n, I hate to tell you this, but word is your man, Webb, bust off on the police something terrible and he on the run. Now the whole projects is on fire because police got shot and the only one who lived … it don't look good for him either. So we know Webb ain't coming back. So far, nobody saw your girl. Webb didn't tell you about dealing with them scandalous hoes?"

Jason stood quiet while he listened and instead of answering the question, he went into his cell to lay down. He was filled with stress and wondered how he went from being on top of the world, to having to beg for help. He stared at the grimy ceiling of the cell and thought of how the help he needed came from the one person he never did anything for. He wondered why so many people that he helped never reached out to help him, not even his own mother.

Over and over he tried to figure out a way to reach Zeida, but he couldn't remember any of the numbers except for her beeper. He wanted to get his lawyer to track her down, but he didn't want his lawyer to link him to the events on Hughes Avenue. He thought of how the things he gained fast were gone just as quick and he wondered what the future might bring, but he still had faith in Tasha.

The next day Supreme came with more bad news for Jason. "Have a seat Young'n." Supreme looked him right in the eyes. "I'm gonna drop this science on you *one* time. They just found your girl

Tasha half dead on the B.Q.E. right on the side of the highway. Somebody raped her, worked her over real bad and then set her car on fire. She laying up in Jamaica hospital in a coma, and it doesn't look like she's gonna make it because half of her face was peeled off from somebody dragging her against the pavement while her car was moving."

Supreme waited while his words sunk into Jason, and Jason was thinking that his only hope for leaving was over, but there was worse news to hear.

"Word on the street is that the god, Powerful from Edgemere, lost the four bricks of dope you got popped with, and in an effort to pay him back, Tasha gave him your whole stash. She was trying to move in with the kid afterwards. Some gods said they saw her and Powerful drive off in his Benz, and they never came back. Young'n, you need to know that you can't never turn no hooker into a housewife. You listening, homey?"

"Yeah, yeah, so how I'ma get out of here?"

"These are your options. You can be a rat and try to weasel your way out. You can take the case to trial and with four bricks of dope, you looking at fifteen years for every brick if you blow. Or, you can cop out and go to the mountains. Time moves and don't shit change in the hood but the people. You can love the hustle, baby boy, but the hustle ain't gonna ever love you back. The game uses niggas up and throws them away in one of two places, the cemetery or the penitentiary."

Supreme God was in preaching mode and Jason was still reeling from the news.

"What was I doing out there? I can't believe this. I can't believe my life is over."

"Nah, your life ain't over yet. You just got to put things into perspective and move forward. You see young'n, you was lost and turned out, throwing your life away for material things that can't do you any good now. A simple-assed postman got a better life than we do in here, but we thought he was a square because he had a job. Look at us now? The man that flip burgers for a living get to go home to his family safe and sound every night while we live like animals in the jungle. You here me, gee?"

Jason broke down like a bitch. "No man, nooo. Why me?" he began to sob. The pressure came down on him.

"Don't wipe your tears because you got a whole bunch to shed when you doing time in the pen. Time flies up in them mountains if you trying to better your life. If you going up there, get yourself together mentally, physically, emotionally and spiritually. *Don't* gamble, use drugs, sell drugs, or get involved with what people think about you. You ain't there to be liked because they got the pettiest haters up in them prisons, and you ain't got nothing to prove to nobody. Just get your weight up, young'n. If you scared, turn Blood or sign into protective custody. If you need somebody to think for you, turn Crip, or you can suck a dick and be a fag's puppet. If you want to be better than when you went in, read every book you can get your hands on. Teach yourself about business so when you get out you can take control of your life. Our people don't understand the simplest things. If you can run a drug operation, you can run any company in the world. Most of all, little homey, you got to endure till the end, no matter how bad it gets, because in here, it doesn't get better, it gets worse by the second. Focus on going home at all times."

Supreme left Jason so his words could sink in. Jason thought about everything Supreme said to him and how he was lost and all alone. His own mother and sister were useless. Tasha was probably dead, and the way she crossed him, there was nothing he would do about it even if he could. Zeida was dead or somewhere in a hospital just as lost as he was.

The following week, Jason went to court and the District Attorney offered his lawyers fourteen years, minus time served during the wait at Rikers, if he plead guilty. He threw himself on the mercy of the court and plead guilty to possessing drugs that were not his.

Fourteen

Summer of 2004

Jill was searching. She was deep into one of her favorite past times until the phone rang. Looking at the caller ID she contemplated whether or not to answer or just return the call later or the next day.

When she hit the talk button on the cordless and said, "Hello, Diane," she heard the thick accent come through without even a hello in response.

"Gal when you gonna come outta de house?" Diane asked.

Jill replied, "I can't talk now, I'm trying to look something up on the internet."

"Chu mean ya can't talk? De dam ting can wait, me hav more important ting fe chat bout."

"How's business?" Jill asked trying to change the subject.

"Speaking of dat, you need to come check 'pon you business."

"Diane, we are not going through this again. That's your business. You paid me back the money, so stop calling it my business."

"You tink we name it Dimple's because a me? No girl child, it name dat because a you nick name pon de top a de sign, so come check pon you business and maybe you find a man before you crotches dry up."

Jill laughed. "I got what I need right in the bathroom, can't no man take care of me like I can take care of myself."

"Well, don't tell me you no get tired inna de house all de time, gal?"

"No, I've not gone out since Sharief was alive. I don't have the desire. The neighborhood has changed. The thugs have taken over the streets. It's really nothing out there for me. Between working out, the internet and cable TV, I don't need a man."

"Yeah, yeah, me know de story before it done 'cause you tell me it over and over again. I guess I see you Wednesday so me can do dat hair, and you can put it inna de same donkey tail you a wear as soon as I finish."

"*That's* me," Jill said sarcastically.

"Me swear one of dem days, gal. But right now me have a client so one love. I'll call you later."

Jill smiled as she reflected on the conversation she just had with her best and only friend. Diane was right, since the death of Sharief, to say that she didn't have much of a social life was the understatement of the millennium.

Jill had met Sharief Clayton when she was nineteen years old. She was working at Gray's Papaya in mid town on the cash register trying to earn enough money to buy a few pieces of the designer clothing that she loved to wear back then. She was taking classes at the City College hoping that the money to get into Rutgers across the bridge in Jersey would somehow fall from the sky or that at the least, a student loan would come through. Sharief was thirty-nine at the time and was already one of the most successful businessmen in Harlem. He owned his own real estate company and several other businesses that he never bothered explaining the ins and outs of to Jill.

Back then she was living in her mother's crowded apartment with her three sisters. Each day back then was like a bad dream for her. Constantly having to deal with clothes that were borrowed, but never returned, missing money on the occasions she foolishly left it unhidden and with four women and the flow of men coming in and out, there was never enough food in the house. Her mother had been sickly and was always asking upon Jill, mostly because no one else would respond to her request. At times she felt like the ghetto Cinderella.

Sharief had come along like a knight in shining armor and rescued her from it all. She often recalled the day she had met him as she walked down 125th Street past the Apollo Theater.

"I been in these streets for years and I swear I didn't know they let Queens walk through Harlem," he'd said to her.

Sharief had sat on the hood of his brand new 91' Lincoln Town Car reading a Wall Street Journal. Jill had been caught off guard. "Excuse me," she'd said coyly.

"You heard me, miss," Sharief shot back in a gruff tone yet with a smile. "But that's just a play on words, little lady... *Queens* as in the borough, *walking* through Harlem, get it? Anyway, you're moving kind of fast; where are you rushing off to?" he'd asked as if he was entitled to the information. "And I don't mean to intrude, so please forgive me if you find my speaking to you a little forward, but a woman as lovely as yourself deserves every compliment that a man can afford."

Not used to being approached by such an articulate brand of man, Jill found herself stopping and talking to Sharief. She was usually too shy even though she was exceptionally beautiful in every facet of the word. Jill's father was half black and half Puerto Rican. Her mother was Dominican. The blend of ethnicity left her with the best of three worlds. She had a glowing bronze complexion, dark brown, wavy hair and a body that often stopped traffic on the block.

Sharief was no slouch himself. Though Jill took him for a businessman at first glance she quickly recognized that he had a sense of style reserved for men of extraordinary means. The tailored suit, the crocodile shoes and the three hundred dollar fedora hat he sported gave away the fact that he was class and money. Though he'd impressed her with his appearance, his words and demeanor had been much more impressive.

After telling him that she was on her way to school, Sharief had offered her a ride, which she turned down. To her surprise he was right there waiting the next day to offer again. Though she declined him more times than she could remember, she began to do so with a smile on her face. Then one day about two weeks after she had first seen him, one rainy morning, she accepted his ride. "Oh so you take a ride to get out of the rain, huh?" he'd joked. "Well that's smart because only a fool doesn't have the sense to take shelter from the pouring rain."

Jill didn't know it at the time, but Sharief used that metaphor to reel in the object of his desire.

For years in Jill's life the rain had been constantly pouring. Being the most attractive of her sisters made her the object of jealousy and sometimes things got physical. She was never much of a fighter and often caught a beating at the hands of her sister Gayle, who felt that violence was the best way to get her point across.

Making it worse for Jill was the fact that there was no one for her to turn to. Manny, the one serious boyfriend that she had, had become mostly abusive and hardly interested once she'd given him her virginity on her seventeenth birthday. Though he filled her head with promises he never intended to keep, Jill decided she was in love and tried to be content with the shards of conversation and sex that he gave her. Soon afterwards, Manny caught a handful burglary and weapons charges and wound up getting seven to ten upstate. Though he never treated Jill well, he was the only person who paid her any attention at all, even if it was short lived. As beautiful as she was, Jill quickly realized that the boys and men that she came in contact with only wanted one thing from her.

The loneliness that she felt everyday of her life since she'd been old enough to remember, had just begun to suck the life out of her until the day Sharief had stopped her on the sidewalk. Though she protected her heart as best she could, she found the protection and the life that Sharief offered her impossible to turn down.

Three months later, she moved into a brownstone one a tree-lined street in Brooklyn. Sharief had purchased the place a week after meeting her hoping that one day she would live in it as his wife.

She had long grown tired of facing the projects everyday. From the first day Jill spent in his company, Sharief did everything in his power to win her heart. He first exposed her to a world she knew nothing about. Dinners at fine restaurants were only the beginning. Shopping sprees on Fifth Avenue, days of pampering at a spa and tickets on the front row to see Dream Girls were all overwhelming to Jill. By the time Sharief showed her how he lived like a king and expressed that he wanted to treat her as his queen, she was more than willing to at least try. Jill wasn't in love with him but she loved the way he protected and provided for her.

As a child, she often daydreamed of having a house with a yard where she could sit on the porch and drink lemonade with her husband. With each passing year her dream lost its color like an old picture and she began to give up on the hope of ever having such a life. Now, in the blink of an eye, Sharief had come and offered it all to her in a manner beyond her wildest imagination. She believed everything he told her because he delivered on promise after promise. The last thing he promised Jill was that he would take care of her forever.

Over the years, Jill and her family grew distant. Her sister, Sheryl, got married to a drug dealer from South Philly and disappeared. Her other sister Gayle, held down a job at Columbia Hospital but she was battling her addiction to crack cocaine and had been estranged for quite some time. Her youngest sister, Pat, had lived with her for a while after Sharief passed away. Jill took care of Pat and her baby and paid for her education at City College.

As soon as Pat got on her feet and married the Italian owner of a construction business, she was never heard from again. Jill didn't even receive an invitation to the wedding.

Fifteen

As the whole scene unfolded before him, Jason thought of the intro to the Stevie Wonder song *Living for the City*. After nearly fourteen years, it was if he was seeing New York City for the first time. He stood on Eighth Avenue and 42nd Street at the Port Authority. He was shell shocked that Times Square had changed so much since he'd been away.

As he marveled at his surroundings, he felt a sense of exhilaration and fear at the same time. He didn't know how he was going to make it. He'd lost everything and everyone while inside. His sister had married a pastor and told him that she would not be able to continue writing a convict who had chosen to serve the devil. The last thing she sent him was a bible and a picture of their mother. His mother had taken ill and the last word he got was that she was taken by a friend to live down south.

As Jason moved up the sidewalk toward the corner, he was mesmerized by the huge televisions and the scrolling lights. He found himself jarred from his staring by angry *excuse me's*. People wanted to get by and had nearly resorted to shoving him out of the way. When he took notice of the people moving and standing around him, he suddenly felt naked. He felt like the pedestrians who looked at him knew that he was just released from prison.

In his paranoia, he looked into the faces of the people moving closely by him to see if they were staring at him, but after a quick assessment he realized that they were not and that his mind was playing tricks on him. Jason was self conscious. Here he was around all of these professionally dressed people and he was standing there in a tight, state-donated tan polyester suit, with a cheap clip-on tie and fake leather shoes that hugged his toes.

His low hair cut, the last one was free, along with his tapered beard didn't totally hide his handsome features, but even the women who looked at him, saw his suit, and kept moving. He was standing with a loaded pillowcase in his hands, and that didn't make his appearance more appealing.

He walked two blocks to report to his parole officer. Jason had a non-violent drug case, so he would have limited supervision for a few months. He could have been home a year earlier on a work release program, but he didn't have a residence for his release to give to the prison plus a disciplinary record from having a fight with a disrespectful C.O. Since the officer provoked the fight, he didn't receive a new charge. But the prison authorities didn't appreciate the broken nose he gave to the prison guard so they tagged him with a destruction of property for a shelf he knocked the guard into.

The cool air in the parole officer's building felt good to Jason's sweating forehead. He walked up to the directory and found the name on the card. Women walked by headed for early lunches. Fragrances of perfume, cigarettes, and hair spray filled his being. It had been a long time since he could fully appreciate the traits of femininity. From the smells alone, he was becoming sexually aroused. But Jason made an oath, that only the right woman would cure his sexual cravings.

He found the office and after knocking, a voice told him to come in. Jason stepped into the office which was actually a small cramped room. The stacks of disorganized folders piled on the desk, a small black table with metal chairs and a rusty pole that rode the side of the wall made the room more unbalanced.

A pot bellied, balding man, wearing checkered pants, with tape keeping his eyeglasses together on the sides, sat before him. The disheveled man's attention went from the stack of papers, to Jason. "Mr. Faust?" he asked peering over his glasses.

"Yes, sir," Jason replied.

In a raspy voice, he said, "Let's get right to it. I see here that you had a rough beginning during your fourteen... let's see. It says here you did ..."

"Thirteen years, sir," Jason interjected.

"Yes. Like I said you had some trouble early it seems but then you turned it around and took advantage of all the programs the prison system had to offer? I even see you have an associate's degree in business, carpentry experience and you even did some teaching. It was obvious to Jason that the man was the type that told people things instead of asking.

"Yes, I decided a long time ago that the prison system was beneath me and no place for me to live. Therefore, I had to critically analyze my methods of behaviorism, and adjust accordingly, so that I could properly integrate in society, and become a productive citizen, and a successful business owner."

The man snarled. "How many times did you rehearse that before you got it right?"

"No, sir, I…"

"It doesn't matter," he said as the vein in his right eye twitched. "I've been working parole for twenty years. I've seen it and heard it all and I've come to the conclusion that talk is cheap. You just report to me on a weekly basis until you put all that mumbo jumbo to work and find a job."

Jason pulled out a manila file. "I have a resume and few certificates that I received."

"Ah, nobody out here cares about that stuff. All they want to know is if you have the credentials to get the job done. I have you staying at the men's shelter in Harlem. I see you requested not to be sent back to Queens. Good for you. If you even step on the wrong side of the street, I will violate your ass, send you back to prison for the next year and a half until you finish your sentence. Do we understand each other?"

"Yes sir, Mr. Townsend."

He stood slightly foaming at the mouth. "You can cut the *sir* jive out. You hear me?" The parole officer handed him a specimen cup and told him to go piss. You had a drug conviction and if you consume alcohol or any other illegal drugs, I'm gonna know about it. If you come in my office and those funny looking blue eyes of yours look red like that hair on your head, I'm sending your ass right back upstate to the penitentiary."

Jason's eyes glared at the man and gave him a look that sent a message that he couldn't quite put his finger on. "Yes, sir… I mean Mr. Townsend."

"Boy, are you a mutt?" he asked as he took a closer look at Jason. Drop off your piss and have a nice day. You have a curfew. Be in before ten o'clock. Good luck in there. Hopefully, I'll see you next week at this same time, and if you're late I'll send your ass back to the pen, you hear me?"

It took all of the discipline and patience he learned while he was away to keep his emotions in check. Being back on the street was like the end of a long nightmare and the beginning of a fantasy so he stayed focused. Jason was free. Nothing could bring his spirits down.

He saw an outdated burgundy suit in the window of the American Man men's shop. The reflection of the snickering women behind him proved to him what he'd already realized, that he was dressed like a nut. Women he passed by would first look into his eyes with interest, but when they looked at the rest of him, their heads turned in disgust. The message was clear that he had to do something about his wardrobe.

He walked into the store and his assumption was justified. The salesman recognized that he was just released from prison. The tan state polyester suit was a dead giveaway. For four hundred dollars the salesman promised him a deal.

The price seemed high but knowing he needed to do something to upgrade his appearance Jason accepted the deal. He walked out wearing a new suit, now the proud owner of two new shirts and ties, and a new pair of shoes. At the souvenir shop next door, he bought a small nap sack to carry his belongings. Out of the twelve hundred dollars he saved while he was inside, he was left with seven hundred fifty.

Johnny Hustle, his many women friends, and his plush living entered his mind as he walked by the Marriott Marquis. *Johnny was probably dead by then* Jason thought. He wondered if he should go find out. Suddenly, the oath he took to stay away from anyone in his past life became a reminder. Jason swore off the criminal lifestyle, and he knew that fast money was an addiction he had to stay away from. He reaffirmed that he was one associate away from going back to prison, so he picked up his step and moved as far away from Times Square as he could.

He had to be at the shelter on 143rd Street on Fifth Avenue before 6 p.m. Instead of taking Mass Transit, he decided to walk up Eighth

Avenue to pursue one of the fantasies he had while in prison. The smell of the fresh roses that vendors sold went straight to his gut. He embraced sounds of the buildings under construction. And the sight of the women dressed in designer suits put his senses into overdrive. Gone was the monotony of walking in circles around the prison yard.

He reached the first opening and walked into the park and made his way to a knoll. Then he looked around to see if anyone would object to what he was about to do. He took off his hot suit jacket, along with his shoes and socks. He laid the jacket flat, and fell on top of it. He let his toes play in the grass. For thirteen years, he thought of the day he could feel grass again. The time that he spent in Sing-Sing, Clinton Danamora, Sullivan, and Woodburne correctional facilities, he was unable to climb a tree or lay in the grass.

No one paid him any attention. After all, it was Central Park, New York, and people did what Jason felt was a big deal all of the time. An hour had passed and so did a beautiful white woman with brunette hair, and a tight Rocawear jogging suit. She chased her dog. The black Labrador retriever ran up to him and put his paws on his pants. Jason burst out in laughter like a kid in an arcade. He thought of the many years he fantasized about petting a dog, and out of no where the dog appeared.

The bombshell ran up to him apologizing for her dog's behavior. The look in her eyes showed that she was intrigued by his attire. "Excuse me, do you live around here?" she asked as Jason studied the D-cup breast that surely had to have been created in a surgeon's office.

Jason petting the dog answered, "No."

His answer wasn't enough when her proper tone said, "My name's Dorothy, it's just that I'm new in the city," she pointed at two buildings across the street. "I work over at AOL Time-Warner and I live a few blocks over."

Jason wondered why she gave away so much about herself, as he pet the dog. She seductively wiped the sweat from her neckline drawing his attention back to her cleavage. "You're awfully quiet, and your eyes are sensational," she took a step closer.

Jason smiled, "Sorry."

Then out of no where she said, "I've got to get ready to run but…
you think maybe we can get together later? If you provide me with
your number, I'll send a car to pick you up from where ever you are."

Jason gave a polite smile. "Thanks, but…I'm not in any position
to date."

"Oh, you're married, I'm sorry," she said. "I'm so embarrassed.

"I guess you can say that," Jason lied.

He knew being with a woman after so many years would have
been nice, but a woman would be the least of his concerns at this point.
The new jacks in prison that were fresh off the streets had told him
story after story about how women were more aggressive and
downright desperate for men nowadays. They gave him many accounts
of how things were much different than when he was out.

He was still petting the dog as the stranger continued to flirt. "I
own a Japanese restaurant in the AOL building, and I don't know many
people in New York, so I was just wondering if you were interested?"
She subtly rubbed her firm legs, and passed her hands over her crotch
giving him a seductive smile.

Staring at the woman touch herself, Jason zoned out again. He
thought of how he had studied the art of mastering the desires of
women for years. He wanted to try his new techniques and knew
pleasing one would have been an easy task, but then he thought about
his sexual discipline. For twelve of the thirteen years behind bars,
Jason didn't masturbate and definitely didn't succumb to homosexual
acts. He was too focused on his downfall which allowed Tasha to use
her sexual prowess to control him. So he made sure that he stayed in
top physical form in order to master his lower desires. When he saw
that the woman in front of him was persistent, he figured he would say
the one thing that he was sure would chase her away.

Jason put his hands in his pockets and looked into her lust filled
eyes and said, "Look miss, I see that you find me attractive and I am
honored. You are appealing as well, but I'm fresh out of prison and
this is my first day back in society and I have to find a place to stay and
get myself together."

With a shocked look on her face, she said, "I would never have
guessed, but I can tell by your solid structure that you are a fitness
guru. How much time did you serve?"

He couldn't believe she was still standing in front of him after telling her the truth. "Thirteen years," he answered.

"You mean to tell me that you have been stored away from the opposite sex for thirteen long years," she said changing her facial expression. She reached for his hand and continued, "You have to let me help you, come on upstairs so we can get you *re-acquainted* to the fairer sex."

Jason pulled his hand away giving up in agony. "Miss, I'm sorry but I'm simply not interested."

She looked at her own body and asked, "You're *not* interested?" She grabbed the dog's leash in anger. "You must be a fucking homo. You're not interested in this. I've heard it all now," she mumbled that and more insults while walking briskly out of the park.

Right then, Jason knew all the training he put himself through was going to be tested. If he had to endure this much in one day, he imagined how rocky the road would be for him to remain focused and stay out on the streets. With thoughts racing, he grabbed his things, and headed for the shelter for men.

Sixteen

Jill began her usual routine. First, she turned on the six o'clock Eyewitness News to hear the tragedies from the night before. Next, she slipped into her Baby Phat sweat suit to prepare for her workout. She began to pound out on the treadmill first and then the Stairmaster. After a solid hour of butt kicking sweat, she dropped off four hundred crunches, like nothing. She was determined to maintain her six-pack.

Though her thirtieth birthday was clearly in her rearview mirror, unlike some women, Jill had truly grown more beautiful with time. Still, she understood that time and gravity worked against her. She refused to die the way that her mother and husband did, their bodies giving out way before they should have. She attributed both of their deaths to the foods they consumed, plus their lack of exercise, so she lived the opposite of how they did. Although she'd built up a wall that seemed like it would be too thick for any mortal man to penetrate, Jill did actually hope deep down inside that a good man would come along, though she never went anywhere to meet one. Since she would want the best he had to offer, she was willing to lead by example and do her best in all levels of her body and her life.

Her workout was done and she disrobed. She took a soothing shower, while watching the Regis show on the plasma screen mounted in the bathroom.

Since the sun was out and the weather was nice, she figured she'd do things differently that week, like wear a new outfit on her weekly errands. She pulled out her Calvin Klein underwear and sports bra to fit her thirty-six D cup breast. She put on a white silk zip down blouse, with a pair of chocolate silk slacks, with chocolate high-heeled sandals and a matching Salvatore Ferragamo purse.

Although she usually only ventured out once a week, Jill didn't feel that a real woman should ever leave the house without her hair, nails, and face being done in a presentable fashion. With everything in her attire to her satisfaction, she picked up her keys and placed a pair of brown Gucci sunglasses on the top of her head and she headed for her kitchen downstairs.

As soon as she was on the other side of her front door, the anxiety hit her. *"Walk, girl, walk,"* she said to herself. It happened every time she left the house and every time she overcame it.

Jill wasn't crazy. It was just that the five years she spent with Sharief had changed her. Once she'd moved into the house, he had pressed her into marriage. After the marriage, Sharief began to take complete care of Jill to the point where she no longer had to even think for herself. Sharief's love had turned into control and he no longer allowed Jill to leave the house without his knowledge.

By the second year, she found it hard to make even the most basic of decisions without doubting herself. Having never truly had a chance to develop into a woman without Sharief, Jill put her whole energy into being the dream wife that he'd always imagined. Sharief wanted her to bear his children and stay locked away from the rest of the world. Jill tried for the children as best she could, although sex was not that enjoyable for her, mostly because Sharief had a small penis and he came too quickly for her to ever truly get into it. After his death, Jill mourned not only for her husband but for her failed attempt at motherhood. She never re-established a connection to the outside world. The one she remembered was never that great anyway and she took refuge inside her huge brownstone.

Jill was a loner before Sharief and after his death she was left with no link to other human beings. Other than Diane, her Aunt Lana, and the nameless and faceless people she met on the internet, Jill lived in a world that resembled a prison. It wasn't so much that the world and people terrified her, it was simply the fact that she preferred the comfort and protection of the world that Sharief had forced her to grow accustomed to. On the occasion that she had to leave home she was reminded that in her solitary existence she felt safe and comfortable. She had no reason to step outside of it, except on Wednesdays when she went to get her hair done.

Since she was at home all of the time, she found a whole new world surfing the Web. She had conversations with people in chat rooms from all over the world. She had a few on-line sexual relationships with her anonymous suitors. Her computer gave her the ability to be whoever she wanted to be. She would tell the men on-line the things she would do to them, and what she wanted done, knowing it was only a fantasy. If she were feeling sensual, she would allow the fantasies of the men, who she never planned to meet, to spark her appetite until she went into her Jacuzzi to satisfy herself. This was Jill's life and she convinced herself to believe that she was content with it.

Her finances were in order, as she began to run Clayton Realty from the privacy of her home. Monthly, she would receive several financial statements from the accountants. Instead of a thorough, examination, she quickly glanced over them, then filed the reports away. For the eight years since her husband's death, the company continued to make a significant profit, and after sending her donations to various charities, Jill still brought in a hefty six-figure salary. To top it off, she took ten thousand dollars in the late nineties and began on-line trading. By buying risky but profitable stocks, her portfolio increased from the net worth of ten thousand, to well over a million dollars in less than six years. Jill had made a fortune that she didn't need.

With her phone in hand, she called her favorite cab driver from the local car base to pick her up. Long gone were the days when one of Sharief's drivers named Roger came to get her. After Jill began to stay in the house all of the time, Roger stopped coming to pick her up since she had no use for him. Whenever she went out, she used the local gypsy cabs. The last she heard, Roger had bought a small fleet of cars and was driving around young drug dealers from the Bronx.

Jill took the cab ride from Brooklyn to 110th Street on Broadway. Instead of getting out in front of her aunt's flower shop two blocks down, she preferred to walk by the Korean fruit stand on a 109th Street to purchase her organic fruits and vegetables. She had always picked up something for her Aunt Lana.

The chimes to the shop rang and Jill locked eyes on Lana. Jill could see that her aunt was up to something. The look on her face told her that she was going to have a conversation she didn't want to have.

"Hey, Auntie Lana," Jill said filled with suspicion.

Lana limped around the tall wood counter, saying softly, "Hey child, I was just thinking about you. I have those Asian Jacks in the Pulpits, along with the Platinum Pearls for your garden. I was hoping you were coming in today. Just like clock work my baby done walked through the door."

Jill looked over the plants she ordered and waited until her aunt was done serving a customer to see what else she had in store.

Lana adjusted the silver chain on her reading glasses, and slipped the bifocals into her gray wig. "Yeah, I heard from your sister, Pat. That child got some nerve. She gone and went and married that Italian and got the nerve calling here talking like she come from Italy. That girl done forgot where she comes from. Got that jungle fever and left us here stranded cause she living the good life. I asked her for one favor, and what she does? She tell me she got to discuss it with her husband, like I ain't family. I told her to keep her husband out of it, and that Jill would take care of my problem for me 'cause *you* know what family means."

Jill reached into her shoulder bag and removed her checkbook. "What is it this time Aunt Lana, and how much does it cost?"

Lana lowered her head. "Child, hush your mouth, I don't need Rose to be hearing *our* business." Lana pulled Jill out of ear shot from her only employee, Rose. "Yes, girl, I heard from Gayle. She back in rehab. I asked her to call you, but she said she didn't want you judging her and…"

"Aunt Lana will you please get to the favor you were talking about." Jill was losing her patience. She didn't need the extras. She had made up her mind that she would be there for her family whenever they called, though none of them had ever done a thing to show her any appreciation.

Lana waved at the air. "Oh child, that ain't no big deal. You see, FTD is squeezing things, and the competition is getting fierce. I'm only making a real turnover on holidays, and with Valentines and Mother's Day gone already, the summer crowd is slowing things down.

I don't want to sell the shop 'cause your Uncle Ernest, God bless his soul, would turn over in his grave if I did that."

"Lana, stop beating around the bush. I told you five years ago that you ought to renovate so that customers will see the shop in a more professional light, and you told me no, so how much is it gonna cost to get you on your feet?" Jill said calmly.

"Oh, it's only $25,000, and I'm sure I can pay you back. You know everybody ain't as smart as you, girl. Me and your uncle opened this shop long before you was born, and my own son should be here running it and helping me, but he up in the Bronx hooked on that dope."

Jill interrupted and handed her the check. "Aunt Lana, here. You don't have to pay me back, just get on your feet. If you need me to handle anything else just call me and let me know."

Once the check was in her hand and she scanned the amount, "God bless your soul," she said. Her expression suddenly changed to business. "So, are you going off somewhere? Those plants cost me $63 and I'll order the rest when you come in. I don't want to hold you up or anything."

Jill could take a hint when she heard one. She pulled out $65 to pay for her plants and her aunt handled her like a regular customer. She knew she was no longer needed. "I'll be in next week for a few flowers. Let me know when those Welsh Poppies come in. Bye."

Jill walked out of the shop heading for the 1 train knowing that she was being used again. Her family had become the kind of leeches her husband despised and warned her against. She learned quickly that having money was a constant headache, because everyone she knew figured that because of it she had no problems. She had to admit that she was hooked on having it, and she loved the idea that she was able to do what she wanted most of the time. But what everyone else didn't know was that she would trade in all her wealth for love.

It had been a couple weeks since Jill had last come to see Diane at the salon. "Yes, boss, it's about time you come check pon you shop," Diane yelled while turning around the styling chair. "You see say everyting irie and we a blow up the spot. Yes, come in and sit inna me special chair and make me do a new style pon you head."

"It's a pleasure to see you too, sweetheart," Jill said. "Hi, everybody," she turned speaking to everyone.

"So wha happen to you?" Diane asked, feeling Jill's mood.

"I just came from Lana's and as usual she had her hand out, like a charity case, but what else is new?"

"Gal, you gotta know when to say *no* to bad-minded people. Me know say you have sense, so use all dat schooling you got in dat pretty head and work pon the people who try and bring you down. You nuh see when you do bad, none a dem a go check fe you. When you a go find a man, if him take advantage a you, at least you can say you get something outta it?"

Jill sighed. "Why we go through this every week, Diane?"

"'Cause you crotches a go dry up. You young and you look damned good, and everybody need somebody fe love. Tell me, who you a wait pon? Prince Charming only come once in a lifetime and fe some him never come."

With folded arms, Jill admitted her desire for love. "I just want to meet someone that fate will bring my way. I need someone that doesn't know me from anywhere. One that when we see each other, we'll both be swept away and I won't have to work to impress him and he wont have to for me."

"Dats all?"

Jill laughed, "Somebody tall, handsome, and filled with love. Not these fake playas and little boys who play games as a career. I need someone who knows what they want for my children and me. Now you tell me where I'm gonna find all that?"

Everyone in the salon that listened to Jill's description started clapping, especially the gay stylist. Then they waited for Diane's response.

Diane stepped center stage for her audience. "Yes, you bright, but not so bright dat you don't know dey man you look fe, he don't exist 'cept fe in you dreams. You betta go to a prison or find a young boy and make him into way you want 'cause dat mahn you a tell me you want, dem don't make no more. Dem mahn de stop manufacture years ago, so in de mean time, find one who can suck, grind, and tek out de gar-bidge."

The whole shop was in laughter and everyone began clapping. Jill blushed. Jill always welcomed Diane's advice. She knew she was right in regards to her family taking advantage of her, and that she needed companionship, but now she wanted to discuss other things.

It was six o'clock when she reached her door. Jill looked down at her mail stack and saw that a small brown package had arrived. Since the box was small she figured it was a DVD she was waiting for, or something else that she ordered from the Internet. A new package was delivered almost daily since she did all of her shopping off the Internet. When she looked at the box she saw that it came from Hollywood, California, so she knew what it was.

She picked up the phone to let Diane know that she had arrived home safely. She prepared steamed Japanese vegetables, chicken breast cutlet, and sliced tomato for dinner. She carried her food up to her loft to view the news. Once the last of her meal was in her mouth, she headed for the shower.

Jill was still naked and dripping from her shower when she closed all the drapes in the loft and lit the candles she had on her mantle. She pulled her covers back from her canopy bed and pulled her bedspreads half way down. On her bedside table she reached in her drawer and pulled out her ben-wa balls and her vibrator. She placed her toys on the bed, and headed over to her DVD player and inserted the disk. Before pressing play on her remote control, she laid back and began deep breathing.

With each breath, Jill focused on all her sensual energy. In line with what she'd learned about Tantric sex, which focuses on what's happening in your mind, not your body, when you make love, Jill focused on sending her internal heat from her toes, to her pelvis, and then up her spine and to her head. When her juices started flowing and her body was warm from the power of her mind, she could feel her internal juices flowing faster. Her nipples perked up, and her mouth was getting dry, which meant it was show time. She pressed the play button and the movie started with two women sun bathing on a beach. They playfully threw sand on each other and when they had too much sand on their bodies, they headed for the shallow blue water to wash each other off. Seductively the women began to wash each others breast and then their hands traveled down to each other's crevices.

Jill sat in the Lotus position and focused on every detail of the film. The women pretended to be naïve as to what the other was doing. The actors made it appear that it was their first encounter, and Jill adored their innocence. The women laid on the beach while the water touched their feet and they kissed passionately. The bikinis fell off of the women and now they were in the nude kissing every part of the other's body. Jill watched as the blond woman used her tongue to lick the other in between her legs, placing her tongue inside her hole.

Jill got hot, but resisted the impulse to touch herself. Her juices flowed and her body reacted to the visual stimulation. The camera did a close up, and she saw how the woman stimulated one another's clitoris with each lick. As they moved into the sixty-nine position, there was a double camera shot of both women's clitorises being stimulated and devoured by the other. When the women had their orgasms, Jill had her own, and restarted the movie again.

In her hands, Jill rolled the two golden ball bearings so that the friction could create warmth. She placed the two balls into her vagina and began to squeeze and flex her vaginal muscles until the two balls touched and sent an internal pulse of stimulation within. She continued to squeeze while she opened her legs and licked her firm nipples. First one, then the other, and then she placed both of them in her mouth at the same time while she squeezed the silver balls. The oral stimulation and the sound effects of the tape made Jill go into her second orgasm, but she knew she hadn't hit the big one yet.

When the close up of the woman's clitoris being licked came on again, Jill cut on her vibrator. She placed one of her fingers inside of her to touch the ben-wa balls so they could clang and send vibrations that aided her stimulation. She then placed her vibrator directly on her clitoris with her other hand and moved it in circles as she fantasized about receiving the same type of oral pleasure that she was witnessing though she had never had it done to her.

This round, she rotated the vibrator on her clit, with fantasies of her mystery man. She wished for the day when he would come to please her like the video freaks were doing for each other.

"Ahhhhh, aaaahhhhhh," Jill yelled out in pleasure. When she reached her climax, she dropped the vibrator on the floor and flopped back on her bed panting for air. When she caught her breath, Jill wept as she thought of her loneliness. She wondered if she was being punished, but still she had faith that someday her prince would come.

Later on in the night, she would satisfy her sexual appetite once again and cry her lonely self to sleep.

Jill knew she was lost, but she convinced herself that she was safe where she lived and no one could penetrate her force field. Staring at the ceiling, she tried to imagine ways how she could change her life around. She thought about adopting children but feared doing it alone. Realizing that she had caused her own life to come to a standstill because of her fears, she wished for the courage to change. It now seemed that she'd been telling herself the same lie forever and a day. One day she'd find someone special was what she'd told herself over and over without realizing that that day had turned into years.

Seventeen

When Jason walked into the men's shelter, it reminded him of his first and only trip to Rikers Island. Men were posted everywhere. He was greeted by the so-called tough guys who acted like they were in charge of the place. He was issued a bed in the large gymnasium turned dorm room. In an effort to have some peace, he rolled his cash and all his belongings into his nap sack, and put it under his head to use as a pillow.

When the large halogen lights went out, he dozed off, but the sleep only lasted a few hours. In the middle of the night, Jason tossed in his bed. The shelter was far more unsanitary than prison, and he felt like little bugs were feasting on his skin. He jumped up, only to get the attention of the fat under-worked guards and the attention of thieves who were sneaking around looking for people they could steal from.

It was 4:30 a.m. when his sudden movement upset the peace. He didn't know the rules of the shelter, but word was out that he had done years in prison, so up to that people had stayed out of his way. He took all of his belongings and headed for the bathroom which smelled like old urine. When he looked around the grimy bathroom, he noticed that the showers were broken. The only things that worked were the four toilets and the two large beige public sinks.

Two men lurked around the entrance in search of their next victim. Jason ignored them and stripped down to his boxers and began to do pushups. At one thousand, he rolled on his back to do crunches.

Peeping inside the filthy restroom, the two dull-witted robbers had considered Jason for their next target. They were quickly deterred by his cut-frame. With one look at Jason, they about-faced and rolled out of the door. His six-foot, two hundred-pound body sent the message clearly. Messing with him could cost severely.

Jason washed up with the soap pieces he found laying around. He dried off with brown paper towels. He said his morning prayers and asked God for the strength to get him through the day. Without asking anyone's permission he gathered his things. Normally, the shelter had a specific time before anyone could leave, but with his suit and tie on, Jason looked more like an employee or a supervisor of the place. The security guards didn't say a word to him when he walked out the door.

Lenox Avenue was filled with the buzz of the working class beginning to head out for the commute. Jason wondered momentarily if they knew how fortunate they were. They all had so many things that he didn't. He didn't know how, but he knew it was just a matter of time before he was going to be on his feet again. He wasn't looking for any handouts but Jason refused to even think of using deception or committing crime to get on his feet, but he knew one thing for sure. He was not going back to that shelter.

As the women switched by, he thought of the time when he wouldn't have hesitated to stop them in an effort to spark a conversation. But now his oath of discipline replayed in his head.

He reached the blue and white building known as Harlem Hospital. An older janitor told him that the personnel office wasn't open that early. With no place to go, Jason walked across the street to Pan-Pan's diner.

The cramped restaurant filled with stools and a large metal grill sent the aroma of good cooking to Jason's stomach. His eyes hit the grill, and he was dazed at the fresh eggs that fried. It had been a long time since he ate fresh eggs. Immediately, he ordered a vegetable omelet, hash browns, and a tall glass of freshly squeezed orange juice. The whole restaurant listened to his grunts as he ate. When the cook saw the way he was devouring the food, smiling, he took it as a compliment and gave Jason an extra serving for free.

To Jason, the people in the diner had not the slightest idea of the luxury they had by being able to eat whatever they wanted. For years, Jason dreamed of being able to eat any food he wanted, so he enjoyed.

The bill for fifteen dollars left him confused. *What the hell did I order?* Jason thought.

Prices had sky-rocketed since he'd been gone. This was all new to him, because his former employment did not warrant a budget. Prison commissary came at a reduced price. And anything else that could be smuggled was paid with pack of cigarettes. He shrugged it off in an effort to avoid trouble. He walked out of the diner and stopped at a newsstand for a copy of *The New York Times*. He was determined to find an apartment, room, or some form of adequate shelter.

He reached the hospital's personnel office and the dark woman with droopy eyes sitting behind the desk had major attitude. He figured he could put on his charm to soften her. "Good morning, fine lady," he said with a smile.

The woman took a look at his face and asked in a tired and unimpressed voice. "What *do you* want?"

"Oh...um... I have my resume here and I was wondering what type of positions of employment you all have available?" Jason clumsily replied.

She slammed down her papers, and to no one in particular she sarcastically asked, "So this is how my day is gonna start off, huh?"

"What do you mean?" he asked filled with honest curiosity.

"I mean you come in here like the world is alright, talking about you want to work in this dump? Where have you been? Don't you know the economy is shot and the city is cutting back?"

With raised eyebrows, he said, "Yes I'm aware of..."

"Then are you aware that po' folk are the one's to feel the fire first? I bet ain't a damn soul at Lennox Hill hospital getting laid off right now, but if master got to choose between Lennox Hill and Lenox Avenue, who you think gonna feel it first?"

He didn't want to lose his one opportunity to get employment, so he fought himself from being frustrated and tried to be as patient as he could. "Let me see that resume. I'm sure I'll get a kick out of this one."

He unfolded and handed the wrinkled sheet of paper to the woman.

"Um...yeah...yeah...yeah, okay?" the woman sarcastically commented while she read. She then looked up at Jason and rolled her eyes. "Okay. I'ma keep it real with you. I hope you wasn't in prison for something crazy, because after I tell you what I'm gone tell you, if you go postal up in here, I will have the police and security all over your yellow ass." She exhaled, "Now listen, I have *never* before seen someone put a prison employee as a reference on a resume. You don't have an address for us to contact you, and I don't see a phone number on here either. Now I know you trying to get on your feet and do the right thing, or your parole officer is on your ass like my brother's officer needs to be on his, but if I send this upstairs they gonna laugh at me and then at you."

She stood and extended the paper. "So, go get an address, find a phone number, and straighten out this resume with a better reference before you drop it on anyone else again. And try to find a place with some security whether the economy is bad or good because the city ain't hiring."

Jason's first impulse was to reach over the counter and snatch the woman over to the other side because of the sassy tone she used on him but then at the same time he appreciated her raw honesty. He was sure no one else on the outside was going to be that real and honest with him again. He took the resume back from the woman and walked out of the hospital.

When he stepped back on Lenox Avenue, the summer heat was beginning to beat down on the asphalt. Jason loosened his tie, walked to the steel garbage can on the corner, and dumped all the copies of his resume in the trash.

Going back to Queensbridge and finding someone that he knew to accept a phone call for him was a thought. He knew for sure that someone from his old neighborhood would at least give him a room to stay in, but then his parole officer, along with the oath he made to himself to stay away from the people of his past haunted him over again. Zeida's house floated through his thoughts, but he figured that she had to have moved after all of this time, plus she hadn't tried to contact him the whole time he was away. He also wanted to find her when he had something to offer, if she was still alive. As Jason took two more steps, he was standing in front of the AT&T store. He took it as an omen when he read:

Cool Deals to Whip the Summer Heat. A New ATT Wireless Phone for FREE."

He knew that only a few things in life were free and most of those were liabilities, but Jason walked into the store anyway. He was not prepared for the one hundred and thirty dollars he had to spend to get a phone. He paid the bill and reaffirmed the fact that he would be on his feet in just a little while. Since the phone would help him find employment, he saw it as a needed tool. He gave the store a bogus address in Queens, and checked to see if he could pay his monthly bill in person. When he was told that he could, he knew he was in business.

"I know a lot of women are going to be calling that number, huh?" a chunky saleswoman joked.

Jason's leg started shaking. As he calmed himself, he said, "No. This is for business, you know, I have to catch up with the times."

With a jagged smile she asked, "Well then maybe you can make an exception and let me help you catch up?"

"What do you mean?" he said as innocent as possible.

"I mean, maybe I can call you for pleasure, and we can get down to some serious business?" She extended her hand and said, "My name is Samantha." Jason noticed that she needed a manicure badly.

Thoughts of Zeida's direct approach many years ago came back. He was stuck in a daydream wondering where in that big city she could be. He wondered if she ever had the baby or made it out of the hospital alive.

"Am I that boring that you won't listen to a word I'm saying? Hello… your phone is ready," she said holding his contract.

He reached over the counter for his phone. "Nah, I just went somewhere else for a minute."

"So can I call you or what Jason? I can lose my job for this, but those eyes got me going, and that suit you're wearing is telling me that you ain't a thug. So can a girl get to know you or what?"

With nothing else to say, he grabbed the manual for his phone and said, "Sure, call whenever you're ready" and he walked out of the door.

Everything had changed on 125th Street. He noticed the smallest differences before heading towards the post office on St. Nicholas Ave. Instantly an idea crossed his mind. Purchasing a post office box, gave him a sense of accomplishment. He had at least had a mailing address now for his interviews.

Jason had high hopes. Strolling through Columbia University gave him a feeling of pride. He thought of the new plans he'd made for his new life. In a year from that day, he wanted to incorporate a business that he could run out of his apartment. Working the nightshift, he could take business classes during the day.

He reached the busy corner of 109th Street, and something in his spirit told him that the neighborhood was where he needed to be. Jason stopped at a neglected blue Buick and thumbed to the classified section of the paper and placed it on the roof. After calculating that he had half of the money he was released with, he came to the conclusion that he was not going to be able to afford the rent, securities, and the other necessities that came along with having an apartment in that area. He didn't see anything advertising furnished room for rent, so he decided that finding work was his new first priority.

Store after store, Jason stopped into each one looking for work. The storeowners on one side of the street denied him, so he walked over to the other side until he reached 125th Street. He considered how his image was being received. In the fish and fruit markets, a man in a suit trying to find work sent the wrong message. When he walked into the supermarkets, management looked at him as if he was overqualified for a job. Finally when he reached a bar on Broadway, the owners informed him that they had a job for him.

Jason was overjoyed, but then the boss explained to him that he wanted him to show up at midnight for work. With absolute hesitance in his voice, he explained to the man that he was on parole and had a curfew he had to follow or he would be sent back to prison. For him going back to prison wasn't going to happen. After further discussion he expressed to the man that he had no place to live, and that he needed room and board as well.

The bar owner seemed to understand what Jason was asking of him, so he told him of an old welfare hotel that charged thirty dollars a night. It was only two blocks up from the bar on Broadway. He then explained to Jason that he wanted him to be there at noon and that at nine o'clock he would allow him to go home. Jason agreed to the man's generous terms, shook his hand, and went on his way to find a room.

The ragged Regency hotel stood seven stories high and had many busted windows and an old neon sign that barely hung in place. Jason tried to think of it as better than any prison as he walked into the tiled lobby and was met by a solid cage of wood on the bottom, and chicken wired steel fence at the top.

A white man was beating what appeared to be his woman. The mulatto children screamed at the top of their lungs, while the security guard ignored the disturbance because his eyes were glued to the television showing the Jerry Springer show. When Jason stepped up to what was left of the check-in desk, the clerk observed him with his beady eyes from head to toe. Before Jason had a chance to say anything, the man reached for a key and said, "You just came home and tired of the shelter, huh? Well, it's gonna be thirty dollars a night until your welfare comes, and it'll be extra if you're ducking your P.O."

He smiled with teeth like an alligator. "My name is Harold, but everybody calls me the king. I'm the king of this castle and if you don't have my rent money your things automatically belong to me. Don't even fart wrong 'cause I won't hesitate to make a few calls and have you sent back up to the pen. We ain't got no towels, we got cable but no TV," he cackled when he said that and went on, "No free soap and toothbrushes. I ain't room service so don't come down here for none of those types of things."

Jason couldn't believe the welcome he received. He paid the man sixty dollars. He joyously spun the keys as he took in his surroundings. The old hotel was like one big shelter with rooms. He reminded himself that anything was better than a prison cell, and to stay focused. He made it a few feet away when he heard the clerk say, "Hey, blue eyes, in case I didn't tell you, and if I did then let this be a reminder, I'm king of this castle. I'm the clerk, manager, concierge, and owner of this spot. If you want to get your nuts out the sand, just call me. If you want to get high, I got whatever you need. I see you work out, so I can get you them steroids too. If you need a gun to take care of some overdue work, I got one of those for you too. Everything for a fee, *nothing* for free. Have a nice stay, and lock your room. In here, you sleep at your own risk."

Jason nodded. He pressed the up arrow to the elevator and was quickly reminded that it didn't work unless the king of the castle wanted it to. His only other option was the creaking stairs.

On his way up to his room, groups of women stood in the hallway on each floor waiting for any type of action. Just like he did in prison, he wouldn't get familiar with anyone because his stay was temporary.

Jason opened the fragile door and was greeted by a mouse. It stopped to see the trespasser, and then ran under a radiator. The room was hot and smelled like cigarette smoke, mold, and musky sex. He thought of Tasha and the way they used to have sex until their room smelled exactly like the one he was standing in. A squeaky sound under his feet broke his dreamlike state. To his surprise, a used condom was stuck to the bottom of his foot. Jason was sick. He quickly opened all three weak dusty windows. He pulled back the bloodstained sheets on the bed and went to check on the bathroom. The tub was painted with nasty stains that would keep a crime lab busy for days.

Deep breaths of the muggy air kept him focused. Jason searched for a clean place to put his clothes. There were none. He had one thought; getting to the store to get some cleaning supplies.

In route, a little hustler wearing a red doo-rag, an all-blue Sean John sweat suit and a platinum chain approached Jason in the hallway. He was on his cell phone but interrupted his conversation to run his spiel down to Jason, "Yo, boss, whatever you need, you need to holla at me first," he said. Jason was amazed at his mature voice. He smiled at the character before him. "How old are you shorty, and what's your name?"

The youngster told the person on the other end of the line he'd be home later, and then paused, "Save the shorty speech. I'm old enough to know what's right for me. And yo, just know that questioning me is wrong for you. My name is what you want it to be, but I prefer to be called *Paid* if you gotta call me anything. Now what you need?"

Nodding his head, Jason knew the life the young kid had to live. It was all too familiar to him. "New sheets, a plastic mattress pad, Ajax, incense, cleaning supplies, a radio, maybe even a TV depending on the damage, bubble bath solution, a Loofa sponge, Dove soap, a pack of extra large underwear and a cheap alarm clock," said Jason.

"Hold on, hold on, you speeding." The boy pulled out a Palm Pilot and entered the list. "Now, I got you, but the TV is on lease without the option to buy. That lame downstairs that calls himself the king can't know what we doing, so I'm gonna pick all this up. The building is rigged for stolen cable but he's going to want to charge you for the TV plus the cable if you go through him. Have my paper when I get back or you getting evicted. One of my assistants will be here with the stuff, so don't be *scurrred* when he knocks on the door 'cause he's a big mufucka. I'll be right back."

Jason scratched his head in a state of disbelief, but when he looked at the young man he saw himself back when he was around twelve years old. It was hard for him to believe that this young kid was living the life he was, but he quickly rationalized that some circumstances forced kids to grow up way too fast.

After waiting for a half an hour, Jason heard a knock at his door. When he peered through the peephole, a hulk of a man with his shirt open revealing a black hairy chest filled the hole. He opened the door and a giant was holding a twenty-inch color television with a remote control and cable box. The gorilla didn't ask if he could walk into the room. He placed the television on the old dresser, and then hooked up the cable wires. At the same time, the little man brought his other items.

"I see you met my assistant?" he said as if he owned the place. The boy opened the bag and said, "I got everything you want and I threw in a few towels, a bath mat for the tub and this throw rug right here. Plus I threw in my cellular number in case you need something in the middle of the night." Then he reached into his backpack and pulled out a brand new dead bolt lock and a bolt chain. "I got to charge you full price for this, but it's worth it. You can change a lock right?"

Jason nodded, "Oh yeah."

"Yeah well if you don't change it, you won't be able to leave shit in this rat trap. Here use this, but I'll be back to get it in a little while," he said as he handed Jason an electric drill along with bits for it. Then as he was about to leave, his voice dropped to a timid whisper when he declared, "My sister is a ho-fessional. So if you need company let me know? She only seventeen, but her country-ass pimp won't find out she with you 'cause she always tries to stack a little paper on the side."

Jason didn't want to believe what he was hearing, but he knew the truth was sometimes a harsh reality. "So what do I owe you?" he asked.

"Since you just came home, give me sixty and another ten for the use of the television. Plus, like I said, the full price for the locks. Another twenty."

Jason wondered if a sign was on his head that read, *Newly Released Prisoner*. "Cool, now tell me your name so I know who to ask for. And little man, how you know I just came home?"

The young man waited until his assistant was out the door. "Dudes on the street ain't got that up north glow you got boss. The smog down here makes your face look depressed. That fresh air in them mountains give y'all life. Plus, you all cock diesel when you peeled out of your shirt. Any dude that looked like you would'a been on his feet by now. Too many chicken-heads that got cribs in this city need a man. The way you look boss, you suppose to be out in the Hamptons or the Waldorf or something," the kid cracked.

He took the compliment from the young hustler. "Yeah, okay, I got you, but you didn't tell me who to ask for if I call?"

"You mean *when* you call," the kid said sounding a little too cocky. "I'm Peter, and before you start preaching, I'm thirteen. A little short for my age, but big things come in little packages, so wise up boss and get at me when you ready."

Jason slapped his hand and the little man walked away. He walked over to the television and put it on CNN. He became addicted to the news on the inside. He knew being informed was going to work to his advantage when he got out, so he always listened. He also listened to the news to improve his speech. He studied the way the newscasters spoke and pronounced words, and while mimicking them, his vocabulary improved.

He cleaned the hotel room the way he cleaned his cell. He filled the basin with hot water and poured the bubble bath liquid on a towel. He then dipped the towel in the water and wiped down the walls, the ceiling, the furniture, and the windows. When he went into the bathroom, he scrubbed the fixtures with Ajax until they were white again. By the time he was done, the entire room had a whole new freshness to it. He then set the bath for him to wash away the sweat that was pouring off of him from the sweltering heat. He lit the pack of incense, and got down on his knees to thank the Lord for shelter.

His phone rang as he soaked in the tub. Suds fell to the floor as he ran to answer it. He pressed the talk button as he got back into the tub. Samantha from the AT&T store was on the line and her syrupy voice gave him an erection. "Hey bright eyes, what's good?" she asked. "Nothing really, just coolin' out," Jason responded.

It only took ten minutes into the conversation before Jason got turned off. He heard children in the background. He also discovered that she had four kids by three different men. It wasn't much of an issue except that then she invited him to share her bed that night, knowing that she didn't have a clue about who he was, or what type of damage he could do to her children, so he put the brakes on.

She spoke and he thought about how he did his time without a woman in his life. He knew that the women that wanted him now would have never come to visit him in prison. So his standard was set high. The type of woman he wanted was one who found the time in her hectic schedule to better herself mentally, physically, and spiritually, the same way he had. He wanted someone like Zeida who had everything in her life except a good man. He wanted a woman that was going to be an asset and not a liability in his life.

Samantha began talking about her man being away in prison and Jason knew he could never deal with her. When she paused to light a cigarette, she was instantly disqualified. Under no circumstances was he going to deal with a woman that wasn't concerned about her health, and that would deal with another man while her real man was down on his luck. He politely ended the conversation and shut the phone off hoping she would never call again.

Eighteen

Jill awoke suddenly in the middle of the night. The nightmare of lust with her mystery man felt so real that she awoke with disappointment. She grabbed a bottle of wine from the small fridge in her kitchenette area, and headed up to her roof. She sipped her wine and stared at the freshly planted flowers from the day before. Tending to her garden, she thought about the things missing in her life. She asked herself if she was really happy and answered herself by shedding a few tears.

After she'd gone back to bed and finally fallen into a deep sleep, the phone rang. When she checked her caller I.D., she saw the number to Diane's salon and knew what was in store. She reluctantly answered the phone. "I just went to sleep, so make it quick so I can go right back."

"Just get back to sleep? Wha, you tellin' me you finally get some wood and a mahn keep you up all night?"

Jill rolled her eyes and in her deep groggy voice said, "No, me no tell ya dat," she said mocking Diane, "but what you want this early in the morning?"

"Me no need a ting from you gal. You need watch you fresh mouth. Me call ta remind you 'bout de party we a havin' over at Webster's Hall."

"Is that *girl* and all of your friends gonna be there?" Jill was referring to one of Diane's lesbian friends who had tried to seduce her the last couple of times she had been out with Diane. The woman was so pushy that she wouldn't take no for an answer and had actually gotten Jill to give her her phone number.

"Why, you ready fe switch? You know you lead de poor child on and make her tink se you gonna give her some. Why you so bad Jill? De poor child a still tink 'bout you, so me will mek an excuse so she no come. But plenty man a come, so mek sure you come Friday night. So don't cha play no games. One love."

Too many thoughts were racing through Jill's head as she stared at her ceiling trying to think of an excuse so she could wind up not going to the party. In all truth, Jill knew a party was exactly what she needed, but she didn't feel like being around a bunch of strangers that she may have nothing in common with. After another hour of debating with herself, she turned on her television and decided she would go.

On Friday morning Jill awoke with butterflies in her stomach. She was actually anxious about Diane's party. She reached into her closet and pulled out a red silk and chiffon-laced corset top by Vanessa Bruno, a pair of white silk slacks and a pair of red Miu Miu heels. Jill's plan was to carry her outfit with her to the shop, get her hair done and get dressed at Diane's house.

"Give me something fresh like a Mary J. Blige look." After her detailed description, Diane got right to work.

"Yes, de donkey tail style get soft? About time you change up. Some ting big a go on tonight, eh?" Diane commented when she prepared Jill's hair for a wash.

"Why does it have to be all that?" she asked. "You invited me to your birthday bash, and now I want to change up my style and you still have something to say?"

"Okay, me just hope your crotches get wet tonight. Dat way dem can't dry up. Some money mahn a show up tonight, and you need to be sure dat you mix and mingle."

Jill wiped the cleansing solution from her face. "Well, since I didn't get the chance to give you a birthday present yet I'll give that to you. I promise that you'll see me dancing."

Everyone in the salon that knew Jill began to make comments when they heard her promise. The gay stylist was convinced that Jill was gay, and when she made that statement, figured she was playing. Deep inside, she thought she was lying to herself, but she had no idea what cupid had in store.

By the time Jill's hair was highlighted with auburn streaks and put into flowing curls, it was time for them to go to Diane's house. Diane had moved into a loft at Union Square, so that she could be close to her salon. When they reached her house, Diane's woman was walking around half-naked. Diane and her lover embraced in front of Jill, the way a man that was hard at work came home and embraced his wife. Jill found the passion between the women to be erotic. After Diane told Jill to make herself at home, she and her lover went into the shower together.

Jill sat in a barber's chair positioned in front of her entertainment center. She could hear Diane's woman moaning out in ecstasy. Instantly, the images of the two women from her adult movie entered her mind. She replayed the thoughts of the women in her DVD and her nipples grew hard. She thought of how Diane's girlfriend was probably licking on her in the same fashion as the two lesbians in the movie and moisture settled between her legs. Unconsciously her legs parted in the chair with erotic moans echoing in her head.

As a result of the stimulation, a wet spot had formed in her jeans and Jill was shocked that she actually wanted to touch herself. By the time the moaning stopped, it was hard for Jill to contain herself. Diane stepped out of the bathroom, and Jill jumped out of the chair, headed for the hot water.

The warm steam and scent of magnolias in Diaine's bathroom calmed her sexual tension. She wished she were at home with her toys.

She lathered her body and discretely touched her firm sensitive nipples. Diane didn't have a door to her bathroom, and the gigantic shower stall was encased with a transparent glass, so at any moment someone could walk in and see her showering. When she washed her vagina, the soft wash cloth massaged the area until her finger slipped right where she needed it to be. The soothing hot water, the Herbal Essence body-wash fragrance, and the erotic images behind her lids took her where she wanted to go. As she began to climax, Diane's lover walked into the bathroom to grab something from the cabinet. She turned her back to the woman glancing over her shoulder. The woman seductively smiled, and slowly walked out. Jill's mood was gone. She was still aroused and wanted to cum, but she felt violated, so she rinsed off and exited the shower.

"You want me fe do you makeup, Jill?" Diane asked.

She nodded to accept the offer, "Yeah, please."

Diane had a way of accentuating Jill's best features. Jill looked like a runway model, once she was done.

The three women walked out of the loft and onto the city streets looking like flames in bonfire. Although Diane was a plus size, she had a flare for style that drew attention her way. Since her lover was a masculine lesbian, Jill and Diane out-shined her. Upon reaching Webster's Hall, they noticed a gathering crowd. Diane played hostess, while Jill and Diane's lover made their way inside.

Beyonce's *Nasty Girl* blasted the hall. The semi dark room had high ceilings, but still managed to provide a cozy atmosphere. A lot of drinking went down that night, but Jill ate instead. She helped herself to the buffet table several times. She ate crab cakes, wafers, and miniature Romaine salad bowls that were placed on serving platters. When her stomach began poking through her corset, she grabbed two glasses of the champagne that waiters were circling the party with and drank them down. With a third glass, she mingled amongst the guest. The alcohol had an immediate effect on her. Jill felt warm and tingling inside and rushed to mingle before she got herself in trouble.

Diane introduced Jill as the owner of Dimple's, over her protest, to a handful of gay Hollywood celebrities, who lived in New York. Jill gave up trying to explain that the salon belonged to Diane and went with the flow. After meeting more people, she felt like she was on display. When, the well-known R&B Diva, Shawn Simmons approached her and asked her for a seductive dance, she told herself that it was time to find a dark corner another drink.

For an hour, Jill sat in the corner alone frustrated. She was sure she would still end up alone before the night was over. The gay couples paired off, and those who weren't, were in their own little social clicks. Diane and her lover were accepting gifts and being good hostesses. Everyone looked as though they were on the prowl to find a man or woman to take home. Jill heard the deejay yell through the mic, "Alright, we're about to take it back for the old school lovers in the house."

She thought her whole night was wasted until a handsome man caught her eye from the distance.

Then her heart fluttered when she saw that the caramel complexioned man was headed in her direction. He wore an all black suit and had his hat tilted to the side as if he were the second coming of Super Flyy. As he moved toward her like a tiger closing in on its prey, she looked around to see if she had neighbors and seeing no one close to her, Jill realized that she was the only person he could possibly be after. Once he was upon her, Jill couldn't help but take in his attire. He had on a pair of crocodile shoes that were shining as if a marine had buffed them. She was almost blinded by the glare from his pinky ring and she noticed that his suit was made of the finest silk.

In a simple and graceful move, he removed two glasses from the serving tray of the waiter that cut off his path. She saw how he reached, spun, side stepped, and didn't miss a beat while holding both glasses in one hand, and wiping his forehead with his pink lace handkerchief with the other.

Jill burst out in a drunken laughter. The brother was too smooth. When she was certain he was coming her way, she braced herself to look more appealing, straightening out her back and tilting her head slightly to the side.

He licked his lips, and in his a smooth but high-pitched voice said, "Pardon me, my dear, my name is Cashmere, and I would love to keep that smile on your face so you never shed a tear." He handed her the champagne and added almost singing to her, "Now I hope you can hear that my words are crystal clear, because in your arms I belong and when I'm there, have no fear."

Jill tried to contain the explosion of suppressed laughter. Cashmere's voice reminded her of the short pimp in *Friday After Next*. To control herself and not embarrass him, she grinned.

"Now why don't you swallow that down and come stretch your legs. I can tell you don't get out enough because you've been looking uptight and uncomfortable in your own skin all night. But no need to worry any more, you see, being in the presence of a man like me will do wonders for your ego."

He grabbed Jill by the hand while *Before I Let Go* by Frankie Beverly and Maze played in the background. With much effort, Jill stood, and noticed a familiar face. It was the woman that Diane promised would not be there, the aggressive lesbian friend, who had a crush on her. She wanted to turn Cashmere down, but she knew that the woman would be persistent about trying to go home with her. Jill didn't want the drama so she stumbled her way to the dance floor.

Jill expected to go onto the floor and have a routine spin until she could make her way to the door and home. Instead, Cashmere gave a performance to the rest of the crowd. Before she knew it, it seemed that the whole party had made a circle around them just to watch his every move. He glided across the floor, his body moved in sync to every beat, and most of all, he made her look like a star. When Diane saw her having a good time, she yelled out that Jill kept her promise. By the time the third song came on, *Ain't No Half Steppin'* by Big Daddy Kane, the room was too hot for Jill. Without her saying a word, Cashmere grabbed a cold flute of champagne. With his free hand he placed the cold glass to her sweaty spine. Instantly, Jill was aroused. Jill's back was to Cashmere's crotch and his erection proved that he hung low.

When the DJ put on *Olivia* by the Whispers, Cashmere slowed down perfectly, spun Jill around to face him, and fed her his drink. He pressed Jill's body into his, gripping her lower back. Her head found comfort on his shoulder and so did his erection between her legs.

Jill hadn't been that close to a man in years. Cashmere took his time making love to her, all while fully dressed. He eased his leg in between hers, and through both of their silk garments, he could feel his penis in between the lips of her vagina. He moved in a rhythm that was so subtle that Jill embraced him more and dug her nails in his back while her vagina dripped in lust as he sang softly in her ear, *"Lost and turned ouuuuuuuttttttt, Lost and turned ouuuuuuuuttttttt, whaatttt is the world coming to, so many used and abused."*

Slow jam after classic slow jam, he moved her closer to the darkest part of the dance floor. She felt like a floating cloud. He moved with the beat of the songs, but she didn't know how she ended up from one end of the floor to the other.

When they had reached an obscure spot near a column Cashmere reached his hand down to Jill's firm behind. He pulled her closer while he slipped his erection between her newly wet pants. He then whispered, "Relax. Relax. Let it go sweetheart, let it all go and exhale."

Jill let out a soft moan while she felt her hips moving slowly. She was mesmerized by the erotic sensation of her body moving onto his firm manhood. The thin layer between the two organs added to her pleasure. Slowly she shifted her body, rotating to the beat until her body tingled. Her nails dug into his back, and her teeth bit into the salt of his neck while she was cumming. "Don't be afraid baby, I can tell it's been a long time, hold on and enjoy the ride," Cashmere whispered.

She obeyed his words. The slow grind continued until she was done and no one was the wiser. She looked around the jammed floor to see if anyone had noticed. Gay couples were doing worse acts right out in the middle of the dance floor. She looked up and her dance partner, Cashmere, smiled at her. He then handed her another drink and said, "Come on."

On the way out, Jill grabbed her purse and waved to Diane while swallowing another flute of the bubbly. Diane was so drunk that when she saw Jill leaving with a man she started clapping and all her friends joined in. Cashmere walked Jill outside. The alcohol had her head spinning yet she was still somewhat conscious of what was going on. "What are we... wait," she asked.

He motioned with his hand and a shining black car pulled up in front of them with an Asian woman driving. Jill reached for the back door. Cashmere grabbed her hand and motioned for her to wait. The driver jumped out quickly and came around to the back door and held it open for them to be seated. They sat in the car and *Hey Love* by the Delfonics was playing. After getting comfortable in the plush seats, she looked around the car and asked in a slurred voice, "What...what the hell kind of car is this? The seats are so plush."

Cashmere laughed and said, "It's a 2003 Bentley Arnage T." He motioned for the driver to wait before she pulled off. He turned to Jill and asked, "So where do you live?"

Jill was surprised when she yelled out her address and the car didn't move. Jill didn't think she heard her until Cashmere folded his legs and said, "Su Kim, take us to Brooklyn. The address is on Decatur and Patchen Avenues."

In a drunken haze, Jill leaned over to Cashmere's ear. In a whisper she asked, "What's wrong with her? Didn't she hear me when *I* said it?"

Cashmere put on a serious face. "No, she's trained to listen to me, only."

"*Trained*? Like you train a dog?" she asked.

He looked at the glistening road and said, "Exactly, the way you train a bitch, but some dogs are more rare and expensive than others. Hopefully you will learn to understand. I think you should lay back and sleep the alcohol off. I'll wake you when we get to your home."

Jill leaned back on the plush seat and rested her head. She closed her eyes, far from asleep. Her mind reeled from what she heard. He hadn't whispered his response so his driver couldn't hear, she thought. Then she wondered what type of man he was. The internal debate began. *Should I let him stay, or should I not?*

By the time they reached the Brooklyn Bridge, Jill was telling herself that Cashmere knew things about her that no one knew, and that she didn't have to tell him. She thought of how he knew that she wasn't with a man in so long. She rationalized that by those words alone that he had to know how to take care of a woman. She thought that maybe he was the prince she was looking for. She thought, *God won't steer me wrong.* She made up her mind that she was going to invite him to spend the night, but first she had to stop off and buy some condoms.

The neon sign from an all night smoke-shop caught her eye so she asked, "Could you pull over here?"

The car kept rolling. "If you need something, Su Kim will get it for you. It's dangerous out here so it's best that she go. What do you need?" he asked.

She was uneasy about the answer. The whole ordeal had a sobering effect. In another whisper she said, "I was going to ask you to come up," she said nervously, then went on, "I wanted to get some...you know...some protection."

Cashmere had a look of surprise on his face. He tapped her hand when he turned to her and said, "Oh? That won't be necessary." He turned to his driver and said, "Su, take this lady home and speed it up."

She was sure then that Cashmere had been prepared. She sat in the seat and gave him the instructions to her house. She was sure he would be impressed when he saw her home, but when Su Kim came around to open the door, he looked up at the house and said, "This is decent. You live here alone?" She nodded while leading him by the hand to the basement entrance. She had it all planned out. The bedroom on the bottom floor was going to be used for her sexual escapade.

When they reached the threshold, Cashmere took a step back and said, "I had a good time with you. I'll be here tomorrow evening, well rather later on this evening to pick you up around eight."

Jill was stuck, but not too drunk to be shocked when she asked, "Oh, I thought maybe we would spend some time together now?"

He stepped back and said, "Oh no, sweetheart, it doesn't work like that. I have business to take care of tonight, and I play for keeps. So think about that and I'll see you in a matter of hours. Please don't keep me waiting." Cashmere stepped off, stopped suddenly and asked, "By the way, hun, what's your name?"

Reality hit her like a ton of bricks. She was willing to expose herself and allow a man to enter her home that didn't even know her name. Filled with shame she said, "Jill...Jill Franklin-Clayton."

He smiled at just hearing the facts and said, "Okay, eight o'clock Jill. Eight o'clock."

Without a kiss or a simple goodbye, Cashmere walked to his car and waited for his driver to let him in. While she looked on, the car sped away and was gone before she turned the key in the door. Jill was filled with embarrassment. She felt like she had already had sex with him, and that he didn't like the experience, based on the way she literally had an orgasm in his arms. Dealing with lust, passion and then rejection was too much for her to handle in one day. She entered her home, climbed the steps to her room and fell asleep fully clothed. Before she had a chance to let one tear fall, the alcohol took her to another place.

When Jill awoke in late morning her head was still banging to a beat that wasn't music. There was only one cure for her hangover and she was grateful that she had that luxury.

She grabbed a can of tomato juice and quickly popped two Aleve tablets. Jill then disrobed and headed straight to the comfort of her huge tub. During her soak in her Jacuzzi, she relaxed and thought about Cashmere and the events from the night before. Just thinking about the way he handled her on the dance floor got her aroused all over again and the mystery of the man made her more enchanted.

What kind of man would turn down a willing conquest of her caliber? she thought. The voice in her head told her not to worry because soon she'd have Cashmere in her bed. She was tired of not living and having to do things to herself for pleasure. Since her orgasms were the only thing that made her feel truly alive, she decided that it was time to have a man to make her life complete.

She prayed for a while after she got out of the tub but then she felt like a hypocrite because nothing was going to stop her from having sex with Cashmere.

Jill's date was in five hours. As she selected her outfit, her phone rang. "Bow, bow, Jill, big up to me, girl," Diane yelled, filled with enthusiasm. "You have ta tell me every single detail."

"Is sex the only thing on your mind, Diane?"

"So you feel bright dis morning? As if you wasn't sexing all night?"

"That didn't answer my question..."

"Yes, me know, gal. Me have sex pon de brain. So tell me, him pee pee big?"

Jill wanted to lie but she didn't. "Yes it's definitely big." She could hear Diane screaming and clapping her hands. She could hear silence in the salon. "But we didn't do anything," Jill said.

"Wha? You mean say you no do nothing? Den how you know him big, you push him wood inna you mouth?" Diane asked while laughing.

"No silly, but that's none of your business." They broke out in laughter. She didn't know what to tell Diane so she said, "He was the perfect gentleman. He dropped me off at my door and scheduled a dinner date. We'll see what happens later."

"Yes, finally your crotches a go get balanced out tonight."

"I didn't say all that."

"So tell me, why you never mek him spend the night? You better know. They say him rich and have a reputation fe make all the gay girls go straight. As soon as dem deal wit him, nobody ever see dem again. Dem say he send dem go California to live inna him mansion. You sure know how to pick dem rich one eh?"

Jill was stuck for words. She didn't want to tell Diane that she was rejected. "Yeah, I guess so," she said as they laughed.

Jill wanted to get a few things done before her date so she said, "Girl, I gotta go. I don't know how you woke up and got to work the way you were drinking, but I'll call you at home to let you know how things went."

Jill sat with the phone in her hand wondering where this experience would take her. *Jill, will you end up being trained like a dog too,* she thought to herself. Then looking in the mirror she spoke out loud, "Something has got to give, so I guess there's only one way I'm gonna find out."

Nineteen

Jason treated his job at the bar with the utmost respect. For all practical purposes it was his first job outside of the prison. The owner had him cleaning the place and due to his muscular body and his ability to keep his cool, he had him also supplementing as a bouncer on the weekend. Every night he received a hundred dollars cash. Jason was also in his hotel room before ten o'clock.

Slowly but surely Jason began to feel like his life was gaining a sense of order. He saved every dime and only spent money on his meals. It made him feel good when he received extra respect from his boss when they found out that he didn't want to consume any alcohol. He had made a promise that he would never drink in public again, or be in a situation where his senses were impaired. He knew he was one error away from going back to prison, so he made daily affirmations to stay focused.

After being released for a week, it was time for him to go visit his parole officer. He was dressed to impress in his newly dry cleaned suit, thinking that Mr. Townsend would be impressed when he arrived.

Jason walked into the crammed office and his parole officer handed him a cup for a urine sample. When he returned with the full sample, his parole officer had his handcuffs in his hands and Jason started to panic.

Mr. Townsend saw the fearful look on Jason's face. "Oh, these aren't for you. It's for the next spick asshole I got to see after you. Think he can go to a party without asking me, huh? Well let's see how he likes to party in Attica."

Jason watched on as he shuffled some papers around. "You got a job yet?" he turned to Jason.

"Yes, sir," he said filled with pride.

The P.O. scribbled a few notes on his file. "Okay. Lets see how long that's gonna last?" He handed Jason the file. "Write down the name and the address to the place, and at the end of the month I want to see all your pay stubs." Jason grabbed the sheet. "How's life in the shelter?"

Jason had forgotten his housing arrangement was a factor. He considered lying, but he didn't know if Mr. Townsend had been there to check up on him. "I moved from there and found a run down hotel on the upper West side."

He thought that maybe the parole officer would be proud of him. "Upper West Side? *I* can't even afford to live on the Upper West Side. I can violate your ass right now. Have a seat."

His heart began to pound a hip-hop beat. Jason stared nervously at his officer. "You changed addresses without notifying your parole officer? Didn't you read the manual? You don't move an inch without me knowing. Next thing you know you're gonna be shacking up with some ghetto queen and I'll have to track you down all over the city. Write down the address. I'm giving you your first and final break. If you consider moving out of that hotel, you better get my approval first." After Jason recorded his information, the nasty officer snatched it from his hand. "Now get out of my sight," he growled.

Jason walked out of the office smiling to himself to avoid crying. As he fought back the tears, thoughts of the cold nights when he cried in prison ran through his mind. Like the times when the mess hall food wasn't edible and all he had to eat was bread and water for dinner.

Then he thought of the racist officers who yelled with their tobacco breath right in his face. The same ones that were so petty and vengeful that they often made the simplest of issues turn into a test of wills that would usually end with the inmate going to the hole. Jason convinced himself that if he could make it in prison with those miserable officers, then Mr. Townsend was going to be a piece of cake.

For a whole week everything in Jason's life was in order. He was able to bring his savings back to a thousand dollars. Under the carpet in his room, Jason loosened up a floor board and used the space under it for his safe. He thought his boss was going to have a problem with paying in checks and taking taxes out of his money. When he explained the situation, his boss understood and they came to an agreement that he would receive a weekly check on Mondays.

Jason's goal was to save five thousand dollars and then move into a studio apartment. He priced paint and wallpaper, and made a connection with a furniture store employee who agreed to sell him repossessed furniture at a reduced price. At the rate he was going, within six months he would have the money he needed.

He calculated that after being out for a year and a half that he could have at least thirty five thousand dollars in cash saved. He wanted a mate or partner that would be able to invest in a restaurant and bar with him. He'd walked the Manhattan streets for hours just looking and he knew the concepts he had were different than anyone else that was out in the business, so he was sure that within two years, he would make a huge profit on his money.

The following week, when he went to see his parole officer, Jason had a feeling that he was about to receive some bad news. After the urine sample, Mr. Townsend said, "Have a seat."

Jason figured that he was going to violate him and send him back to prison simply because he could. He owed the state another eleven months, so he made up his mind that he was ready to go back to prison. At least when he was released again, he wouldn't have anyone to dictate his life except him. "Come on, no need to beat around the bush, just hit me with the nonsense 'cause you been on my back since I been out," Jason said adjusting himself in the chair.

His discipline went out the window and his parole officer had a big smile on his face. "Oh, you sound frustrated. Looks like you're lacking patience? That's good. That's usually the first sign that I will be locking your ass back up in no time, but not today. You have to find another job. I didn't realize that you worked in a place that sold alcohol. To me that's the same as a drug, and since you went up for drugs, I can't have you in that environment, so find another job."

He sat in the seat and contemplated what he had to do. Crime wasn't an option, so he figured he'd have to take a step back, to take a few steps forward and live off of the money he saved.

After his talk with Mr. Townsend, he headed out the door with his spirit needing a crutch. He tried to figure out how he could convince his boss that he had to leave. His boss had grown close to him in such a short time. The man could tell that Jason was used to having, but that he was just down on his luck, so he treated him with the respect of a fallen soldier.

He walked into the bar and everyone knew something was wrong. He explained to his boss about his situation with his parole officer. The owner of the bar offered a way that Jason could get over on the parole officer, but he treasured his freedom too much and decided to quit. With his severance pay in hand, he headed to the safety of his room.

The Regency Hotel was bustling with activity. Jason looked over at Harold's desk and he had a smile on his face. "Hey, homeboy. I see you went out all decked up today? Musta been time to report to your P.O., huh? Well, let me know if everything is alright with your room upstairs?"

Jason tried to figure out why Harold was trying to be so nice to him. He had never showed any real form of respect, and he was sure it wasn't possible for people like him to have any. He met hundreds of Harolds when he was on the *inside*, and most of them ended up getting thrown off a tier, or shanked to death.

He cut the corner from the steps on the fourth floor landing and he saw a light that he wasn't supposed to be able to see. The closer he moved down the tattered floor, the more he could see that the door was hanging from the hinges. Jason raced to his door, pushed it open and it fell completely off. In a state of panic he ran to check under the carpet, and in total shock he saw that his money was gone. The television and everything down to his cosmetics had vanished from the small room.

A tornado of feelings twirled in his body. He wanted to hurt someone badly. It was like a man who was violated in prison by a sneak thief, only to see that his whole cell was stripped clean. The only difference between a sneak thief in prison, and one on the outside, was that the one on the outside could easily get away, but Jason had an idea who it was.

He raced down to the lobby and Harold, the king of the castle, was sitting with a grin on his face.

"I was robbed." Jason yelled at the top of the stairs.

"Oh yeah, that type of thing happens all the time up in this place. I'm sorry to hear that," Harold responded with a devilish grin on his face.

Jason tried to contain himself. The man couldn't look him in his face while he spoke. "So that's it, you don't do a search or nothing, huh?"

"I told you what I am. I do everything around here, but the one thing I ain't, is the police. You free to call them, *if* they come. But I know a convict like you don't need that kind of heat. You don't look like no snitch, so I'll give you a few minutes to look around. Since you can't pay the rent, and I don't have any other rooms left except yours, I guess you ass out of luck?"

Jason leaned closer to the cage. "Maybe I'm talking to the thief now? Ain't you the king of all this?"

Harold looked Jason in his eyes, flicked out a toothpick and said, "Maybe you are? But right now, you just talking and I ain't got a problem picking up this phone and dialing 9-1-1, if you jump bad. So you gonna keep singing, or are we gonna dance?"

He knew when the odds were against him. He wanted to wrap his muscular arms around the man's throat and choke a confession out of him, but he was in a no-win situation. Jason walked out of the Regency, only to hear Harold say behind him, "Come on back when you get some more money. I'll make room for you. We ain't had a guest as good as you in a long time," then Harold let out a belly laugh that really tested Jason's patience.

Tears were in his eyes when he cut the corner onto Broadway. He was lost again, and had to start from scratch without a clue on how to do it. He had considered going to the AT&T store to terminate his service since someone else had his phone at the moment. But he didn't want to see Samantha, so he shrugged it off. He wasn't going back to the shelter. Since his parole officer had his address down as the Regency, he was stuck between a rock and a hard place.

He walked over to the diner on 110th Street and had a seat by the window. His reflection told him that it had been some time since he had taken a shave and trimmed his hair. He thought of Diane and the days he used to go get his hair cut by her and wondered if she was still there. A part of him wanted to jump in a cab and go to the shop, but then he thought of how much money he had and cancelled that idea.

When he exited the diner on a full stomach, his feet carried him to Riverside Drive. He didn't know where he was going, but he crossed the pathway into the park and headed for the Hudson River. He continued walking until he reached a dock. He sat and thought about his whole life. He never had a mother or father who was a real parent. He wondered where his sister was, and if she had a family of her own. The fact that he had never had a Christmas gift, a birthday party, or that his mother never came to any of his school graduations was crippling. He thought of Webb and Tasha and wondered where they were now, and how the consequences of his simple choices had changed his whole life drastically.

Thinking, meditating, and then praying all helped him control his emotions. It was pitch black on the dock and he found himself lying down and falling asleep. The cool breeze, along with the sound of the tide coming in and hitting the rocks had a soothing effect on his mind and body. He slept on the dock by the waterside under a pale moon and the stench of the Hudson River.

In the middle of the night, he got up to leave and then reminded himself that he had nowhere to go. By five o'clock in the morning, he felt a tug on his suit jacket. When he opened his eyes, he saw two river rats the size of cats. One was walking on his chest and the other was nibbling at his pockets. In a frenzied haste he jumped up. Chills ran through his body, and he had a serious need for a shower.

During his trek up the hill to Broadway, he thought of returning to the hotel for a quick shower. Suddenly a group of athletes from Columbia University ran in the street. A light bulb went off in his head and he headed for the campus of the prestigious university. He walked through the security post, and followed the path of the gray sweat suits ahead of him. When he walked into the building to the gymnasium, the sprinkling from the showers came from the basement, so he headed in that direction.

Like any student that attended classes, he walked in, grabbed a stack of towels and a bar of soap. He opened the first empty locker he saw, sat in front of it, and began to disrobe. Again, his image in the mirror stared back at him. He didn't recognize himself. His hair had grown, and his beard was unkempt and had grown to a disheveled length. He made the image disappear by slamming the locker door, and headed for the area he heard the loud voices coming from.

Jason walked into the exclusive shower room with his socks and underwear on. All conversation came to a halt. The skinny, pale men looked at the muscular black man walk in partially dressed and a quizzical look came over all their faces. Jason looked at them, gave a polite nod, and then walked under the soothing water that pounded his back. He lathered his skin and the feeling of the soap on his body gave him a sense of dignity and life. As he did in prison, he washed his underwear while they were still on his body. He slipped off his socks and washed them as well. Then he slipped off his underwear. Once he was fully exposed, a few of the boys made a dash out of the shower, while the others looked in awe at how well hung he was. Jason saw the commotion, but casually minded his own business.

After all his under garments were washed, he scrubbed his body. When the soap disappeared, he reached on the ground and picked up the scraps that were left behind. When his audience saw his desperate act, they were sure that he was not a part of the student body. One by one they abandoned the shower like roaches seeing the light. Two minutes later he looked up and two black security guards were standing with a white student that pointed his way.

Jason was exhausted. He didn't care if he was arrested. He had hit rock bottom and had nowhere to go. When the security guards called to him, he ignored them until his shower was done. He was sure that they thought he was a bum off the street, and he reminded himself that they wouldn't have been that far off with their assumption.

Carefully, he wrapped a small white towel around his waist and another over his shoulders. He walked over to the guards with an explanation that he only needed a shower and didn't have anywhere else to go. He weakly explained that he had been to a shelter and how he was robbed at the hotel. His entire story was told while he was getting dressed, but he left out the fact that he was recently released from prison.

The lighter of the two round men told him to remain seated on the bench in the locker room. Jason was convinced that he was going to get the police so they could lock him up for trespassing. After ten minutes, the guard returned with a blue gym bag with the campus logo on it. In a covert move, he handed Jason the bag and told him to disappear. Without hesitation, Jason left the way he arrived and walked back towards the diner for breakfast.

In the comfort of the hard vinyl booth, he opened the bag. It revealed a pair of old jeans, a few bars of soap, a towel, a tee shirt, and a sweatshirt. All the items of clothes had the Columbia logo on them. He was sure the lost and found bin was missing a few items, but Jason was still grateful. He ordered breakfast, contemplated on how he was going to find work, and how his life was going to pan out for the next few days.

For two days Jason slept on a park bench on Riverside Drive. He began a new routine where he would walk on the downtown side of Broadway and stop in each and every store to ask for employment. On his first day he walked all the way down to 42nd Street before he took the train back uptown. His free time was spent near the hotel in case Mr. Townsend stopped by. On the following day, he repeated the same routine. That day brought a little success. A restaurant owner by Lincoln Center asked him to wash the windows for twenty-five dollars. When he asked for a permanent position, the owner said frankly that he preferred to hire immigrants. Jason knew he meant illegal immigrants who he could pay a third of the minimum wage.

As nightfall set on the third day of his journey, he hung around the hotel. He saw Peter. "Hey, little man, what you got good?" Jason asked.

Peter was walking with two of the other assistants he employed. Peter hardly recognized him because of his out of control hair and beard. He paused. "Damn, boss, what the hell happened to you?"

Jason's eyes fell to the pavement. "Hard times in the hood, youngblood."

"I heard the so called king pulled a gank move on you and you broke out?"

"A gank move?" Jason asked confused.

"Yeah, I heard he robbed you for like a grand or something, and then tried to call the fucking police. Boss, sooner or later that buster got it coming to him. I thought you woulda murked his ass by now?"

Jason shook his head. "Never let your emotions supercede your intelligence, shorty. If I kill him, I go back to the pen probably forever this time, and that would be a worst violation than anyone else can do to me. Out here I can rebound no matter what someone does to me because I'm blessed. In the pen, the rules are different and seldom followed."

"Damn, Boss, that was deep. I like the way you dropped them jewels on me. Let me talk to you."

Peter held Jason as if he was the younger one. He pulled him out of earshot of the other two men. "Listen, man, I got the TV back and we even. I see you messed up and you don't want to go back to prison, so listen here. If you want, you can crash at my crib with my girl and me. I'm squatting and I got a room that can be all yours. Just pay me twenty a day or hit me off when you get on your feet. I can *smell* you need a place with shower. If you interested, meet me on Manhattan Avenue on a 107th in an hour, but don't tell nobody where you going and make sure you ain't followed."

"I thought you lived in the Regency?" Jason asked.

"What? Man you couldn't pay me to live up in there. I just hustle in there and check on my sister and my drugged out moms. Holla at your boy if you with it. I'll see you in an hour if you down."

The little man walked away and Jason began an internal debate. He asked himself what type of living situation could a thirteen-year old kid possibly be in. He then weighed his options and thought about the alternative, and the park bench did not appeal to him.

After making a total observation of the place, Jason walked down to Central Park West and had a seat on a park bench until the hour passed. When enough time elapsed, he walked up the street and waited on the avenue. Most of the homes were maintained well and there was only one house that was neatly boarded up.

While leaning against a lamp post, he saw the red and white Fubu Harlem Globetrotters cap bobbing his way. Peter carried two shopping bags of groceries in his small hands, busy looking behind him to make sure he wasn't being followed. When he reached Jason, he didn't acknowledge his presence. He just nodded for him to follow while he led the way.

They walked down into the block of 107th Street. Peter made a quick dip into an alley on the side of the boarded-up house. When Jason saw him disappear, he picked up his pace and followed the red cap to a beautiful cherry wood door. Peter turned his key in the lock and walked up a flight of stairs that was right in front of the open door. Jason rushed in behind Peter.

"Lock it behind you." Peter walked on. When he reached the landing, Jason was totally blown away at the sight he saw.

A bright stainless steel, fully operational kitchen was in front of him. Peter emptied the contents from the shopping bag and loaded the fridge. In an instant, a pretty, dark-skinned Ethiopian girl, who was well shaped, came down the steps and into the kitchen. Jason guessed that she was around seventeen years old. When he looked closer he noticed that one of her hands was deformed. She looked at him with suspicious eyes. "Who this?" she said with an accent.

"This is my man I told you about that just came home." He turned to Jason. "Meet my wife, Imani. Before you want to start asking, I met her at the Covenant House before they closed it. Since we was both runaways, we decided that it'd be best if we survive together, ya' feel me? She my wife, and the queen of this castle."

"Please to meet you," Jason respectfully replied.

"Now let me give you a tour and show you your space," Peter said as he led Jason to the room next door to the kitchen. "This is your room, Boss. You got a bathroom down the hall, and the kitchen is right here. You eat something, you replace it, or you give Imani the cash. The king-sized mattress is decent. I got all the linen in the closet, from the Waldorf, the Plaza, and the W hotels. That crate is your nightstand, and you can pick a closet for your things. That old boom box is mine, but you can use it. If you need a TV, you know the fee. The hot and cold water works, and the whole place is air-conditioned. If the lights go out, don't sweat it. I'ma introduce you to Grady, my butler. He fix anything in here that goes wrong. He upstairs in his room, come on."

Peter walked with Jason up the burgundy carpeted steps. When they reached the first room on their left, Peter opened the door. Jason looked in and saw an immaculate room with another king size mattress with milk crates underneath. The bed was made of fresh linen spreads, and the blanket on top was laced with an oriental design. The drapes in the room were a perfect match to the spreads, and the red carpet was of the best quality. Across from the bed were three twenty-seven inch televisions with different programs showing on each. A hotel phone was sitting on the floor, and two glass tables and lamps were on each side of the bed.

Peter looked at Jason beaming with pride. "Proper, right? Yeah, boss, as soon as I heard them planes hit them two towers, I was with my workers in a moving truck on the way down. Who was gone question the kid? I can retire off of what I racked up on down there. Them offices and them hotels that were abandoned was a gold mine. Then them people was leaving they cribs for months because dust was everywhere? Man I blew dust off of mad shit and kept it moving. Especially when I found out the steelworkers and the doormen was in on it too? Man, if we get another attack, I might be able to get Imani and me a mansion when I'm done. Come on."

Jason realized that the young boy was always on survival mode. *Who else would think of capitalizing off of a national tragedy other than the government and the wealthy,* Jason thought. Then his mind was filled with visions of looters in Watts and Chicago and then the more recent L.A. Riots. Everyone did it given the opportunity.

"This is Grady." Peter introduced Jason to the fish eyed man that looked to be about fifty years old.

Jason took a quick glance around the man's room trying not to appear nosey. Grady's room was done in the same expensive hotel décor.

"Now let me show you what every kid my age dreams about." Peter walked Jason to the last room on the top floor. "Bam," Peter shouted. "How you like this?" The room had a giant leather couch with gold buttons and an office desk. Across from the couch was a sixty-inch plasma television. On the floor were a Play Station 2, an X-Box, and a Nintendo Gamecube. Next to the TV was a studio sized audio rack system. On one side of the wall was a rack of more than a hundred CD's and on the other side was a DVD player with over a hundred movies. Jason was impressed.

"I know you don't know nothing about this, so when you ready to watch a movie or play a game, wait until I'm home and I'll show you the ropes."

Jason stopped him in his tracks. "Listen, this is cool, but whose house is this and who is Grady? What's up with Imani if the police come messing with us for squatting?"

Peter removed his cap and took a deep breath. "Listen, Boss, this house belonged to an old white man I used to run errands for. When he kicked the bucket, his rich kids took to long to sell it. Crackheads robbed it blind, and Grady was in here sleeping on the floor. The kids wound up boarding it up and broke out. Grady and me made a deal real quick, so I put an official door on it, and gave him a key. Turns out Grady was a handyman, yo, and yo, the man loves to clean. He treats me like his son, so I let him do his thing. He done rigged the phone, gas, and the electricity in the basement so we ain't got no bills. We just can't use the phone whenever the church on the corner is open, so Imani uses her celly. She's seventeen but when she get eighteen in a couple of months, we moving and getting us a legit spot. I already got the section eight hook-up for a place on a 112th and St. Nick. Now, if the cops roll up, which they ain't done in two years, we going to court under the squatter's law. Now let's go."

They walked downstairs and Peter left Jason alone for a moment. As Jason scanned his new surroundings, he couldn't believe that a kid was helping him get on his feet. When Peter walked into the kitchen, Jason pulled out the hundred dollars he had in his pocket and handed it to his new landlord. He wanted to make sure he had a roof over his head no matter what. The feelings he experienced on that park bench and sleeping on the dock almost sent him back into a life of crime. He never wanted to feel that way again. Since he was used to fasting in prison, he figured he could skip food for a day or so and still survive. Peter did a great thing for him Jason thought, but he knew the young boy was a businessman. As the elder, Jason felt it was his responsibility to make moves so that he wouldn't become a leech.

Jason sat on his new bed and thought of his current lifestyle. His life had always been one of extremes. As far back as he could remember he would have nothing one day and too much the next. As he looked around the room he thought that Peter would never understand what his help meant to Jason. It was by far the biggest bed and the most space that he had for himself in the last thirteen years and was provided by a boy that was a baby when he went to prison. Jason would never forget the kindness that was bestowed upon him.

Twenty

Eight o'clock came fast for Jill yet not fast enough. She was so anxious the entire day that she could hardly think, yet she was nervous as a schoolgirl before the prom.

She didn't know where Cashmere was taking her so she didn't know what to wear. After trying on two different outfits, she settled on a powder-blue D&G dress. She twisted powder blue yarn around her hair, and skipped the underwear. The last step was the Gucci perfume. Finally a horn beeped outside her window. She ran to the front of her loft.

Cashmere arrived in another glimmering Bentley. This time it was Continental GT with paper tags on it. Jill was impressed and rushed downstairs in excitement. She put lip-gloss on her lips and did a quick touch-up to her face with her makeup. On her walk downstairs she thought about Sharief and Cashmere's similar ways.

Sharief too had been a man of extreme elegance. When she had married Sharief she hadn't known exactly how wealthy he was. Though he'd pampered her with gifts and his affections, there was no way of knowing that the company he owned, Clayton Realty, had been worth a small fortune. What had been obvious was that Sharief had come from the streets and had an edge that made him fearless and confident. He had introduced her to some notorious characters, Johnny Hustle, Brave Dave, and the young man named, Money, who she was sure sold drugs. During the time that they were married, he'd exposed her to some elements of the streets that she'd never paid attention to. She saw that same *'I am the master of all I survey'* swagger in Cashmere the only difference was that Sharief had never turned her on the way that her new suitor had. She chalked it up to her own budding sexuality and decided that she'd just enjoy it.

The night air was warm but not muggy. Even a breeze danced across her shoulders as she stood at the door of the car waiting for him to open it. Instead she saw him bobbing his head as he sang to the Whispers track, *In The Mood*.

Cashmere didn't move an inch to help Jill get in the car, and she stood there feeling foolish for a few seconds before she realized he wasn't going to play the role of the gentlemen. Finally she reached for the door and climbed in. Before she said hello, she asked, "What happened to your driver? Does this mean we'll be alone tonight?"

He put the car in drive like a cabby with a fare. "My ladies drive my sedans, and I drive my coupes," he said without observation. "We don't have a long way to go so I decided to take the wheel." After a brief pause, "You don't know how to say hello and show a man love when you see him?" he asked.

Jill smiled and reached over to give him a kiss. He put the back of his hand to her lips. "Thank you, I knew you had some manners."

She laughed to herself to hide her shock. When she looked at his outfit he had another suit on like the night before only this time she was amazed that he had a blue handkerchief that was close in color to her dress. Jill broke her silence. "It's funny how we're matching today. What, are you reading my mind?"

He looked at the road. "Not at all my dear, it's just that I make it a priority to be in tune with a quality woman and I am sure that soon I will know you better than you know yourself. That's my job isn't it?"

She was flattered, subconsciously patting herself on the back. She was right about him knowing what a woman needed. "You are definitely right to a point, and speaking of jobs, what do you do? I notice you always wear suits?"

Cashmere looked into her eyes. "I have a few occupations, but my main thing is that I make money the best way I know how. For right now I'm the President of a prestigious gentleman's organization. Our membership is on both coasts." He turned to Jill and asked, "You ever heard of the American Express slogan *'Membership has its' privileges'*?"

"Actually I have."

"I said that to one of our members once. Of course I was referring to our organization. Nevertheless, he liked it so much he called me from his office and asked me if he could use the phrase for an advertising campaign."

"Are you for real?" Jill asked.

"Oh, I'm real, baby. Never question that. And I told him sure, go ahead. Of course I got a little compensation and the rest is history."

"Wow. So do you live in the city? You don't sound like you're from New York."

"I'm what you call a resident of the world community but I tend to spend my summers in New York, and my winters in California. I have a home there. Maybe you'll be interested in doing what's needed to live there with me?"

"Time will tell," Jill said.

"Indeed it will," he shot back. The classics played on while she thought about his question. The things Diane said about him sending women away to live in his mansion popped into her mind. Jill knew she would never be one of those women but she was intrigued at the business he owned. She wondered what the gentlemen's organization was about, but the only thing on her mind was how the date would end.

"If I may ask, how old are you?" Jill placed her arm on the back of his chair.

"I don't know. I stopped counting at thirty. I'm sure it wasn't long ago." He snapped his fingers to the melody as GQ played on the CD.

"So, I see you like listening to classics?" she said.

"I listen to this because it's music. None of that electronic stuff that they make today. The sounds have to take me back to when players played and ladies appreciated a man. Today things are different so you can consider this music my little time machine."

Again she was swept off her feet. "Oh, I see, because I was wonder..."

"Don't finish your statement, we can do that inside." He cut her off and climbed out of the car before she could react to her shock.

Jill looked out the car window and saw a valet reach for her door. Before she exited the vehicle, she looked around and discovered that she was at the world famous Plaza Hotel. Her foot hit the pavement and she leaned back and looked up at the roof of the building and asked, "You're staying *here*?"

Cashmere smirked while walking around the front of the car. "No. I *live* here," he said, and slipped his arm around her waist leading her into the hotel.

All the trappings of wealth were before her as they walked through the lobby. Louis Vuitton luggage was stacked high on the rollers as bell boys scurried past followed by the clack of expensive heels moving from the elevators. From what she could see, they were the only black couple in the place. When they stepped into the brightly antique elevator car, Jill observed how the help catered to her date's every move.

Their journey ended at the Presidential Suite. Su Kim, a gorgeous red head, and two waitresses were waiting for them. In the middle of the room, a dining table was set for two. A bottle of Freixenet sparkling wine sat in the center on top of the white tablecloth. Jill heard Cashmere call to the redhead in what she thought was Russian, and the woman left the room.

Jill was seated, and instead of joining her, Cashmere stood over her waiting for something. A second later the red head came back into the dining room with a smoking jacket and a pair of hard bottom slippers.

To Jill's amazement, the woman was on her knees undoing the laces of Cashmere's shoes. Su Kim was helping him put his jacket on. When he was dressed to eat, the women kissed his hand. Almost on cue, one of the waitresses filled the each glass. "Leave us," he said, and they disappeared into another room.

The look on Jill's face told him that he had some explaining to do. "Something wrong?" he asked, motioning the waitress to refill his glass.

"It depends on how you look at it," she calmly replied.

"Well, lets get it over with so we can have all your questions answered. But there is a catch to it."

Jill shook her leg under the table to avoid losing her temper. "Oh really, what's that?"

"I'll answer yours as long as you agree to answer all of mine."

With premature security Jill shot back, "Fine," and took a sip from her glass. "So what's up with Su Kim and the other woman and was that Russian you were speaking?"

Cashmere huffed, placing his hands on the table. "Su Kim is a business associate of mine. Like all businesses, I provide a service to many people. The proceeds from that business takes good care of her and her family, and for that she rewards me with her undying loyalty. I've owned her since she wandered in from the docks and I gave her the opportunity to drive for me. The other woman is Natalia, and yes, that was Russian. She's indebted to me for other reasons. They, like most women, have submissive natures and take pleasure in the fact that I have relieved them of all the responsibilities in their lives. I take care of the overhead and the liabilities, and they compensate Cashmere with loyalty and service." Jill sat attentively as he went on in an amazing fashion. His tone shifted up a notch in excitement when he added, "Just imagine not having *any* responsibilities and always being taken care of? All of us thirst for that child-like existence though we all can't attain it. Luckily for them, they have, and I guess I'm the father in all of this."

Jill was speechless but she had to admit that she was no different than the two women. Her whole life she looked for her father in the men she dated and Sharief had come closest. She was stuck in thought. Leaning back and folding one leg over his lap, Cashmere responded to her silence with, "My turn. So, Jill, tell me. Who taught you how to think?"

Her face twisted a bit as she came back with, "How to think?"

"Exactly, who taught you what was the truth and what was right or wrong?"

Again she was speechless. She didn't know how to answer the question. She pondered the question over in her mind but kept coming up with a blank.

"Let me help you out," he said pouring her another glass of wine. "It seems that you have some degree of higher education? Which means you probably didn't know what true thinking was until you went to school. After four years of *education* you may now think the way the faculty of the institution programmed you to think. The rest came from your upbringing, which I'm sure was the ghetto. And I'm sure you're the product of a single-parent household. Am I right?"

Again she was stunned on how he knew her. Jill didn't know if she was receiving a compliment or an insult, so in her own defense she responded. "Well, you sound like you went to school, so who *programmed* you? And why are you asking me all of this?"

He smiled. "No need to be defensive, you're not under attack. I'm simply inquiring because you appeared to be very disapproving of my family and to two of the people that have been most loyal to me. Where we have gone and arrived is a tragic story that I'm sure many can't comprehend or endure. Then you took the luxury of coming into our home and being judgmental because they do things different than some other women?"

He rubbed his chin and continued, "And to answer your other question. I went to the school of Hard Knocks and have a doctorate in the Game of Life. Everything I know came from the streets, and since I knew that white people made the rules of the game, I decided to be smart and master it."

The food arrived and Jill was glad that it came. She felt intimidated by Cashmere, and wanted to apologize for offending him and his family. She decided to remain silent while the food was uncovered.

A giant sized stuffed lobster, a baked potato, and some type of spinach sat on the plate. Cashmere was starring at her, so she closed her eyes and said her grace. When she was done, she attacked her food while he sipped on water and continuously refilled her glass with wine.

"Now, answer this Jill, I promise this will be easier, tell me your life story."

Instantly she began to feel comfortable. The wine and the music in the background were beginning to sooth her. On top of that, she was put at ease by the fact that Cashmere was still interested in her at all, let alone her life story. No man had ever been that concerned about her before. She suddenly felt emotional but held back her tears. His words and compassionate tone made her feel something deep in her soul. Her legs trembled like she was standing on breaking ice, while she thought of where to start her story she wondered aloud. "Why are you asking me this?" she asked.

With a handsome grin on his face he said, "You see, you're already violating the rules. You agreed to answer all my questions. But before you do, remove your shoes while you eat and know that I ask only to better understand your nature."

One by one her feet slid out of the sandals. The next thing she knew she started talking about her father, and what he meant to her, and how he and Cashmere had a lot in common. After two more drinks, nothing could stop her from talking. She was under a spell and receiving the best therapy in her life. While she told her story, she was analyzing why certain events in her life took place. Since he was an excellent listener, she continued on and was completely honest. She revealed how she felt about him and how long it was since she'd slept with a man.

At the end of her story, she was feeling vulnerable and wondered how he would look at her. Cashmere leaned back in his seat with two fingers on his cheek. He kept a poker face while starring into her eyes and listening to her every word. He pushed his chair back and stood. He then reached for her hand and said, "You have lived an incredible life. I hope you are proud of your accomplishments. I see you and I are no different in regards to the laws of compensation. Your husband did what a man of his character had to do for you. It is a pleasure to be in your presence. Now I hope you'll allow yourself a different type of pleasure?"

A fresh bottle of Freixenet was in his hands when he led Jill through double doors of a bedroom. He closed the door to the room and sat her on the bed. Gracefully, he waltzed over to the stereo system and pressed a button. The room was filled with the voice of Teddy Pendergrass' crooning *Come On and Go With Me*. They stared at one another.

Instantly, her nipples became swollen and the aching between her legs started up. The effects of the alcohol had her itching to have him deep inside her. She knew her desires were going to be met, and the one thing she did feel with her new lover was an overwhelming passion.

Cashmere walked over to the lounge area of the room and took his slippers and his smoking jacket off. He removed his jewelry and shirt exposing his chiseled body. She had waited too long for this moment and she was going to enjoy herself even if it was only this one time.

After dimming the lights, he walked over to the bed. She reached to kiss him and he put her hands to her side. "I don't do that baby, kissing is a little too personal, but I want to do something real special, but *you* have to give me permission," he whispered.

The combination of his seductive voice, the alcohol, and the music made her feel totally relaxed. Cashmere put her hand on her breast. "I want you to do a few things...*for me*. You think...*you* ...can think differently for me?"

Jill nodded, "Yyyeeesss," she whispered.

"Cashmere wants you to imagine. Imagine it's all about *you*."

She began to rub her breast and in a pant she said, "Yes...yes...oh yes."

"Good, I need you to lose your inhibitions and grant me my wishes, can you do that?" Jill nodded while licking her lips. "Good, I'm so proud of you. So close your eyes and breathe. Make your mind a blank screen."

When she closed her eyes he leaned her back onto the mattress. "Now I need you to think of all the pleasure you want to receive as you're breathing deep for me. Concentrate and imagine all that you want done to you."

Her body began to tingle and the hairs on the back of her neck stood. She saw all the images of the pornographic DVD's she watched when she masturbated. She began to breathe harder when the video images of the two women came into her head. She thought of the two women in the other room and wondered if she had the nerve to tell him what she was thinking. Her body was on fire.

"I want you to be different. I want you to be brave and new with me. I want you to let go of what you think is wrong. And just feel what you know is right. Take off your clothes," his voice was soft and soothing, yet commanding.

Jill quickly removed her dress unfastened her bra. Her eyes were still closed. Part of her was hoping that Cashmere would take one look at her 36-26-34 body and lose control. Instead he guided her through each movement.

"Run a finger from behind your ears to your mouth and lick it." She obliged him and herself at the same time. "Take that finger and run it down your neck. Imagine it is my tongue. Take it down to your breast, but don't touch the nipples. Not yet."

"Ohhh yesss," she panted out.

Minute by minute he had her guide her own hands down across her belly button and to her hips all the while telling her how much pleasure to feel. She felt as though she'd been placed under a spell. For minutes her hands roamed her body but did not touch the areas he said were forbidden.

She finally felt him move to her and she opened her eyes just slightly. Her vision felt strained. The room was dimly lit but she made out his movements. He had put his hands into a bowl of warm water and toweled them off as he moved toward the bed.

Cashmere descended upon her and without warning he pinched her swollen nipples and pulled at them. She didn't know how he knew that she loved her nipples bitten and treated roughly. Delicate kissing or caressing did almost nothing for her. She had married Sharief and not once had he ever yanked on them like Cashmere. He then stepped away for a moment and she almost cried out in agony for the distance he put between them.

In one swift movement he had turned the lights out completely and lit a candle. Now she was in a daze because his fingers dug into her thighs and parted them. She was breathing in a labored manner as she anticipated what was coming next.

Her body was inflamed with so much passion that when he finally touched her clit, spasms shot through her body. From just one touch to her wetness, she screamed in ecstasy. She wanted to stop it. She had never cum so easily and didn't think it was possible. Her toes curled and her mouth widened as she moaned out in pleasure. Her hunger for more of his touch alarmed her.

Jill looked up and realized for the first time that the top of the canopy bed was a giant mirror. She admired her own nakedness, which turned her on even more. Cashmere was still partially clothed when he handed her a fresh glass of sparkling wine. She'd already had too much to drink, so she swallowed down the whole flute without giving it any thought.

He laid next to her and whispered, "Yes, sweetheart, I'm so glad you allowed me to witness your pleasure, but we have only just begun." He reached for her hand and led it to her clitoris. He placed his hand on top of hers and said, "Show me how you need to be pleased."

"Okay," she said not believing that she was doing this in front of anyone.

Jill laid back and opened her legs. She imagined he was inside of her and began to pleasure herself. He told her to suck her nipples and she did. He told her to lose all control, and as if she was working toward the last orgasm she'd ever have. She began to rapidly move her fingers in and out of her vagina. She rubbed all over her body, licked her large nipples, and tasted the wetness of her vagina off of her fingers. "I want you to cum harder than you ever have before." He placed two of her fingers so deep inside her that her wrist almost went in.

He told her to bend her finger in a circular motion until she felt her G-spot. He then reached for her other hand and parted her vaginal lips to expose her clit and asked her to rub it with her middle finger. He poured the wine straight from the bottle into her mouth and the overflow splashed onto her neck and breast. While her two hands were occupied, Cashmere reached for her wet breast and put it in her mouth so that she could lick the taste of the wine off of them. She looked up at the mirror and knew she was having the most incredible experience of masturbation possible.

She had followed his directions and lost all sense of time and space. She worked her fingers just as directed finding a spot inside of her that she hadn't known she could reach until now. The sensations began to send her into a frenzy. It was too sensitive for her to continue, yet she was powerless to stop plunging her fingers inside of herself. She felt so many emotions. She was putting on a show for him and pleasing herself shamelessly in front of him. She wanted him to watch her.

She imagined that he was fucking her with the huge dick she had grinded on at the party and suddenly Jill felt an internal tug deep in her uterus. Her whole body convulsed and it felt like she was about to have a seizure, but then she felt the tingling sensation intensified to the highest degree. She fell back and moved her hands away. A power inside, greater than her strength, was on its way out. At the top of her lungs, she yelled in pleasure. She could feel her cum squirting out of her the same way her high school sweetheart used to ejaculate in her hands.

A river of pleasure poured from her, and she couldn't stop cumming. She bent her legs back to her chest in an effort to make it stop. Her head was light, and she saw bright spots in the darkened room. She turned over on her stomach realizing that she had trouble breathing. Jill gasped with her head in the pillow.

"Breathe, sweetheart, breathe. Enjoy a new experience of life and come on home to pleasure," he whispered to her. "No man but Cashmere has made you feel like this."

"No, no, no, no, noooooooooo," she barely could speak words as her ultra-orgasm continued to wrack her body with one convulsion after another.

"No man after me ever will," he added. She believed every word.

Jill was losing consciousness, but reached for his pants. She wanted to return the favor. He politely moved her hands away and put his lips close to her ear. "When you're ready to evolve into the creature I need you to be and make me your master, then and only then will you experience my manhood inside of you. In the mean time, relax as you come down and get some rest."

Her eyes were too heavy and her body too relaxed to fight the feeling. She closed her eyes and felt satin being thrown over her shoulders. Cashmere turned the music off, and went into the other room.

Jill fell asleep in Cashmere's bed and awoke to a breakfast of waffles and fruit. Once she showered, she was surprised to see that a fresh set of panties and a bra were waiting for her in the room along with a linen skirt and blouse that had come straight from Barney's. Cashmere instructed her to dress and once she did, he whisked her off on a series of errands with him.

They spent the following two days together but both nights ended with disappointment. She found herself being dropped off at her front door. On both occasions she invited him into her house, and dressed seductively in an effort to make love to him. He was more pleased with sharing her company and they drove around the city as he took care of his business. Whenever she took matters into her own hands to make sexual advancements, he was clear about her having to live to please him before he'd touch her.

Jill didn't want to have a complicated union. She was only focused on finally having him completely satisfy her. After he had showed her the greatest sexual experience she ever had taking it to the next level was all she could think about.

On Wednesday morning, she was awakened by her doorbell. On the third ring she jumped up in her nakedness and saw that the clock read ten o'clock. She walked to the front of her loft and looked out the window. Cashmere was standing in her courtyard.

Jill snatched her silk peach robe from the closet, and then ran back to the window. When she opened it, she told him that she would be right down. She knew he didn't like waiting, so she moved like Flo Jo.

With a devilish grin on her face, Jill untied the robe and opened the door. Cashmere stepped in the door, "I got a surprise for you, so get dressed." She was surprised that her naked body didn't faze him, but reminded herself that the morning was still young.

She swayed her way to the stairs. "What's this surprise about? I hope it will be a pleasant one?"

His eyes wandered. "I have to seal a deal and you play a part in it, so I came to get you."

They reached the cluttered loft and Jill dropped her robe and climbed back on top of the bed. She was sure her nakedness would convince him to get undressed and attack her body. She had planned for that moment with a box of condoms in her nightstand. When she peeked out of her partially opened eye, she saw that he was looking for something. She sat up and put her hand on her crotch. In a playful voice she said, "I don't know what you're looking for but I think it's right here."

Her words meant nothing. "We have things to do and I'm looking for the remote control."

She searched around in the bed until she found the remote. Not hiding her frustration she handed it to him, slamming it into his palm. She took deep breath and prepared for the worst when she asked, "Are you a homosexual?"

He turned the TV to CNBC. "Look, I tried not to treat you like all other women, but I see I'll have to. Just like them, you only hear what you want to hear. Perhaps you feel that I'm joking when it comes to my desires, so let me repeat it for you. I play *for keeps*. When you are ready to make me the central part of your existence and leave the rules of this sad world you been taught to follow behind then and only then will you experience all of me. *If* and *when* you do that, understand that you are my family and that I am willing to live and die for my family and that isn't offered to just anyone. Today we will see if you're content with being just anybody or if you want to finally step up and be *somebody*. Now shower and get dressed."

He was listening to the CNBC reporters discuss the future of the Dow Jones index. When she heard the reporter she was reminded that she was missing her workouts and losing money in the stock market ever since she started spending time with him.

The outfit he picked out was to her taste and she knew he was a ladies man for sure. Jill was about to put on makeup, but he told her that she was going to a salon from there.

After the car pulled off Jill noticed that the driver had a clean shaven head. Jill leaned over to Cashmere. "What did that girl do to her hair?"

He looked at Jill and then stared out the window. "Su Kim, tell Jill why you don't have hair anymore."

"Me disobey. Me show humility to master. I most loyal," she said as she licked her lips.

Jill's eyes popped out of her head. Her hand went to her mouth. She looked at Cashmere. The look on Jill's face registered and in a calm voice he said, "Don't even think about looking at me like that. The bitch was disobedient, and she chose her own consequences. She's an adult, and I had nothing to do with her decision. This will be the last time I explain my actions to you." He then tapped Su Kim on the shoulder. "Take us to Diane's shop, and turn that up." Jill had an attitude. He sat back and enjoyed the sound of Gladys Knight and the Pips.

When they reached Diane's salon, Cashmere walked in and gave his greetings to everyone.

Within an hour Jill fit the exact image Cashmere had in his head. When Diane was finished the three of them looked in the mirror and he said, "You see, all she has to do is listen and let a man be a man and I will bring out the best in her."

On her own Jill would have never chosen the style she wore. The job that Diane did made her admit that she looked better than she did in a very long time. Jill and Cashmere said their farewells and Diane signaled with her hand for Jill to call her later so that they could gossip about the day's events.

The car headed uptown and Jill asked, "Where are we going?"

"We're going to a meeting. I'm trying to acquire some land on the coast of Florida. This older gentleman is hesitant about meeting my terms and I think you'll give me good luck."

On the way, Cashmere showed a different side of himself as he serenaded Jill. She was delighted but every time she looked at Su Kim's head, it reminded her that there was more to her man than the eye could see.

The car stopped at the Trump World Tower across from the United Nations building. The valet rushed to Jill's door. She took a step forward but heard Cashmere tell her to hold on. Just like that Jill stopped in her tracks. When she looked down behind her into the car, she felt him reaching his hands under her skirt. Jill simply stared at the valet and doormen in embarrassment as they stared back at her. Before she had a chance to panic, her panties were down to her knees. Panties in his hands, he stepped out the car, and pushed them in his jacket pocket.

"Your skirt was showing a panty line. We can't have you looking tacky. All eyes will be on you searching for a flaw. A flaw in you represents a flaw in me." She was stunned but was growing used to Cashmere's controlling ways.

They were escorted to a room with a gigantic oval table that seated twenty. Jill was surprised to see that the room was empty and wondered what kind of meeting they were having. Cashmere said, "Sit here." Then he slid her chair a foot away from the table and said, "Cross your legs."

When she did he pulled her miniskirt up an inch. If someone sat across from her and looked in between her legs they would most likely see a glimpse of her vagina. When she turned to Cashmere to protest she heard the door open.

An overweight white man with red cheeks walked into the room sporting a cowboy hat. He had what looked to be his clean-cut black lawyer trailing and carrying two briefcases behind him.

Jill quickly noticed that the cowboy could not keep his eyes off of her. She was surprised that she didn't feel cheap or used. She was actually having fun torturing the man with her sensuality. Here he was supposedly conducting business and yet all he could do was ogle her. It became pitiful when the fat man began to sweat and was licking his lips in lust while staring a Jill's shiny legs. Cashmere leaned in and whispered, "Now you're getting it. Turn it up a notch and he is all ours. Soon enough we'll all get what we want."

With a slight smile on her face she pushed with her toes so that her sandal dangled off of her right foot. Continuously she repositioned her legs so that he would get a quick glance between them. Surprisingly Jill became aroused instead of insulted that the man viewed her as a piece of meat. She had never experimented with her sexual power before and the control she had over the man gave her a thrill.

Cashmere negotiated for a lower price for a sixty-acre ranch. When the man wouldn't budge Jill looked him in his eyes, seductively licked her lips, and in a lingering motion gracefully re-crossed her legs. The man put his face in his sweaty palms and agreed to Cashmere's offer of 2.4 million dollars. The property would have been a steal at 3.5 million. Jill was happy for Cashmere and hoped that now she would get what she wanted.

After a few finalities the meeting concluded. Cashmere stood and took her hand and she stood and nodded at the two gentlemen. Before they exited, the cowboy called Cashmere over. When he walked away Jill noticed that he had dropped his billfold near the chair where he was seated. When she picked it up she couldn't help but take a peep inside. She laughed under her breath when she read his name.

Looking over at the two men, she could see that the cowboy whispered into his ear while looking her way. Jill stared. For the hell of it, she turned her back allowing the cowboy to take a look at her rear hoping that Cashmere would come to his senses about what he was missing. Moments later she felt a hand on her elbow and again they were escorted by the employees to the running car.

Cashmere seemed nervous when she handed him his billfold. With a name like *Shirley* she understood. When she celebrated on how she had the man in the palm of her hands for the entire meeting, Cashmere didn't join in on the celebration. He said with a poker face, "I've secured one deal for the day, now I want to conclude my most important deal."

Jill recognized the seriousness in his demeanor. Jill braced herself and Cashmere faced her. "I see that you liked the power of holding a man's attention. Since I met you, I spent a lot of time with you, and my time is money. I didn't think you were interested in living a life like ours but Su Kim told me you might be worth the effort, so for her sake, she better not be wrong."

She looked at Su Kim through the rear view mirror and made eye contact while trying to figure out what was going on. "Natalia also feels you will be a great addition to our family and since you want to make love to me, I feel tonight could be your night. Based on how professionally you performed in that meeting, working within the Gentlemen's Organization might be right what you've been looking for."

Cashmere rubbed Jill's cheek with the back of his hand. "Ed, the cowboy offered me five thousand for an hour of your time. I told him you were not in my stable yet but he wants a good time. Once he drops his load he's sure to be off to sleep. Seeing how you handled him, you could probably make him cum without taking your clothes off quite the same way I did to you. So, tell me do you want into my family or not? You're a natural winner, baby, but you have to get in the game." He was cold as ice. "So what's it gonna be?"

Jill thought of how much time she'd spent with Cashmere and how she desperately wanted to be with him. Maybe she'd do this for him just one time and once he'd made love to her, Jill believed that he would never want another man to touch her.

Her face was the picture of confusion. In a careless manner, he handed Jill a card key and said, "He's waiting for you in 2205. When you hear this pager go off, meet me right here with the envelope. Don't count it in his presence. It's insulting." Then he pushed her door open. As she stepped out of the car, she realized that amongst the many things that Cashmere professed to be, he was in fact a pimp.

Twenty-1

On Wednesday morning, Jason was getting dressed to visit his parole officer. He called to confirm his appointment time not wanting to be late. On the other end of the phone the secretary told him not to come in because his parole officer was out sick and he was to report on the following week. He had received a blessing. One extra week meant he had more time to come up with something before Mr. Townsend found out that he was homeless.

He was determined to make the most of the time he had to go out and find a job. In his mind he was willing to do anything to keep from being violated. He thought about how he could shower on his own time now that he had his freedom and how, thanks to the kid, he actually was in a place clean enough to really relax and groom himself properly.

The bathroom Peter provided came without a shower curtain but it was fine by Jason. He grabbed the thick hotel towel and placed it next to the tub. While standing on the cool surface of the tub, he thought about the scented candles and the bubble bath flakes he used to use when he had his own home. Immediately thoughts of his old life invaded his mind.

Thoughts of Zeida gave him an erection. He thought of her voice, her smile and he even swore that he could recount the scent of her body. He laughed to himself, wishing he would have known the world would be so fascinated with J. Lo's ass, because he would have put Zeida's ass on a video. Right there he decided that he would go to Zeida's job and see if he could find her.

Jason grabbed the clothes that the security guard from Columbia had given him. The pants felt a little snug. The sweatshirt was too small, but that didn't stop him. He put on the tee shirt the guard gave him and allowed it to hang down to his pants. The sweatshirt was placed on his back and he folded the two arms across his chest. He looked in the mirror and believed that he could pass for a preppy college kid except a few things were wrong.

His reddish brown hair had grown into a curly afro and his beard made him look like a modern day Muslim. He didn't have a toothbrush or body oil to help his ashy face. He licked his palms and wiped his face with his saliva. Though he realized that he wasn't at his best he still walked out of the house filled with anticipation for Zeida.

He wanted to catch the nine o'clock crowd that went into Zeida's office building, just like on the first day he met her. He looked around and considered his options.

Harold, the self proclaimed king of the Regency, walked past and he considered asking him for five dollars. Jason's ego mixed with a little reality hit him and he stopped himself. He looked around the bustling avenue. The streets were crawling with traffic. As he saw storeowners opened for business he wondered about a job.

He ran to the Korean fruit stand and began to help the man unload the truck without asking if he needed help. The Korean storeowner and his wife looked at Jason suspiciously and wondered if he was a drug addict, or a robber. Jason picked up their vibes and put a disarming smile on his face. He hoped it would work. His smile always worked in prison when he ran into an insecure guard. The people thanked him for his help and the man removed three dollars from his pocket and put it in his hand. Jason was overjoyed but he needed at least one more dollar to afford his trip.

Across the street at the supermarket he saw the store manager sweeping in front of the store. He dashed across the Broadway traffic in his slippery hard bottom shoes and almost caused an accident. The store manager saw him approaching and pulled the broom closer to his small body. He looked at Jason with a frightened expression on his flat face.

Jason gently took the broom from the man and said, "Good day, sir, I'm sure you have more important things to do in such a successful business. It just doesn't look appropriate for you to be doing such a menial job as sweeping the sidewalks." He began to sweep the sidewalk. "You're the manager. Why not allow a simple citizen such as myself handle these tasks that are beneath you? Please move, I'll tell you when I'm done and will accept any form of gratitude you bestow upon me."

He continued sweeping while the short man adjusted his glasses onto his beak and stuck his chest out. The way the short man walked away nodding told Jason that the man had a sudden boost to his ego.

The sidewalk was swept in five minutes. He held the broom up at the window indicating to the manger that he was done. The manager said, "Thank you, I'm sorry, but I don't have any money in the register yet to pay you with." He moved closer to Jason and whispered, "But I'll let you get a couple small items you want and you can sell it on the streets."

A light bulb went off in his head. He leaned in closer. "Here's a better deal. Why don't you slide one dollar from your pocket to me now, and then right before closing, I'll come back and sweep again and see you for the items?"

The manager looked at Jason and reached into his pocket and handed the money to Jason. "Sounds fair enough."

Jason took the dollar and shook the man's hand before he walked away.

Many things changed after Jason went to prison. It took him five minutes simply to figure out how to purchase a Metro card. The machine cards were new inventions to him. Finally an older woman helped him figure out what to do. While waiting for the train, he pulled an old *New York Times* out of a garbage can. Jason had trouble focusing because he couldn't get Zeida out of his head. He wondered what she would say to him. Did she still love him and would she accept him back into her life?

The crowded train didn't move fast enough for him. He was bursting with anxiety and anticipation. He reached the Chambers Street stop, raced off the platform and headed up the stairs. Jason felt that he was one step closer to his true freedom. He wondered to himself why he had waited so long to try to find Zeida. He imagined hearing her voice telling him, *"Everything will be okay."*

Like a bird on a limb, Jason stood perched at the side of the entrance to the building he robbed many years ago. His keen eyes scanned every face that walked in. He saw women that resembled Zeida in some fashion, but when he walked up to them, he was disappointed each time. For two more hours, he stood in front of the building just in case Zeida was late. When the morning rush slowed down to a trickle there was still no Zeida. He walked away, head down.

The thought of asking security for her, or going up to the floor her office was on, crossed his mind, but he looked down at his appearance and figured that he would come back when he was on his feet. On his way back to the train station, something caught him out of the corner of his eye. A woman with long hair wearing a business suit had a behind that was similar to Zeida's. Impulsively, he ran through the crowded city street. He reached the woman and grabbed her arm. When she turned around, he greeted her with a smile on his face. His gracious smile turned into a frown because the stranger who cursed at him was definitely not Zeida.

He kicked himself for pulling a stunt like that. As he walked away he chastised himself. *Instead of trying to find Zeida, he should have been looking for a job,* he thought.

Broadway was busy with the noon traffic when he reached uptown. He stepped out of the subway and up the stairs into the summer sun. Out of frustration he removed the snug sweatshirt and threw it in the garbage can. He looked down in embarrassment at his outfit. The old image of himself started to play on his mind. He began to think that he could do one robbery and never have to look back. He could take the money and cop a pistol and get back to work.

All he had to do was befriend the manager in the supermarket, and then take him when his guards were down, he thought. He was sure that once he cut his hair and shaved, the victim's description wouldn't hold.

Jason sat on a milk crate on the side of the Korean fruit stand, shielding himself from the powerful rays of the sun. The Korean woman felt sorry for the way he looked and threw him a peach. He attacked it like a pit bull annihilating his prey. The fruit only frustrated him because it showed him just how empty his stomach was.

For an hour, he sat and tried to meditate so he could calm himself. When he tried prayer to get the robbery out of his head, he gave up. He thought of how Peter could go with him in the supermarket that night and play the part that Webb used to. He would show his gratitude to Peter when they got the money.

Jason began to run the entire game in his head. He counted how much he thought customers had spent by the size of their bags. He figured that at the rate the store was raking in money that they could easily make two thousand dollars in a day. He made up his mind that he was robbing the place that night by himself and nothing was going to stop him.

He was biding his time sitting on the crate. His mind was set and the consequences of going back to prison became an afterthought. Jason was frustrated and his discipline had all but disintegrated. His eyes stared directly in front of him at the supermarket and he began to go through the ritual he did when he planned a robbery.

He was totally focused on how he would be successful in his heist until a pink and blue blur crossed his vision. When he looked up his eyes followed the trail of a gorgeous goddess that was wearing a pink hat, blue jeans and old Nike sneakers. When he looked at her from behind it was like a scene from a Spike Lee movie. Though the world moved around them, both he and the goddess were still.

Unwittingly, he was off the crate and following the path of the most beautiful woman he'd seen since he'd gotten out of prison, or maybe even in his lifetime. Her graceful walk led him like a drum major with a marching band. When the miracle before him crossed the street, he stood on the corner patiently waiting to see where she would wind up.

She walked into the flower shop on the corner so he crossed the street and stood at the window. Everything in his being told him to go inside and introduce himself, but when he took a step closer to the window, he heard his shoes scraping on the hard concrete. He looked down at his attire. He was wearing sweats with hard shoes and a T-shirt. He knew there was no chance in hell the goddess would take him seriously so he walked away feeling even more determined to get some money.

He crossed the street heading away from the fruit stand but a voice in his head told him to wait. Listening to his intuition, Jason stood against the wall looking into the shop from an angle. He was surprised when he saw her kiss the lone employee in the flower shop.

With every move the woman made, his head followed. His heart beat with her steps, as he watched her exit the shop.

Jason panicked. If he could have disappeared through the wall he would have. Although he didn't know her, he didn't want the woman to see him like this. Quickly he turned and headed for the fruit stand. He picked at the assorted fruits and vegetables, hoping she would come near him. He struck up a frivolous conversation with the storeowner at the cash register, his eyes focused on the window.

"Are you alright, sir?" the owner asked. Jason turned slightly keeping one eye on the door.

"Yeah, I'm cool. I um need some roughage, that's all."

Oh shit! Here she comes, he thought. Jason almost went into cardiac arrest. Sweat began to form on his neck. It was as if she was headed straight for him.

The storeowner and his wife made reference to Jason's sudden condition, or so he assumed. They snickered at his shyness. He lifted his head and she was two feet from him. Staring into her eyes, he was mesmerized. The woman didn't seem alarmed, but she looked him up and down and smirked. Jason dropped the item in his hand and headed for the door. He glanced back to avoid being hit by a garbage truck. The Korean woman was at the curb with his angel, pointing at him. She spoke in the poorest English dialect. Jason exchanged glances with his angel before disappearing.

Jason had one thing on his mind, seeing Diane. When he walked into Hairs to You beauty salon, he crashed through the door like a bull. Everyone was caught off guard. Everything came to a halt. Thinking he was a robber, one customer reached into his waist for his gun. Jason wasn't phased by it. Alicia, the owner, was the only face he somewhat recognized.

"What you want?" the gunman said.

With a sound of hesitance he asked, "Di...Diane here?"

The sexy, full-figured woman, who he recognized as the owner of the place from way back, asked in a high soft voice, "Diane? Jamaican

Diane? She doesn't work here any more. Could you please close my door before we have a mess up in here?"

The door was closed before the woman had a chance to finish her sentence. He crossed over to the downtown side of 7th Avenue. All the hustlers were out getting their cars washed. A feeling of nostalgia came over him and his frustration was at an all time high. He remembered the day he and Webb drove there Zs up to Harlem for the first time to get them cleaned.

Jason was shocked when he noticed the same old man that used to wash his car. The man he'd called Pops hadn't appeared to age much in the fourteen years since he'd seen him. Not wanting to be seen while he was down, Jason tried to avoid eye contact, but the man saw him anyway. Jason nodded casually hoping the man wouldn't recognize him.

"Hey. Hey, you, hold up."

Jason turned around at the corner and saw the old man coming his way with a towel in his hand. When the man reached him he didn't say a word to him. The car washer looked into his eyes for awhile. The old man closed his own eyes digging through his own memory bank.

When his wide eyes popped opened he said, "Porsche 911. Before that was a 1991 300 ZX. Yellow," he said laughing and proud of his memory. "Gave me two hundred dollars once just to throw some water on it and wipe it down, I never forgot it. Pops might don't remember a name, but I never forget a face and the cars that go with 'em." The man looked concerned. "How you doing, man? You look like you down on your luck?"

Jason held back the tears. So many emotions were running through his mind. "Hey, Pop, it's been a long time. I ended up doing a bid, almost fourteen years, and things ain't been the same since I got out a few weeks ago."

"Oh, that's all, huh?" The old man replied.

"That's all?" Jason asked sarcastically. "Man, I don't know if I can make it out here."

"Maybe not. I'm no fortune teller. What I do know is you got good principles and you was a man even when you was a boy. A prison ain't no place for a man like you to be. You ain't like these young rappers with they Ferraris and they Lamborghinis. Thinking somebody owe them something. Like we all was born to be washing they cars. These cats today ain't got no respect. *You*, though. You was from another breed. What you feeling is what you suppose to be feeling, 'cause if you can't handle the bad, then you don't deserve the good," the old man looked Jason over from head to toe.

The weathered man adjusted his apple jack, jingled the change in his pocket and said, "Now hear this. It's always darkest before the dawn. Some get stuck in the darkness, and some know how to make the sun come up a little faster. Take this and get the sunshine back in your life." The old man forced a wrinkled, damp bill into Jason's hand and said, "It ain't much, but for a trooper like you, that's all you need to get you through the day. I'll see you when you come through with one of them new rides. I got to go finish that young punk's Maybach over there."

"See you around Pop," Jason said as he turned his back headed towards 125th Street. He opened his hand and saw a twenty-dollar bill. Considering the priceless words the man told him. He knew then that God was watching over him. *Strange how God sends his angels in all forms*, Jason thought.

Jason struggled through 125th Street and was headed through Morningside Park. He cut through the desolate park and headed for the campus of Columbia University. By the time he reached 110th Street, it was late in the evening and almost dark. Broadway slept, so he sat on a milk crate next to the supermarket until it closed. When the employees were gone, he tapped on the window. The manger saw that it was him and he indicated with his skinny finger for Jason to come around to a side door.

"Oh it's you again?" the manager said. "I'm glad you waited until the other employees were gone. The broom's right there. Do me a favor and break down that stack of boxes and put them in the dumpster. Just knock on this door when you finish. I'll be in the office closing out. I'll let you grab a few items when you finish."

It took him twenty minutes to take care of the task and by this time it was completely dark. The manager let him in and said, "Grab a few things. I have to do something really quick in my office." Then he walked to the back of the store to grab his belongings. Jason knew what he wanted and he knew what he needed the most.

When he reached the elevated office he heard the man say, "Holy cow, you scared the bejesus out of me. I'm sure glad you're not a robber because no one would ever hear you walking up. Did you get all your things?"

Jason heard not one word of the man's question. His attention was on the stacks of cash on the floor. The safe door was open, and from the quick glance he saw what had to be thousands dollars. His criminal instincts were aroused. A couple of blows and the manager would be out cold. The man looked strangely at him, then when he noticed the cash was exposed, he grew nervous.

"Hey guy, did you hear me? I was asking if you got your things, but I can see that you did, so let me see you out."

The manager turned for Jason to leave but he didn't budge. The things he could do with the money were turning the cylinders in his head. Then just like that he thought of the words the old man, Pops, had told him and he smiled and said, "Oh yeah, I'm sorry."

Jason and the manager were headed for the side door. The manager nervously said, "I see you're a man of your word. Why don't you take one of these, and check back with me from time to time to see if I have some work for you?"

"You sure?" he asked looking suspicious.

The manager nodded and handed him a pack of the Fruit of the Loom boxer shorts from the sale rack. They were a size too big but Jason didn't care.

It was getting late, and although his parole officer didn't know where he lived, he still followed his curfew. He made it into the house and headed to his quarters. Jason dropped his items on the bed. He had a lot more things to do. His stomach was growling and although he had the money from Pops, he decided to fast for the day. He grabbed a single stick from the bag of incense and the things from his bed and headed for the bathroom. After sticking the lit incense in a small hole in the wall, he pulled out his scented candle, dropped his bubble bath flakes in the tub, and hung up the new shower curtain.

He submerged his body in the hot water and replayed the power of the day's events. The thoughts from the old man had weighed heavily on him, but the real reason that he had decided not to rob the store was because he didn't want to have to hide and not have the chance to see his goddess again. He realized that time had passed and he knew that he wouldn't be able pull the pieces together with Zeida. She probably was married anyway he figured.

But his goddess wasn't. And if he never saw her again he knew now what he would be working toward, a woman like her. Beneath his eyelids, he recaptured her face. He promised himself to be on point if they ever crossed paths again.

Twenty-2

Jill had reached a breaking point. She had become so hard-up for a man, namely Cashmere, that she had almost done the unthinkable. She realized that she was not in her right mind when she rode the elevator up to the fat bastard's room. The entire time she tried to convince herself that this would be the only time that she would do anything like this for him. If she could really get the cowboy to cum in his tight pants without touching him, then her reward would be worth it. What she didn't realize until she stepped off of the elevator was that the cowboy had a few tricks in store for her. As she wandered around the floor looking for his room she saw a group of four more white men enter a room, all rough looking types and one even had a video camera. She casually stepped back and watched them enter.

When she saw the number on the door as she walked up on it, she realized that she had set herself up to be raped or even possibly killed. It took the shock of that to cause her to snap out of her craziness. She stood looking at the door trembling for a second before she ran for the elevator. When she reached the lobby, she didn't know whether or not to call the police or a cab. She was a complete wreck.

"Ju okay, meeze?" the cabdriver asked as he drove her to Brooklyn.

Jill only nodded as she whimpered uncontrollably in the back of the cab. When she got home she downed half a bottle of wine before crawling across her bed. Before she could fall asleep the phone rang. "Hello," she answered.

"I see you don't have what it takes," Cashmere's voice came through her line.

"Fuck you, you piece of shit. I'm not one of your whores and never will be."

"You watch your tone, young lady. I have every right to be upset with you. You disappointed the cowboy. I had to send a couple of my other girls over there to compensate. But, hey I want to give you a chance to make it up to me."

Jill was irate but kept her cool not wanting him to know that she'd been shattered into pieces, "Listen, I appreciate the offer but if you ever contact me again I will inform the FBI of your little organization and give them your tag numbers which I've written down and your real name," she said assertively.

First came a low, sinister chuckle. "Cashmere is not afraid of the authorities," he said coolly.

"Yeah, well maybe Shirley Whittenburg Junior is."

"Hey, now listen sweetheart, there's no need..."

"Like I said, don't ever contact me again," she shouted and hung the phone up on him. She was changing her number the first thing in the morning. Jill had cried herself to sleep in disappointment. She couldn't deny that she had hoped to be making love to Cashmere instead of threatening him.

A week later and things were back to normal, almost. The day before Jill had run her weekly errands and resumed working out. She had come to some realizations and made some tough changes.

First she had gotten rid of all of her sex toys and porn. She had decided that she needed to be strong and not ready to jump at the first hard dick she came across. A vow of celibacy until the man proved worthy, or at least checked out, would make a lot of sense. She might even hand out an application. *Check here if pimping, drug use, homosexuality or prison is in your past.* She laughed when she said that she might even have to recount the bit about prison.

Second, she decided that even though she'd had the bad experience or nightmare with Cashmere, she was still going to make an effort to get out and start meeting people.

Third, she was going to become more involved in the business that her husband had left her to be more constructive with her time. She had done so little with her life simply because she had the money to sit back and collect. If nothing else there were at least some sick children she could spend time with.

As noon approached, Jill was feeling sleepy and she prepared to take a nap. No sooner than she shut her eyes, the phone rang in her quiet loft and disturbed her. In a sleepy voice she asked into the receiver, "Diane, I'm tired. Can I call you back?"

"Why, you gonna act like you up all night wit a mahn?"

"There you go again."

"What? I know you not still blamin'..."

"No, I'm not blaming you, but *I was* up all night."

"Wha? You let him back in?"

"No, I couldn't sleep. I threw Mandingo and the rest of my gadgets away. I need sexual discipline girl."

"You coulda send dem to me. It not like you and somebody else use dem, plus you hardly get ta use the right way."

The two friends laughed then Jill said, "I'm telling you. The one night I tried to get to sleep without an orgasm, my body rebelled against me. I'm telling you, I swear my eyelids were on strike and I was so tempted that I had to pray. I think I'm going to switch my workouts to nights or workout twice a day or something?"

"Any ting good always hard to do."

"Don't I know it? My body is craving so much that every time you say the word *hard* only one thing pops in my mind. I better get a man quick cause I don't know what I'm a do at this rate."

"You have somebody in mind?"

"No, but did I tell you about this man that I think was stalking me?"

"Sound hot, tell me more."

"It's the funniest thing. I went to see aunt Lana and I saw him. He was tall and built real well, but he looked homeless or strung out on something. I'm still trying to figure out which it was."

"You talkin' bout a bum in de street? Oh my, gal I tink you are desperate fe real."

"No, it's not that. It was weird because honestly he was too clean and too fine to be a bum. He was black or mixed or something 'cause he was a few shades lighter than me, but he had the most beautiful blue eyes I ever saw. I *never* saw blue eyes on a brother before. His hair was dark brown but he had like a reddish freaky tint to it. It was exotic, and he freaked me out 'cause he wasn't dirty or anything, and when I went for a closer look he was gone."

"One time me did have a damn good customer who favor de mahn you a just describe. What him name again? John? No Jay, yes, Ja-son. De boy fine, him fine, him fine. De mahn so fine me was ready to give him some and you know say me never let a mahn touch dis yet. Me wonder wha happen to him cause him just disappear. But you know how dem money-mahn stay, dem either dead are dem go a jail fe a long time."

"Well girl that man was a freak of nature. Just thinking about him gets... I ain't going there so lets change the subject," she caught herself. "I'm not leaving this house until Wednesday, I got a lot to do. I decided to stop doing the pony or *donkey-tail* thing so make sure you got a good style for me."

"It's about time. Me see you a take a new lease pon life, huh? That's good. Listen, me have a client, call you later, one love."

Jill hung up the phone grateful that she had a friend like Diane. She replayed the conversation in her head, and wondered how a black man could have blue eyes. She dismissed the thought and closed her eyes to go back to sleep, but that wasn't working. She cut on the TV and turned it to CNBC to check on her stocks. While the reporters discussed the Standard and Poors 500 Index, thoughts of Cashmere entered her mind so she changed the channel. She channel surfed for a few and stopped at the learning channel. *A Baby's Story* was on and she sat the remote control on the bed.

For an hour she watched as the pregnant women went through each stage of their pregnancies. She saw how the babies were born, and she wondered if she would ever be a mother to a child. Thoughts of the two rooms downstairs haunted her.

She then opened the windows in her loft and started cleaning up. An hour later she headed down to the rooms of the kids she never had and that's when the drama began.

She cleaned the girl's room and everything was fine. When she went into the boy's room, thoughts of having children, what she saw on television, and feelings of inadequacy filled her body. She reminded herself that her biological clock was ticking and that she had to have some validation of her life. She began to cry uncontrollably. Her sobs brought her to her knees. Her legs were shaking while she thought of how lonely her life really was. She asked herself if she died how many

20

people in her family would even show up at the funeral, and she could only think of her aunt Lana, and that wasn't a definite.

She wondered what was wrong with her and why was there such a shortage of good men. She asked herself if she should go out and get a job, or start running Clayton Realty on her own. She felt that maybe if she went to work everyday then maybe that would fill the void in her life, or maybe she could meet a progressive man to share her life with. Jill was upset, and with no where else to go, she decided to head back to bed.

Twenty-3

Jason was giving himself a pep talk while getting dressed in the mirror. *All you got to do Jay is walk right up to her and tell her that you think she is the most beautiful woman in the world. Focus, when she replies, tell her that you would like to get to know her better, and that's it. You got this.*

Staring at his reflection, he even wished that he had a pair of clippers so he could cut his hair. But he had too many other needs to concern himself with spending twenty dollars on a cut. That morning he was up and ready to change his life. He wanted to take his destiny into his own hands that day by making something positive happen. The woman he'd seen the day before stayed on his mind. He envisioned that he would see her again and when he did he was going to approach her and convince her to take him seriously.

Peter poked his head into Jason's room before he left, "You doing alright, homey?"

"Yeah, I'm fine," Jason lied.

"Cool. Yo, I heard your man Harold the king ganked another cat for his belongings. The same way he got you. Homeboy went off and tried to issue him a beating."

"Oh yeah," Jason said getting angry all over again.

"Yeah, but the cops just happened to be right there on the scene and they locked the nigga up. Homey got sent back to the pen. Well, I'm out. I got moves to make. I see you still looking for a job, huh?" Peter pointed to his suit.

"Yeah, still looking."

"Good luck, I'm out," the youngster gave Jason a pound and hit the streets as he often did from sun up to way after sun down.

Once Peter left, he looked around at the house and thought about the situation. If Peter was doing the impossible, living like a king, even though he was technically a homeless delinquent, then why couldn't he? When he came to the notion that there was *no* reason, his will was fortified.

With the same suit that he'd worn for days without cleaning, he headed up to Broadway with the intentions of meeting the woman of his dreams. Thoughts of Zeida were now the farthest thing from his mind. He prayed that he wasn't being silly in his pursuit knowing that in his predicament, he shouldn't have been concentrating on a woman. Not once was he directed to give up his hope of seeing the woman. Instead, the voice in his head told him that she would in fact be his angel. The idea that his search for Zeida had led him to this woman seemed to warm him inside.

When he reached Broadway, it was 10:30 a.m. He knew the woman he was looking for passed by around noon the day before. He had two hours to spare, but he didn't want to miss her in case she changed her time. He had considered walking into the flower shop to ask the owner who the beautiful lady was, but he was afraid of the description she would give of him.

Sitting on the crate, Jason convinced himself that his dingy suit wasn't dirty. Although the slight stains and the wrinkled white shirt were noticeable to everyone else, in his mind it wasn't all that bad. His hair was getting longer by the day, and his beard was at least three inches long. The fact that he hadn't worn deodorant in days didn't help at all.

He sat under the canopy of the fruit stand again. When his anxiety took over he stood and walked over to the steps of the subway station. He continuously looked down to see if she was coming up. His mind bounced around a few theories as to why she hadn't shown up. Maybe she was a professor or a student at Columbia. He considered going up to the campus to look around but didn't want to take the chance of not seeing her if she showed up so he planted a seat on the milk crate and promised himself that he wasn't moving until she arrived.

By noon he was pacing back and forth while watching the clock that hung in the window of the fruit stand. He reasoned that she was on her way so he walked to the far corner and headed back towards the fruit stand. This was for the sake of making it seem like they were crossing paths, and it wouldn't seem like he was waiting for her. After pacing for an hour, his stomach was growling. He hadn't eaten in two days.

By three o'clock, he reasoned that she wasn't coming and was ready to give up. He walked over to the flower shop. When he stepped inside to inquire about her, he lost his nerve and walked right back out. He walked back towards the subway and took a glance down the steps but the woman was no where in sight.

Not even realizing how much time had slipped by, Jason's stomach was flipping off beat when six o'clock came. The rush hour traffic cluttered the sidewalk. By then, his suit had new lines in it, he was exhausted and he'd finally made up his mind that it was time to eat.

At the diner on 110th Street, he sat at the corner booth ready to order a special. The waitresses that were working didn't want to serve him. They assumed the bum in the corner booth didn't have money to pay for the food let alone to leave a tip. Before he was allowed to place his order, Jason had a visit from the cook.

The Greek man showed up with a meat cleaver in his hands asked Jason to show him his money. When he pulled out the crumpled twenty-dollar bill, the man turned and said, "Sorry, we get a lot of people in here who run out on the bill. No offense."

The nervous waitress came over with a fake smile to take his order. "It wasn't my idea," she said.

Jason's face showed no expression. He was beginning to get a headache from the hunger. Otherwise he would have left. Jason ordered a bowl of vegetable soup, a tuna sandwich with a side order of fries, and a tall cup of fresh-squeezed orange juice in a take out cup. While he was impatiently waiting for his food to arrive, he daydreamed about his past life.

He thought of the money that he had back in the day, the way he used to spend it recklessly, and how he had nothing to show for it. He thought of how he was doing time and lost his home because it wasn't even in his right name. Then he compared his past life to the way he was living in the present. Right there he broke down and cried to keep the anguish from sending him over the edge.

The tears poured down his cheeks. Everyone that heard his loud sobs assumed he was mentally disturbed. Jason sat at the table with his head down and with his hands holding onto both sides of his hair. The pressure was too much for one man to take. The emotions from the day before combined with his misery for the day had taken their toll. When the waitress delivered the food to him, she fearfully sat it on the table and rushed away. He sat wondering how he had been reduced to the level of a third class citizen.

Jason paid his bill and asked for another orange juice to go. Three dollars was all he had left so he left it on the table as a tip. His nervous waitress saw him leave the tip and a genuine smile surfaced on her face. She remembered the tears he cried, so she ran out of the restaurant to catch him.

Jason was standing in a trance on the corner with his newly emptied cup. As he was shaking around the ice in the bottom of the cup he felt something drop into it. When he looked up he saw the waitress smiling at him. "You're such a sweet man. Thank you, but I think you need it more than me. I hope you find your way," she said.

He spun ready to protest but a passerby, who resembled a professor, dropped loose change into his cup. He was offended by their gesture and he didn't know what to do because panhandling was below his moral code.

Just like that another passerby dropped change, followed by another one with a bill. On many occasions in the past he had dropped hundred dollar bills into the cups of the poor. He had looked down on them, now here he was officially a part of the panhandling union. When he was ready to stop collecting donations, he reasoned that at first he had nothing, and that cup gave him something, so he better stay there and collect the acts of charity.

When stores on Broadway closed, Jason began his journey towards Manhattan Avenue, still holding his cup out in front of him as he walked. A small bulge was in his pocket and he saw that his appearance caused people to continue giving. He had no idea that people gave as much as they did, so he had a new agenda for the next day. He was going to panhandle until a job came along and he had a sure-fire way to get the attention of the woman he was searching for. Nineteen dollars and fifty-four cents was his take for the day. He wondered how much he would have made if he'd started earlier.

It had been close to ten years since her husband's death, and the thought had never entered Jill's mind to do what she was thinking. Sharief's clothes were still enclosed in preserving bags in the closet. She felt the day had come to let them and him go. *If you're going to move on with your life, then there's no time like the present,* she said aloud.

Jill cut off Sunny, her favorite deejay on Hot 97, and put in her Rachelle Ferrelle CD. The words to the song, *"You Send Me"*, moved her to make a change. It was time to clean. Ridding herself of her past ties wouldn't mean destroying memories. It would merely give her the strength to create new beginnings.

Singing the words to the song she grabbed his suits first. She found many unworn, still with price tags. She carried ten at a time down to the bedroom on the bottom floor. By the third trip she had a large stack lying on the bed. She found shoes by the dozens and couldn't remember Sharief having so many pairs.

Her mind began to drift to the days leading up to his funeral. The incredible trials she gone through when she found out that Sharief had had other 'kept' women. A couple of them had even had the nerve to contest his will.

She began to feel guilty because she felt like she didn't pay close enough attention to the details of her husband's life and had perhaps pushed him to wander. As she made the last few trips up and down the steps Jill wondered how many other women had his clothes in their closets and had gone through the exact same thing that she was. She easily beat back the anger and continued to move the last of his things. She piled all the shoes she could in three empty North Beach Leathers shopping bags. It took her over an hour to clear his entire wardrobe. The bed was lost in the large pile.

Jill went back to the bedroom where she wiped down the closet shelves. With the first part of the task done, she placed all of her husband's jewelry with hers. She exited the closet and walked around to her mini-fridge for something to drink.

On the ground floor, she became overtaken with emotions as she pondered what to do with all of his clothing. It wouldn't make much sense to simply store it in the closet of the basement bedroom.

She went through all of the pockets in each suit. By the time she was done she'd collected a dozen cigars, a stack of business cards, phone numbers, a couple of lighters, a switch blade and $777 in cash. The phone numbers grasped her attention. They were the names of women who tried to be with her husband, Jill was sure.

Looking over at the pile of clothing, she noticed an envelope that she'd missed when going through his clothes. It was sliding out of the pocket of one of his suit jackets. She walked over grabbed it. There was a letter written on hotel stationary. It was a letter addressed to her, dated three days before Sharief's death.

My Queen Jill,

I'm sitting here in the lobby of the Waldorf with probably my last stiff glass of Remy Martin. I just left the doctor's and they've told me for he last time that there's nothing else they can do. I need to stop smoking cigars and drinking immediately. Even still, I could last one hour, or one year. In either case, I don't want to risk not putting these words down for you.

Jill, when I first saw you, I knew I had to have you in my life. You made me feel young again. Though you had no money, you offered me something so much more valuable. You gave me purpose and value. We have been so connected in so many ways since that day. Through the ups and downs. I may have accomplished much, but one thing is true, and that is that I was most proud of being your husband. I can truly say that you have been my true soul mate.

I know now that my time, our time, here on this Earth is nearly done. I'm sick in body, yet well in heart because I've known you and I've felt true love. It has been an incredible blessing to have you as my wife. I am leaving you well taken care of. Be respectful, but please don't mourn me for too long. While I love you dearly, it would sadden me for you to stop living your life because I'm no longer with you in the physical.

Only do me the honor of one thing, after I'm gone, that is. Make sure that any man you choose will be worthy. Never settle. I truly pray that when I'm gone that you find happiness and be with someone who lives to please you the way I wish I still had the time to do. Remember, Jill I changed your life and gave you something when you had nothing. I know I never talked about it, and I'm not saying it now for any reason other than to teach you. Allah did the same thing for me. Now with whatever I leave you, I hope you reach out and give something to someone that has nothing in the material sense.

I ask that you forgive me for any pain I may have caused. I'm leaving you soon and it was just too difficult to tell you these words.

Loving you always,

Sharief

The tears poured from her eyes. She calculated the time the letter was written. Sadly, it would be the last time she saw her husband alive. Right after they had an argument. She had always wanted to know how he really felt about her. Now that she knew, there was no way for her to tell him that although she was never really in love with him, she appreciated everything he did for her.

At that moment, the words to the song that played in the background, *'You can't get until you learn to start giving'* put a beating on her soul. She raced to the phone. Before she heard the dial tone, she punched Diane's number.

Twenty-5

Jason got dressed early so he could catch the morning rush hour pedestrians. He needed eleven more dollars to take care of what he wanted to accomplish for the day. Jason wondered if he would violate parole if he was caught panhandling as he walked the block headed for Broadway, with what he now considered his lucky cup. When he had nothing, that cup gave him something. With just a few hundred dollars, he was sure he would be able to get on his feet.

On the bustling corner of 110th Street, he was the new charity event. He placed the fifty-four cents he had from the day before into the cup and shook it around. He kept his nineteen dollars in the cheap shoes that were beginning to wear out. Harold the king swaggered by on his way to the dump he called a palace, placed a dollar in his cup, and looked at Jason with a smirk. Jason was too focused to lose his cool. What Harold did not know was that he was helping him reach his goal.

He was hot as hell, but kept his suit on, figuring that people would be more willing to give to someone that looked more respectable. His new darker skin made his blue eyes standout more. At certain times his eyes looked gray, and at others, green. Either way they had always had a hypnotic effect on people. He fixed them on quite a few women who all incidentally wound up dropping money into his cup. Some even tried to see past the dirt and grime to gaze at the handsome face buried beneath nearly four weeks of losses and trials. Jason didn't care that the woman all saw him as a bum, his focus was set only on one woman and now he hoped she didn't walk by before he made the money he needed.

By noon he took a short stroll towards Amsterdam Avenue on 109th Street. He placed all of the cash he received on the sidewalk. He had earned $41.32. He felt like he had hit the lotto.

His new found riches added an extra pep to his step. To complete his task all he needed now was an accomplice. Walking along, he spotted Peter swaggering on the other side of Broadway.

"Yo Peter," Jason yelled from across the street.

Peter walked with his two employees and seemed to be breaking in a third. He stood admiring Pete's business savvy and believed that the young man could easily run a legitimate business given proper training. Peter looked like a real boss in a brand new, bright-red, sweat suit with a red Yankee's cap. His little hands heeded his workers to stop. "What up?"

"I need to ask you something real quick."

Peter looked at his watch, "Make it quick, I got something to do."

"I need a favor," Jason asked in desperation.

"Listen man," he spoke in an all business tone. Jason was a little shocked when Peter asked, "Don't you think I'm doing enough for you?" Then he added, "I hope this ain't about the rent, 'cause homey I can't go any lower."

"No, it's not that. I need you to go on a little mission *for me.*" Jason looked around realizing that he was in the vicinity of where he'd seen his angel. So he quickly scanned the area to see if his queen was coming.

Peter frowned as a passerby dropped money in Jason's cup. "Boss, you out here begging for shorts? Are you crazy? Man, if I would of known things was that bad for you, I would'a gave you a job. As a matter of fact, I'm about to tell that old timer over there that he's fired, so I can make room for you."

Jason stopped Peter in his tracks, touched by his empathy. Peter said, "We about to go down to the Ritz-Carlton and put in some work. My peeps tell me that they are replacing a bunch of televisions and the drivers get real sloppy when they get deliveries like that for the right price. So the more hands I got the better. So drop that cup and come on get some real paper."

Jason pointed diagonally across the street to Lana's shop and said, "Listen, I told you I'm not going back to prison and I'll do *anything* before I do that. Just do me a favor. Go in that flower shop, tell the old lady in there that you're looking for a sister, well she might be Puerto Rican, or even Dominican…," Jason rambled and caught himself. "Just say you're looking for a woman that's beautiful and came in on Wednesday. She was wearing a pink cap, jeans, and a tee shirt. *Nobody,* and I mean *nobody* else that goes in there looks like her." Jason handed him the money and said, "Take this. Tell her you want to buy the lady two dozen yellow long stem roses and you want them to stay at the shop until she shows up. Then tell her to put, 'to my angel from Jason' on the card."

Peter's face shriveled like a prune as he stared at the money. "Nucca is you bonkers? You ready to trick out when you ain't got a dime? And damn, you can at least buy some deodorant and get you some clothes? Why can't you go over there?"

Jason looked at Peter and they both looked at Jason's attire before he said, "Come on, please, man. I need you to do this for me."

Peter looked at his appearance and got the message. "Aw'ight, I got you. You lucky I like you." He nodded towards his employees and said, "But keep your eyes on those three. I'll be right back."

Jason put his panhandling mission on hold and watched Peter go into the store. He waited filled with anticipation. As Peter walked back towards him he turned his back to avoid the woman's eyesight.

"Shit, I never been interrogated by anybody like that in my life," Peter said. "Them old women in there put more pressure on me than the police. I went in there and did what you *told* me to do. Then I had to go through twenty-one questions. The chick you looking for is the owner's niece. Her name is Jill. She didn't even want to accept the dough unless I told her who you was." Peter laughed and elbowed Jason in the ribs. "You know I had to do the damn thing and not rat you out? So holla at your boy 'cause I ran that Gucci game on dem. They in there thinking you my boss, some big time executive or something. I want to see this bitch. If she got a nucca going hungry just so she can have some flowers that's gone die anyway, she gotta be banging."

Jason grabbed Peter's wrist with a firm grip. "Don't call *her*, or any respectable woman, that. How would you like someone calling your mother that?" he said defensively.

Peter twisted his lips and said, "My moms *is* a worthless bitch." He saw the seriousness in Jason's face and added, "But I got you, Boss. I hear where you comin' from. All y'all brothers go up north and come home on some black power stuff. But I got you, son. It's all good, no disrespect but watch that grip."

Jason quickly let him go and said, "My bad. I didn't mean to grab you like that."

He looked down at his wrist that was growing numb. "Can I go now? If it's alright with you, I'm going to get some real paper, so yo, I'll catch you later."

Jason waited patiently for his angel, Jill. Now that his one goal was achieved he looked forward to the next scheme. He was excited knowing that Jill would soon know of his existence. For him that was all that mattered, at least until he had the opportunity to stage the big approach.

By the end of the night, he was well fed. He had twenty-two dollars in his pocket. He headed home with his proceeds from his day of begging. When he reached Manhattan Avenue, he noticed a crowd gathered by the house. The street was filled with paramedics and cop cars. Peter was hiding behind a tree and when Jason crept over to him he tapped Peter on his shoulder. "Daymmn, man. You *scurred* the hell out of me," he whispered in a tone that showed his excitement.

"What happened to the house, youngblood?" Jason asked, trying to hide like Peter, but from what he didn't know.

"Man, Imani just popped me on my cell and told me that Grady died in his sleep."

Jason eyes widened. "Grady? Damn, how did he die?"

"What you mean how he die? His damn heart stopped beating, that's how." Peter shook his head and said, "You bugged out. He dead man, that's all that matters, and police is all up in *my* crib."

Jason could see that Peter was holding back tears. He loved the old dude. "So where's Imani? Is she okay?" he asked changing the subject.

Peter pointed down the block. "Look, she sitting in the police car. Damn, I got to get to my stash. I got five gees up in that spot and I got to get it, like right now."

"Five gees?" Jason asked in shock. "Imani didn't get a chance to grab it? What you think they'll do to her?"

Peter went into a silent zone without answering him. Jason could tell that he was plotting on something. "Listen man, my baby is a trooper. We planned things like this out a hundred times. She can do the impossible, so I'm not worried about her right now. You wouldn't even believe me if I told you about her. But right now, I got to get to my stash."

"So how come Imani didn't get the stash?"

"She only got one hand man. And that ain't part of the plan. She the boss of the crib and what she says go. She know we gonna survive regardless of what. But my fake papers, ID's, and what she need to stay up in another hotel for a few weeks is all we need in an emergency situation."

"So what we gonna do?"

"*We*? I ain't French, homey. What *I'm* gonna do is move all my stuff out that spot and drop it in storage. You on your own now, homey. I'm just as homeless as you are, but the difference between me and you is, I know how to stay in one of them five stars without being noticed. I got my man coming with a U-haul from the Bronx. They are going to board this spot up in a minute and bounce. When they do I'm breaking back into *my* crib. We need the help because I got to get rid of them flat screens I got the other day so if you want you can go get all the stuff in your room and keep it, sell it, whatever, but I know your scary ass is worried about parole, so the choice is yours. Poe-poe is moving. I'm gone, man."

Jason stood there watching Peter make his way to what he felt was his home. *"Yeah you right man, you are so right,"* he said sadly.

With no one to help him, and not enough money in his pocket to do anything serious about his situation, he sat on the crate in front of the Regency Hotel. He refused to walk in. For the whole night, he sat dealing with the reality that he was homeless all over again.

For days Jason, panhandled until he couldn't stand on his feet anymore. When he got to the point of exhaustion, he would walk down to Riverside Drive and nap on the park benches. He was unable to shower, shave, or take care of his hygiene. He would use the toilet and make futile attempts of washing up in the bathroom of the diner where he ate his meals. He purchased a toothbrush and deodorant that he carried in a small brown bag. He continued to tell himself that he was homeless and not worthless. On two occasions he was ready to go back to the Regency. He was sure that if he went back that he was going to wake up in jail from killing Harold, so he felt the park bench was safer. Jason was under the impression his parole officer had already found out that he was homeless and was going to violate him. On Wednesday morning he made up his mind that he was going to report. Whatever the man did to him he was going to deal with it. At least he knew he didn't break the law and that was all that mattered. If he was violated then he would tell his story to the judge. He couldn't believe that a man who had lived by the code of the streets was ready to trust in the mercy of the courts.

Early that morning he made an attempt to clean himself up, but his clothes were moldy and his shoes had given out on him. The right one now had a hole in it. He looked at himself in the restaurant mirror and thought of his man Webb. While staring at the reflection he told the image that looked back at him that he was a soldier. When he stepped out the diner he was all set to take the train downtown, but first he had something to do.

The brass chimes to the flower shop rang as Jason walked in. He approached the counter. The two women behind the counter stared at him. "Excuse me, I'd like to buy a dozen orchids please," he said as he pulled the money from his pocket.

The taller lady frowned at his disheveled appearance. She stood a few steps back with her hand on a baseball bat. When she recognized that the money he held was legit, she suspiciously filled his order.

Jason cleared his throat. "I was wondering if I could leave a message and have them delivered?"

He was reluctantly handed a gift card. "Here, fill this out and tell us the address and the name of the person."

Jason wrote and the cashier was amazed at his penmanship as his hands glided across the card. The note read, '*You are my angel, here to save me. I'm sorry I couldn't see you face to face, and I may be gone for awhile, but I'll be back for you one day. Until then, please enjoy this small token from me and know that love can be found.*

Truly,
Jason

"You didn't write an address," she said.

"Oh, the address won't be necessary, I need it to be delivered here to a customer of yours named Jill," he said handing her the card.

"Jill?" Lana asked in shock. "That's my niece. For the past few days this man named Jason has been sending in gifts for her. Now he sent you in here too? Well my lord, I'm sure glad she'll be here today to get all this. What type of man delivers flowers to a damn flower shop? Okay, tell him you did your job. What's the matter, he ain't got the nerve enough to walk up in here?"

Jason shrugged his shoulders and tried to slow the pace of his heartbeat. When he heard that she was going to be there that day, he almost passed out. He turned from the counter and walked out of the shop, never responding to her question.

He stood out front and actually contemplated his options. The chance to see Jill, or his parole officer. Jill was not a sure thing right now. And he had to clear up his parole situation. So unless he wanted to risk his chances of having her in his life at all, he knew he had to drag himself to the parole office.

It was 9:30 a.m. when he reached the parole office. He walked in the door and Mr. Townsend sat waiting for him. He took one look at Jason. "Wow, I see you couldn't do nothing with that mumbo jumbo you were running on me, huh? Have a seat, I've been waiting to see you, because I have some news for you, smart guy."

Jason eased in the seat. He folded his legs and hands waiting to hear his punishment.

"I went by the Regency Hotel. Harold and me got along real well. He gave me some valuable information on you. I see that he likes you, but you were a bad boy. He said that he heard that you were sleeping on the streets, and from what I can see, he heard right. The problem with that is it means you've violated your curfew," Mr. Townsend paused. "Ow," he said, grabbing his heart.

"You alright?" Jason asked feigning concern.

"Yeah, better than you. It's just gas. Now back to what I was saying. Your curfew is given to you for a reason. I was waiting for you to get arrested, but since that didn't happen, I'm sure you got away with what you did, for now. Since a precinct didn't notify me, today is your lucky day. See, Harold and me worked out a way for you to stay put. All you have to do is go to the Regency and he has a job for you. From there you can get a room and get yourself together. This wasn't my idea and I'm ready to violate you, but I'll let you do it to yourself. It looks better for me at the end of the year if I keep you straight but most of you guys ain't worth the effort. Let's take a walk."

Jason followed the man into a bathroom. Once inside, Mr. Townsend pulled out his gun and handed Jason a small specimen cup. Jason stared at the gun, unsure of why he had it out.

Mr. Townsend said, "Piss in that, and if you try to run, I will lay you down like a dog. Make it quick."

"Sir, do you think I'm on drugs?"

"Never mind what I think. Just do what I said and don't try anything." Jason complied and reached for his zipper. Mr. Townsend walked up behind him in the toilet stall and put the gun to the back of his head. He peeked over to see Jason's penis in his hand before he said, "I want to make sure you're not dropping any vinegar or water from a balloon. I learned that one from this Spic I had once. Boy you animals come up with a new twist everyday. Come on and shake it quick."

Nervous at first, Jason became numb, tired of Mr. Towsend's shit. He couldn't urinate because of the pressure he felt. He managed to get a small stream out. When Mr. Townsend saw the yellow liquid he said, "That's more than enough, come with me."

He walked Jason back to his office. He then pulled out his handcuffs and hooked him to the railing. Once both of Jason's hands were immobile, the parole supervisor walked in with another officer.

The supervisor nodded at Jason. "We're just going to test your urine. If you're clean, you can leave, if not, you know the rest." A female officer was assigned to watch Jason, until the test was completed.

"Mr. Townsend and I will be back in a short while," the supervisor promised.

Jason closed his eyes. He thought about the things he could have done differently when he first got out and about the guys that would laugh at him when he returned to the prison. Then Jill came to mind, he felt relieved knowing that one day, he would have her in his life.

In what seemed like an hour, the men returned. The supervisor uncuffed him. "Well, you're clean. I reviewed your file and I see that we only have you for a few more months. I see you haven't broken the law, and that's good, son. A lot of men would have, before they let themselves go. So, Mr. Faust, you will follow the guidance of Mr. Townsend. You have twenty days or so before the month is out. By then, I'm sure Mr. Townsend will have you on track, or back to the slammer you go. It's all in your hands." He nodded to the other two parole officers. "He's excused."

Jason looked over at Mr. Townsend who was still holding his chest and wondered if perhaps all the hatred inside of him was giving him heartburn. He walked out the door thrilled that he had been given another chance.

Jason walked into the Regency. He was determined to deal with whatever came his way. At least he had secured somewhere to live. When he walked through the door, Harold was sitting at the desk. "My man, freaky eyes. I see you back, huh? What's up, my man?"

"I just came from my P.O. so run it down to me."

"Yeah, man, that Mr. Townsend. A good man, I like a man I can reason with. I hope he told you that I saved your ass, huh? Well, well, I see they always come back to the king." He chuckled, but Jason's face showed contempt. He truly wanted to strangle Harold. "Okay, this is the run down, I don't need your help, but Mr. Townsend ain't got to know that. Him and me worked it out so you gonna pay me twenty dollars a day starting Monday. You want a room, that's fifty a day. Stay out as long as you want 'cause I'm your new curfew and parole officer. As long as you pay, everything is all right downtown. If you don't pay, I call the cops on your bummy ass, and you go back to the pen. I got you covered homeboy, now you can get out my face and have that money for me on Monday."

Jason laughed to himself, looked at Harold and said, "So let me get this right. You want me to pay you everyday without having a room, and if I don't, you call the police? No job, no room, and I still got to pay?"

Harold kicked his feet up. "Sheeeit, you learn quick cuz..."

Jason was out of the hotel before Harold had a chance to finish his statement. In a fit of anger, he threw his suit jacket and tie in the garbage can on the corner. He walked across the street, over to the man in the bar that he used to work for. He asked the owner for work and his request was fulfilled immediately. For two hours he scrubbed the walls, and cleaned the dirty glasses from the night before. By the time he was done, he locked the bathroom door and took all of his clothes off. He used a half of bottle of hand soap and cleaned himself from head to toe.

He dried himself off with the paper towels from the bathroom, and threw away the soiled underwear, socks, and tee shirt that he wore for days. He exited, with his pay in mind. The owner paid him salary plus ten dollars extra. With the sixty dollars in hand, Jason raced down to Lenox Avenue.

He remembered the Salvation Army on Lenox from the time he sought employment at Harlem Hospital. When he walked through the door everyone inside could tell that Jason needed all of the salvation they he could get.

There were piles of clothes in wooden bins all over the place. It looked to Jason like a group from a church had just dropped off some clothes so he headed in that direction. He found two button down shirts and tucked them under his arm. He then looked for a suit, and after putting five against his body to size them up, he found a half-decent one that looked like it would fit. He picked up two pairs of socks and found a decent pair of wingtip shoes that looked like they were worn just a few times. He searched around for a small bag, and found an old Avon gift bag. He walked up to the register and all of his items came up to $22.00. He found a place in the back where he could change his clothes, and when he stepped out, he looked like a new man. Another mission accomplished.

On his way back up to Broadway, he stopped into a discount store and picked up a new toothbrush, toothpaste, deodorant, a small wash cloth, and a pack of boxers.

When he reached the diner on 110th Street, he placed his order for a fish burger deluxe, a double order of fries, a milk shake and an apple pie. The waitress didn't hesitate to put his order in. With his cosmetics in his Avon bag, he headed for the public bathroom.

Just like every other respectable customer, he walked into the bathroom and took his suit jacket off. None of the men saw anything strange with his behavior, but when he began to remove his pants in front of the mirror, the men made a quick exit. Jason slipped on a new pair of underwear, feeling like a new man. He then washed under his arms again and applied deodorant. Feeling even fresher, he stepped back into the diner.

After gobbling down his meal, he left a five-dollar tip for the waitress. She didn't protest or make the effort to give it back that time. Now that his stomach was full, the next part of Jason's plan had to go into action.

He walked around the corner to Amsterdam Avenue and headed uptown. He walked with the confidence he had back when he was in the life of crime. When he reached his destination, he turned into the Columbia University campus and headed for the library. He sat in the library under the small lamps and read a newspaper. By closing time, he walked into the bathroom and waited. By the time everyone was out he slipped back into the library and moved into the corner and fell asleep. The cool air conditioning and the plush lounge chair would do just fine for the night. A handful of students trickling in broke his sleep. He got up and left.

For four days Jason hustled the bar, the supermarket, the fruit stand, and he panhandled in his clean suit. By Monday morning, he paid Harold his money for two additional days in advance. On Wednesday morning, he dressed feeling something special in the air. He purchased a bouquet of wild flowers for Jill, and he decided rain or shine, he was going to introduce himself to the woman of his dreams.

Twenty-6

Jill was so anxious that she woke up at six in the morning and couldn't get back to sleep. Finally she had to call Diane. When Diane got on the line, Jill began to hit her with her story in a rapid-fire sequence.

"Whoa, slow down, gal. First, me can't believe you call *me* so early inna de marning? Is every ting all right?"

"Girl, I can't believe I'm so nervous. For three weeks, this man has been sending me the most beautiful flowers. I swear today I'm gonna finally meet him. I don't know why, but my intuition is telling me that I am going to meet this man today."

"How you know se it no Cashmere?" Diane asked and laughed.

"He got too much of that playa-pimp stuff with him to be that sweet to a lady. Plus this man always signs it as Jason."

"Hum, me tell you before me did have a client name Ja-son. And you tell me de mahn who a stalk you did have blue eye, so it probably de same Ja-son. But den again me know him would never be a bum, plus if you did a get stalk you would see him again, no true?"

"Well, ain't no stalker taking days off, so I don't know who it could be. Think real good Diane, we don't know any other Jason's?"

"Me nuh know no many mahns, so you goose is cook now. Can't believe say a mahn have you a go on so. Serve you ras, you so bright, figure it out child."

"Well whatever I do, I hope he's a good man inside. I gotta go because I want to see if he left me something else. He called me his angel and said 'I was here to save him.' I wonder what that meant?"

"Time eh tell."

"Yeah, you right. Girl, I'ma call you later."

Jill got ready for what she believed to be her special day. Her horoscope confirmed what her spirit told her. The planets were about to send her into a period of new beginnings. But then the horoscopes always said things that were so general that they could mean anything. She went into her closet and prepared for the cool cloudy day. She decided on a pair of Paper Denim Jeans, a lime green tight fitting short sleeved sweater and a pair of multi-colored Jimmy Choo sandals. She grabbed a small Prada backpack and secured her ride.

During the cab ride she had butterflies in her stomach. She had her cell phone in her hand ready to call Lana to find out if Jason had left something there for her. She convinced herself that a surprise would be better, so she didn't call. When the cab pulled onto 110th Street, she rushed out and forgot to pay the cabby. She backtracked, handed the man a fifty-dollar bill and left half the change as a tip.

When she crossed the street, her eyes canvassed the area. She nearly lost her breath when she noticed her blue-eyed stalker as she passed the fruit stand. He was tall and light sporting a rumpled suit. She nervously dug in her bag for her phone.

"Diane, Ohmigod. I just passed the stalker. He's got a different suit on, but he's the same one that was following me before. Girl you got to get me some mace, because he is stealing glances at me like he wants to kill me or something."

When Jill reached the flower shop, Diane asked, "What does his hair look like?"

"Unkempt. That's what."

"No chile, what de color of it?"

Jill turned and nervously looked at him and he was nervously pacing behind her.

"It's brownish red."

"Put him ras pon de phone. Me want to chat to him," Diane demanded.

"No way. What am I supposed to do? He looks like a homeless person. He might run off with my phone."

Diane laughed. "You silly, gal. You got nuff to buy a new one if you right and I'm wrong. Put him pon de line."

The anticipation was killing Jill so she turned around and walked towards the direction of her stalker. Only feet away she said, "Stay on the line in case he attacks me. Hold on… where did he go?" Just like that he'd vanished. Part of her was relieved and part a little scared that she wouldn't find out if he was in fact, the mystery man.

"He's gone," Jill huffed.

"What you mean de mahn is gone? I don't believe you, Jill…"

"Look, I'm crossing the street to go to Aunt Lana's." One more glance and she said, "Wait, let me look back and see...oh shit. He's right behind me and he's got this crazy ass look in his eyes. I'm going into the shop. I'll call you later. Jill started a slight jog when she saw him pick up his pace. She made it in the shop just in time.

Lana gave Jill a big smile and started in immediately. "Oh, good Lord, I don't know what type a man wants flowers delivered to a flower shop, but he sure got the hots for you child. Here take these."

"Wow, they're lovely," Jill said.

Lana handed her the wild flowers. "Listen, I don't never get in your business. Girl whoever this Jason is, he's persistent but shy."

"I just don't know what he's waiting for to reveal himself. It's getting a little creepy."

"Creepy, no. Romantic, yessss. Hell, the man is treating you like a lady and that seduction has even got *my* old juices flowing. You make sure you give that man a chance, you hear?"

"We'll see."

"No *we'll see*. I don't care if he fat, ugly or handicapped. It's about time you start getting some loving in your life and make me some grand nieces and nephews. I'm out your business now, so how you doing otherwise?"

In the safety of the shop, Jill now stood in a trance holding the wild flowers. Her smile was as wide as Broadway and she took her time in the shop expecting to hear from her mystery man that day.

When Jill walked back towards the 1 train on Broadway, she kept her hand on her phone, and her eyes scanned for her stalker. She looked behind her, no stalker. She moved briskly toward the train. Feeling like she was being watched, she suddenly she turned around, and bumped right into a firm chest. Her eyes were glued directly to his. Fearful for her life, she was about to run for the subway. As she moved toward the first step she heard the man say, "Hey, I didn't mean to scare you. I just didn't know they let Queens walk through Harlem."

Jill was so stunned by his words that she spun around, tripped over her own feet and began to fall backwards toward the subway steps. In what seemed like slow motion, her dead husband's words flashed in her head. She felt the firm grip of the stalker grab her by the front of her collar and yank her from a forty step tumble towards certain injury or even death. Her heart began to race. He pulled her towards him, back onto the sidewalk. Once he had her firmly on solid footing he shook his head and said calmly, "There's no way I would allow Mother Nature's work to go to waste and let you harm a hair on that head."

"You…you…you…save…you saved my life," she said catching her breath.

"And you saved mine without even knowing it," Jason replied.

In the middle of the excitement, Jill couldn't believe that she had been so scared of the stalker at first and then after almost falling, she had an urge to use the bathroom.

"I don't get it." She was confused. "So do you know who has been buying me all the flowers?"

"Yes, I guess you can say that," he said with intense disappointment. He peered down at his appearance and understood.

"So who is *he* and where is he?"

He looked away towards the Korean lady who was behind Jill. In a whisper he said, "Right here."

"What? I didn't hear you?"

He looked into her eyes. "*I* said, I'm right here. *I'm* Jason."

Jill's jaws dropped. She couldn't believe what she was hearing. Diane had assured her that the Jason she remembered was a money man and could never have been a bum like the man before her. She looked him up and down and assessed that he looked extremely healthy although scraggly. Didn't resemble a druggie a bit. Trying to piece it all together, she began to speak.

"You just said that I saved your life?" she asked confused.

"Yeah, you did." When he told her that he was ready to give up on everything until he saw her face and felt her spirit, she realized the words she heard coming from him were the most beautiful ones she had ever heard. It bothered her a little that suddenly she found herself lost in his blue eyes. "You…you…called me an angel in your cards and that thing you said about queens walking through Harlem?"

"That was a …"

Jill finished his sentence, "… a play on words."

"Exactly."

Jason smiled showing his teeth and they both laughed briefly. Jason looked away to the oncoming traffic, fighting to maintain his courage. "As far as me saying you're an angel, that's what you are. From the first time I saw you, I can't explain it, but it's like the heavens opened up and dropped you down here just to keep me going."

"I really don't understand all of this?" Jill replied.

Jason surrendered, holding the flowers that she'd dropped in one hand. "I can explain everything if you want." He pointed at the benches. "If you give me five minutes of your time, I'm sure it will all make sense when I'm done."

Jason's polite manner made Jill feel safe. So she figured a few minutes would not matter. Besides, her curiosity got the best of her. She often looked at bums on the street in sympathy wondering how they had gotten there.

"Okay, five minutes is all you got, starting now," she said watching the time.

"Here, sit here." He guided her by the hand.

She kept her hand on her cell phone in case he attacked. Once he saw that she was willing to listen he started. "Okay, this isn't easy, so please bare with me. Your beauty has me mesmerized, so if I stutter, just be patient."

He took three deep breaths and knew he only had one shot at getting to know her. He decided to be completely honest with the notion that a real woman always accepted honesty.

"My name is Jason Faust. I was released from prison a few weeks ago. I was convicted for a crime I didn't commit. Since coming home, I swore never to go back to a life of crime. But there's been one bad break for me after another. I've been reduced to scum. It's been extremely hard but I refuse to break the law and go back to prison."

Seeing he still had her attention he took a deep breath, never breaking eye contact, "I'm a positive person now, but my world seemed hopeless, until I saw you. I know this sounds strange, and I wouldn't believe it myself if I was in your shoes, but I looked at you and saw everything I needed in my life. And I don't know you and don't know if you have a man. I really don't care if you're married, because in my heart, I knew that you were meant to come into my life. I was ashamed of how you would treat a man you perceived as a bum on the street, so I sent you the gifts to speak for me." All other thought fled his mind so he finished with, "I have long ways to go, but I know I'll get there. Now you can leave, laugh, or say what you have to say, but my life is now a lot brighter, and I feel like a weight has been lifted off of my shoulders since I spoke to you."

Jill sat with her mouth open. She was convinced that his words were true, but felt that a healthy man would not allow himself to be reduced to that state no matter what.

"Well my name is Jill ... Jill Franklin-Clayton, I am pleased to meet you. I think what you said was sweet and I really appreciate the flowers but..."

Her phone rang. It was Diane. She had forgotten that she'd left Diane worried. She excused herself to answer the call.

"Gal you have me worried sick and you no call?"

Jill kept looking at Jason and didn't want to talk about him in front of his face. "I'm alright. I'll explain everything when I come down," she said keeping it short.

"Me tink de stalker catch you and take you someplace."

She glanced at Jason cautiously. "Yeah, he did."

"He did?" Diane asked in a state of shock. "Wha you mean he did? You all right? What happen to Ja-son, de flower mahn?"

"I'm talking to him now," Jill whispered into the phone.

"Who? De stalker or Ja-son?"

Jill looked at Jason and then slightly turned her head. "Same person."

"Jeez um peas," Diane wailed. "The man Ja-son is de stalker? The same bum pon de street?"

"Ah huh."

"Him have blue eye and a reddish tint to em hair?"

Jill looked at Jason again almost drowning in his eyes. "Yep."

"Him right there?"

"Ah huh, on the bench."

"Lord a massy, put him pon de phone," Diane yelled.

"Put him on the phone?" Jill blurted out.

"Gal move you backside and put de mahn pon de phone. If him nuh kill you yet then him nah go kill you now. Put him pon de phone."

She looked at Jason again. "Hold on. Here," she said tossing the phone to Jason. "Now I'm gonna sound like the strange one, but my friend wants to talk to you."

Jason was shocked. He hesitantly took the phone from her and looked at it with caution as if it was going to bite him. He placed it to his ear. "Hello?"

"You de mahn called Ja-son?" Diane asked.

"Yes."

"I know a Ja-son one time, but he no sound like you. What you a do wit me friend a send flowers all over de place and a stalk after her?"

Jason's eyes got wide. Jill wondered what Diane could be saying on the other end. He said, "Hold on, hold on. Your voice...is familiar. Is this Diane?"

Jill was shocked. She was sure she never mentioned her friend's name. That's when she heard him ask, "Is this Jamaican Diane that was a beautician on a 125th Avenue on 7th?"

Diane listened closely to his voice. "Blow wow, a you yes. Jaaaay-son. How you doing, boy?"

"Diane, I just went looking for you last week and they gave me a hard time."

She was filled with excitement. Jason had to pull his ear from the phone as Diane shrieked from joy that it was the man she once knew. "Jas-son. Me tink you been dead all dis time."

"No, I have been..."

"No-no-no," she cut him off. "Nuh talk nuh more. Me want to see you now. Pass Jill de phone. I will see you soon."

Jill could hear Diane tell the entire shop that the most handsome man was on his way. Considering Jason's condition, Jill looked into Jason's face and tried to see past the scruff and wear. "Hello," Jill finally said.

"Go catch a cab now and bring Ja-son to me. Ya hear, gal, just hurry up and come." Diane was emphatic.

"Okay, okay," Jill said curious as to why Jason was the cause for such excitement. Jill didn't know what to do or say, so she turned to him and said, "I don't know if you have other things to do, but Diane wants to see you right now. If I show up without you there's going to be hell to pay, and I don't want to go through that, so please consider coming."

Jason shrugged his shoulders and with a joyous smile he said, "Lead the way."

During the ride to Dimple's Jason went into further detail about what he was going through, and how he reached the point of desperation. He told her where he was from and his rise and fall in the life of crime. Jill purposely danced around the fact that he was attracted to her because she was numb. He sounded like a nice guy to her, but when she looked at the dingy suit, the curly Afro, his unkempt beard, and raggedy nails, her mind was having too many emotions for her to understand. So she remained silent.

Diane almost knocked Jill down trying to get to Jason. She hugged and kissed Jason on his cheek, jumping up and down, holding both of his hands. The entire salon was wondering why Diane was kissing on a bum off the street. What they failed to realize was that Diane saw what she was going to create, not what was in front of her.

Immediately she led Jason to her chair. Jill felt jealous pushed off to the side. She thought that some of his story must have been true since he knew Diane the way he did. By the way she carried on had Jill wondering if Diane was changing her sexual preference. Since everyone in the salon had eyes on Diane and Jason, she grabbed a copy of her latest novel *I Shoulda Seen It Coming* by Danette Majette.

"I read that. Loved it," one of the stylists said to Jill.

"It's good right?" Jill responded. But the whole time her eyes were drifting back to the shampoo bowls.

Before Jason had a chance to protest, Diane poured what seemed like a whole bottle of all-natural, peppermint and aloe, Stimulator hair treatment into his hair. Instantly Jason's scalp began to tingle and his sinuses were wide open. She toweled his face, her hands and then stopped to reach into her pants pocket and pulled out her wallet. She pulled out a platinum credit card and handed it to the gay stylist, who was finished for the day. "Honey child, do me a geeganteek favor, tek dis and go to de store and pick out a nice outfit fe me friend. Top to bottom." She then leaned in, "Ja-son what size shoe you wear?"

He was embarrassed. He didn't want to be a burden to anyone so he looked at the gay man and said, "Nah, bro that's alright. I'm okay, Diane."

Diane turned his chair around, and looked right into his face and said, "Listen, Ja-son, you was a special client a mine back inna what... '91 me tink," she said as she shaved his beard and left only a mustache and slight goatee. Diane went on, "Dem time me used to depend pon every cent dat come to me chair. Me did a do bad, bad, bad, and one day dis fine mahn, *you*, come and give me a couple hundred dollar fe cut him hair. Every few days after, you bring fifty or a hundred dollars. I swear to ya, back den, me did need every dime me could get. Now times a little better, so me have fe do unto others, as others do unto me." She turned to Jason and asked, "Now, what bloodclot size shoe you wear?"

"Twelve. I wear a size twelve," Jason said to the gay stylist.

"Girls, watch me work this something fierce. I got you head to toe, love. Give me an hour," he said with a two-finger snap, and switched out the door.

After massaging his scalp with the moisturizer, Diane sent Jason to the spa side of the salon. Two women were waiting for him. When they took off his clothes, they couldn't believe that a man off the streets could have a fine sculpted body like his. The women scrubbed his body with an exfoliating mud soap and lemon solution. They gave him an acupressure massage and touched places that he was sure wasn't a part of the program, but he enjoyed every bit of it. His bones cracked as a result of the hard places he slept. When they turned him over on his stomach he had a full erection.

Diane walked in to see the progress her employee's were having on her client. When she walked in and saw Jason's erection making a tent out of the towel, her eyes were fixated on his large member. She quickly ran out to get Jill, so she could take a peek, but Jill had an attitude, so she left her with her book.

Next, the two women gave Jason a micro-dermabrasion facial, and when they attempted to cut and wax his pubic hairs he stopped them. He stepped out in a robe with a pre-wash solution dripping from his curly Afro and his long beard when he was done. Since his well-defined chest was sticking out of the top of the robe, everyone in the salon looked at him.

All of the excitement, got Jill's attention. She slowly moved the novel from her face. It dropped to the floor along with her bottom lip. *Now this is a man I could take home,* she thought. Jason shined like new money. His skin and face came alive. He had a new glow to him, and Diane hadn't even touched his hair yet. Jill knew how Diane could make a miracle with hair. So she, and everyone else in the shop were dazed at the makeover in progress.

The manicurist came over and began to work on him. Diane had a smile on her face the whole time. Once she did someone's hair, she never forgot the details of it. She knew every swirl of Jason's hair. She reclined his head in her shampoo bowl and gave him a thorough washing using a plastic scalp massager. Her fingers felt so good that Jason couldn't help but moan a little, "Ohhh, wow."

"Feels good, eh mahn," Diane said proudly. She then gave him a Mizani conditioner, rinsed, repeated and then dried his scalp. Even after blow drying it, his hair remained baby soft.

Diane snipped and cut his hair to precision. The continuous motions of Diane's hands drew everyone's attention inside and outside of the shop. A couple of pedestrians gathered at the window. Other than the music playing through the system, the entire salon was quiet. People in the neighborhood knew of Diane's celebrity clientele, and figured Jason was a star. By the time she applied a dab of gel, and brushed it a few strokes, the curls rippled like ocean waves.

Already feeling like a spectacle, Jason declined the manicurists offer to get a pedicure. His feet were one part of his body he didn't want exposed. "They were in bad shape," he said.

"Non-sense, Jas-son. Do them. Heat the water and get the hot wax ready. He'll be back in a moment." Diane wasn't taking no for an answer.

By the time Diane put the finishing touches on his hair, Jill was in awe. She stared without regard and her heart fluttered a bit. She was definitely amazed by his transformation.

The gay stylist strutted through the shop breaking her lustful state. "I'm baaaaacccck," he said as he sat the bags in the chair. Diane laughed.

Diane gave Jason a few finishing touches to his eyebrows and exclaimed, "Beautiful, if me don't say so me self." She removed the smock from over his head and led him to the back so no one could witness the last phase of his makeover. She wanted to have the thrill of introducing them to the Jason she knew. The difference between the man she remembered and the one with her now was that the old Jason was many pounds lighter and over a decade younger. Now standing before him, she had a chance to look into his face. He looked ruggedly handsome, yet he still had the face of a man in his mid twenties. He no longer had a lean boxers frame. It had been replaced muscles with that made him look like a calendar model.

They went into Diane's office. Jill tried to get in, but Diane locked the door and told her to wait outside like everyone else. "Put de clothes on, mahn." He took the robe off and stood naked in front of Diane. For some reason, Diane's mouth watered when she looked down at his penis. She took a deep breath and had to remember herself. She quickly reached into a cabinet and grabbed some deodorant for him. Jason reached into the bag and pulled the clothing out.

He tried to hold back his excitement. As she scanned the bag, he kept saying, "I don't believe this."

"Believe it, Ja-son. You been down fe a time, but dat time pass now. You in what dey say, de company of fam-ih-lee."

Jason quickly wiped away a tear of happiness that had been welling up in his eyes. There were new socks, underwear and T-shirts. The Calvin Klein boxer briefs felt strange once he slipped them on. They were so soft and gave him support that boxers hadn't. Everything was a perfect fit as he slid the sand blasted jeans on. Then he put on the white, collared, dress shirt, which hung in a Banana Republic bag, and then slipped on the cushioned socks. Jason reached into the box and pulled out the Prada loafers and for the first time in years he slipped his feet into a pair of shoes that were comfortable. Lastly, he put on the blazer and he looked like a real model.

"Don't forget de belt, mahn," Diane picked up the thick buckled Prada belt and tossed it to him. Once he put it on, he stepped back and looked at himself in the mirror and shook his head in disbelief. His mind took him back to the days of his childhood and the one time his grandma had taken him shopping for Easter.

"How do I look?" he asked.

"Like one million," Diane laughed out. She then turned and reached for the door.

The anticipated audience waited as the door slowly opened. When Diane gave Jason the cue, he took one step and she beamed like a proud parent. Jason glided in clear view of the onlookers. The outside spectators applauded Diane's work.

Jason's new look definitely resembled a dress-down professional.

Jill was speechless. A tear escaped from her eye because of her premature judgments of him. Oddly, she felt intimidated by his new look. In her mind, he had been elevated to a higher social level with the make-over. She worried that he would no longer be interested in her.

To calm the excitement, Diane asked Jill and Jason to follow her to her office. Everyone went back to work.

When they stepped into the office Diane wanted to know how Jason ended up the way he did and what he wanted to do now. She was willing to help. For what seemed like the tenth time, Jason explained everything, including how he lost his house. The only thing he left out was part about Zeida. Diane asked him where he was going to live and he told her he didn't know but that he would be all right. Diane made him promise that he would come in once a week to get his hair cut, so that it would be easier for him to find a job. She also told him she would ask her rich friends if they needed someone, and then she remembered.

"Jill, you tell me one time you did have a whole heap a Sharief clothes pile up at de house?" she asked.

Jill angrily looked at Diane, and unsure if she wanted to answer aloud she said, "Yeah…yeah, I still have them." \

Diane winked at Jill. "Fine. It's all settled then. Jason you go with Jill a Brooklyn and pick up a few suit and shoes."

Diane raised both of her eyebrows, knowing her girlfriend would not deny her a personal favor. Jill had mixed feelings. Even though he was one of the most handsome men she ever saw, and was a friend of Diane's, she really didn't know him.

She turned to Jason. "Excuse me, you mind if I have a word with *my friend* over there. We'll be right out."

Jason stepped out without hesitation. As soon as the door closed, Jill went off. "How you gonna just invite a stranger to my house and offer him my husband's clothes without checking with me first?"

Diane was losing her patience. "Stop blood clot front and don't be a hypocrite. Sharief tell you inna de letter to do fe somebody de same way him do fe you? Nuh you say you want somebody who want you fe you an don't know how much money you have? You a de same one who cry say me did right when me tell you fe come outta you shell? Dis mahn, he is a good man. Him tell you more bout himself than any a de mahn you claim you love, and please no make me mention Cashmere. Take de mahn home, give him de clothes, and see if you want to give him a place fe stay. You have to decide what is at stake in every situation. Now come outta me shop, me have more work fe do."

She hated to admit that Diane was always right, but it really didn't take much for her to decide to do exactly as she'd been told.

Trying to seize control of the situation and be at ease at the same time, Jill grabbed Jason by the arm as if he was her possession and led him out of the shop. They caught a yellow cab straight into Brooklyn.

It was drizzling when the cab pulled up to Jill's house. Jason carried her flowers while they both ran to her courtyard to shield themselves from the mist. When Jill put her key in the door, he figured she lived in the basement of the large home. When they stepped inside, he noticed a set of steps. *It must be a three-story home* he thought.

He followed her up the stairs and into the kitchen on the floor above. They discussed his life in more detail and Jill explained briefly where she grew up. They placed the flowers in a vase and when she sat them on the dining table, Jason saw that all the other flowers and cards he'd sent were right next to each other.

In a moment of uneasiness, they spoke at the same time, "Let me ask you something?" hearing themselves they both laughed.

"Yeah, you go first," Jill said.

"Okay, I heard Diane say something about a Sharief. Do you live here alone?"

Jill walked over to the dining table and had a seat. Playing with the pedal of an orchid, she said, "Yes I do. Sharief was my husband. He died years ago and left me this house. He was a good man who did what he had to do from time to time, I guess."

"I noticed how you said that, you sound a little bitter. Did you all have a good relationship?"

"No, I'm not really bitter." His question made her feel vulnerable. She pondered a few minutes before she spoke. She knew that honesty was best. "In my life, I've experienced a small amount of different kinds of relationships. Relationships where I was dominated and relationships where my only job was to simply shine like a trophy."

She wasn't sad but the bearing of things that she'd kept in caused her to feel an overflow of emotions. He looked into her eyes as she continued. He saw a tear roll down her cheek. One first, then they began to get more steady.

"I've always heard of relationships where someone loves you for you. For your mind, your spirit, sometimes simply for the sake of loving you and each day them proving worthy of your trust. The type of relationship where someone loves you for your humor, your madness, your flaws, even your insecurities and through it all they still encourage you to fulfill your dreams. I know that's rare, but that's the type of relationship that works, and I didn't have that. I've never had that."

Jason moved his chair closer to wipe away her tears. She rested her head on his chest. "While I was away, I thought of the ways of people. I felt that I could never love someone that knew me when I was up, but couldn't be there when I was down. I always felt like I would be bitter towards women. I know I'm going to make it, but I didn't want someone who would be with me for what they could get from me. I dreamed of being with someone who was willing to give, and love me when all I had to give was love."

Jill nodded and Jason fought the craziness her scent sent through him. Staying focused on his thoughts he sad, "I was lost Jill, lost and turned out to the street life. Now that I've been blessed, I want to rise from the ashes and share my blessings. You are a wonderful woman, with a lot to be proud of. The relationship you want you can have, all you have to do is give yourself a chance. Maybe give me a chance."

Jill leaned her head into his chest while she sobbed. The comfort of her head on his firm chest was soothing. When she felt like she was drifting she lifted her head, stood, and said, "You must think I'm an emotional wreck now, huh?" She stood up and moved to the fridge, "Are you hungry? I'm starved," she said changing the subject.

"Let me," he said following her. "You did a lot today, so let me show my appreciation."

He grabbed a knife out of the holder and walked over to the fridge. He removed an onion, peppers, cabbage, carrots, and grabbed the elephant garlic out of its bag. Jill had a seat and watched Jason go through her cabinets and remove brown rice, and two salmon steaks from the fridge. He placed an apron around his waist. "You don't have to stay here and watch me. I'm sure you have something to do? Go slip out of those damp clothes before you get sick. And oh, if you don't mind, could you put the radio 101.9 FM for me?"

Damn, he's such a man, she thought. First the honesty, then the cab ride, the dinner, and now the commands. She was actually thrilled to death. She always thought it was appealing for a man to take charge.

Jill adjusted the radio to the station he requested and headed up to her bedroom with some apprehension. For the first time since she'd had the house, she closed the door to her loft. She hopped in the shower with a lot on her mind. *It has to be fate, that brought this man in my life,* she thought. The roses, the heroic effort to save her life, him knowing Diane and the way he looked after his transformation all sunk in her head.

Jill brushed her wash cloth over her breast and her nipples sat out like headlights. "Damn, I'm hot," she whispered. One hand caressed her breast while the other traveled down south. The beating of the water on her ass did not help. She stroked and rubbed, preparing to go somewhere she'd promised not to. "Old habits were indeed hard to break," she said. "There is a stranger in the house. Be disciplined girl, snap out of it," she coached herself.

The aroma of curry hit Jill as she slid into her cut off sweats and Escada T-shirt. In the kitchen, she found him pushing carrots through the juicer while pouring sweetened condensed milk into a container. He operated like a real chef. Jason didn't realize he was being watched and when he turned around and saw her legs and then her braless breasts it sparked an instant erection.

"Ah…do you have any nutmeg?" he asked turning towards the counter.

"Why are you so jumpy?"

"Oh, no reason, I'm cool," he said.

Jill peeped the bulge in his pants way before he could hide it. She smiled uncontrollably. Feeling embarrassed for him, she pointed him towards the spice rack. "It's against the brick wall," she said sitting on the stool. The pungent odor of the spices gave her home an aroma that made her hungry.

"Is it almost done?" she asked.

"Yes, you may have a seat, now."

They sat at the table and Jill was taken by his presentation. It was just like dining in an upscale restaurant. The salmon rested on a bed of rice, and fancy-cut seasoned vegetables surrounded the plate edges. They bowed their heads in unison.

From the first bite, she was impressed. The food melted in her mouth. He watched as her eyes widened when she sipped the carrot juice.

"Jesus, this food is good. Where'd you learn to cook like that?"

"I hope you didn't mind me using the Vodka in the freezer? I haven't had a drink since I been out, so I only added it to yours."

"God, no."

"Oh, about my cooking, I had to cook for myself growing up, and when I went to prison I spent a few years in the food service department."

She nodded with raised eyebrows. Her mouth was too stuffed with food to speak.

After dinner, they chilled in the living room. The Vodka made Jill mellow. They sat on opposite ends of the couch, enjoying the mellow sounds of a Smooth Jazz CD. Boom. Thunder shook the windows, and Jill cowered.

"It's getting late, do you want me to show you the clothes?" she asked, regaining control.

"Sure. Lead the way."

After taking Jason into the room where she'd deposited the clothes she announced, "Here they are."

"Whoa, you gots to be kidding," Jason was amazed at the mountain of clothing." He held each item up to him one by one. The suits were finer than the ones he'd worn for Zeda. He took as many items as he could hold and went in the bathroom. He opened the bathroom door and a foul sour odor knocked him backward.

"Oh no, I forgot that the water isn't working in there. Close the door quick," Jill said. Jason placed the clothes on the bed and walked over to the sliding door to let in some air. "I can fix it for you if you give me the tools."

"I'll call the plumber. Just use the bathroom upstairs where the kid..."

He looked at her surprised. "I thought you didn't have any children?"

"I don't...it's just...you may not understand. Just follow me."

The cash that she left on the bed fell on the floor, when Jason gripped up the clothes. They both looked down.

"Oh, keep that for yourself," I found it when I moved this stuff downstairs.

"I couldn't do that."

"I insist. If you don't I'll flush it just to prove that I have no other desire for it."

Seeing that she was serious he nodded in acceptance.

They walked upstairs and Jason stopped at every painting along the way. He was captivated by the colorful abstract images. Jill eventually led him to the guestroom decorated for the nonexistent nanny. When he walked into the room she said, "I'll be right upstairs, give me a holla when you're done trying on the clothes."

Jason saw that no one had ever used the new room. The television, the cable box, and everything else were new. He walked into the bathroom, and there were no signs of it being lived in. He thought of the other two rooms that had closed doors and wondered what secret Jill hid.

He tried the suits on and they all fit to a tee. Jason felt like his old self again, as he checked himself in the mirror. Once he finished trying on everything, he called for Jill.

She appeared barefoot. "Did everything fit?" she asked leaning on the Mahogany banister.

"Like they were made for me. I want you to know that I sincerely appreciate everything you've done."

"Don't sweat it, the clothes, that is, I was getting ready to call the Salvation Army so they could come and get them anyway. Thanks for the compliment. Let me get a bag so you can put them all in."

The sweat from Jason's head became profuse.

"Damn, you sweat kind of easy."

"Yeah I do, and I left my deodorant behind. You mind if I take a bath?"

Jill was stuck for words. His request meant that he would have to get naked. Honestly, she was uncomfortable with it but let it go. "Put the stuff in the bag and I'll be right back."

Before she walked away he said, "Wait a minute. Do you have bubble bath, lotion, Vaseline, and a razor?"

"I can help you, wait right there."

She bounced up the steps and found his request to be a major turn on. She wondered what type of lover he was, and if he knew how to treat a woman well. Everything he did that day seemed to be perfect. The fact that he lived on the streets still bothered her, but she didn't have a legit reason why.

"It's getting late, I don't know what time you may have to be back to where you're going, but take your time," Jill said while handing him the things for his bath.

He took the things from her and headed to the empty room.

"Call me if you need anything, I'll be right above you."

She sat on her bed in silence, wondering if she should offer him a room. *Where did he live,* she thought. *Where was he going?*

In the midst of Jill's daydreaming, she heard a sound that struck her attention. It was coming from underneath her. She got down on her knees, putting her ear to the floor. She couldn't quite figure out the words. So she crept down the stairs, to get a clearer sound. Like a magnet she was drawn to the melody. She placed her ear to the door.

"Darling you ou ou ou, send me. I know you ou ou, send me. Darling you ou ou send me baby. Honest, you doooo. At first, I

thought it was infatuation..." she heard Jason sing in a deep soulful voice.

She raced upstairs and dialed Diane's number.

"Yes Jill, wha you want? You give my boy some yet?"

Out of breath, she whispered, "Diane, I don't understand why this man came into my life? He's in the tub singing *my* Rachelle Ferrell songs. This is too freaky. He can cook, he can sing, and he is fine like I don't know what, but what's the problem?"

"Yes, you a de bright one. You need a good mahn. Me tell you say de mahn is a friend a mine, and him have everyting you need in a mahn, but you nuh know what is de problem right?"

"Exactly. He's too perfect, or something, is that right?"

"All right, me only go say dis once. Jill, you have money and you don't know what it feel like fe do someting fe somebody unless you a benefit. You want a mahn to care fe you, so you have one who need take care of, and it new to you. Maybe you cheap, maybe you tink every mahn suppose to have some ting fe you?"

Jill was silent. Diane went on, "All me have to say is a mahn is there, and when love too perfect we always feel someting not right. Me hangin' up now 'cause you seeming selfish. You can call me tomorrow and cuss me, but me will still call you a fool. One love, me dear."

Jill was startled from a knock on her door. She opened the door, and there stood Jason, wrapped in a towel exposing his wet chiseled body.

"I was calling you from the tub, and then from the bottom of the steps, but you didn't answer, so I came up," he said.

"Wow. You have a very nice loft up here," he said peeking through the doorframe. "Anyway, do you have an extra toothbrush? I hope you don't mind?"

She was flustered. "No...no...oh...God, I mean yes, wait right here."

As soon as he walked back down the steps she whispered to herself, "God, I'm going crazy," she said, as she laid her hands in between her legs. She bit down on her pillow trying not to moan. Having Jason around was like one long lasting tease to her. She wanted him out of the house.

Jill was getting too weak, and time was moving too slowly. She was afraid of how the night would turn out. She knew what Diane said was right, but this was just too much for her to handle. She wanted to maintain some kind of self-respect. She couldn't see herself sexing a man who had been a homeless bum the day before.

Jill was mentally exhausted from the words of aunt Lana, Diane and Sharief that kept re-playing in her mind. She was tired of fighting herself and considered just giving into her lust. She had gotten to the point where she hoped Jason would walk back into the room and take her. Or maybe, she would be the aggressor and get naked for him. The box of unused condoms in the drawer could be put to good use.

"Jill," he called, breaking her erotic fantasy. He surfaced, draped in a tan suit.

"Do you need me to call you a cab?" she asked.

"No that's all right. I'm not sure where I'm going, but at least now I can get on my feet. Once I secure an address and get another phone, I'll be straight. I'm never going back in the streets and I have you to thank for that."

"Just get in contact with Diane. I'm sure she will find you work," Jill said feeling guilty.

He held her soft hand. "Again I want to thank you. I see you're still a little uneasy around me, but trust me I meant everything I wrote on those cards. You will forever be my angel. Oh ... and are you sure about the money."

"One hundred percent."

"If it's the last thing I do, I'll return it to you."

"No need..." He leaned to kiss Jill on her cheek and startled her. Between his soft lips and masculine scent, she didn't know *which* made her want to lose her mind. Her left hand reached for his pants, she thought about it, and went for the doorknob instead.

"Thanks again."

"You're welcome," Jill said.

When she opened the door the rain was beating down ferociously. The thunder was still booming as the sky lit up with lightning. Water was pouring off of the roof like a waterfall. She immediately slammed it shut.

"I can't let you go out there in that. Put the bag down and you can stay in the guest room until tomorrow."

Watching her rear sway from side to side as she locked the door and moved toward the steps, Jason felt his heart flutter with excitement. *It's gonna be a long night,* he thought.

Twenty-7

Jason couldn't sleep. It was too quiet. His thirteen-year prison experience had conditioned him to sleep under some form noise. Knowing that the woman he desired more than anything in the world was just up the steps was torture. Imagining having her caused him to stiffen. Without realizing it he began to stroke himself. Up and down his hand moved until his eyes rolled back in his temple. *Stop,* he thought. He couldn't go on. He'd made a promise he wasn't ready to break.

Unbeknownst to Jason, Jill was having some problems of her own. She'd been fighting the urge to put her fingers deep inside her every since she'd gone up to bed. Every time she closed her eyes, visions of sensual sex scenes replayed in her head. She envisioned Jason on top of her taking her like a man escaped from prison. She resisted for fear that she wouldn't be able to control her moans and finally dozed after four agonizing hours.

At a quarter to seven, Jill was stirred from her sleep by the pounding beats of rock and roll music. She was not accustomed to noise in her house unless she was the one making it. She hopped out of the bed, put on her sports bra, and grabbed her robe. She headed downstairs and was surprised that Jason was indeed listening to rock music.

When she cracked the door she saw Jason's sweaty body on the floor in his boxers doing crunches. Every time he leaned back, the split in his boxer-briefs offered her a peak at his soft member. Yawning she said, "Will you please cut that off, or down, or something, as a matter of fact, I want you to stop working out. In five minutes come, take a walk up to my room."

Jason felt guilty for waking her up and was worried that she regretted allowing him to stay. He sat on the bed for two minutes and contemplated getting dressed before going up. She'd already seen him in his underwear so he figured that he couldn't hurt his chances of seducing her by showing her his chest up close and personal.

He started up the steps in his boxers. At the top of the landing, he found a set of folded clothes, some shorts and a tank top and a pair of athletic socks. Assuming they were for him, he put them on and walked into her room. Jill was bent over, stretching her hamstrings and back. She wore a purple and black workout suit that rivaled something Serena would wear. Jill's flexibility was impressive.

She did not skip a beat. "Now, let me show you how to really work out," she said.

Jason laughed. *Hell, now I know she's the woman of my dreams,* he thought. "Okay, let's set it off then."

Jill had purchased a DJ Envy mix tape so that she could have the latest hip-hop songs to work out to. She popped it in to show Jason that she was a little hood. Fat Joe's *Lean Back* came on first and she got started.

They pushed their bodies for almost an hour. "Inhale on the crunch and exhale at rest," he coached as she worked her abs. He took off his shirt and grabbed Jill's hand. "See, put your hand on my abs. Now watch how they, contract. Now stick your finger in my belly button and you will feel my abdominal walls working."

Captivated by the intensity in his eyes, she lost focus. Before coming up on the third crunch, Jill had straddled him with a blank stare on her face. Jason's body accepted her weight and he smiled. Then instinctively he reached for her to come closer. Their lips met for the first time and when they touched Jill melted.

He slid his hands into her workout suit, palming both cheeks. She felt him hardening between them.

"Wait…wait…wait," Jason panted.

He instructed her to lie in front of the mirror. He slowly scaled off her pants. And with his teeth, he ripped off her thongs. Jill relaxed and let him do his thing. "Shit, your body is beautiful," he said, studying it.

Jason started from the top. He patiently licked her earlobe. "Ooh," she moaned out as his tongue and lips brushed her lobe. Wasting no time he slipped his fingers deep in her. Surprised and turned on by the sudden onslaught Jill grabbed her hair in ecstasy. Jason wanted to take his time. It had been so long since he'd had a woman's body to fulfill his desires. Now that he had one, it meant the world that he didn't have just *any* woman.

Jill was then taken by surprise at how masterful he was with his hands. He teased her clit with his index finger until she felt as though she was ready to cum on his hands and then he stopped and began to slowly slide a finger inside of her. He found her G-spot and began to massage it the way that Cashmere had taught her to.

He sucked her neck while his fingers worked her middle. Never removing his hands from her vagina, he moved from her neck and sucked her plump nipples. Jill began humping his hand.

"You like that, baby," Jason whispered.

"Oh my god…oh my god…oh my god," she began to yell out.

Jill pulled his hands up and sucked Jason's fingers clean of her juices. The action turned Jason on though he was stunned at how sexual she was. Desperate for more, she began biting on her nipple, and Jason took the other one in his mouth. He watched in the mirror. The sight of seeing herself being freaky was too much for her to handle.

Jason then placed both of her nipples into her mouth so she could stimulate herself. "Don't stop until I tell you to," he said.

Brushing her stomach with his lips he lowered his head until his mouth reached her opening. He slipped his tongue across her lips and onto her clit and then began to press on it with a back and forth motion that sent her to the moon. "Ahhhhhh," she screamed. He licked her box as if he were kissing her mouth, taking his time to apply just the right pressure. Once he felt her vaginal lips and clit were swollen, he gripped the meat around her clit with suction and he locked her clit gently between his teeth. Then he led an assault on her with rapid flicks of his tongue and his warm breath. Two straight minutes of his licking and she felt herself beginning to spasm from her first oral orgasm. "Oooooohhhhh, baby, please, Jaaaassssson, don… donnnnn…. Dooooonnnnn't stooooop," then her body began to quiver and convulse. "Oh, shit, I'm cumming," she yelled grabbing his head.

Jason was pleased that he was doing his thang. "Cum all over my face," he begged. His words sent her over the top and she grabbed his head and pushed it into her center and obliged him. Her juices flowed into his mouth as he continued to lick and plunge his tongue inside of her.

"Fuck me, please," she begged when he brought his face up. She didn't want to wait another minute. She needed him deep inside her. On many nights over the years Jason had laid in his prison bunk fantasizing about this very moment, so he intended making the moment last as long as he could.

Jason kissed her so deep he almost made her gag. Jill loved every minute of it. Jason led her to the bed and put Jill on her back. He stood up and pulled his underwear down. His dick was at attention. Jill took one look at it and began to masturbate. After a few jabs, he removed her hand.

From her view, his pubic hair was curly and finely trimmed. "Damn I can't wait to taste that," she said.

"It's all yours," he responded. Jill sat up and grabbed the remote to the CD player and hit the shuffle button. She had a mix of love songs that she had planned to play for Cashmere but realized that they were perfect for the man she finally had in her bed. Next she anxiously climbed on top of Jason. The look on her face gave away that she wanted to devour him. She leaned over and reached into her drawer, broke open the box of lubricated condoms, and slipped one onto his rock-hard dick. As soon as she straddled him, she felt her one hundred and twenty-pound body being lifted into the air.

Jason entered her, scooped her thighs, spun around, and stood up in one motion. He rocked her body from side to side in midair. Her vagina did circles around his stiff shaft. With each motion, he sunk himself in a little deeper. By the time the base of his shaft was deep inside of her, they were in front of the mirror again.

He said, "Open your eyes and watch." Jason sunk and withdrew in rapid strokes.

Her body jerked like a washing machine on spin cycle. Propping her legs in Lotus position, he never pulled out of her. He stroked her like it was his first time.

"Ohhh damnn," she screamed. Her vagina felt tighter than when she was a virgin. She was grateful that she worked out and was flexible because it felt like Jason was deep in her stomach. He moved extra slow and she held on while taking glances at the mirror.

His pace got stronger and harder. Jason took deep breaths as he fought to keep his balance. He grunted and moaned her name. She knew he was having an orgasm. His love muscle vibrated. To Jill's surprise, it stayed hard. Jason continued move in and out of her and after a minute, he unfolded her legs and carried her over his shoulder to the bed. "What are you doing to me," she cried.

She looked down at the condom. "Didn't you cum?"

"Yes I did."

"It's still rock hard. But how could..." Jill was about to ask.

He whispered "Shhh," and he entered her in the missionary position. He kissed all over her. Joss Stone's *I've Fallen in Love With You* played through the speakers. Jason began to grind in a motion that opened her up. The heat from their pelvic thrust was building and as he pounded into her she moaned, "That's it."

"You like it like that?"

"Oh, yes. Just like that," Jill was staring into his eyes.

Jason grimaced and struggled hard to keep his composure. He couldn't believe that he had a queen beneath him when he looked down into her face. Sweat dripped from his neck as he continued in and out. The smacking sounds and the scent of sex were driving them both wild. He hit a spot that sent a shock throughout her body and she dug her nails into his back. "Cum for me please, baby... cuuuummmm," she cried out.

"After ... you," he said.

She grabbed hold of her breast and put her nipple into his mouth. Her other hand held a firm grip on his ass. She pulled him deep inside of her taking control of her own pleasure. She arched her back and met his thrust and her walls began to contract. Her teeth clenched and she felt it. The backs of her thighs trembled as her orgasm worked its way from her middle throughout her body. Tears formed and rolled down the sides of her eyes. She was so happy. Her body felt so fulfilled and her heart felt safe. Something in the way that he made love to her let her know that he appreciated her in a way that no man ever had.

Now her gaze was on him. She was breathing in short breaths as her body continued to spasm, "Iyyy, Iyyyyy...," she moaned.

"Ohhhhh, Jillllllllll. Ohhhhh, babeeee," his body locked and the muscles in his chest rippled. Jill reached up to caress his hard nipples and he exploded. His orgasm felt so good that he swore he was having an out of body experience. "Yesssss, ohhh shit, yessss." He stroked until his penis tingled so much that he had to pull it out. In a daze he fell flat on his back and sucked air like a marathon runner.

In the still of the afterglow, they held each other thinking the same exact thing. *Where have you been all my life?*

Jill and Jason were still lying in bed at nine o'clock that evening listening to music while feeding strawberries to one another.

"Who is this? I like her accent," Jason asked.

"A group called Floetry," Jill responded.

"I like that. That's a beautiful song... kinda sad though."

"Heeeeeeyyyy yooouuuuu, sorry that I had to leave... I'll try to come back," Jill sang with a smile. Jason didn't smile. It reminded him of what he needed to say to all the people he'd left. He thought of Webb, Zeida, his sister and even his mother. He was really shocked when Tasha popped into his mind. Now that he was home things just seemed different. Too real.

Trying to snap himself out of it, he asked Jill a question that he really wanted to know the answer to. "Tell me something, what does happiness mean to you?"

"Wow. Good question. Happiness to me is peace and the ability to share love with those around you and of course being loved back."

"Hmmm," he said and nodded. "So what are your dreams?"

Jill blushed. "Ummm."

"Come on tell me, what have you been dreaming of?"

"I hope this doesn't come back to haunt me. I dream of being with someone who will take care of me. I don't mean financially, but you know, the way *you* make love to me. It feels like we're tapping into the powers of the universe. It's like we belong together...doing this. I guess I dream of that real love. I know drama comes with it, but I also believe that love that can *endure* anything as long as two people work together. I want children. I want to get into my art." She paused then asked, "You know those paintings you saw when you were coming up the stairs?"

"Yeah, those are hot," Jason said.

"Well, I want to be somewhere that I can showcase my art, maybe teach underprivileged children to paint."

"How many children?" Jason questioned.

"How many children what?"

"Do you want?"

"Oh, two. A boy and a girl," she smiled.

"Then what?"

"Just me barefooted and pregnant because *I* choose to be. I want to cook for my *husband* so when he comes home from work he can leave that world behind and come into ours. You're a regular Barbara Walters, now, why don't you answer some questions?"

"Oh, you trying to flip it?" he asked. After a pause, he spoke. "Well, I want to have as many children as I can afford, but I'm getting old. I also want to open a franchise restaurant where good vibes exist. And I want to be that man, *that husband*, that comes home to you. The one who will supply your every need. You know, be by your side during the hard times."

Jill looked into his blue eyes and asked, "How do you know this so soon?"

Jason exhaled. "Look Jill, I've been trying to tell you from the start that I know you are right for me. From the minute I saw you it was like God spoke to me, and I am not into religion, but I ain't stupid either. I can make things happen once I get on my feet and I figure in twelve years I'll be a billionaire."

"A man that aims high, huh?"

"I sent you flowers when I was homeless and sleeping on a bench. I went after you when it should have seemed impossible, now look, I have you here with me. Can't get much higher than that, and since I been to the bottom, why not stay here at the top?"

Jill was stunned when she thought about what he'd said. He interrupted her thoughts, "So where are we going with this?"

"You been away in prison deprived, how are you sure another woman won't capture your eye?" Jill asked, feeling insecure.

"Another woman *will* garner a glance or maybe two, but only you have captured my soul. The least of my problems is finding a woman. What I *need* is balance and focus in my life. I've been away too long to settle for less, and if a woman couldn't be there when I was down, then I don't need her. What I *need* is what's real and that's you. If my eyes wander, I rather pluck it out before I violate what we have."

Jill sighed, looking down at her hands. "You asked me where we are going with this. I've been asking myself that from the moment you made love to me this morning. I'm afraid, but someone did something for me, and I would like to do the same for you. Please just don't play with my heart, because the way you've been playing with my body I don't want you to go anywhere. But life is more than physical, and we have a life outside these doors. So I'm just gonna follow some advice given to me for once. I just hope you can be trusted and learn to trust someone besides yourself. I know it will be hard for the both of us, but I'm willing to try."

They sat up and discussed each other's lives in detail. Jason told her about Zeida and the conditions of when he last saw her. She suggested that he track her down to make sure he wasn't still in love. He was falling in love behind her advice, because she confirmed how real he knew she was.

The next morning she awoke to Jason's soft strokes. She eased in closer. He wrapped his arms around her as he penetrated. Their bodies danced to their natural rhythms.

When the lovemaking was done, he jumped into the shower. Jill anxiously rushed to his room to hang up his clothes. *My man is staying,* she thought. She even laid out his clothes he would wear that day.

Upon entering her bathroom, she found Jason using her toothbrush. She felt that was so romantic. She walked up behind him and relaxed her head on his back. She lightly pressed her waist into his ass, kissed him, then headed for the shower.

Jason whistled a tune as he stepped out of the bathroom. He saw the clothes lying on the bed. He smiled to himself thinking how giving flowers had changed his life, forever.

Jason searched through her clothes and pulled down an outfit for her to wear. Jill laughed at the gesture, glad to have a man to make the suggestion. He had unfinished business to take care of.

After they were dressed, Jill placed her watch on her wrist and stopped Jason from going downstairs. She walked back into her closet and opened an old make up trunk. Inside was all of Sharief's jewelry. She removed the matching TAG watch, and placed it on his wrist. As she did, the phone rang.

The caller ID revealed it to be a long lost friend of Sharief's. The ID said Marriott.

Jill sat down and took the call, "Hey, stranger. Long time no hear from."

Jill laughed and said, "Johnny, when are you moving out of that hotel? You need to invest in some real estate. What? No, no, no. I pulled out of Tate Industries. What, oh, no. This is why I told you to diversify your investments, but you want to listen to X-man. No, no, no. Don't you listen to the Bloomburg? You have too much capital floating not to stay informed."

She kissed Jason on his lips, motioning him to wait. He overheard her say, "Listen, the wire says Ashley isn't coming back. Yes, I know you know what's going on, but X-man is throwing snowballs in hell right now. I have my sources. Yes I know you the man, but when it comes to investing you are lost. What? It's only money? So why is your hustling butt calling here? Yeah, because I was the only one on this line that made a bundle off of the war in Iraq. They don't call you Mr. Hustle for nothing? Well Mr. Johnny Hustle, Northrop is up for now. Well, I wouldn't count Martha Stuart out just yet." On a normal occasion they could go on for a good hour or more but Jill didn't want to upset Jason.

"Listen, I have to go, *my man* is waiting on me. What? It doesn't matter to you who he is. Your boy? Your boy has been gone for years, rest his soul. Please do not lecture me about relationships as if you're the authority on love."

When Jason heard Johnny's name he pointed at Jill to hand him the phone. She looked at him in the state of confusion, so he reached for the phone and took it out of her hand. She overheard him saying, "Hey homeboy, do any cleaning lately? Yeah…this is me…been home a short while now. Been rough but things turned around. Nah, you keep that. I'm out of the game for good. Well for me it's over. Yeah, thirteen long ones. Nope, haven't heard from your nephew. I really would like to know where he is, just to make sure he's safe. Listen, maybe some other time, but I don't want to keep the lady waiting. What? Yeah, fo sure. I'll let you know when the wedding is. No I don't want the ring from you. Man, I'll catch you later."

He handed the phone back to Jill who was standing with her jaw on the floor. She couldn't believe that he knew two people in her small circle. When she put the phone to her ear, Jason overheard her saying, "Yes, *it is* a small world. He's a young don, huh? Well I don't select them they select me. He's your family? Don't threaten me, you thug," Jill giggled out.

"Oh yeah that's right, excuse me, *businessman*. Yes I'm going to take care of him. No I'm not after his money, I beg your pardon? I should have his kids? You just finished telling me your partner's body wasn't cold yet. I love you too, but I have to go. Yes, pull out of Tate Industries. Goodbye, Johnny."

"Small world, huh?" Jason asked.

"Yes, and if I didn't know before, I know for sure now that we are not an accident."

They walked down to the kitchen where they had breakfast.

"I'm gonna stop by Diane's to get my hair done and then do a little shopping. Can you call me later and let me know if you want to hook up, or if you want to meet me back here? You may want to come in early so let me know when you call."

"Yeah, I'll like to take care of a few things uptown, and then work out a few odd ends." Jason was grinning as he spoke.

"What?"

"What, what?" Jason asked.

"Why the big grin?"

Jason shook his head and said, "You just have no idea. From the things I've suffered through to being here with you. It's like I feel human again and it's like my whole life is ahead of me because of you. Woman you just don't know what you did for me."

"Well, you did a lot for me, and I want you here. Since we said we're going to trust each other, wait right here."

Jill took a walk down to the bedroom on the basement floor. She opened the door on the right-hand side of the desk where the safe was located. Sharief had always kept petty cash in the house in case of an emergency. She never saw the sense it made, but when he died, she left it there. With the information Johnny provided about Jason, she had no problem doing what she was about to do. She removed three stacks from the fifty thousand in cash and headed back upstairs.

She walked into the kitchen and found Jason washing dishes. "Here, Jay, this is for you," She put the money on the counter and his eyes nearly bugged out of his head. "I need you to do a few things for me. Stop by the DMV and get some ID. Pick up a cell, and please use this address. I'll have a job for you by the time you report to your parole officer. My heart is in your hands now so I hope you don't drop it."

He looked at the cash in his hands and thought of the times he used to do the same thing for Tasha. He put the cash in his jacket pocket. "Thank you, baby, you won't regret it," he said confidently.

Almost like a light bulb coming on in his head he came up with, "Listen, do you have the number to a cab service that I can use for a few hours?"

"Give me a minute. It's been a while since I've called him. He'll be glad to hear from me," she said. Jill called her driver. "He'll be here in fifteen or twenty minutes. Handle your business and call me when your phone is activated." Jill scribbled down her address and phone numbers and gave it to him.

They sat at the dining table while waiting for the cab to arrive while discussing their experiences with Johnny Hustle.

In twenty minutes exactly, a silver Audi A8, pulled in front of the house beeping it's horn. Jill escorted Jason to the car. The driver met her at the curb with open arms. She landed an innocent kiss to his cheek. Jason stared at the man, but not for obvious reasons. His face was familiar.

"Roger?" he said. "You used to drive the Lincoln?"

He looked Jason in the eyes. He snapped his fingers several times trying to jog his memory. "Jay? Jay, right? Used to have the Porsche, hung with Webb?" Once he knew that he was right his voice rose in joy. "What's up, homeboy? Man I was wondering what happened to you? I was thinking about that time on Wall Street the other day, and I was rolling. Man I'm glad to see you."

Jason indicated with his eyes to cut the details short and Roger caught on. "Jill, how are you, pardon my rudeness ma'am, I was just happy to see Jay."

Jill looked at the two men with one hand on her hip. "It seems like all my friends are just tooooo happy to see him."

They pulled up to Diane's salon, and Jason got out with her. "Give me about ten minutes, Roger," he requested as he slammed the door.

They walked into the salon and everyone greeted them. "Yes, de love bird dem show up. You could'a at least hang up de phone when you a screw down de place." Diane said out loud in the shop. Diane had called and caught them in the mix the day before. Jill couldn't recall whether or not she hung up the phone.

Jill held her hand to her mouth in embarrassment. Jason turned red. To break the tension, he walked up to Diane, kissed her on the cheek and then gave her a big hug.

"Sit down ere' an let me give you a shape up," she told Jason.

Turning to Jill, she said, "Yes, Miss Bright. Me see say you nuh so hard headed and you give tings a chance eeeh? If me never wrong bout a woman, wha mek you tink say me wrong bout a mahn?"

Jill looked around and saw that Diane wanted to put on her regular performance so she said, "Yeah, yeah, just make my man look fine and we can gossip about him after he leaves."

After re-lining his hair, Jason passionately kissed Jill and the whole shop made their comments. He then hugged Diane and walked out of the door. When he reached the cab, he sat in the front seat and told Roger to take him to a Cingular Wireless store on Fifth Avenue at 40th Street. When he pulled off, Roger said, "Man where you been?"

"Did a long stretch and came home last month."

"Man, ain't nothing the same as when I saw you last, but then the more they change..."

"The more they stay da same," Jason finished for him.

"Exactly. I don't drive anymore full time," Roger boasted. "I only pick up select clients. I own the base now, so if you need a job for your P.O. or a vehicle, let me know."

"In a minute I might need that, but right now I'm just trying to get myself focused, ya' know, and get used to living without gun towers. But right now I'm blessed and I got some serious things to take care of. I'm on my way back to getting some peace in my life."

"I hear you, man," Roger said. "I was just telling your man Webb that same thing he needs to slow his roll and...."

"Webb?" Jason asked emphatically grabbing the dashboard. "Hold on, you just said you were telling Webb? You know where that nigga is?"

"Yeah, I see him all the time. He up in the Bronx on College Avenue. My old client, Dee, he left the game after a whole bunch of drama. He got a soldier named Scooter up there that's off the heezy. So I got Webb an apartment when he came back to the city."

Jason was filled with anticipation. "Listen, after I take care of a few things you got to take me up there."

"Fo sure, fo sure," Roger replied.

They drove to the store to pick up Jason's new wireless phone. When he went to pay for the phone, he counted almost four thousand dollars. He knew for sure what he wanted to do, since he had that type of money. He paid his bill and headed out the door.

After that, Roger took Jason to get his license. It took him three hours to get through the lines and the test. When they left, Jason felt relieved and in an act of kindness, Roger did the unthinkable and let Jason drive is car.

The Audi A8 headed to the Bronx. During the ride, Jason was debating with himself about seeing Webb. He knew he could be violated just for being seen with him, and since Webb was on the run, he didn't want to be associated with him. But Webb was his brother as far as he was concerned. He was sure that once he told Webb that he was done with crime that everything would be fine.

They crossed the Macombs Dam Bridge and made a right at Yankee's Stadium. They drove up the Grand Concourse. Jason was familiar with the Bronx, and when he cut the corner, he was familiar with the drug lifestyle he saw.

On the corner, there was one man that stood out amongst the rest. He was over six feet tall and weighed over two hundred pounds. Jason watched the man closely. He had another man pinned against a wall and it looked like a confrontation was taking place. The man looked over at Roger's car and did a double take when he noticed that Jason was driving it. A grimace appeared on the man's face and he and Jason made eye contact. Instantly his instincts from the yard kicked in and Jason gave a glare back as if to say, "What the fuck you lookin' at?"

Roger followed Jason's eyes. "Oh don't sweat that, that's the dude, Scooter, I was telling you about. That dude got more bodies under his belt than the morgue. He basically owns all of this. It used to be Money's but some drama went down and now Scooter runs it all. He's a nice guy once you get to know him. Wait right here, you in the safest car in the world on this block. Come around and get in the passenger's seat."

Jason watched as Roger disappeared into building number 1405. He looked over to his right and saw the man they called Scooter studying him. He talked into a two-way radio.

After waiting ten minutes, he saw Webb coming out of the building with Roger. It was the same old Webb. The only difference now was that he had long braids in his hair and was sporting a jacket that was much too heavy to have on in the summer. A smile appeared on Jason's face. Webb kept a tight grill until he got into the car.

"The door opened, they sat in the car and Webb said, "Pull off, Roger." He then smacked Jason in the back of the head and said, "What's up, baby booouy? So I see they finally let my homey out, huh? Finally out, huh?"

"Yeah, finally."

"Dayumn, baby boy, you done swole up in them mountains." Webb smacked Jason's chest rapidly nodding. "Yo Duke, Duke. I love the way you didn't fold and send them at me Duke."

"C'mon, man, did you ever consider that I would?"

"Nah, Fuuuck no," Webb barked.

"So, what the hell happened to you? Where you been?" Jason hollered.

"Yo, you got bagged and I didn't even know, homey. I didn't even know. Little homey, P.R., he looked out kid, he up North, and Lord still in the hood doing music or something. But on that day, Duke, I came out and the pigs tried to press me. So, so I had to twist something, had to twist a few pigs something terrible. Too bad all them cocksuckers ain't die, now if I step foot anywhere near B.K. or Q.B. Anything could happen. See?"

Webb lifted his jacket and he had two seventeen-shot nine-millimeter weapons, four extra clips in a pouch, and a body armor vest on. "Real easy, Duke, real easy. The kid ain't living in no cage, and the next time, I'm laying them all down fo real. My aim is perfected, Duke, my shits official, Duke. This thing is rough though because I can't drive, I can't stay in one place too long, and I got to eat."

Jason asked, "What *I* want to know, is how you got away? The police was saying you disappeared in thin air or swam across the river or something?"

They all laughed and Webb said, "Pigs is square lames, baby boy. I went through the hole in the fence in Baby Park. You know the one, you know the one. They had ghetto birds flying over my head and the whole nine. I jetted to the river and just did a dip, and since the tide was right, I swam over to the sewer drain. You know the big one we used to hide our rusty burners at? I swam down there and just crawled until I hit the R&R subway connection we used to go to when we was shorties. Them pigs can never figure out the hood. They lames, they can never figure out the hood."

"So how you been eating?"

"Duke, for a while, I just picked spots on 95 South, and I went there and set up camp. When I found out who the biggest ballas was, I'd go get 'em. I go get 'em, Duke. It's nothing. Richmond, D.C., Norfolk, Charlotte. I've been eating swell. I'm thinking about Vegas next. Yeah, Vegas. I might join a mosque or something."

Everyone in the car started laughing. "So what you doing up on a drug block if you on the run?" Jason asked.

"Roger put me on to this chick, homey, Didn't ya cuz?"

"Sure did."

"Yeah, I needed a place to stay, Duke, needed a place to stay. I was doing bad from the stress, ya feel me. The four walls closing in and shit. But after I got with shorty, she let me get my head right at her spot. I ordered one of them weight machines off the TV and stocked her fridge. All I did was eat, watch fucking videos and jack steel right in the living room. Then while I was laying back, I used to peep out the window and watch the show for like hours on end. I saw how they operation ran on this block, I was scheming to do a lick. But before I could do it... one day when I was coming out the building, this clown tested me." Webb laughed, "Yo, this nigga asked me if I was holding. I asked him straight up what time it was. I was like what time is it, B? I told him if he was gonna stick me up, then just get to it. I got down on both knees and put my hands up on top of my head and told him to do his thing."

"What?" Jason asked.

"Nah, Jay, let him finish," Roger said.

"Yeah, let me finish, B. Let me finish. So this clown starts laughing and calls me a big, bitch ass, nigga as he stands over me with his gat, yo. As soon as the nigga reaches inside my jacket and feels my gat his eyes get big. That fast, duke, that fast. I swing with an uppercut to his nuts hard enough to knock a fucking horse out. He fell back, right, B? Then I jump up and take his gat and slam it in his mouth, so fucking hard I chip all his fronts. The nigga starts to scream like a little bitch, B. Like a bitch. So I had to put him out. Since he was top dog on the block and ended up on a milk box after that, the red carpet rolled out. Rolled right out for me after that. The kid Scooter, he a good dude. He worked for a different team from the cat I smashed, but they was still deep and since I was gonna stay, I needed to team up. The cat Scooter pulled me up and told me he wanted me to work with him. He needed some back up on the block. Duke, he stepped to me real official-like. He got a lot to learn about his emotions, but a stepper always recognize a stepper. Don't get me wrong, I know two bulls can't live in the same pen for long, so I'm just waiting for some loot so I can get something started a few blocks down on 166th.

"I got it all mapped out with my soldiers waiting. I just need some shorts to jumpstart it. Back in the days, the red top crew had that jump banging off the hinges. This kid, Big June, he's doing life now but, yo, he was holding it down back then. Was holding it down, official, homey. But them faggots left him for dead with a shit load of product laying around. The poe-poes got him and as soon as the doctors got the bullet out of his back, he got sent up north. But I'm trying to lock it down like dat."

"But if you blow the spot up, sooner or later something's gonna happen to bring the feds. You and I both know a spot can get you trapped off," Jason reasoned in fear that Webb would get caught.

"Nah, homey. I'm setting everything up proper right now. I'm two steps ahead. Two steps ahead. When the pigs roll, I'll know they coming. I got trap floors and hidden walls and all that in there, so I'm safe even when I'm right under they nose."

"Sounds like you got it all mapped out. But let me ask you this. What's it gonna take for you to get out the game?"

"Good question, homey, real good question." Webb paused for a minute as if he wasn't even contemplating an answer then he blurted out. "I know one thing though. The answer starts with me getting some paper. Some major paper."

Jason told Roger to take him to the Regency and on the ride there Jason told Webb every detail of how he had to live from the day he got out of prison. Jason was shocked to hear that Webb knew Harold the king. "He's a fucking clown. I ought to murda his ass." When he finished telling his partner all that he'd been through, all Webb asked was, "Man it got that bad and you mean you never thought about taking some steel to a nigga or knocking a store in the hood? You know they let you stick up spots in the hood all day. Everybody know that. Just don't hit nothing the white man owns."

"I won't lie and say I didn't think about it once it got really bad, but man I got a whole new perspective on life, homey. I just can't live like that. I was tested and because I didn't fold, I was blessed."

"Yo, that's mad deep. But son, I woulda had to twist cabbage and get mine, homey. Fuck a park bench and a cup, I need meat, gravy and a soft mattress. I guess its good you got tested in the summer time."

They all laughed.

When the car reached the Regency, Webb was itching to see Harold. He made Jason stay in the car. Fifteen minutes later Webb came back to the car with a straight face. "Yo homey, that faggot trick buster want to see you."

Jason wondered what Webb had done. His parole was at stake. He walked into the Regency and Harold was in the cage dabbing a bloody towel behind his right ear, and his right eye was closed shut. He saw Jason and in a pleading voice said, "Homeboy, I wanted to apologize to you for the way things went down." Harold looked like a Cyclops now. When Jason walked in, Harold looked him over and said, "Yeah…" in the meekest of voices. "Homeboy, I wish you would have mentioned Webb from the jump and you would'na even had to pay." He reached down and pulled out a gray steel box. "As a matter of fact, I got a little insurance money from when your room was broken into, hold on."

Jason couldn't believe that it was the same man. He watched as Harold started counting money. "Here is five hundred. Come back and I'll have another five for you tonight. And don't worry about Mr. Townsend. If you haven't heard, he had a stroke, heart attack or something. From what I heard, it don't look like he gone make it, but you could go live in North Korea for all I care and it'll be all right with me. If they call to check, I got you cuz. If you need me to do anything at all, just let me know, okay?" He dabbed the towel and blinked continuously. "Just *please* keep Webb out of my hotel."

Jason took the cash and put it in his jacket pocket. He wrote his new cell phone number down and said, "Give this number, and the other five hundred, to Peter. Tell him to call me."

"Will do, brother man. God bless you. Merry Christmas. Happy Kwanza. Peace, my brother, peace," he yelled as Jason exited the door.

Jason got back to the car, looked at Webb and asked, "Where do you know him from?"

"Duke, Duke...you slipping Duke...you slipping Duke."

Jason shot Webb a smirk and the car kept rolling until they reached the diner. He walked up to the waitress that gave back the tip, and he handed her a hundred dollars. She wouldn't have recognized him if it weren't for his eyes. "Thank you," he said as he hugged her and showed his appreciation. She tried to get his phone number, but he laughed it off. He told her he had to go and walked out.

Roger, Webb, and Jason spent the day kicking it. Jason learned that Tasha was still alive. She was a bartender in a strip club in Jackson Heights, Queens, on Ditmars Boulevard. She had surgery and tried to dance in the club, but too many people booed when they saw her face. With nothing else to do, she tended the bar instead. Webb caught up with her and spared her life because he didn't know what Jason wanted to do. He wasn't as compassionate when he ran into Powerful.

Once Webb had gotten the whole story, he'd made his mind up that he would torture the man responsible for his friend's demise. It took him almost a year and a half to catch up to Powerful. But he finally caught him at his and his girlfriend's home in New Rochelle.

Webb had watched Powerful for a week and had seen him switch cars with a girl everyday out in Queens. Each morning he would see Powerful back on the block in the same car he'd swapped earlier the previous day. It didn't take him long to figure the girl was doing drops so Webb followed her. It turned out she was taking the car straight to a crib and parking it in a garage. Webb figured it was his stash spot.

Webb decided to get a two for one. He waited for Powerful to come to the house that night. As soon as Powerful pulled into the garage Webb crept around the corner on all fours and rolled into the garage as the door slid down.

It was too easy. When Powerful climbed out of the car Webb jumped up and put the pistol to his face. "It can be hard or *real* hard, homey. You choose, homey. You choose."

Webb had walked Powerful into the house and cuffed and bound him and the Jewish girl, who'd been driving the car every day, right next to one another. Powerful had shocked Webb when he begged for the life of the white bitch. It turned out that she was his main jump-off.

"You *love* her?" Webb asked shocked that this grimy street nigga had fallen in love with the white bread.

"Yeah and she's pregnant. So, son, whatever you want... you got. I can make you rich."

Webb had laughed and spooked Powerful when he said, "Nah. I really didn't come for your money. I'll leave that for the feds when they find you. But I am going to rape this bitch in front of you. Strictly fuck her in the ass, Duke. Strictly in the ass. Then I'm going to kill her slow in front of you."

She whimpered and Powerful pleaded. Webb proceeded to slam a lamp across his head, but was careful not to kill him. "If you close your eyes and don't watch, I swear I will set this fucking place on fire and burn you both alive. I'll burn you alive, Duke."

Then Webb explained why he was there. Powerful couldn't believe it. What he couldn't believe was that Tasha had once warned him of Webb and he had discounted her words.

Webb had taken his time and done everything he threatened to do to his woman right in front of him. She had grunted and screamed like a pig being slaughtered with a dull knife. Powerful had cried, like a baby watching his woman be violated as Webb bit into her flesh while sodomizing her a few feet away.

"I'll get you for this. I'll get you for this," he'd moaned and whaled. Webb broke a sweat and even laughed.

When Webb had finish committing the most lewd acts on his woman he grabbed a knife from the kitchen and killed her. Then he took the same knife and slit both of Powerful's wrists and shot him three times in the abdomen. A lung, liver and stomach shot, all purposely targeted. He wanted Powerful to bleed out, but he also wanted him to feel the heat that he was bringing. Webb rolled them up in the Oriental rug that they were laying on. Then he set the rug on fire with enough gas to burn the entire house on fire. Powerful was still alive when the carpet burst into flames. He left through the garage and collected a fee.

Jason actually felt bad hearing the story. Part of him was of course happy that Powerful got his. But there was another part of him that was saddened that Webb had committed the acts in the name of their friendship. *A rape and baby*, Jason couldn't stop thinking about it. They had nothing to do with it.

They dropped Webb off when they reached the Bronx. Jason pulled out fifteen hundred dollars. "You know I don't have much, but save up and go to Nevada, there's nothing for you in the game, but a trip upstate or to the grave even."

"Save the lecture, Farrakhan, but good looking, homey, I'ma make something happen with this. We fifty-fifty on everything I do. Fifty-fifty."

Jason held Webb's hands. "I'm out the game, Webb. Just take that and keep it moving."

"Duke, Duke, I had you Duke. Knee-high to a grasshopper. Come check me in a few weeks, I'm a get an apartment down on six-six, get some paper and then I'm out west. It won't take me long."

They said their farewells and headed for Brooklyn, where Jason couldn't wait to get to the woman of his dreams.

After a night of passionate screams, Vaseline, and whip cream, Jill was dead to the world. Jason was up early so he eased out of bed. He slipped on a sweat suit and a tee shirt. Quietly, he washed up and then headed down to the basement so he could do the same Saturday morning routine he had when he was in prison. When he reached the bathroom on the ground floor, he cracked the window and poured bleach into the toilet. He then searched around and found some tools.

He put the plumbing skills he learned in prison to use. He fixed the toilet and cleaned the bathroom. When he was done, he walked into the bedroom that Sharief used as an office. He laughed at the safe he saw sitting in an open desk drawer. In a few moves with a heavy-duty screwdriver, he could have had it open. He and Webb used to open them all the time when they were kids. He closed the door deciding to clean the room instead.

He went up to the kitchen and boiled several eggs, made two bowls of oatmeal, and prepared sliced fruit. He placed the hot items in the microwave, and left the cold in the refrigerator. He then cleaned the cabinets, washed all the dishes, and got on his knees to clean the floor. By then, he had a bucket out with all the windows in the living room open.

When he got to the next floor he went into the room he had slept in. He removed and changed the linen on the bed, wiped the walls and windows down, and scrubbed the bathroom until it was spotless. From there, Jason opened the two closed doors.

He was surprised when he saw the two decorated children's rooms. There were brand new toys, teddy bears, and everything from cribs to a potties. His mind was spinning, but he did not let his confusion stop him. He noticed the carpets needed vacuuming, so he went to work in the pink room first.

Again Jill was startled out of her sleep. When she awoke, she was so tired she didn't even know she was home. She wanted to go back to sleep badly. It was her intention to put an end to wherever the noise was coming from.

She jumped out of bed in her birthday suit, then headed down the stairs. As she descended each step, her vision revealed that both of the children's rooms had their doors open. Her heart started beating. She felt violated and embarrassed. When she reached the room, she yelled over the vacuum, "What the hell are you doing in here?"

Jason turned with a smile on his face. He turned off the vacuum cleaner. "What?"

"I said what the hell are you doing in here?" she screamed in rage.

He looked at her like she had lost her mind. "What does it look like I'm doing? I'm cleaning the house. It's time you get up because I was on my way up there."

Jill was touched by his kindness on one hand but her anger superceded her appreciation. "Those doors were closed for a reason. I want them closed at all times. I want you out of this room now."

He looked at her for a moment and then playfully cut the vacuum back on. Jill's temper popped. She ran up to him, slapped him in his face, and started yelling obscenities. Jason saw the anger in her eyes, but his own anger took over so he palmed her face and pushed her to the ground.

He stood over her and said, "What's the problem? What's the problem, Jill? You're upset that you don't have kids? You're upset that I saw that you're ashamed of the fact that you don't have kids? I already knew that."

She jumped up and charged at him yelling. "You don't have the right. These are my kid's room. You don't have the..."

He pushed her onto the tiny twin bed and said, "Open your legs."

She kicked at him and missed. He then grabbed her legs. "You want kids, Jill? Is that it? You really want kids?"

She was struggling as Jason shoved his manhood deep inside of her. Halfway in she screamed, "You're raping me, no...no...no, stop."

Jason ignored her and pushed her legs back to her shoulders. He sunk deeper into her and she said, "Stop, this is my daughter's bed. No...no...no...Yes...yes...yes, Jason, oh god please don't stop. Give me my babies."

He pounded away and made sure his member was as close to her fallopian tubes that it could get. He then carried her to the room that was designated for her son and continued ravaging her in there. When he came, he stood her up and took her into the bathroom designated for the kids. She thought they were going to wash up. Instead he leaned her over the sink and thrust into her from behind. When he was done, he sat her up on the sink and held Jill by her ankles and pulled her legs over her head so none of his sperm could leak out.

She stayed in that position protesting for what seemed like thirty minutes. Before he let her legs down she said, "Do me a favor? The next time we fight, make sure we end the fight this way. That was totally awesome." The fact that she had enjoyed the intensity of the argument reminded him a bit of the way he used to do Tasha.

After they ate breakfast, Jason made the bed while she was still lying in it. He cleaned up the entire loft. When he was done, Jill awoke from her nap and they headed for the basement so she could explain to him what he was going to be doing for a living.

They reached the basement and she pulled out the monthly financial statements from Clayton Realty. She handed them to him with a listing of all the properties the company owned. She explained that his job would be to visit all the properties and to recheck the monthly statements to make sure everyone was paying their rent. When he had the stack of papers, he asked to be left alone while he studied the company's progress over the years. She went back to bed and left him to do his work.

Jason returned to the loft two hours later with the papers in his hands. He gave a serious business stare. "Get your accountant on the phone."

"Why, what do you see?" Jill asked alarmed.

Jason looked down at the papers. "Please, just do what I asked you to do first and then I'll explain."

Smiling, she reached through her computer files for the number to place the call. She held the phone out for him. "Uh, yes how are you doing? This is Jason Faust. I'm handling an audit for Jill Clayton from Clayton Realty. Well, I have both copies of the monthly statements. No, not really an accountant, but I have the power of attorney on this matter. Yes I caught it. I'm more concerned about the last five years when you took over the accounts. Yes, I expect you'll be here within the hour with the off shore account numbers, or however you disguised it. Yes, you do know where she lives. Yes, in cash if you prefer. Yes, all six figures. No, I don't use the police. Either my associates or I will come *for* you, or you can come *to* me? It will be advantageous if you came to me, trust me. Sure, I'll see you then."

"What was that all about?" Jill asked worried.

"That was about you not being on your job for the last five years." He pointed down on the papers. "You see here, you have all the monthly statements. You have a copy from the C.O.O. of Clayton Realty for all accounts receivable. Then you have the book keeping statements with the assets, expenses, and the overall location of capital.

"Okay," she said.

"Let me finish. From each property, fractions have been deducted, but when you do the math overall, it doesn't add up. Since it's a very small number from each account, you wouldn't tell the difference unless you were really looking, but I see your C.O.O. was not in on it because all of her numbers add up. Your accountant has been taking a dollar here and there every month, but you never checked. You're supposed to have a non-interested C.P.A. do an independent bi-annual audit on your accountants, but I guess you took it for granted?"

"Where did you learn this, and I'm sending his ass to jail."

"No, we don't send people to jail unless we have to, and that's where I learned all of this."

"So how much did it come up to, and what do we do now?"

He punched in some figures on the calculator. "Let's see. It came up to almost five thousand a month for sixty-three months, probably including this month, so roughly three hundred thousand dollars."

Jill's mouth was wide open. In a raging fit, she began to scream and yell about how she was being robbed. Jason knew just how to calm her but it would have to wait.

When the doorbell rang, she wanted to get dressed in a business suit, but he stopped her. He informed her that leisurewear would put the thief more at ease. As an ex-thief himself, he knew exactly what to do. He did a few push-ups and when his body was fully pumped he walked down to meet the man without his shirt on.

The man walked into the living room and Jason was most polite. Jill wanted blood, but Jason handled affairs by doing what no one did for him, he gave the man a way out.

Jason had a seat, and thanked the man for coming. "I'm sure you have lots to do today, so let's wrap this up expediently. I ran across the error and I commend you on your strategy. Since you've been handling the accounts for over twelve years I take it that something tragic must have happened five years ago, or that you noticed that you weren't being audited?"

"Well this is just one big misunder..." the accountant tried to explain, but Jason cut him off.

"Whatever the case, you need not give an explanation. I am asking for your letter of resignation by Monday, all of the official and unofficial books, records, etc., and the full amount today. Guys like you usually keep the bounty or you're robbing so many people that I'm sure you have what you stole from her. I prefer cash, but I'm sure you understand that if your check bounces then *you* will bounce?"

The man stared into Jason's blue eyes, looked at his muscular body, and wrote down the numbers to his Geneva account. When he handed over the sheet of paper, Jill was expecting a check. She was about to protest, but Jason put his palm on her chest for her to relax. He shook the man's hand and escorted him to his car, where he made the man hand over his driver's license.

When Jason walked into the house and said, "He'll be back within the hour with a cashier's check," Jill did a little dance.

"You are so incredible. I swear you're *my* angel."

The closer he got to her she eased her way down to her knees. He walked up in front of her face and she reached into his sweats and pulled out his manhood. "You know you're the man, right?"

She made an attempt at sucking on him. It was her first time giving head. His eyes rolled back. "You take care of me don't you?" she said coming up for air.

Before he had a chance to answer, she started moving her mouth extra fast. Goose bumps filled his body. She stopped again. "You're bringing the freak out of me. I just hope you can handle everything that comes with it because I never did this before."

Jill grabbed his manhood and led him to the stairs.

By the time she reached the top floor she was naked. She teasingly put her leg up on the railing.

"Okay, you want to play? Okay, wait until I get up there," he said watching her every move.

She walked into the gym area and lied flat on the workout bench. Jason walked over and put his head on her stomach. When she looked down to see what he was doing he put his hands on her ass and scooped her up into the air. He tossed her up and put her legs on top of his shoulders, slamming her against the wall.

Jill watched in the mirror as her lover tasted all of her insides. She placed both of her palms against the ceiling for leverage. When she came, she begged him to stop, but he wouldn't. Her nerve endings were on fire. Jason opened her legs further and ate her until she came again. He then let her down, put her on her knees in front of the mirror and made love to her from behind until she came.

They were interrupted by the doorbell. The accountant had returned with a cashier's check as promised. There was an extra fifty grand included. He apologized again claiming a misunderstanding.

Like old lovers, Jason and Jill slept in each other's arms the rest of the day. On Sunday, they slept in and Jill cooked. They watched classic movies the whole day.

Monday morning, she requested that he wear a suit. She wore her gray pinstriped Armani business-wear. They skipped breakfast, and took a cab ride to 26 Court Street in downtown Brooklyn.

The slumbered office of Clayton Realty came alive when Jill stepped in. A buzz filled the room. "That's the boss," she heard a middle-aged woman say. Jill had only been there on two other occasions after Sharief had passed. By Jason revealing the theft, she felt uneasy about her former business practices.

Stay strong, girl. Show this man that you can handle your business. Let all of these people know who's the boss. You have a company to run, she thought to herself as she walked towards the company boardroom.

The top executives met her there. She explained to them why she was there. She wasn't really the tough boss type, but the employees seemed to long for it. She had two security guards accompany her and Jason into the office.

She pointed to the white C.E.O of the company, whose phony smile made her job easier. Jill walked into his office and shut the door. "Mr. Best, I want your resignation on the C.O.O.'s desk immediately. Security will give you three minutes to gather your things. That which you leave behind will be shipped to you." Imitating an usher, she said, "I would like to introduce you all to Mr. Jason Faust. He will be in charge of operations until further notice. When I'm done investigating the overall performance of this company, restructuring will take place. At that time, I will announce the new leader."

Jill turned to face a short caramel complexioned woman with an extremely well proportioned rear. Jason took a good look at the woman from head to toe. Her eyes stayed glued to his.

Jill interrupted the woman's trance. "Cecile, I need you to make a check out to Mr. Faust for $200,000. He will give you a check for $300,000 of this company's stolen money that has been recovered. I will not tolerate another mishap of this magnitude again. I also want you to give him an employee identification card and an annual salary of $250,000. As the C.O.O., you will receive a one $100,000 raise over your current salary, with a $15,000 bonus. You up for that?"

Cecile was so stunned that she almost screamed out like a kid on a rollercoaster. She nodded her head and said, "Yes ma'am."

"Good. Mr. Faust will sign off on that bonus once you draft it." Jill turned to the rest of the executives and said, "She was the only one who had things in order."

Cecile winked at Jason and rushed to take care of the boss's request. Ten minutes later, Jason was holding a check for two hundred thousand dollars. At the conclusion of the meeting, he pulled Jill to the side. "What do you expect me to do with this?" he asked in a panic.

Jill pushed her hair away from her face. "For one, you need to leave now, go open a bank account, and spend at least half of that on a car because we need to get around." She leaned in and whispered, "With the rest, buy something nice and don't forget about me," she added.

Jason could never imagine that he would hit the jackpot again in his lifetime. The fact that he had come across another good woman with her *own* money was hard for him to believe. One who was willing to put him on his feet was like catching a falling star.

Never in his wildest dreams did he think he would be in this position so fast. *His baby had bank,* he thought. He was finally on his way to becoming a self-sufficient man again. With Jill at his side, he would soon be back on top. His endurance had paid off, so he walked the crowded streets feeling on top of the world.

With pride in his stride and pep in his step, he walked into the bank and opened an account. He asked for a certified check for seventy thousand dollars, and twenty thousand dollars in cash. The bank executive that was processing his transaction wanted to check and re-check his credentials so he waited patiently. He was so proud of his come-up and his accomplishments that nothing could change his festive mood. The smiling executive returned with Jason's request, so he took the large envelope and headed for the door. While leaving the bank, he thought of how his positive choices in the face of despair had allowed things in his life to turn around. He felt like kicking himself for ever entertaining the thought of giving up on himself. Then he thought about it and realized that almost any man would have and most importantly, he hadn't.

He jumped into a cab and told the driver to take him to West 41st Street. During the ride, he watched the city go by knowing he wouldn't be sleeping on benches again. The cab took him to Mercedes of Manhattan. Without being invited, he sat at a salesperson's desk expressing his desire to drive out of the shop with a 2005 model. The woman thought he was joking until he produced the check. Two hours later, Jason was the proud owner of a new all black on black CLS 500 coupe.

The smooth ride and the futuristic technology were much different than the other cars he was used to handling. He had keyless entry and a DVD navigation system. The soft black leather seats gave way to Jason's contours. The smell of the new car, along with the shiny features of the wood dashboard sent his senses into overload.

He took his time driving the car. Even on the rough streets of Lower Manhattan, the car felt like it was floating on air. At the first stop light, he was stuck in a daydream of how his life had changed so soon without much effort. The tribulations he'd suffered through had all been a learning experience in humility, but a part of him still felt like he was living in a dream.

Just like old times, Jason headed down to Ultrasmith's. The owner and staff there asked him a million questions about where he had been, and he lied and told them that he was on the West Coast. After talking with the owner, he persuaded them to start on his car. Immediately the men gave him smoke tint, a remote starter feature and three television monitors. He swapped the rims that came on the car for a pair of chrome AMG 7-spoked ones. They gave the car major bling-factor without being overstated.

Jason had known the second he left Jill where his next stop would be. He parked on West 47th Street and ran into Shenoa & Company on 6th Avenue. His old jeweler, Ira, went off when Jason strutted in. "Where ya been man?" he asked loudly before coming from behind the corner to give him a hug.

Jason explained it was a long story. Then he told Ira what he was looking for. Ira walked him upstairs to his private office. He told Jason that for ten thousand dollars, he could bless him with a marvelous piece. Ira explained to Jason that he was still importing 'select' pieces of jewelry and that he had a nice amount of jewelry that could be had for a fantastic price. Nothing had changed. The old man was still a fence for various jewel thieves.

All that didn't matter because Jason never asked questions in the past and Ira never told him any lies. Ira placed three rings on a purple velvet cloth. One was pear shaped, another was emerald, and the third was a single heart shaped platinum, dripped in diamonds. After careful thought, he selected the twelve-carat heart shaped ring and said his farewells.

He hit HMV music store next. He purchased a handful of CDs by the songstresses he loved and a couple of rap CDs. Jason sat in the car and popped in the latest by Cassandra Wilson. Next he made the mistake of taking the sluggish street of Broadway uptown instead of the

FDR. The car stopped on 108th Street, he pulled up to the curb and got the attention of every passerby.

The attendant looked back when the brass chimes rang as he passed through the flower shop doors. He bypassed the employee going straight to the owner. The old woman looked him up and down as if she was ready to eat him for lunch. "May I have a dozen white orchids please?"

The woman blushed. "Sure handsome man, call me Lana, you can have *anything* in the store you want."

"I sure appreciate that," he said with a smile.

"You look so familiar, I'm sure I would have never forgotten a face like yours, and those eyes, my god I'm sure I know you."

He shrugged his left shoulder. "Well, you never know."

Lana wrapped the flowers without taking her eyes off of Jason. He handed her the money and she handed him the bouquet. "Are you sure you don't want to leave a gift card in the flowers?"

Jason smiled, put the pen and card in the lady's hand and said, "Here, you write it for me." She pulled her glasses off her head waiting for his message. He leaned closer. "To my angel, the world is ours. Nothing or no one can come between us, but us. Love, Jason."

Lana wrote the last words and a frown of familiarity came over her face. When she looked up at Jason, he pulled the card out of her hand and turned his back heading out the door.

"Young man. Hold on, hold on," she yelled. "You talking about *my* Jill?" was all Jason heard while he was walking out of the door. He sat in the car watching Lana reaching for her phone and it didn't take a rocket scientist to figure out who she was calling.

He drove uptown on Broadway. When the car stopped, he rolled the passenger seat window down and beeped the horn. The woman from the fruit stand leaned down to look in. Her eyes lit up when she saw Jason. She waved to her husband. They both approached the car happy.

"I just wanted to thank you for everything," Jason said.

They were jumping around hysterically. "You're doing fine my friend," the husband said.

A few blocks away, Jason saw Peter. He beeped the horn to get his attention. Peter came closer to see the man behind the tinted windows. Jason cracked the window halfway. "Come on in before the light changes."

Peter recognized him and took off running to get in. "Damn, my nigga," he screamed. "You couldn't take it no more, huh? Your ass is back in the game."

"Nah, man. I told you I wasn't gonna do that."

"Man, Harold told me about you coming through looking like a million, but damn, I didn't know my nucca was moving like this. If you didn't start robbing or slinging, how the hell you come up like this?"

Jason put his hand on Peter's shoulder. "No, I followed my intuition no matter how hard it got for me. I endured to the end and never took the fast route. I stayed focused, and the forces I needed to make things complete were drawn to me. Now I can see above water for now. So, where you going?"

"Man you talking some real philosophical shit, but I got to go pull something off for five small. I'm glad you strait. Well you way past straight it look like, yo."

They stopped at the light on 125th Street. Jason pulled out five hundred dollars for Peter. "Change of plans," he said. "You gonna stay with me for the day."

Peter quickly took the money, smiled and nodded. He said, "Daaaammmmnn," again and they headed for Brooklyn. He called Jill on his cellular and told her to meet him outside of the house. She told him that she was back at the office and had just returned from the city, so he asked her to meet him outside on Court Street.

He eased the new sleek ride into the narrow block. The front of Jill's office building was bustling with people. Jason beeped the horn. He and Peter got out of the car, and like celebrities, they got much attention.

"*Very* nice, baby. I see you have some class after all," she said swiping the ride. "Who's the little guy?"

Jason dropped his voice three octaves. "Oh that's Peter that I told you about. *Do not* call him little."

Peter walked her way. "Yo, big man, you can't say 'what up'?" Jill said.

Jason shook his head at Jill's ability to go from sophisticated to ghetto in an instant. He loved every minute of it.

"No doubt," said Peter. "But what up, my name is Peter, and you keep calling me big man, I'm feeling that."

She was amused. "Aw'ight then, my name is Jill," she said as she smacked his hand as confirmation.

"Jill," Peter said a bit too loud. He looked at Jason and said, "Jill-Jill? Ohhhh…yeeeeah." He turned back to Jill. "I'm *def…initely* glad to meet you. You just don't know how glad I am to meet you." Then he clapped his hands in laughter.

"What's that about?" she said focusing on Jason. He shrugged. "Are we going for a drive, or are you ready to go home?" he asked avoiding her question.

During the drive, he handed her the flowers. She looked back at Peter who was bobbing his head to his headphones. She then turned to Jason. "You ever have something happen to you in your life that you know is *oh* so right and you're sure it will always be with you and then it turns out that way?"

He said, "You mean, it's like everything just fits and all the pain, suffering, heartache, and disappointments all suddenly seem worth it because what you have now is better than anything else you ever thought you could have? So you want to do what you can while you have the time, before what you have turns out to be too good to be true? That sort of feeling?"

"*Exactly.* I swear we are on the same level in so many different ways."

He looked at her with a serious face while trying to keep his eyes on the road. He reached into his inside jacket pocket, and pulled out the velvet box. "Now take this and when you're ready to, *you know*, do the whole dress and tux thing, you let *me* know."

She opened the box to an even bigger surprise. She screamed, alarming Peter. The tears flowed uncontrollably. She immediately slid the ring on her finger. "You see...you see, I told you we were connected in so many ways."

Thirty

Jason found that life could never be all bliss on every front. The despair he observed in the projects was the opposite of the prosperity that he was now enjoying. He reluctantly drove to Queensbridge. Everyone in the projects beamed at Jason's car as he cruised through.

He parked on 40th street. He and Jill walked into his mother's building and knocked on the door. Apprehension and hope consumed him as he wondered what became of her. Over the smell of stale beer and urine, he found the courage to turn the knob, and the door flew open. He stepped into an empty space, forced to throw out some junkies who were sitting in the living room on the floor. His heart sank as he headed towards his mother's room.

In the hollow room sat a dirty, pissy mattress in the middle of the floor. In the center of the mattress Jason saw his mother, lying in scroungy underwear and a sweater with the sleeves cut off of it. She was unconscious and obviously in an alcohol induced sleep. A half empty bottle of Wild Irish Rose wine served as her bed partner.

Jason looked into her face and the life was being sucked out of him. If his mother was fifty two, she looked like seventy two he thought. He shook her shoulder. She swatted her arms, mumbling some nonsense about losing her money. She never opened her eyelids. Frustrated, he stormed past Jill, who was jotting on paper.

He always thought that his efforts were going to be a waste of time, but he hoped that just maybe his mother could have herself together for once in his life. He wanted to give her some form of love, but Jason gave up. As far as he was concerned, he no longer had a mother.

Little Lord was in front of the building. He wasn't all that little anymore. He gave Jason a firm hug, looked to him and said, "Damn homey, you the only cat that drove out of the projects in a nice whip, got locked up, and then come back through in a even hottah joint. What you do, go to the park and dig up some cash you buried, 'cause nobody stash is safe after all them years?"

Everyone started laughing. After kicking it for a few with the fellas and introducing Jill as he sent her to the car to join Peter, Jason realized that nothing really changed in the neighborhood, especially in his mom's house. Jason said his goodbyes and left.

Jason jumped on the highway and raced out to the Long Island home he had once purchased. He made his way up the old street, pulled into a driveway and received the surprise of his life. The house that he left was boarded up. He explained to Peter and Jill that it was his home once and he wondered what had happened. He was sure someone else would have been living there. After standing in the driveway for a few moments, a man from across the street came walking over with his bulldog. Jason looked up and saw a familiar face. It was the same retired police officer that he'd know in the past.

The man, who now looked to be in his seventies, told Jason that he'd asked about him and from a contact on the prison bureau he discovered that he had been arrested and sentenced. He told him that the house sat there for four years until the IRS stepped in for back taxes.

He also said they had been trying to sell it for seven years, but from a poor plumbing job the pipes had busted and flooded the basement. The house had mildewed and had really gone down to the point that no one had been interested in it. He had considered buying it and renting it out, but it was too much trouble. Only someone who fell in love with the character of the house would want it. That someone now stood right there.

Jason was happy with the news he'd received.

The man bopped over to his house and returned with the agent's name and number. He told Jason that he could arrange to pay his back taxes, or re-buy the home if necessary. He thanked the man over the sounds of crickets.

Jason handed Jill the card and she covertly slipped it into her pocket book. Jason drove back to Manhattan to show her the Regency. Peter gave her the history, as the car cruised through Harlem. They reached Eighth Avenue, and Jill showed them the projects where she grew up.

When they reached the corner and saw Pops, they both yelled, "Pops," at the same time. Then they laughed at each other.

"Now this has to be a miracle, or maybe Christmas done come early? Hey, Sugar," he said to Jill. "My man, my man, my man," he smiled, turning to Jason. What I tell you? What…did…I…tell…you? You look like a race horse at Belmont, I know a winner when I see one."

"How 'bout a quick wipe?"

"My pleasure." Pops proceeded to tell a few life stories, as he carefully wiped the new car. When he finished, Jason slid him three hundred dollars when he was done.

Then Jason leaned in to his ear and said, "Thank you, man, thank you for making me believe when was ready to give up."

Like a true man of class, the old man put it in his pocket, never giving it a look.

Jason wanted Jill to meet his childhood partner in crime. He reached 170th Street, and the man he knew as Scooter said, "Webb down on 166th Street." Then he rushed Jason off the block for attracting too much attention.

There were no signs of Webb when Jason pulled up on 166th. A group of thugs gathered on the corner watching his every move. He didn't like what he saw, so he prepared to pull off.

"Yo man, let me out. You got the child safety locks on," Peter commanded. "I know these cats."

Pete climbed out the car and walked over to a couple of the guys. Minutes later, he hiked over to building 1105.

Jason wanted to go after Peter but accepted that the youngster knew what he was doing. Peter and Webb returned five minutes later with two unleashed Rottweilers.

Webb looked at the car and said, "Yo homey, what? You was stashing on me or something? Damn this ride is mean."

"Nah, this is one of the perks of living legit, you should give it a try," he bragged as he got out of the car.

"Duke, Duke, you beating me in the head with all that, Duke." Webb leaned his head down and spotted Jill. "Who's the chick?"

Jason bent towards the passenger side and said, "This is Jill, my wifey I was telling you about."

Webb smiled. "Damn, homey. She is definitely bout it-bout it." He shook her hand. "Please to meet you, baby girl, I hope you take good care of my homey here?"

He tuned back to Jason. "Yeah, I see you sent baby boy to come holla at me."

"Yeah, we just hanging out, taking a ride that's all."

"Come on, let's take a walk," Webb said with a suspicious look.

After Jason told Jill and Peter to stay in the car, he and Webb strolled towards the thugs on the corner. Webb stood in the middle of the crowd and said, "These *our* workers right here. They official soldiers, ready to pop off too. I got them running six miles every morning, doing the whole work out. Understand, the whole work out. They want to get down... they got to go through basic training, just like the army."

Webb walked up to the crew of six and said, "This is the general I was telling y'all about. He's our sponsor. Y'all want to drive a phat whip like him? You gotta be ready to put in work. You gotta be ready to put in work. So let's get this paper and stop standing around."

Jason didn't like the surprise, so he backed away from Webb trying to get closer to the car. He pulled Webb back across the street while watching the young thugs go through all types of things to impress him. Jason asked, "Who puts a spot together in just four days?"

"Four days? Four days? This *been* put together. Once I took the re-up money you gave me to Scooter, we blasted off. I figure we'll cover forty grand after a month of work. This is all ours, Duke. All ours, Duke. *Nobody*, I mean nobody can move nothing without me and you getting a piece."

Jason was annoyed. "Homey, I'm out of the game for life. I'm trying to make a family. Plus, I thought you were headed for Vegas?"

Webb followed behind Jason, who was headed for the car. "I am your family. So what chu sayin', Duke. What chu sayin'? We in this together," he said shouting. "You in the game, money stay the same. You either full time crook or square up and turn lame. Remember that, homey? Remember that? You ain't no lame. We in this for life.

Come see me in a couple a heartbeats so you can collect your paper. And Jay, knee high to a grasshopper, Duke, don't make me have to come look for you."

Jason jumped in the car and slammed the door. He was upset that Webb was still risking his life and his freedom and now putting his at risk too. Jill asked what happened. But his silence was the only answer she needed. Sharief taught her that when a man is ready to talk he would.

He blamed himself because he went against his oath to leave his past behind, and to never embrace people from his old lifestyle, including Webb.

Peter had fallen asleep by the time they reached Brooklyn. Jason informed Peter that he could stay in the guestroom on the ground floor. "Nah, I gots to get home to my wife."

After Jason explained to Jill who Imani was, she told Peter that she would send Roger to go and pick her up if they needed a place to stay. "Not tonight but I'll use that ride."

"Okay, cool."

In the silence of the loft, Jason explained everything about Webb to Jill and she understood his loyalty. "Baby, what you have to understand is that if people don't add to your life, then you don't need them in it. Even if its family."

He agreed and made up his mind that he was going to avoid Webb at all cost.

On Wednesday morning Jason wanted to get two things accomplished. He dressed in *his* Hugo Boss suit and shoes, and headed out the door. He parked in the 42nd Street lot on Eighth Avenue. After a little small talk with the Haitian attendants, he jetted to see Mr. Townsend.

Jason knew Mr. Townsend would be upset that he was back on his feet, but he had too much to lose to allow an emotional response to land him back into prison. When he tapped on the door, he observed a young white male who looked to be fresh out of college.

"Maybe I have the wrong office. I was looking for Mr. Townsend?" Jason said.

The man looked startled and asked, "Oh, are you a supervisor here at the department?"

Jason looked down at how well dressed he was and said, "Oh. No, I'm Jason Faust. Actually I'm on his case load."

The man cracked a smile and said, "Oh, Mr. Faust. I was expecting you. I'm Mr. Hancock, your new parole officer."

Jason's eyebrows frowned with surprise, "*New* parole officer? What happened to Mr. Townsend?"

"Oh, I might burn in hell for saying this, but *fortunately* for us all, Townsend had a massive heart attack. He's still alive, but he won't be coming back. You know the stress on the job and all."

"A heart attack? Wow. So now what?"

"Now what?" He motioned for Jason to take a seat. "Do you have a job?"

Jason nodded his head because the news had thrown him off balance. "Yes," he said "I do."

"Do you have a check stub and an employee's identification card?"

He handed the man what he asked for. Then the man said, "I only have you for a few more months before it's all over."

He nodded again. "We have you down for living in the Regency, but I can guess from your attire that that's not still the case, is it?"

"No sir."

"Nevertheless, you seem to check out, and I don't want you to report anymore. My load is heavy enough as it is. Just leave your new address with the secretary and be sure to call once a month and make sure you speak to me. If you don't get arrested, you won't hear from me. Have a nice life, Mr. Faust."

Jason was stunned. This turn of events was definitely a blessing. "That's it? You don't want me to submit a urine sample? No house search, curfew, or new conditions?" Jason blurted, before he could stop it.

The man looked at him. "Whoa...whoa...whoa. That would mean extra work, and that *work* is what gives you stress on the job. I don't want to end up like Mr. Townsend and have a heart attack. Just don't get arrested and we're cool."

The man slapped Jason five. "God works in mysterious ways," said Jason.

Mr. Hancock leaned back in his chair with his feet propped on the desk. "I'd have to agree."

Jason was ready to dance on his way out of the parole building.

Jason woke each morning finding his life impossible to believe. He would look over at Jill, who slept more soundly than she ever had in life, and thank God over and over.

For the next eight weeks Jill and Jason's life settled into a routine that suited them both completely. Jason went to the office of Clayton Realty in the daytime and took real estate classes at the New York Real Estate Institute on West 35th in the evenings. Between studying and working he lived the type of life that, up to that point, he'd only seen in movies. A hot plate of food would be waiting for him when he got home and a massage before he went to bed. For his part, he did everything in his power to shower Jill with his affections. He continued with the flowers and gifts.

Peter and Imani started spending more time with them. Jill convinced Peter to become a ward of the state so that she could legally take him into foster care. Peter insisted that he was still going to have to maintain his independence, meaning he wasn't looking for a mother. Jill agreed and even helped him get an apartment that they put in Jason's name. At the same time, Jill was seeing what she could do to get Imani's immigration papers.

Now that she had a man around to care for, Jill's world was almost complete. It became obvious to Jason that she had no real interest in real estate or her company. She seemed relieved that she had someone to look after it. All she'd ever done was collect more money than she spent or needed. "You take care of it. I'm fine," was her reply whenever he tried to talk business with her.

She'd watched Jason's transformation. She could remember the homeless bum and now she saw a sterling and savvy professional. On top of it, he was gorgeous and the perfect mate. The only thing left for her to do was to wait for him to ask her for her hand in marriage.

The day that Jason passed his test to get his real estate license he was prepared to celebrate. It was a major accomplishment and it was hard for him to contain his pride, especially since it was the first thing that he had done completely on his own since he'd been home from prison. The instructor, Katrina, told him that she'd never had a student work so diligently and become so proficient as quickly as he had. When he explained to her that he was working with his fiancés real estate company as a manager, she was extremely impressed. So much so that she made a call to a friend who was a developer in Park Slope and Williamsburg and told him about Jason.

"He always needs aggressive and talented people. So far you're the first person I've hooked him up with fresh out of this class. He wants to meet you tonight," she'd said.

"Wow, I guess I could do that." Jason was thinking that Jill would want to celebrate with him.

"Meet us at Delmonico's. 56 Beaver Street. Bring your fiancé if you like."

When Jason told Jill the news about him passing, she didn't seem very excited. "I told you there was nothing to worry about," was her response."

Feeling a little dejected, Jason decided not to invite her to dinner. "I have a meeting with this guy, Matthew Leahy. He owns…"

"Matthew Leahy, I've heard of him. He owns the Zone Development Group. How did you get a meeting with him?"

"My instructor set it up."

Jill nodded and without a word more on it she said, "I'm tired. Not feeling too well. You enjoy your meeting. Don't bother waking me when you come in."

Jason thoroughly enjoyed the lobster Newburg and hearing the history of the 172 year old restaurant from Matthew. Jason loved that Matthew was a genius when it came to real estate and making money. At one point he told Jason something that really shocked him and at the same time earned his respect. "Jason, I'm going to tell you something about the new money situation in America. Thirty, or maybe even twenty years ago, you and I wouldn't be having this dinner. I'm white and you're black. Nothing in common. I'm filthy rich... you're not. But all that has changed. I can use you because you're black, talented and hungry. Most importantly, you have a face the working class will trust. You can use me because I'm rich, white and I have the connects to the power structure. It's all about alliances. Call it using each other... whatever. Just always know that in business, money is green. You could make decent money working solely with Clayton Realty or you can become wealthy by aligning with me as well. But remember, I will expect a lot from you. But then, I will be sure that you shit hundreds and wipe your ass with twenties."

For the rest of the time they ate, Jason impressed him with his knowledge and ideas about the market. Ever since he took over he was determined to find away to make enough money to pay Jill back every penny that she'd given him with interest. It was just a goal for him as a man. He needed to build from his own hard work and not from a handout, even if it came from his woman. He wanted to give Jill a check for a half a million dollars one day soon, proving that he was an asset to her and not a leech.

"Jason I share a lot of your views on the housing situation in Brooklyn. One thing I want to ask you is this. What do you see as the forecast? In other words, where would you put your money?"

Jason's answer both surprised and impressed Matthew. "Well, Mr. Leahy, for Clayton Realty, I am working on a project that I think will propel it to the next level. On a grander scale, I think it would benefit your company as well. I am trying to put together a consortium so that we can buy several blocks of Brownstones in Bed-Stuy. Instead of renovating them and re-selling them, I want to turn them into apartments that are affordable.

The city is prepared to grant seventy percent of the cost, which will allow for a profit of nearly six hundred percent to the investors. While most everyone is investing in the luxury condos, I like the idea of creating affordable houses for hardworking people as well as getting rich in the process. Plus, being a part of a project geared at benefiting the working class will do wonders to aid any future projects that need help at City Hall."

Then sipping the last of his wine, Jason added, "At the same time, I plan to find the next hot spot. Park Slope, Williamsburg and

Dumbo are old news. Every big investor in the region is begging to get in over there. The question is what's next? Once I find the answer to that, I'll be ready to supply the other fifty thousand buyers who couldn't get into Park Slope."

"Now that's thinking outside the box, my man."

When they finished dinner, Mr. Leahy told Jason to send him over the plan for his project. Then he told Jason to think big and that he would be ready to back him and take it to the next level. The last thing he said to Jason was, "I have a project or two left in Williamsburg and a few depressed areas of housing that I could use a good front man on. If you're interested in getting on board and getting in where most people can't, I'd love to have you."

"Sure."

"Think about it. I'm asking you to jump onto a train that is already moving toward victory. In return I might ask you to be a fresh face and shake things up. There are a lot of people... community activists, many of them African American, who don't have your vision. What they don't understand is that there's always more than one *right* way to do a thing. I just do them the money way," he smiled and Jason nodded. "I could pick any one to do this, but not one of the people I've spoken to has come up with one idea that will help the working class. As a matter of fact, when they meet with me, the only thing they think about is how much money they can make working with me. You are the one, son."

Thirty -3

For the next month Jason was hardly home and when he was, Jill was hardly any company. It was strange that she seemed less interested in sex. Jason began to wonder if they had moved too fast and were falling out of love. Everything hit the fan when Jason came in after a meeting with Matthew.

He slid into the bed with Jill. For once he wasn't dead tired. He even worked out for an hour before showering. Jill was watching television dozing off. Looking at her in nothing but one of his T-shirts caused him to stir below the waist.

He turned the remote off while Jill watched the news. "You couldn't see I was watching that?"

"It was watching you. Besides, I've got something more exciting than the news." With that he scooted up next to her and his penis brushed across her thigh.

"Not right now, Jason. I'm not in the mood."

Jason ignored her and began to fondle her titties. Her nipples were hard, yet she squirmed away. "What's up, ma?"

"I'm not your ma."

"I know that, but still. I want some."

"Oh, that's romantic."

"You want romance?" Jason said as he leaned his head in to kiss and Jill turned her face away.

"Jason, please."

Finally realizing that she didn't want sex he said, "Shit, what the hell is wrong with you."

His tone sent her over the top. "Don't raise you voice with me. If I don't want it... I don't have to. It's not like I haven't done enough for you."

Jason couldn't believe what she'd said. "Oh, its like that."

Jill leaned up. "What? Did I hurt your feelings? Well maybe, you've hurt mine. All you do is work all day and run the streets with this Matthew all evening. I haven't seen any flowers lately. We haven't been out in three weeks."

"It's not like I haven't asked. You always tell me you're tired. And tired from what? You sit in here and order shit off of QVC and the Home Shopping Network like its going out of style and eat. You're obviously not working out, cause to be honest…your getting a little soft."

"Fuck you, Jason. If you don't like it, you can leave. I've given you enough money."

With that, he got up out of the bed and put his underwear on. She went on. "I'm not talking about this room either. I'm saying you can get your ass the fuck out of my and Sharief's home."

Fifteen minutes later, Jason was knocking on Peter's door. "I'm gonna need your couch for a couple of days."

"Boss, mi casa is su casa," Peter said. Jason looked around the apartment and noticed that once again the youngster had laced the apartment with the best in electronics.

"Thanks a lot."

"Is it that bad?"

"It might be over," Jason said. "She really took it there on me."

Peter looked around his apartment and spread his arms apart. He said, "Don't be no fool."

"It ain't about that. It's about respect."

"Nah," Peter said. "It's about pride with you. It needs to be about love." With that Peter turned the light off in the kitchen and headed to the bedroom. "I'm going to bed."

"You fourteen, son. Where's your energy? I can't believe you sleepy already?"

"I said *bed*, not sleep, nucca."

For the whole night, he laid on the couch with his phone in his sweaty hands. When he couldn't hold out anymore, he broke down and called Jill. She hung up on him. He would have preferred to argue with her than to not talk at all, but he allowed things to remain nasty if she wanted it that way and he went to sleep.

The following day Jason was on edge at the office. He rationalized that Jill would probably show up at the office that day.

During the day, he asked his secretary over and over if there were any calls for him, but none came in. It appeared the entire office picked up on his disgruntled mood. After a while he began to wonder if Jill might be coming by to fire him.

By noon, Cecile barged into his office with unannounced confidence. "Mr. Faust, I took the liberty of ordering you lunch from the new restaurant up the street."

Jason was hungry but hadn't even thought about it. When Cecile brought the food in, the aroma woke him up to the fact. "Place it on the table for me."

"Mr. Faust, are you going to eat now?"

"Yes as matter of fact I am, why?"

"Well, the break room is full and I wanted to know if I could sit in here with you," she said.

"I guess that'll be okay."

She smiled as if she'd won the lottery. "Thanks. Let me turn the Audix on," she turned to head out of the office and dropped a folder she was carrying. "Oops." Papers were all over the floor.

Cecile seductively bent at the waist exposing her DD cups, while gathering them. Jason salivated from her perfect measurements. "You missed one right there," he said. Cecile turned around and she bent wide enough for Jason to get a good look at her heart-shaped rear. Not even realizing that he had wanted to see her in that manner he slowly became erect.

Cecile was flawless. No, thought Jason, not flawless, but tempting. But tempting suggested he had no self-discipline.

During lunch Cecile caught Jason glaring at her breasts several times. She looked into his cheering eyes and just smiled. She ate with her legs crossed. Finally she said, "Mr. Faust, I have a confession to make."

"What is that?"

"Ms. Clayton called earlier." Jason's face turned to stone. "But let me explain. She told me that if I told you that I would be fired. She just wanted to know if you were here and had you come in on time."

"She said she would fire you?"

"Yes, sir, and she sounded deadly serious."

"Well, why did you tell me?"

She looked at him right in the eyes. Then she licked her lips. She looked like a video ho when she did it, but once again Jason's body reacted. "Why do you think?"

Jason tried to play it off as he stood up. He didn't hide his swelling penis. "I'd better get back to work," Cecile said as she wrapped up lunch. On her way out the door she said, "I'll be at my desk, Mr. Faust, and I want you to know that I'm here for *you*... and Clayton Realty one hundred percent in any way you need me."

Jason closed the door to his office trying to make the blood that rushed to his penis go back up to his head. He needed to call Jill, so he walked over to his desk and right there on the glass was a sweaty print of a heart, and an inviting aroma. His finger pressed the speed dial and he hoped she answered, but her voice mail picked up.

Why didn't women understand what rejection did to a man? Jason wanted to know. *A weaker being, would have fallen victim to the breathtaking proposal he received in his office,* Jason thought. In an effort to gain his composure, he sat and day dreamed about his future goals.

Jason finally left the office to take a walk to the newsstand. He wanted to see if the ads for the real estate listings were to his satisfaction. While he was at the stand, he grabbed all seven of the papers that he ran ads in. While flipping through the Village Voice he saw near the center of the paper an advertisement that read:

ANNUAL DELTA SIGMA THETA SORORITY GATHERING
BEING HELD AT AVERY FISHER HALL
@ THE CITY COLLEGE OF NEW YORK.
TUESDAY 8:00 p.m.

Jason instantly thought of Zeida. They had had a great time at the one he attended with her. He wondered if she would be there, quickly dismissing the thought, but something was telling him to go to the gathering.

In his mind, he felt his desire to go was innocent, but then erotic thoughts of he and Zeida entered his mind. He tried to fight off the thoughts of her but his conscious wouldn't let him. He had found it much easier to control himself and his thoughts when he was abstinent.

Now that he and Jill had started with the high-octane sex life, he needed it all the time. Jason thought back to Zeida and the times that they had and his libido kicked in again and his little head began doing the majority of the thinking. Jason was embarrassed and told himself that he had a fiancée at home and that he should stay away from Zeida and let his old life go.

In an attempt to control his sinful thoughts, he called Jill's cell phone and left her messages to call back immediately. When that didn't work, he left messages on their home phone. He didn't want to go home unless he was wanted there, so he spent another night on Peter's couch.

The following day Jason didn't go to work. He wanted to get his hair cut *just in case* he decided to go to the gathering that he was sure Zeida wouldn't attend. He drove down to Diane's salon hoping that he would run into Jill there. He knew she wouldn't make a scene in public.

Instead of Diane discussing Jill with Jason, she asked for his advice on expanding the business and safeguarding her investments. Since he took over at Clayton Realty, Jill had bragged about Jason's cutting company expenses.

Jason left the salon undecided on what to do. Before he started his car he made one last effort to call Jill. She answered the phone, but before he had a chance to get one word in, she told him she was busy and hung up on him. He immediately called back, but she wouldn't answer.

Jason's insecurities were raised and he questioned if she could really be trusted. *Maybe she was ashamed of him for some reason, or wasn't serious about being his wife.* He had reached the peak of frustration. The comment about them living in Sharief's home had stung and Jason couldn't wait for the first phase of funding for the project with Matthew to go through so that he could earn his first percentage. He was going to buy his own piece of real estate just for situations like this.

His payoff was coming. Jason was working like a dog and he was going into neighborhoods where Matthew would be received as a threat and was making major headway. The key part of the deal was that he was doing his business under the guise of being an agent for Clayton Realty. Matthew assured him that within two years he'd be a multi-millionaire as long as he stayed focused.

Jason's mind was made up. He called Johnny and told him that he needed a room at the Marriot Marquis for the night. He didn't want to put it on his credit card and he didn't see any reason to pay four hundred for a room he could get for one C.

"You got that, youngblood. When you hit the front desk, your key will be waiting for you. Oh, and your name is Borne, got it?"

"Yeah, thanks."

"You can leave the hundred at the desk for Mr. Love."

"Okay, I really..." Johnny hung the phone up before he could get his words out.

His next move was to head to 5th Avenue to Saks. He picked up a Tux and they altered it while he went across the street to Kenneth Cole for shoes. Not knowing when he'd be welcomed home he went to Banana Republic and grabbed underwear, socks and a couple of suits for work.

Needing to get the car washed, instead of going to see Pop, he stopped over at the Westside Highway on Twelfth Avenue to get his car washed for time's sake.

He stepped out of the car to get the interior cleaned and a couple of prostitutes walked up on him. He kept his cool. He smiled at all the compliments the women threw at him. One even jokingly asked to pay *him* for his time. "No thanks," Jason said rejecting their appeal.

"Oh what motherfucker, you think you too good?" the women in pink patent leather said with hostility.

Jason knew the streets and what those types of women respected. They had him pegged as a square. So he flipped it on them. "Look, I just came home from a thirteen year bid, so unless you bitches are up for me sticking a broomstick up your asses then get the fuck away."

Stunned, one said, "Damn, you ain't got to get like that."

"Yeah, well I tried to be nice to you bitches now beat it before I get violent out here."

The women stepped off quick and Jason laughed to himself. He wondered why it took him getting like that for them to understand he didn't want to be bothered.

Jason was getting dressed in his room and thought about calling Jill once again but decided against it. He wondered for a moment if it was over between them. When he finished he took a look at himself in the full length mirror and for the first time he realized how far he'd come. When he realized that it was because of Jill's presence that he was able to afford the clothing that he wore, he had mixed emotions. Was he going to stop living if she never came around?

He cruised uptown on the Westside Highway until he reached 125th Street. He made the right onto the Avenue, made the left on Convent next to B & G's soul shack, and pulled up to the tree-lined hill of the City College of New York.

There was a long caravan of cars parked on the street. Spectators were everywhere. Jason pulled up in the sparkling Mercedes, and all heads in the parking lot turned. The attendant asked him for his name.

"Let's see. Mr. Faust... Mr. Faust," he was nervously scrolling a list.

Thinking quickly and knowing his name was not on the list he said, "I'm with Miss Carro," as if the young man should have known who that might be. Then Jason said, "Never you mind, son. Just take good care of it. Here you go." He handed the boy five twenties.

"Thank you, sir," the attendant said trying to keep a straight face. As he exited the car alone, he had the attention of all the single women and some of the married ones too.

Moving mysteriously to the front door, Jason was momentarily the star of the show and he loved every minute of it. It had been a long time since he had received so much attention from a group of progressive women, and he liked it. He told himself that he had come too far to be depressed, and that night he was going to partake in some overdue recreation. Immediately Jason began looking for Zeida's long flowing hair and her perfectly shaped rear, assuming she still had both.

A line snaked around the ancient stone ledge of Aaron Davis Hall. Camera crews were shooting footage there from BET and photographers were flashing away. Beautiful women in their gowns and handsomely dressed brothers in tuxedos were on line. They were standing by as some of the famous members of the sorority were entering. Camille Cosby entered without husband Bill. She walked instead with Nikki Giovanni and singer Nancy Wilson.

Jason was in awe when he saw how gorgeous Natalie Cole looked in her stunning, crimson dress. When he turned the corner into a giant courtyard filled with couples mingling, many people had invites or tickets in their hands. Jason's head turned in every direction, looking for a way in until he made eye contact with a damsel in distress.

The older black woman in the flowing pink gown was five feet nine inches tall, and wore diamond framed granny glasses. At a closer inspection she had too much makeup on her face, and the rocks in her ears could have probably paid for his car. Her smiling face indicated to Jason that she must have seen his distress because she walked over fanning two tickets. She smiled showing her yellow alligator teeth.

She approached Jason with familiarity. In a voice that announced her privileged education she said, "Pardon me, fine young man. You appeared to be somewhat distressed. Perhaps you have misplaced your ticket?"

Jason held his breath to prevent himself from choking. He looked her over and saw that her gown was expensive, but she had two stomachs and the one under her waist favored a kangaroo pouch. He told himself that desperate times required desperate measures so he smiled, put on his Senator Anduzé voice and said, "Before I respond, might I say that your gown is simply ravishing? It fits your sculpted body like a glove."

The woman blushed. "Oh, yes you may indeed say so," she said cupping his arm. My name is Wilemina Cooper. My escort couldn't make it, so if you don't have a ticket, feel free to use my extra one."

"Oh-ho-ho-ho, you are a life saver," Jason said squeezing his butt cheeks tight. "I was so troubled and you came to rescue me?" He kissed her hand. "I am Senator Mark Anduzé. It will be my most honorable pleasure to accompany you to the gathering. Perhaps I can offer you a lift home later in the evening? Or even share a spot of tea at the conclusion of the ceremony?"

The woman's fat cheeks glowed. "Oh, most certainly. If you're serious, I'll give my driver the night off. I just purchased a Cadillac Sixteen from a friend I have on the board at ALCOA and Juan just *loves* to have it for himself. I hope you're prepared for a grand time?" She put her lips to Jason's ear. "Per chance we can even cuddle at my beach house in the Hamptons later?" she whispered. Her eyebrows rose at the question.

Jason tried to keep a straight face without bursting with laughter when he said, "Splendid, splendid. Sounds smashing. Just don't forget to meet up with me before the night is over."

They walked into the hall and Jason was grateful when some of her sorority sisters called to her as soon as they walked in. During his retreat he looked back and saw her blushing and smiling with her sisters, pointing in his direction. "Toodles," he said. Then he walked away as fast and as far away from her as he could.

The dim hall had jazz flowing in the background as prestige networked. Many of the women approached Jason with different offers. Some were decent and others were not so tactful. He knew it would be hard for him to stay out of trouble there when two medical students from out of town gave him their hotel keys and told him to meet them at the Belvedere Hotel.

He put the one flute glass that he had been nursing all night down on a counter and started looking for the exit. He spotted Wilemina glaring his way and made a beeline when the coast was clear. He headed straight up the auditorium aisle for the exit. Rushing to get through crowded room, he bumped into a woman knocking over her glass.

When the woman bent over he couldn't help but notice that she had the perfect rear end. He thought of Zeida, but the woman's hair was cut extra short. He leaned over to assist the woman, and an older Latino man that Jason assumed was her date rudely moved him out of the way so that he could help her instead. A small crowd had gathered to see the outcome of the accident, but they were let down. After the woman turned around and stopped cursing, she froze in silence.

Their eyes locked as they stared at each other. There was a sudden tension between them. Everything slowed down. She was more gorgeous than the last time he had seen her. Like a fine wine, she had gotten better with time.

Zeida blinked. *Am I dreaming*, she thought. Her date stared at Jason trying to figure out why his face looked so familiar. To break the tension that lasted about ten seconds, Jason said, "How...how are you doing, Zeida?"

"How? How...how am I ... I mean *you* doing?" She was amazed.

After all those years, Jason was at a loss for words. "I'm sorry for bumping into you, but history seems to be repeating itself?" There were more seconds of silence as they stared at one another. Jason regained his composure first and came up with, "Can we go somewhere and talk for a minute?"

"You don't need to take her anywhere, pal," said the man who appeared to be Zeida's man.

Jason was in no mood for games. He had come too far to waste his time, so he looked at her and asked, "Who is this clown?"

"Zeida you know this *guy*?" her date asked.

She turned to the man and without breaking eye contact with Jason she said, "This is Jason. Leave us for a moment."

The man's jaw dropped when he heard the name. Like a neglected puppy, he shook his head in disgust and walked off to the side.

"Please tell me that's not your husband?" Jason asked.

"Him? He's a good man."

"Yeah, but you can do better. The insecurity thing's not a good look."

She took a sip from her new flute of champagne without moving her eye. "Well, he's obedient and knows how to come home. After you, I refused to deal with a bad boy."

"Next time you want a clown why not try the circus?"

Her attitude became cold. "For someone who disappeared without a clue, while I was in the hospital dying with a hundred police questioning me, you're kinda out of line."

"Is that what you think happened?"

"How could you leave me like that without knowing if I was going to live or die?"

Jason shook his head. "Do you really believe I would have done that?"

"I didn't know what to think. At first I thought you were angry because I dragged you into all that mess. Then I thought maybe you got killed. When I got out of he hospitals I checked every hospital in the area and when nothing came up... I just stopped thinking. I just thought... I just..."

"Zeida, I loved you..."

"I was pregnant with your child, Jason."

He couldn't believe what she'd just said. A whirlwind of emotion struck him, but he tried to control it. Through clinched teeth he said, "I was in prison for the last thirteen years. My life was upside down. When I came home I had *nothing*, no one and nowhere to go."

Clearly his excuses weren't good enough. "You could have called my job, had someone to come see me, do whatever was in your power to get in contact with me."

"Zeida, you just have no idea."

"Why didn't you find me as soon as you came home then?" She looked away dismissing his excuses. "Your story is hard to believe, and I run into you here, of all places?"

"Please, relax until you hear all the facts. Believe, me I tried all of that. Why do you think I'm here?" Realizing he was making a scene, he lowered his voice. "I can't get into it right now. I feel you should have done the same in trying to find me. I need to speak to you in private. I have a few things to explain. Will you at least hear me out?"

She pushed Jason near the seats in the concert hall. She opened her evening bag, and removed a business card. She folded the card, placed it in his hands and said, "I want to show you something. Come closer to me and look down."

Jason was subtle with his movements. For some reason he showed Zeida's man some respect. Still, he moved so close to her that he could feel the warmth of her breath. He wanted to kiss her so bad, but instead he looked down and received an incredible surprise.

Zeida pulled the skirt and panties to her two piece outfit away from her stomach. When he looked down he saw her well trimmed pubic hairs. His eyes moved up a little and he saw a slash across her belly, and right above it, his name was tattooed across her midsection.

In one move she fixed herself and said, "You could never question my loyalty when it came to you. Come see me tomorrow at my office, I have a lot to show you." She tried to walk away.

Stunned he said, "So do I have a son or a daughter."

"Tomorrow. I'll be there early."

He pulled her back and closer to him and asked, "So, did you start your own clothing line?"

She said, "No. Look on the card. I have to go now. Please. You come and see me and I'll answer all your questions."

Jason was slightly distraught as he watched her walk away in the arms of another man. It didn't shock him at all that she had someone. He would have expected it. But the idea and the reality were two different things altogether. He placed her business card in his pants pocket. He took a step into the aisle and Wilhelmina was smiling, blocking his path with a group of her sisters who blocked the exit.

"Senator, are you ready to retire with me for the evening?" she said smiling with her wide lips over her gums.

She looked over her shoulder at her sisters. She blushed as if to prove that she was indeed leaving with the handsome man. Jason was upset with the way things turned out for him that night, so he looked her in her eyes and said, "Sweetheart, I must find the lavatory. Give me five minutes and then meet me right here."

"I'll be here, waiting." She smiled and nodded her head at her friends.

With that he walked into the crowd and out the door.

Thirty-4

He reached the Marriott and sat in a corner with a bottle of Armadale and orange juice. His mind was playing still frames of his life. As he made his way to his room he realized he was lost. He convinced himself that if Jill didn't want him then he would be all right regardless. By the time the bottle was finished he had fallen off to sleep.

At midnight, his cell phone rang and startled him. He woke to a raging hard on. Hoping it was Jill, he answered the phone with, "Hey, baby."

The voice on the other end was not Jill's. Instead he heard a voice that sounded like Cecile's say, "Hey, Mr. Faust. Or at this time of night is it okay to call you Jason?"

"Cecile?"

"Yes, I was worried about you. We didn't hear from you all day and Mr. Leahy called three times and of course Mrs. Clayton called in secrecy to see if you showed up."

"I see you're good at keeping secrets," he said in a groggy yet sarcastic manner.

"Certain ones I am really good at keeping."

"So what are you saying?" Jason said. He was now rubbing his dick inside of his boxers.

"What do you think I'm saying?"

"Cecile, I'm not up for any games. I'm a grown-ass man. What's on your mind?"

"*Honestly?*"

"Absolutely."

"I want to fuck you. No, let me correct that. I want to fuck the shit out of you."

"Right now?"

"Anywhere, anytime."

"I'm at the Marriot. Times Square. 2804."

"Give me forty-five minutes."

Jason began the tug-o-war in his mind. He had so much on his mind and he saw his life unraveling before him. On one hand he knew he could make it even if Jill left him. He didn't know what would happen between he and Zeida. He loved Jill, that much he knew. She was his angel. There was no way he should have invited Cecile to his room.

The only thing he knew at that moment was that he was horny. The battle raged for forty minutes and when he was ready to call Cecile back a knock at the door came.

He opened it and there stood Cecile. He didn't have to guess what she was wearing under the small summer rain coat. She walked into the room and let the jacket fall open exposing her huge breast wrapped in a see through bra and matching sheer lace panties. All thoughts that of explaining to her that it was wrong went out the window.

If there was any question whether or not Jason still could put it down on any woman, they were answered right there. "My God. Jason. You are fucking the shit out of me. Ohhhhhh. Ohhhhh."

Jason had Cecile's legs pulled apart like a wishbone and he was slamming his dick in and out of her like he was drilling for oil. Jason began to grunt.

"Pleeeaaasssse, that's it. Hit it. Hit that shit. It's yours. Whenever yooooooouuuu want it," she panted.

"Turn over, bitch," Jason growled.

"Oh yeah, you want this from the back. Huh?"

Jason answered her question by slamming into her and pushing the tip of his penis into her uterus. "Ayyyyyyiiiiiiyyyyyyiiiii," she moaned out. Then he dug his fingertips into her voluptuous ass and spread her cheeks. Next he spit on her ass and watch the saliva roll down to her butt crack. He timed the entry of his fingers perfectly. "Ouch, baby. Ouch, baby."

Her ex had liked it rough but he didn't have the size or the stamina that Jason had. They had been at it since 1:00 a.m. It was now almost 4:00 a.m. and they had only stopped for a few breaks in between.

Now as Jason was slamming into her from the back, she felt the sparks shoot up her back as her orgasm rocked her body. Jason felt her going limp and he banged her completely through it. She couldn't take anymore. She screamed out in ecstasy and from the torture of feeling too good for too long.

Jason stopped for a moment and Cecile tried to capture herself. She was weak from the pounding. But instead of a reprieve she felt an incredible pain and sensation. "No, Jason, no, Jason, nooooo." It was too late. He was now inside of her asshole.

She begged him to slow down until an unbelievable amount of pleasure took control of her. She couldn't remember being dogged like this in the bed and she loved it. After five long minutes he pullet out and grabbed her by her hair, the way he used to do Tasha. He yanked the condom off and jerked his semen all over her face and breast.

At 7:00 a.m. Cecile rolled over and smiled at Jason. She tapped his shoulder and saw the look of surprise on his face when he opened his eyes and realized that she was lying next to him.

"So, Boss, do I still have to work today?"

Jason got his senses together and sat up. It took him a minute to digest the situation. He looked at the bottle of Vodka on the nightstand and saw that there was but a sip or two left. Then he realized what he needed to say and do. "Hell yeah, you got to go to work. Ain't shit changed. This shit happens everyday."

Cecile looked confused.

Jason went on, "You wanted to fuck me. I obviously wanted to fuck you too. You're beautiful and you're sexy, but I love Jill. This did feel good, but it was wrong. You understand that, right?"

"I guess. But she don't have to know."

"Women always say that. Let me ask you this, Cecile. Do you love me? Be real."

"Well, no, but I do think you're..."

"No, is the answer. But if we keep this up you will and things will get ugly. That's the only way it can go. Now I was horny as hell and you really... I mean *really* satisfied me." She smiled. "But Jill and

I have something special. We're going to be married. Now what I need to know is this."

"Yes?"

"This is the scenario. You have now fucked your boss's man. You have one up on the woman who pays you. I enjoyed it, but I can't and won't do it again. I will also not allow you to backslide at work, give you a raise behind this or speak about it to anyone. If you do and I lose her behind this I will have nothing to lose. I just came home after fourteen years of state time and now I have a lot going for me. If you ruin that..."

"No, I understand. I could tell you were from the streets... believe me. I don't want anything from you and I respect you. I just really appreciated the way you treat me. I swear."

"Understand that this is not a game."

"I do."

"Alright. It's over. If you want anything out of this say so now, because I can cut you a check today, but after today I will consider it an unforgivable insult."

Without a pause she said, "Just to keep my job. That's all I want."

Jason was quiet for a second and asked, "You sure?"

"Positive."

He was feeling really good about her answer. With that he got up and went to his pants and pulled out some cash. "Go to the office and work a half day. After that I'll call you and you can take the rest of the day off. I know you're tired after all that. Take this, have a good weekend, do some shopping and I'll see you Monday."

She looked at the money. It looked as if it was easily twenty-five hundred. Actually it was eighteen. If she was insulted, she didn't let on. She took the money, grabbed a dress from her bag and hit the door.

Jason let her out and went back to sleep.

When Jason woke up for the second time, he was in a totally different state of mind. He decided that something had to give. That something was Jill. Either they were going to make up or he was going to pack up and move. He was willing to sign over the proceeds that he was going to make with Zone Development to Jill in order to step with a clear conscience. He would pay her interest if need be, but he wasn't going to have her holding anything over his head.

He packed his belongings and drove home.

Thirty-5

Jason was surprised that his key still worked in the lock. As soon as he stepped inside Jill was standing there. He looked at her head and asked, "What happened to your hair?"

Jill had cut all of her long flowing hair down into a short feathered style. She looked a lot like Rosario Dawson only prettier. "I was going crazy without you. I had to do something. I just been all over the place. Do you hate it?"

Before he had a chance to say anything, Jill was hugging him and squeezing his body for dear life. She kissed all over his face and tried to grab his bags, but he just set them down. When they stepped into the living room, she stopped his progress. Jill passionately kissed him with all of her tongue in his smelly mouth. She quickly led him up the stairs until they reached the loft without saying a word to him. She peeled off his clothes, and tossed them on the floor. Jason was so happy that she'd had a complete change of heart that he didn't notice that Zeida's card fell out of his pocket along with his keys.

Jill hastily walked him to the shower and cut the water on. In front of him, she disrobed and then joined him. She washed his body and over the stream of the water, she said, "Baby, I am so, so sorry. I need you, baby. I couldn't sleep without you lying next to me." She kissed all over his chest and said, "I missed you so much. I was dreaming of you every moment that I lay in bed. Damn, Jason, I'm in love. I love you so much and I swear I want to spend the rest of my life with only you and the two of our children."

Jason pulled her away from his body and asked, "The *two* of our children?"

She cut the shower off and reached for a towel. "Yes, baby. I was so crazy and I have just been feeling horrible for the past month. I didn't want to trouble you. You'd been working so hard and I didn't think it was anything serious. Turns out it was."

"I don't believe it," Jason said smiling.

"Anyway, baby, I know I been so evil and crazy lately... I ... I just didn't know what was up with me. I got worried so I went to the doctor. I was still having my period so I never guessed I could be pregnant. Turns out that I... I mean we... are having twins."

Jason was silent listening absorbing it all.

"I apologize for all the things I said. I swear I didn't know I was such a bitch. I thought you were frustrating me, but even after you left, I would start crying for no reason. The doctor said that usually happens in the second trimester. When I took a sonogram and saw two heartbeats. That explained it. Your children were draining the life out of me so that they could survive." Jill giggled hoping to be understood. "Jay, I wasn't in my right mind. I apologize baby, let me make it up to you."

She escorted him to their bed and pulled the covers over their bodies. She made an attempt at oral sex, but then stopped because she wanted to feel him. She positioned herself on top of him and rode him until they both climaxed.

Jason fell asleep. An hour later she came upstairs with a plate of food. The aroma cracked his eyelids open.

Slowly he ate his food. After his meal they both shared the Strawberry smoothie. As they lay, he thought of Zeida. He got dressed to prepare for their meeting.

Jill held Zeida's card in her hand. "What did she say?"

He came out of the closet with a casual outfit and saw the card in her hand. "She said we have to talk. I'm on my way over to see her now."

"Did you tell her about me?" Jill said, pissed off.

"I didn't have the time to. She was with her man, husband, or whoever he was."

"Do you still love her?"

"I don't know. It's been a long time, but I do know I love you and I'm not leaving you or my children."

Jill sat up in bed. "If I ask you not to go will you respect that?"

"Not respect it, but I'll accept it," he responded while putting on his shirt.

Jill sighed. "Well, I want you to go. I want you to get closure in that situation but keep one thing in mind. *I* want you in my life and all that comes with you. You are *my* man, and without the marriage I am your wife in spirit and now in blood." She looked down at her stomach and rubbed it. She looked at him and said, "Keep us in mind with whatever you do today." Jill jumped out of bed, kissed him on his lips, and then grabbed the serving tray, headed for the kitchen.

Jason got dressed and walked outside without saying goodbye.

Too many nights Jason slept in the hell of prison dreaming of Zeida. Now that he was going to see her, the only thing he was sure of was the fact that he was no longer in control of himself when it came to her. As he parked, he prayed for strength.

Jason reached 350 Fifth Avenue and stepped into the Empire State Building. He stepped off the elevator on a tower floor. He followed the arrows and walked to the door that read "Carro Incorporated" in gold letters. When he opened the door, he was buzzed in by a receptionist and was told that Ms. Carro would be with him in a few moments. In what seemed like an instant, he saw two Italian men and a short oriental woman with a French accent leave Zeida's office.

Zeida indicated with her finger for him to come to her. She was wearing a pink, silk, mini-skirt, Zoë outfit, similar to the outfit she wore on the day they first met. Her office had windows taller than him. Jason noticed long stemmed white roses sitting on top of her desk.

Instead of sitting behind her desk she walked up to him and put her tongue deep into his mouth. The sexual tension between them was enough to bring a building down. Four hands fell everywhere. Before he had a chance to do anything, she had him bent over her desk. She had her hard nipples on his back as she breathed heavy into his ear. Both of her hands were in his pants. She pulled them down, along with his boxers, and began to kiss each cheek. She turned him around, grabbed his shaft, and licked it rapidly as if she was licking an ice cream cone that dripped on the side of her knuckles.

Jason was squeezing onto the edge of the desk so tight, he could have cracked it. He was overtaken with pleasure. It was driving him crazy. The thing that he missed about having sex with Zeida was that she made him feel like she had to have all of him.

She stopped sucking on him. He watched as she pulled a lounge chair right up to his knees and pinned him in with the desk. She got on her knees on top of the lounge chair. She hiked her skirt up over her rear, ripped her own stockings from behind, pulled her panties to the side, and then guided him inside of her. Jason couldn't move. Zeida got on the tip of her toes and while she held the back of the lounge chair she pushed her body back and forth. She used him for her pleasure it seemed, as if he owed her. She came in three minutes. When he felt her cumming, the thought of Jill brought him back to reality.

"Cum for me," Zeida moaned. Jason stopped his rhythm and pushed her forward.

"No," he said as she went headfirst over the lounge chair.

She chuckled, and peeked over the chair. "Less than five minutes. You are the only man that has the ability to make me cum in less than five minutes. I wish you only knew how much I love you."

He fixed his pants and moved the lounge chair back to where it originally sat. Jason felt guilty. This was different that fucking Cecile he reasoned. He cared for Zeida. This was an emotional betrayal.

Zeida reluctantly asked, "What's wrong? I don't turn you on? After all those years away from me, I thought you would devour me. Que pasa Papi? Ya no te gustá está mujer caliente?"

"I came here to talk. I need to figure a few things out," Jason said keeping his distance.

Zeida sat at her desk. She smiled at Jason and said, "Jason, so many nights I sprinkled your scent all over my bed and got dressed in your clothes just to feel some form of comfort. You don't know how much I needed you. I was all alone, having to deal with so much responsibility all by myself. All those nights home alone in my bed crying myself to sleep. But... it made me strong." She paused and walked over to her window and looking down she finished, "So, let me say this, if you're ready to come home, I'll let Roberto know that he has to leave."

Jason couldn't believe his ears, and then he asked in jealousy, "That's the man I saw you with the last night?"

"Yes, I waited six years for you to come home. My final theory was that I thought you feared I would rat you out for killing my brother and those Ching-a-lings. I didn't know why you left me, but I knew you were gone. I met Roberto six years ago, he's financially stable, owns a record company for Cuban bands, and he loves me. He knows the whole story with you and that I will never love another. You were the only man to tame me. Now Roberto is my pet and he obeys very well. It will crush his heart, but it would hurt me more not to have you in my life."

Jason thought about what Zeida had just told him. Something in her voice sounded cold. In response he said, "I met someone that changed my life. She was there for me when no one else was. I can't be a traitor to someone who was loyal to me when I was down and out. I know I love you, but..."

"Hold your words. After you take a ride with me then tell me what you want to do." She pointed to the things on the desk and said, "By the way, these are for you. I only ask that you open the briefcase when you get to wherever it is that you call home. Are you ready?"

She got herself together and they left the office. When they reached the parking lot on 32nd Street, Zeida walked ahead of him, looked at the Benz and said, "2005 CLS 550, with the AMG package. Now that's nice, I see you have matured."

"A little, I guess," he laughed.

Jason looked around and was about to ask her how she knew that was his car but changed his mind.

Zeida jingled her keys. "We're taking my car. I'll bring you back. What we have to do will only take a couple of hours, and I have some unfinished business to handle when I get back."

He put the briefcase and the flowers in his trunk. They walked a few parking spaces down and hopped into a black Lexus SC 430.

During the drive they talked over the radio the entire time, making up for the missed years. Zeida told him that she had her tubes tied so that she couldn't have any children, and when Jason asked about the pregnancy, she changed the subject. He figured that she had either lost it or had an abortion. She asked him details about Tasha, Jill, and the twins that were on the way.

"So did you ever start your own clothing line?" Jason asked.

"No, but it's still in the works."

"Well, from the looks of your office you seem to be doing big things."

"I'm a consultant for Nigo in Japan for Bathing Ape clothing. In New York, I work for Demitris Bragg and Diamond Girl. They're my two largest clients and between the two of them I'm really swamped."

By the end of the conversation they were on Central Park Avenue near Scarsdale.

When she pulled into the same driveway from years back, he leaned his head back. "If I would have suspected that you lived at the same place after all this time, I woulda came straight there when I was released from prison. They reached the elevator and the same man was there. He recognized Jason immediately.

They stepped off the elevator and Zeida turned the key in the door. Everything in the place was different. Roberto came out of the back room. Zeida asked Jason to sit on the terrace, and told Roberto to go back into the room. Both men fulfilled her request.

While sitting on the terrace, Jason thought about the sexual things he did there. A few moments later, Zeida walked in with a gorgeous girl that had the hair and complexion of a Puerto Rican, but facial features similar to Jason's. He almost fainted.

Zeida said, "Jason? This is *Jada*. As in Jason and Zeida equals Jada?"

He was speechless. The girl walked over to him and Zeida walked away. Jada said, "I heard so much about you. I knew you would come one day. Mommy never stopped believing. Papi, can you take me to the movies, and to amusement parks, and to school, and on long trips around the world?"

Jason's heart was broken. He hugged Jada as tears rolled down his cheeks. "Yes, yes, yes, where ever you want to go."

Zeida walked back in with a small garment bag. She handed the bag to Jason and said, "It's all there. Every picture of special events, every report card, every time she went to the doctor, everything. Your daughter is a genius. She's in her second year at the Bronx High School of Science and she's only thirteen. A bunch of private schools want her overseas, but she was waiting on her Papi. I made sure I got copies of everything. I represented you wherever we went. I got things in there as if you were home because I knew one day you would come back. Jada even has all of your clothes in a trunk in her room waiting for you."

He couldn't believe what his eyes were seeing. A part of him didn't want to believe that it was true. Another part of him didn't know what to do, but he made up his mind that whatever he did, he was going to have to do his best to make up for not being there for his child.

Jason spent an hour talking to Jada. He answered all of her questions, and was completely honest with his answers. He made a promise to spend as much time with her as possible.

When he and Zeida were leaving the house, she placed a copy of the house keys in his hand and said, "Whenever you're ready."

They jumped in the car and Zeida asked him what he was going to do. He told her about Jill's condition. Zeida asked to meet Jill so she could explain her position in relation to their child. He didn't know what Jill would say to that. And based on her emotional state lately, he didn't know if she would be able to handle it. For the rest of the drive he looked at all of Jada's things until his cell rang breaking his thoughts.

"Jason," Matthew Leahy was on the line.

"How's it going?" Jason replied.

"I'm not working you too hard am I? I've been trying to reach you for two days now. I thought you might have taken a vacation. Yesterday your secretary said she hadn't heard from you. Today I couldn't even catch her."

"I think she left early."

"How early? I started calling at nine and then had my secretary calling every thirty minutes after that. But anyway, I need you to swing by the office. I have some things to review with you and I have something I think you'll be glad to hear. The first phase of funding is going through on Monday. So by next week this time you'll be sitting pretty."

Jason was elated by the news but a little pissed at Cecile for playing him and not showing up at all. He wondered if she was going to start slacking and trying to take advantage. Then in his mind he figured that she was probably exhausted from the three and half hours of sex. He was tired himself.

When he got to his car, Zeida kissed him delicately on the cheek and told him she'd be waiting to hear from him.

Jason walked through the door of the house, stopped in the dining room and placed the roses in a vase. He carried the briefcase and the garment bag up to the loft. He walked through the door and Jill was naked in front of the full-length mirror rubbing cocoa butter on her belly.

Jill looked at her man and knew by his mood that something was wrong. She sat down with him on the bed, held his face. "How did it go?"

He shrugged his shoulders.

"Before you answer, I've been sitting here all day trying not to listen to my ego and only concentrate on how I feel about you. A lot of women let their pride, ego, or their friends get in the way or come between them and their soul mates. I know I love myself more than anyone else. I make my own decisions and I'm skeptical about people's motives and that's why Diane is my only friend. I took a deep look within today, and I asked myself how much would I compromise and if compromising was the right thing to do?"

"So here it goes," she sighed.

"Jason I don't think I can compromise my values, but I feel you are worth adjusting the way I look at things. From the moment we've been together you have done just that. So, I've made the decision that I can move on without you, but I would be devastated if that happened. I want to make this thing work. I want a fiftieth wedding anniversary. So, tell me everything and don't keep anything from me. I promise I'll try not to get upset or hold it against you."

Jason kissed her on her lips. He realized Jill was a remarkable woman, and that he didn't want to lose her. He picked the briefcase up, put it on the bed, and together they opened it. It was filled with cash and a note. They held the note in their hands together and it read:

Jason,
I've been holding this for you for all these years. I didn't
need any of it because I have my own, and what's mine is yours. As

you may know, I am the type of woman that takes care of her man. I am that helpmate that the Bible speaks of... I leave this with you because you may decide to run away after seeing Jada. If that is how you feel, then take this and go far far away. I don't want to lie to her, and I don't want her hopes to be in vain.

If you decide that you are going to be the man that I know you are, then use this to get on your feet, or do what you have to do. There is more where that came from if you need it. I am here for you, and I just ask that you allow me and Jada to have whatever part of your life you can share.

Love always,

Z.

Jill had tears in her eyes. She saw some things in Zeida that she didn't have herself before she met Jason. She saw in the letter that her man had the ability to bring out the best in people. Then she asked, "Who's Jada?"

Without saying a word, Jason closed the briefcase, held it up to eye level, and placed it into her hands. He reached for the garment bag and put it on top of the briefcase. Cautiously, he told her every single thing that happened from the moment that he left the house that morning until he arrived in front of her, leaving out only a few details that he knew she wouldn't really want to hear.

She was about to say something, but he placed a finger to her lips. He got down on his knees, kissed her toes, and then looked up into her eyes and said, "Will you marry me?"

Jill cried, nodding yes.

Jason and Jill spent the weekend making up. On Saturday after Jason met up with Matthew, he and Jill hit the Turnpike and made their way to Atlantic City. They checked into the Borgata and got a six-hundred dollar Fiore Suite that was equipped with plasma screen television, marble bath and a big comfortable bed.

They both gambled for a few hours and while Jill won six hundred on the slot machines Jason dropped ten thousand on the crap tables and another four thousand at black jack. While they ate the complimentary meal, Jason joked that they needed to enjoy the Peking Duck because it was costing him seven grand a plate.

On Sunday they went to the spa to enjoy a sensuous soak coupled with foot and scalp massages. They were so relaxed that they almost stayed a second night. Jason knew that he had so much to do to prepare for next wave of work that was coming his way.

Jason had the last three homes to negotiate the sales on, which would give Zone Development a span of four blocks of homes. As soon as he completed the negotiation, Matthew was going to make the announcement of its' initiative to preserve affordable housing in the 'new' Brooklyn and proclaim itself, along with Clayton Realty as the trailblazers and procurers of sanctuary for the working class.

They would look really good and grow rich in the process. Jason didn't care how much Zone was making. He was thrilled that he would indeed become a legitimate mogul. He had plenty of ideas of things he would do with his money.

On Monday the alarm went off. Jason put the pillow over his head. Jill pulled on it and asked. "Do you mind me using your car?" Jill asked lying dazed in the bed.

"Jill, never ask me if you can drive the car. *Tell* me you need the car and take the keys," he said as rubbed his eyes. He got up to use the toilet and brushed his teeth. He jumped into the shower and got out soaking wet and asked, "Where you headed, to see Diane?"

"No, actually, I have to go to Queens. By the way, Thanksgiving is next week and *we* have plans so don't make any of your own."

He stopped at the door. "Oh yeah, what type of plans?"

"The type of plans you don't need to concern yourself with until that day. Let a woman be a woman, baby."

Since she took the news about Jada well and accepted his wedding proposal, he figured he'd just keep his mouth shut and go along. He called Roger and got a ride to work.

At the office things were bustling ever since Jason restructured management. He'd wisely put people in the positions that they wanted to be in, and he produced more with fewer staff. Cecile was there in a new outfit. She stared at Jason more than she should have but she kept things on a professional level, but made it clear that she was still willing to do *anything* for him.

Jason walked into his office just in time to answer a call from his private line. "Jason," Jill's voice was filled with fear. "That man is sitting on our front stoop dressed like a damn marine or something. What's his name? Webb? He asked to come in, but I told him you weren't here and he said he'd wait until you showed up. Come home, I'm scared."

"I'll be right there."

Jason hung up the phone raced out of the door and hailed a cab. He had the driver rush to get to his house and tipped him well. When he turned the corner, he saw Roger's car parked. Webb was sitting on the top step of the house wearing an all black army jacket and black cargo pants. He did indeed look like a soldier of some sort.

Jason hopped out of the cab and walked up on Webb. The nozzle of a MP-5 machine gun hung out from the bottom of his coat. Next to him was a full, plastic, blue GAP bag. Webb moved towards Jason as he came up the steps.

"What you doing at my crib, man?" Jason asked looking at the faces of Webb's counterparts. He scowled at Roger for bringing the thugs to his house. Roger held his hands up to surrender and moved his hands back and forth to say that he didn't know it was wrong because Webb was family.

"Duke…Duke, if I'm gone do all the work, Duke, the least you can do is come pick your paper up. I had to come all the way out here. All the way *out here*. You know I can't even be in B.K., Duke."

Jason stopped in front of the house. "Yo, Webb. I'm telling you, homey, we got to stop this. I'm out of the game. I thought you needed paper to go to Vegas? Take whatever it is you got for me and go. You gonna end up doing life, or worse losing yours." He grabbed Webb by his shoulders. "Listen to me, man. We ain't kids anymore, man, we thirty plus. This bullshit has got to stop. You may not care about life, but I'm your family and I don't want to see you die. In the game, you gonna die or go to the pen. There ain't no other way. You can't survive in the pen, trust me. A nigga like you, you'll stack up bodies in there and never get out. I've seen it. You haven't." Jason's voice was firm and for the first time it seemed to him that Webb was hearing him. "Go. Join that mosque, surround yourself with them good people that's out there and nobody will know that you even existed in New York. Fast life is a dead end, my brother, pull out."

Webb moved Jason's hands off of his shoulders and said, "Little grasshopper telling me how to stay up, huh? Man, what happened to you in the pen?"

"I woke up, and I could not have done that without going to the joint. We were like slaves to greed. We were twisted. The things we did for paper were insane. Man…I was lost and turned out to the point that I never even considered that my mind could make me more paper than the streets ever could. Look at me, homey? I'm all right. The moment I stopped sweating paper, the paper came and it's nothing. Nothing. Go to Vegas and make you a family."

Webb walked back to the car ranting, "Yeah, yeah, you beating me in the head and I left my helmet at home." He and his soldiers started laughing. Then he added, "Homey, it's all good, baby boy. It's all good. Another hundred gees and I'm out. These soldiers will be Fed-Exing me paper after that. I got you, Duke. But don't make me have to come back out here to give you your cut."

He slammed the door and they drove off.

Jason ran up the steps and grabbed the GAP bag. He ran back down and entered the house from the courtyard.

"What did he want? Why is he coming to our home?" Jill asked.

"Webb is Webb, and he does things Webb's way. But today I'm putting an end to it. Get all the cash in the briefcase and count that cash in that bag."

"Count that up, Jill, while I get dressed."

By the time Jason was dressed, she had counted $140,000. Jason scooped the cash into the briefcase. He kissed Jill. "I'll be right back."

Jason headed for College Avenue in the Bronx. On the way, he stopped to pick Peter up. He didn't want to drive the car onto the block with all that cash so while he tracked Webb down he wanted Peter to stay in the car.

When they were a block away on 165th Street on College Avenue, Jason pulled over and said, "You drive."

"What? You want me to drive?" Peter asked filled with joy.

"You know how to don't you?"

"Yeah, move over."

Peter handled the car without a problem, but he was a little too heavy on the gas. Jason was glad they didn't have to go far. They parked on the corner of 166th Street on College Avenue. When they looked through the windshield they saw Scooter and Webb having a discussion in front of a bodega.

Across the street at 1105, Jason saw drug addicts on a long line. Six of Webb's soldiers were directing the drug traffic, and Webb's dogs were circling his feet while keeping customers from going into the bodega. It was clear that he and Scooter were discussing business, but when Jason looked closer, he saw that Scooter was wearing the same type of outfit as Webb.

Jason turned to Peter and said, "I'm going over there to have a conversation. If shit gets hectic pull off and go straight to Jill, you got me?"

"No problem," Peter said.

He took his time walking across the street. He didn't want to alarm anyone. When the soldiers saw him, they didn't know if they should salute, or keep their eyes on him, so they watched for Webb's reaction. Webb saw Jason, "What up, homey, what up? You change your mind after seeing that paper, huh?" He hugged Jason, and then

Scooter gave him five and hugged him too. Jason looked at Webb and said, "I need to talk to you."

Webb shook his head up and down. He turned to Scooter and said, "Yo Duke, step inside with me while I hollah at my homey for a second." Then he turned to Jason and said, "Come on."

They stepped into building 1108 and occupied the lobby. Webb lit a blunt, took two long tokes, and offered it to Jason. Jason refused, so Webb handed it to Scooter and with smoke coming out of his mouth he said, "All right, I got my helmet on, hit me."

Jason knew Webb better than most so he said, "Yo, you told me once you get a certain amount of paper that you'd be done. Cool. I got that amount of paper for you. We can drive to Philly right now and you can get on a plane and be gone. I know you got a stash, so with what I give you, plus that, you have enough to eat real swell. Here is your opportunity. If you can't do this... then we dead. We over, no more family. I can't let you take me down after I worked so hard to get up, homey. I love you, but I got to be more loyal to my family and myself than I can be to anybody else."

Webb looked at Scooter and said, "You here this? Homey is lunching. He just don't get it. Jason, man, you and me is married to the game. We go when death do us part. I been trying to wait on you to get your nerve up. I know you nervous after the stretch you did. But I always had your back. Now you want to turn your back on me. On this here," Webb now had a grimace on his face as he was barking at Jason. Spit was even flying out of his mouth. "Nigga, I raised you in this game. Put it on the line for you. Time in and time out. I bled, raped and blasted muthafuckas in your name. What? What?" He yelled in Jason's face.

"Yo, you need to calm down. I'm trying to bless you."

"Nah, homey, you trying to turn pussy."

"If that's the way you see things, but don't come around my home again. I got a family and kids on the way."

"What you gonna do. What chu sayin'?"

"You know what I'm saying. I got a family."

"Man, fuck you and your family."

With that Jason threw his hand with lightening speed and it landed in a firm grip on Webb's throat. Webb was surprised at how strong Jason was as he was driven into the wall.

But just that quickly Webb reached into his belt and pulled his .380 out of his belt and put it in Jason's face.

Scooter jumped at Webb. "Hold up, hold up." He pushed the gun away and separated the two. "Yo. You can't go out like that. Webb, this man right here is *you*... and you *him* for life. You kill him and your soul is dead. You'll never come back from that. You been talking about your brother Jason for as long as I known you. The fuck is your problem?"

There was silence. Jason's eyes were glassy and Webb huffed trying to calm his breathing down. Scooter went on, "Your man sound just like my homey, Dee. He my heart, Duke, and we came up together. I'll twist a cabbage quick and get laid down for him in a heartbeat. That's how much love I got for him. Just like you. Let me tell you, my homey? He just wanted to go to school. For years, I couldn't understand him, but then he met this white bitch and his whole life changed. You hear me? From one move. Dee's whole life changed because he listened to himself and never lost focus. I mean yo, I'm rich and all that, but look how I got to walk around because I choose to stay in this jungle?"

Jason watched as Scooter opened his jacket. Inside he had body armor over his midsection and groin, two .41 auto magnums on his waist, and a Calico machine gun dangling under his arm. In the pants pockets of his army fatigues were extra clips and speed loaders.

"This ain't no way to live, and I'm sick wit it. But Yo, Webb, I ain't on the run from the pigs. I just got massive drama in the jungle."

Scooter sucked air through his nose, "Yo, this is all I know. I can't do nothing but get money in the streets."

"That ain't the point. You can always do you. The choice is on you homey. All your man is saying is that you always got new opportunities. If you don't take them, you stuck in the jungle. As for me? I don't need no company, so breeze if you want to."

Scooter smoked the rest of the weed and stared at Webb. Jason could tell that Webb was expecting Scooter to say something different.

Webb looked at the two men and said, "Let's be out, Duke, my head is spinning. Y'all beat me in the head so hard y'all got my brain hurting."

When they stepped out of the building, Webb and Scooter made a left and bounced to the corner where their dogs and soldiers were gathered. Jason looked to his right and a police car was coming down the wrong side of the one way street. He spotted the huge CPR letters on the patrol car, turned around and yelled, "Yo, yo, porky rolling."

Webb and Scooter turned to see what Jason was yelling about. On their blind side two other police cars stopped right in front of Scooter and Webb. Simultaneously the police yelled, "Freeze."

Jason's hands went up in the air. He looked over at Webb and Scooter and the men calmly frowned and began walking away. When one of the uniformed officers was walking to apprehend Webb, two of his soldiers stepped in between them and Webb said, "Handle your business."

Jason saw it before it was coming so he dropped to the ground. The two soldiers reached for their weapons and tried to shoot, but the police gunned them down. Shots were fired at the police from the corner across the street. The officers spun with their backs turned to Scooter and Webb and returned fire. Scooter saw the opportunity and calmly walked across the street towards the supermarket.

Webb used the opportunity to remove the cannons from his hip. Seeing his two shorties go down for him put him in a rage. He aimed the tips of each weapon to the backs of the officers in blue. The hot lead spit and Webb's deadly aim once again made him a cop killer. The hat flew off the head of one of the officers as the bullets tagged him behind the ear and in the neck. The other fell to the ground only stunned from the impact. Webb knew they wore vests and that a kill wasn't a kill unless there was a headshot. A witness was bad, but an officer as a witness was worse.

Jason put his head down and folded himself into the fetal position. The war between the street soldiers and the police sounded like a firefight in Iraq. Scooter and Webb rushed into the supermarket. Together they shook an isle until it tipped over and blocked the entrance to the store as the officers approached. "Get the fuck down on the floor," Scooter yelled as he shot over the head of the lone cashier.

Webb was walking ahead of Scooter and grabbed a pack of knee-high stockings for each of them and put them into his pocket. Webb found lighter fluid and squirted it all over the floor near the entrance. He then grabbed plastic bottles of bleach and ammonia and emptied them all over the floor. Meanwhile, Scooter lit another blunt, took a drag and flicked it to the floor into the fluid.

The market ignited in a blaze and the caustic fumes prevented the police officers from entering. Scooter and Webb escaped through the fire exit in the rear of the store. They slipped through an alley and ended up one block down on Findlay Avenue. They walked down 166th Street like two people that weren't in a rush.

Police car after police car zoomed into the area and right past the two men who toted on a blunt. When they reached the corner of Clay Avenue, a police car went past them, and then stopped suddenly. When the car came to a screeching halt, Scooter and Webb looked and saw reverse lights. Webb passed one of the stockings that he removed from the pack to Scooter. Together they slipped the black nylon over their heads reached for their weapons. They looked around for refuge and the only place they saw to run to where they wouldn't be pinned was an abandoned factory. Webb's heart began to pound as the adrenaline started to fuel him.

With the police car coming in their direction, Scooter went into the middle of the skid-marked street and met the officers with a hail of gunfire. He filled the trunk of the car with holes, and saw the two officers get out and scurry towards the hood of their car with their weapons drawn. Webb had already run for the door of the old helium balloon factory. He had to shoot the lock off. The building took up the giant space between Clay and Webster Avenues. Scooter covered Webb by spraying shells in the direction of the officers. Once the old metal door was open, they jetted into the unlit space.

Because of his street smarts, Webb stepped into the cold damp space and felt around the floor with his foot until his pupils adjusted to the darkness. The smell of gas was everywhere. Trying to breathe through the stocking cap made it more difficult to stay calm and alert for them. A small fraction of sunlight was peeking through the door, so they were able to see that a huge gas tank of some sort was in a far corner. Under the tank was a liquid that they assumed was some chemical compound.

"Yo, see if we can get out on the other side. You know they trying to get us surrounded."

Webb was looking all around while Scooter kept his weapon pointed at the door. Webb saw a steel staircase, by a far wall. It led to another door that had an old halogen exit sign over it. He called Scooter and pointed to his right. Scooter gave him the hand signal to wait, and he began to reload his weapon. Webb pointed his machine gun towards the door while he continuously nodded his head out of nervousness. They turned around and headed for the stairs, but a police officer was entering the door.

The officer fired seven shots, hitting Scooter in the shoulder twice. "Oh shit," Scooter screamed out.

The officer didn't see Webb who returned fire and sent a bullet into the top of the man's head as he tried to duck. While Webb was checking on Scooter's condition, he watched as a uniformed arm reached in the door and dragged the dead officer out.

"Ahhhhh, you fuckkkkaaaas, you fuckkkaaas," Webb screamed.

"Yo, we can't go out the door. They probably out there," Scooter yelled. They could now hear a helicopter.

They could hear when the S.W.A.T. teams arrived and were assembling their men. The whole neighborhood was flooded with officers from the 44th Precinct. The officers were set up and ready to move quickly. When their commander gave the order, a group of three moved in on the entrance to the factory in single file. The first officers walked into the darkness, and they were greeted with blind fire. They retreated back out of the factory. It sounded like the fourth of July in the place.

The potent odor of gunpowder permeated the air. Officers were in streets on bullhorns asking citizens to cooperate and to clear the area. They were foolishly expecting cooperation from the same people that they usually abused. Clouds suddenly set in and hid the sun.

Six more tactical unit officers teamed up with the original three. A half an hour passed, all nine tried to rush in. More shots were fired. The officers didn't have a clue where the two assailants were perched inside. Going in was proving suicide. Webb had become an expert shot and Scooter even with one hand was capable of deadly aim. One officer gave a bad account of where the fire was coming from and when they rushed in five of them were hit as they scrambled around trying to make it out of the door.

Snipers were on the neighboring roofs trying to get a target but it was too dark inside. The whole building was closed off to the outside with the exception of the small door under the exit sign. When the firing stopped, seven officers were pulling the bodies of five wounded officers out of the building.

The media being on the scene frustrated the commander. Four news helicopters were above the building, and the police helicopters were trying to get them to leave. In an effort to get some type of control of the situation, the commander pulled all his men back from the scene and re-established a perimeter. When they analyzed the situation, they found out that the structure of the building was unstable, and that it had been condemned because it was determined that it might collapse at any moment. Since it was in the middle of the ghetto, the importance of removing the possible disaster in a timely manner seemed to have been repeatedly overlooked. Records showed that the building had been scheduled to be demolished six years earlier.

Mayor Bloomberg and Raymond Kelly were on the phone with the commander. The police commissioner was giving the Bronx police commander official orders to bring an end to the drama that the two street thugs had created. Against his own wisdom, he ordered his men to use flash/bang grenades. He gave the orders to launch them into the building and for the squadron of men to storm the structure during the launch.

The commander followed police protocol and ordered the crowd to disperse. The men from S.W.A.T aimed their weapons and they launched the grenades. Three officers were storming the building and when the grenades ignited, the flash hit the gas that was under the huge tank, and the tank exploded. The building shook as the windows blew out. The building erupted in flames and in less than a minute it became clear that it was collapsing.

Two of the three officers who'd stormed the building had been wounded and were quickly dragged back. People in the street screamed and started running. The police cars that surrounded the huge building all backed away to avoid igniting from the burning debris. After what seemed like five minutes, the roof collapsed with a bang just before the walls gave way to the heat. Suddenly a deafening creaking sound echoed out and the building folded. Dust and rubble was everywhere and scene reminded onlookers of the way the Twin Towers collapsed. It would take hours for the dust to settle.

Jason was handcuffed on the sidewalk. He looked around as the ambulances pulled off and as the coroners did their jobs with the bodies that were up the block. His stare was fixed on the car and finally he saw Peter drive off and turn the corner. He felt a level of peace then, hoping that within the hour Jill would know what had happened to him. He was placed in a police car and taken to the 44th Precinct.

When he reached the precinct, officers were waiting for his arrival. Before he had a chance to do anything, a few of the officers started kicking and punching on him. He didn't know why he was being handled that way, but then he heard the buzz in the station house about what Scooter and Webb had done.

"Are we sure he's one of them?" The desk sergeant asked the officer that was signing his name into a book.

"Not sure. He was clean, but he was seen in the company of the two perpetrators moments before they started the whole mess," said the officer.

"Take him upstairs to the holding pen until we figure out what to do with him."

"You got it, Sarge."

While he was in the holding pen Jason said, "Officer, I know you have a job to do. I just ask that you allow me a phone call at your earliest convenience."

"Shut up, scumbag," an officer walking by said after he smacked Jason in the face.

He sat in the holding pen listening to the chatter of what Webb and Scooter had done to the police. He sat there thinking how history had repeated itself. The block would never be the same. Webb would go down in history for having shot more cops than his idol, Larry Davis, the Bronx legend who shot his way out of an apartment in 1986, when six officers came to kill him.

Jason now realized that his predicament was completely his fault this time. He had no business going to a high crime neighborhood. The station was in an uproar as off-duty officers were called in to cover the crisis.

While the plainclothes officer that brought him in was filling out a report, Jason asked, "Excuse me, sir, do you mind if I make that call before things get too busy around here?"

He had to be polite if he wanted to get something from the man. The officer, who was the only young black one he'd encountered during the entire ordeal, looked around to see who was watching him. No one was there. He then pulled out his gun. He let Jason out of the pen and with his gun he pointed at the phone and said, "Listen, from what I can see you're clean. There's a file on the activity of that block that goes back four years and your name isn't anywhere on it. We should be letting you go, but they claim to have seen you with those maniacs that cost officers their lives. Cops don't like that. I know you're clean and by the way you're dressed I don't know why they're associating you with those other two goons. So hurry up."

Jason called the house and the phone picked up on the first ring. "Baby?" Jill said.

"Yeah, this is me."

"Oh thank God, thank God. Where are you? Are you all right? What did they do to you?"

"Calm down, calm down so you can do what I need you to do. Now watch what you say on this phone. You hear me."

Jill was still hysterical. "Peter called from his cell and told me that the police had you… people were shooting… that everything went crazy and that…"

"Listen baby, calm down. Think about the twins. You can't help me if you're hysterical. I need you to call a lawyer named Troy Yancey."

"Troy?" Jill asked. "Who is he, I have some lawyer friends…"

"No, listen. I need you to call Troy Yancey. Write it down. T-r-o-y. Yancey, Y-a-n-c-e-y."

"Troy Yancey?" Jill made sure.

"Yes, she's a lawyer in Manhattan. Tell her where I am and what happened to me. She will know what to do."

"I'm gonna do it right now, baby, I love you."

The phone cut off. The officer heard some of his fellow officers coming back up the stairs. He put Jason back in the pen and then sat back at his desk like nothing ever happened.

The Irish captain walked through the door and asked the officer, "This the one?"

The plain clothes officer nodded his head while the other two officers that accompanied the captain looked at Jason salivating. The rose-faced captain walked over to the holding pen. He put his lips between the bars and in a bad Irish attempt at Ebonics he whispered, "Your two ,homies are dead, you homeboy. Just make it light on yourself and confess to shooting at my officers. Whadda' you say? You want to make a statement?"

Without hesitation Jason said, "Sure, I'll write it all out nice and neat, and you have your officer there to sign it."

The red faced captain smiled at all his men and said, "All righty then, that was quick. You boys see how a pro works? Someone get this young man a pen and statement sheet." He looked over at Jason and in another coffee and rum filled whisper he said, "Hey, I'm not supposed to do this since it's banned, but you want a smoke?

Jason saw where things were going, so he walked up to the bars, looked at the captain's nametag, "Listen, Captain O'toole. I do something for you, and you do something for me, right? Because I'm not going back to jail hungry."

The captain leaned in and in a whisper said, "Go ahead. Whatever you need, homey, just as long as I have a statement from you about your participation in my officers getting killed. You get whatever you want."

Jason leaned closer to his ear and said, "I want a fish sandwich with fries and an ice cold orange juice. Tropicana. I can write better on a full stomach."

The captain lowered his voice. "Say no more. This is your... lucky day. The best fish sandwiches around are just up the block at the deli. Give me a few minutes, I'm gonna handle this one *personally*. I'll be *right* back."

Jason laid on the hard bench in the holding cell and thought about his life. He replayed everything Webb and Scooter did in his mind so that he could prepare his statement. Twenty minutes later, the captain came back with his food. "I kept my end of the deal, so you keep yours. Eat your food. I even picked up a shortcake for you. Just gimme that statement as soon as you're done eating."

Jason knew he was going to have to deal with the savage court system for at least two days. Once his parole status came up in the computer, he knew he was heading to Rikers Island for a long time. He was sure the media was going to be all over him, so he wanted to make sure he had a decent meal before his new journey began.

As he picked the crumbs from his teeth, the captain walked in and announced, "Your lawyer called here. Boy, you must be pretty important because we didn't even let you get a phone call yet. She's on her way over from Brooklyn. I told her you made a statement, so write the statement and let my officer sign it. That was our deal."

The captain handed him the necessary stationary. Jason picked up the pen and pad and said, "Sure." He wrote:

My name is Jason Faust. I am the C.E.O of Clayton Realty in Brooklyn, New York. I was in the Bronx attempting to solicit tenants for a new program that I am heading up in conjunction with Zone Development. Mr. Matthew Leahy has recently commended me on my ability to reach the people who are in neighborhoods that are normally ignored because of crime. On the above date I entered an apartment building on College Avenue in the Bronx.

I went to several apartments, and received no responses. As I was preparing to go to another building I stopped to talk with two young men and asked them about their housing needs. They expressed no interest in real estate so we parted ways. When the officer in car 5240 told me to stop, I followed his order and immediately cooperated.

My head was down at all times, the officer was standing right above me with his weapon shooting, and I never left his presence. I heard shots being fired and the officer kneeled a foot away from me and reloaded. I was afraid and cowered in the fetal position, until the handcuffs were placed on me. I am now in the precinct, but I have not been arrested, because I did not commit a crime. I was threatened by Captain L. Otoole to write a falsified statement to reveal information that I am unaware of. Jason Faust.

He handed his statement to the lazy plainclothes officer, and without reading it, the officer signed and dated it. When Jason asked for a copy, he couldn't believe his luck. The officer walked over to the copy machine and made a copy for him. Jason sat on the bench. He slipped the copy under the insole of his boots. Ten minutes later, the captain returned. "You finished my statement?"

Jason looked the man in the eyes. "I sure did."

"It's here on my desk," the officer said.

The captain read the statement and began to turn a darker shade of red. He looked at the officer that was watching Jason and said, "Shit for brains you fucking signed this shit? This is my career you're talking about." He ripped up the statement and said to Jason, "You better sign another statement that you shot at my officers. I'll produce the gun. Write it now."

Jason flipped his middle finger at the man and all hell broke loose. "You no good piece of shit," the captain shouted. "I lost men today," he said and charged him.

Two other officers ran into the pen at Jason and he had a flashback from when he served time. He blacked out, a threw a series of punches to defend himself. A hook landed and one of the officers was knocked out cold. The other officer was swinging his stick and he caught Jason in the groin. Other officers from downstairs came running up, and they all got a piece of him under the guise of subduing him. Jason put up a good fight on the floor, but then a fat detective jumped on him and landed his three-hundred and fifty plus body on his rib cage. Jason screamed out in pain as he felt something inside him pop with a cracking sound as he was being beat in his head. He couldn't breathe and then it grew dark.

Jason came to with a headache a few days later handcuffed to a hospital bed with his feet shackled to the railing. When his vision cleared, he saw an overweight black police officer sitting next to him watching *Oprah* on the wall mounted television.

"Don't move," the officer said as he saw Jason come to. A few moments later he saw his lawyer walk in with a nurse.

The tall, gorgeous attorney walked in wearing long immaculate dreads. She smiled. "You and your buddy just can't leave the streets alone can you?" she said in a thick New York accent.

Jason winced from the pain. "Then how would you stay in business?"

"I'm glad you're awake today. I've been up here twice already, both times you were still out. You still look like hell though."

"Nice to see you too, Ms. Yancey, what happened?"

"That's what I need to know?" his lawyer asked holding a legal pad.

"Where am I?" Jason asked.

"You're in Lincoln Hospital. You've been heavily sedated. You suffered broken ribs, a punctured lung, and those things along with a concussion have had you seriously out of it for a couple of days. Your fiancé and girlfriend, or somebody is outside. I don't know how you boys do it.

Anyway, you've been charged with assaulting a couple of officers, aiding a fugitive, and some other minor charges. I spoke to a Mr. Hancock at parole, and he said he wouldn't violate you unless you received a conviction. I guess he likes you. So, what happened? The news is all over this, thank you."

Jason explained every detail to his lawyer. When he was done, she immediately requested Jason's property from the cop.

"It is not being withheld as evidence. I'm sure that if you make your request to the administrative nurse she will comply. Please be quick about it, and can you have his family step in?" she told the officer.

The officer walked out and the room door flew open. Jill and Zeida walked in. They both went to opposite sides of the bed. Jill gave Jason a passionate kiss, and then Zeida kissed him on his forehead rubbing his head. His lawyer rolled her eyes. He looked at the two women and asked, "What are you doing here?"

Jill caressed her enlarged womb. She cut Zeida off. "After I found out you were in the hospital baby, I didn't know who else to call. I wanted Jada to know in case something terrible happened, so I called Zeida." She tapped Jason's leg. "She's the bomb, baby. We had a long talk out there and she knows you belong to me, so you're not in trouble."

They started laughing. Zeida said, "Papi? Why you still getting yourself into trouble? If you go to jail again what are we supposed to do?"

Jason got ready to speak, but the police officer walked back in with a Jason's clothes."

Jason remembered the ordeal and the copy of the statement. "Hey, check the left boot. Under the insole."

The lawyer reached for his boots and pulled out the written statement. Jason felt an instant sense of relief. When she read the statement she asked, "You went to prison and became a better criminal, huh?" She reread it. "You actually remembered the car number and you convinced an officer to sign this? How, was he a rookie?"

Jason chuckled slightly but it hurt, "Don't ask me."

She turned to the two other women and said, "Listen, you guys hold tight. I'm going to drive down the block to the D.A.'s office. It's the day before Thanksgiving, but we know each other. Once I explain the lawsuit I'm filing we'll see what happens next. I'll be back in a few hours."

The lawyer turned to the police. "Here's my card. These two ladies are investigators for my firm. If *anyone* asks, they work for me and they are investigating facts for the defendant." She winked her eyes at the two women and was gone.

"What happened to Webb and Scooter?" Jason painfully asked.

"No one knows," Jill whispered. "The building collapsed and it's gonna take days for them to dig through the rubble. A few officers died so the whole world is watching."

Zeida added her two cents. "They're telling the media that the men are dead, but they still haven't found any bodies. Usually dogs can smell through that type of stuff right, Papi?"

Jill looked over at Zeida as if to say, *Don't get too comfy with the Papi stuff.*

Jason assumed Webb was either dead or on a plane headed for the West Coast. Knowing Webb, he probably came up with some desperate escape through a sewer line or an old shaft all dressed up like a S.W.A.T officer.

When the 6:30 news came on Jason, Jill, Zeida, and the police officer were all watching to see if they finally found the bodies of the two men. The reporter announced that special hound dogs, that are trained to smell incinerated human remains, were flown in from Kiln, Mississippi, but there was no trace of the two suspects. Jason rubbed Jill's stomach and started laughing again, but the pain from his ribs forced him to chill. Jason began mumbling under is breath. When everyone else in the room looked at him, they wondered if the medication was getting him high. Then the phone rang.

The police officer was the only person allowed to answer the phone. They overheard him saying, "What? Yes sir. Yes sir. But are you sure? Well, I'm gonna do it, but you have to come sign the book on this one."

The officer hung up the phone. He looked at Jill and Zeida and said, "You have to leave this room immediately. You can meet your lawyer friend downstairs, but you have to leave now."

"Where are you taking him?" They both asked simultaneously.

He held the door for the two women. "I'm just doing my job, you have to leave. Now."

The women kissed Jason and then left with promises that they were going to wait for his lawyer.

"They moving me to Rikers?"

"Just relax," said the officer.

Jason knew the routine. He figured that he was going to the hospital ward in the jail for bed rest. Then he watched the officer unlock the shackles and the handcuffs. That wasn't unusual. He would have to be re-cuffed if he was leaving the hospital, but then the officer said, "You're no longer in police custody. It appears your charges have been dropped."

"What?"

Just as he was about to ask for more info, Troy walked back into his room. "All your charges have been dismissed but you really need to stay here for a couple more days."

"Oh hell no, I'm not staying in here for Thanksgiving."

"Well, even if you go home, you're gonna need some bed rest and plenty of pain killers."

Jill popped back into the room. "So, we goin' home, daddy?"

"Yeah, right now that's what it looks like."

Troy Yancey went over a couple of legalities. Jason blew a kiss at his lawyer as she headed for the door and said, "The check is in the mail. And I promise you that when it comes to criminal matters you will never hear from me again." He was very confident of that.

"Time will tell," she shot back. "Will I be filing a lawsuit against the Police Department? I already have the head of the P.B.A.'s ear."

"Let's talk next week."

"Fair enough," she said. "Have a happy Thanksgiving."

"Same to you and hey," he paused. "Thanks."

She winked at Jason and sped up the hall.

Jason and Jill had a visitor for Christmas morning. Jada had spent the night on Christmas Eve and when she woke she found a tree filled with more gifts than the law should allow. Jason had been surprised that Zeida had let her stay and spend the night with them but he was grateful. When he and Jill heard her screaming for joy they walked down the steps to video tape her excitement.

"Thank you, daddy. Thank you so much. I can't believe you got all of this stuff for me. My friends are going to hate me when they see all of this."

There were boxes of clothes from Macy's, Bergdorf, The Gap, and from most of the stores in between. She hadn't even finished opening them. When she got to the box from the NBA Store she put her hand over her mouth. "I know this isn't..." she dropped the box but held onto the LeBron James jersey. "Yesssss." she screamed.

Five minutes later and she was finished with all but one box. Jason said to her, "You almost forgot one."

"Where?"

"Right here," he said as he pulled the box from behind his back.

It was a box from Harry Winston. "What is this?" Jada asked holding her heart as if she were about to pass out. "Oh my gawwwd," she said as she lifted the necklace out of the box. It was a classic platinum chain that had three charms on it. There were two diamond encrusted letter J's and a three karat diamond heart in between them. "This is beautiful," she said. Then she walked over and gave him a hug. Then she hugged Jill, "Thank you too, Jill." Half of the boxes had been from her.

"You're quite welcome."

"What did you get Jill," Jada asked.

"I really didn't know what to get her. She has ev-ver-ry thing," and they both laughed. "But that's hers right there. Hand it to her."

He pointed to a box big enough to contain a pair of shoes sitting underneath the tree. Jada grabbed it and said, "Here."

Jill took the box with a thank you and pulled the bow off. It was from Gucci. When she opened the box, inside was a sunglass case. She pulled them out, "How do I look?"

"Fly," Jada said. "I like those." Jill then pulled a wallet out.

"This is nice too, Jason."

"There's one more thing in there."

The last box was flat and it had a pair of driving gloves in it, "I needed a new pair of these. Thanks, honey. You did great."

Jason laughed. He couldn't tell if she was really satisfied or if she was feigning her happiness. "I'm glad you liked it. You are really hard to shop for."

"Well you did fine." Jada looked at Jill and then at her stuff. She felt a little guilty that she had gotten so much compared to Jill. She didn't want to come between them.

Jason smiled and said, "I forgot to tell you, you should have looked in the wallet."

"Why is there money in there?" she laughed.

"Just look."

Jill picked the wallet up and inside of it was a small card with a Mercedes emblem on it that said simply, *'Seasons Greetings, Drive Safely'.* Then she looked back at Jason as he dangled a set of keys in his hand.

Jill moved toward him and he pointed to the window. Jill turned without a word and took a look outside. "Ohhhhhhh, Jayssssssonnnn. You didn't."

"I did."

"Ohhhhh my gooooooodnesssss."

"You and my babies have got to be safe out there." Jill walked to the door in her bathrobe and Jada was at her side.

Jada yelled out, "That is phat."

Jill stood motionless taking in the mocha black 2005 Mercedes G55 AMG with a huge red bow on it. "Are you serious?"

"It's serious."

"Okay, so you want to play like that. Get dressed. We're taking it for a ride."

"Let's do it."

Twenty minutes later they were cruising out of Brooklyn in the brand new SUV. "So how far are you driving?"

"Why you have somewhere to go?" Jill asked sarcastically.

"Hey, just askin' … Merry Christmas to you."

Jason was in the back seat and Jada was messing with the radio. She was trying to find a station on the satellite radio. When she found a hip-hop station she was satisfied as Nas blared through the speakers.

After a while Jason began to take notice of where they were. "Hey," he said.

"Why don't you do me favor."

"What's that?"

"Drive past my old house. I've been so busy I never got a chance to check on it."

"Baby, it's Christmas and we have to get something to eat. We can come and do that on Monday. You know I'm eating for three."

"Okay, alright." He sounded disappointed and Jill picked up on it.

"Alright you big baby. You lucky I'm enjoying my new toy."

Jason smiled and began to give her directions. In fifteen minutes they turned up the street. The leaves were gone from the trees yet the neighborhood still had character that made it look like the perfect place to call home. When Jill eased up she asked, "Which one?"

"Right here on the left. Not this one the next…" Jason's words were frozen when he saw the sign in the front yard that said SOLD in bold print. "Oh no," he said. "Someone bought my house."

Jill stopped the car in front of it. There was a white minivan in the driveway and Jason's whole mood had sank. "It's a nice house," Jada said. "You used to own it?"

"Yeah, I really loved it."

They sat there for a couple of minutes. Then he said, "Whoever owns it had to have put a lot of money into it." The landscaping was impeccable and the front of the house had new brick and there appeared to be an extension on the back. They had a new fence around it. Jason had a real sense of having lost out.

Jill began to pull off slowly and then stopped. "I have an idea."

"What."

"Well, baby. We've got plenty of money."

"Yeah... and."

"Well why do you go make them an offer. How much over the value would you pay for that house."

"I don't know. One hundred, maybe two hundred."

"Wow, you must really love the house."

"I do."

"Well go make them and offer. The hell with it. You only live once."

The truck hadn't moved. "You serious?"

"Do it. I know you aren't afraid, Mr. Faust. Who knows you may make their Christmas. And the worst they can do is say no."

That was all he needed. "You're right. What good is money if you don't use it for the things you really want?"

"That's right," Jada laughed.

"You two coming to the door with me?"

"No way," Jill said laughing.

"I'll go," Jada said.

Jason and Jada were at the door and he fought off his reluctance to ring the doorbell. He hit the bell and looked down at his daughter and smiled. They heard someone on the other side as the locks clicked.

When the door opened Jason's heart skipped a beat as he had to adjust his eyes. "Merry Christmas."

"Merry... Christmas," he said and kept staring. The woman before him wasn't drunk and looked clean and healthy.

"Are you going to just stand there or are you going to come in and give your mother a hug?"

The door swung open and Jason embraced his mother and began to cry. The tears rolled down his face and he bawled like a baby. All the years of pain, he emptied from his eyes.

He barely made out his sister, Daisy, as she walked out to hug her brother as well. "Oh, I can't believe this," he said in a whisper. Jill was behind him crying as well. All tears of joy for once in his life.

Jason pulled himself together enough to introduce Jada to his mother and sister. They all embraced like the long, lost family they were.

Over brunch, Jill handed Jason an envelope. "I'm sorry baby in all of the excitement I forgot your gift."

He opened it and saw the deed to his house. Jill had given him everything he wanted and some things that he never dreamed of having. "Thank you," he said. "You are my angel. You saved me and you keep saving me."

"I always will," she said.

For the first time he believed in happily ever after.

Jason got the word that Crackhead Mike had turned his life around. He was working at a youth center in Queens part-time and he also was an on-site counselor at a drug treatment clinic in Jamaica near Hillside. If it was true he wanted to see for himself. One reason was because he wanted to bless Mike with some money for funding.

If anyone or anything could get him turned around and bring him back from the land of the walking dead then they deserved some money at the very least. While Jason knew nothing of rehab work he had seen the difference that a detox program had made for his own mother.

Luckily for his mother, Jill had spent forty thousand to send her to one of the best programs in the country. But not everyone could write a check like that. Jason wanted to reach out to the have-nots who had a problem and yet no where to turn.

He drove through his old neighborhood and parked in front of the youth center where he was told Mike worked. It was incredible that they called it a center. There was nothing for the children to play on other than a merry-go-round and a single basketball rim that had no backboard.

Jason parked and walked up to the door. He was in casual attire, Rocawear Jeans, Air Force Ones and a Northface jacket. He looked like a neighborhood dealer. He was in Jill's truck since there was snow on the ground. He walked to the front of the center and hit the buzzer.

Sure enough, the man who came to the door was Mike. "Can I help you?" He looked at Jason and tried to make him out.

"You don't remember me?"

Mike's body language showed fear. "Hey, man. I'm changed now. Plus I have children in here with me…"

Jason cut him off, "I'm not here to hurt you, bro. I'm here to help you."

"Help me?"

"Yeah, I'm Jason. Used to be with Webb. You used to …"

"Watch your car..." Mike smiled. He was missing two teeth but he looked healthy. As healthy as someone who smoked crack for ten years can look.

"Yeah."

"You look good, player."

"You too. Check it. Little Lord told me about you and what you been doing and about how you changed you life." Three kids went running by.

One of them said, "Mr. Mike, can we get the balls out now?"

"Yes, Bianca..." he turned back to Jason, "So you doing well, huh."

"Yeah, pretty good. I want to help out. I want to know what you need around here and I want to know what treatment center you went to in order to get clean."

"Man, you want to see a list? I've had a work order in with the city for going on two years now. There's thirty thousand dollars worth of things around here we need. I've asked them for..."

"Gimme the list. I'll have a crew out here within ten days."

Mike's mouth dropped, "You for real?"

"Believe it. What about the facility?"

"No facility would take me. I went to the Word Church on 146th. They have a small center in the basement. Sister Benita Rawlins runs it."

"What do you think they could use?"

"They can use anything."

"Okay, I'll send them a check and it will be a donation from my company but in your name," Jason said. "Get me the list and the number where I can reach you."

In two minutes, Mike came back with a list and a card with a number written on the back. "I'll call you the middle of next week and let you know when you can expect this to be taken care of."

"Thanks, Ja...son. This is really nice of you."

"It's no problem. One more thing. I want you to oversee the whole thing. So for that, I will pay you in advance. You may not see me out this way much. I have babies coming and I'll be busy. But you take this and get yourself something nice."

Jason handed Mike an envelope containing five thousand. Mike looked at it and saw a thick stack of bills and a smile came across his face. Then he said, "Man you could have written me check. I do have an account now. You trying to get me killed in this neighborhood."

Jason smiled back. "I think you still have enough street cred to make it home with that."

Mike stood there staring at Jason as if he had just seen Jesus Christ. "That boy keeps some damn money," Mike whispered to himself. "Always has." Jason didn't look back and therefore didn't catch the tears rolling from Mike's eyes. Though he'd been working hard, money was tight for Mike. He was behind in his rent and scheduled to be evicted from the first place he'd ever had in three days. Like a gift from above, Jason had saved him.

Jason turned the corner and when he reached the light, he saw a woman walking up the street with two kids beside her and pushing a stroller. While he was stopped at the light he watched the woman as she struggled with her kids. She looked as if she was trying to tell the kids to hurry up. Suddenly the woman popped one of the kids and began to yell.

He hated to see that type of treatment of children. It personified all that was wrong with the hood. No love and patience with the kids. When the woman stepped off the curb to cross the street he couldn't help but notice her huge behind. Partly because it was dragging behind her and partly because her tacky pants were hot pink. She looked like an out-of-work hooker. Jason shook his head, disgusted from the display. The woman was moving slowly and the light changed. The person behind Jason hit the horn as she and her kids were in front of his wife's truck.

She looked at him and said, "I'm moving, you muthafuckin' buster." Their eyes locked and he saw that it was Tasha. Her face was scarred badly and she looked like life had given her the short end of the stick. Jason glared at her for a moment and she called his name. "Jay? Is that you?"

Jason looked at her and without thinking, he simply smiled. Then he began to pull off and when there was nothing but three feet and a piece of glass between them, he winked at her. "Wait," she called out. "Jason," she called his name again, now sure that it was him.

He pulled slowly on by and shook his head 'no'. It looked like all of the air and life left her body. What ever spirit she held on to left her as her whole life flashed before her eyes. If only she had taken care of Jason the way he'd done for her, she'd be living in a house in Long Island, raising their children, instead of a roach infested woman's shelter.

In the rear view mirror he could see her screaming out his name hysterically while her children wondered what was wrong and looked like they were suddenly crying too. Jason was filled with a rush of emotions that he didn't know he'd held on to for all these years. Knowing how much it crushed her to see him looking like a million bucks gave him a sense of pride that he didn't deny. On the other hand Jason wondered just how ashamed she was of how beaten she looked. He couldn't believe the turn of events.

For all the times he had thought of getting her back he hadn't had to. By overcoming all the odds... he had done what he dreamed of doing for years on end. He had finally evened the score with the woman who had left him to rot. His revenge was living well.

Thank you for reading. Please be sure to check out these other titles from Nvision Publishing!

Also by Zach Tate
No Way Out

Before I Let Go
By Darren Coleman

Do Or Die
By Darren Coleman
A novel by D

The Sequel to the smash hit Before I Let Go
Don't Ever Wonder
Available June 28

Coming soon
I Shoulda' Seen It Coming
By Danette Majette

Fast Lane
By Eyone Williams

Also included in this book is an order form with titles from our sister company, Life Changing Books

Nvision Publishing Order Form

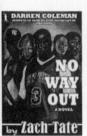    

Don't Ever Wonder
the sequel to BILG
Available June 28

Add $3.95 for shipping via U.S. Priority Mail. Total of 18.95 per book for orders being shipped directly to prisons Nvision Publishing deducts 25%. Cost are as follows, $11.25 plus shipping for a total of $15.20.

Make money order payable to Nvision Publishing. Only certified or government issued checks.

Send to:
Nvision Publishing/Order P.O. Box 274
Lanham Severn Road, Lanham, MD 20703

Purchaser Information

Name_____

Register #_____
      (Applies if incarcerated)

Address_____

City_____ State/Zip_____

Which Books_____ # of books_____

Total enclosed $_____

Life Changing Books Order Form

A Life to Remember

Double Life

New! Bruised by Azarel

Hits Stores 6/15

Add $3.95 for shipping via U.S. Priority Mail. Total of 18.95 per book for orders being shipped directly to prisons Nvision Publishing deducts 25%. Cost are as follows, $11.25 plus shipping for a total of $15.20.

Make money order payable to Life Changing Books. Only certified or government issued checks.

Send to:
Life Changing Books/Orders P.O. Box 423
Brandywine, MD 20613

Purchaser Information

Name_____

Register #_____
(Applies if incarcerated)

Address_____

City_____ **State/Zip**_____

Which Books_____ **# of books**_____

Total enclosed $_____

About the Author
Zach Tate, the interview

I recently sat down with Zach Tate to get some insight on what it is he's trying to do in the game. Here's a piece of that conversation.

D: So look man your new joint has finally hit the streets, what are you looking to do now?

Zach: Yeah, it's about time too. This publishing game ain't no joke, huh? D, you had everybody waiting, Especially in Ellenville and spots like that. But, yo, now... I'm just trying to do numbers, take care of business and change this game.

D: Yeah, the so called hip hop fiction game is hurting. What is it that you feel is missing, or that you're bringing?

Zach: Those are one and the same. I'm bringing what he game is missing. Just because it's hip hop or street fiction, whatever you want to call it... that shouldn't mean that the stories all have to be the same mindless, recycled trash. There's more to the hood than drugs, and violence. There's some struggle, and some loss but there's some victory there too. That's what I'm about. Just because you make someone think doesn't mean you can't entertain them at the highest level.

D: I feel you. So you're coming with some depth.

Zach: With twice the drama... twice the heat. Plus, I give sex tips.

D: Yo, them joints work too! Any words for your fans?

Zach: Yeah. Thanks for the support. Spread the word for me and please start demanding more from these 'so-called' writers. I love ya'll. Zach is the King of the Urban Epic Tale. Recognize.

For more of the interview hit the Nvision Publishing website. Click on *Lost & Turned Out.*

For info on availability of this title go to
info@invisionpublishing or
phone (202) 262-6217